Pawsitively Betrayed

A Witch of Edgehill Mystery

Book Five

MELISSA ERIN JACKSON

Pawsitively Betrayed

Copyright © 2021 by Melissa Erin Jackson

All rights reserved. This book or any portion thereof may not be reproduced or used in any manner whatsoever without the express written permission of the publisher except for the use of brief quotations in a book review.

This is a work of fiction. Names, characters, places, and incidents either are the products of the author's imagination or are used fictitiously. Any resemblance to actual persons, living or dead, businesses, companies, events, or locales is entirely coincidental.

ISBN: 978-1-7351500-9-3

Front cover design by Maggie Hall.
Stock art via Designed by Freepik, iStockPhoto, Shutterstock.
Interior design and eBook formatting by Michelle Raymond.
Print formatting by Alt 19 Creative.

First published in 2021 by Ringtail Press.

www.melissajacksonbooks.com

To Diamond, the sweetest girl

Previously in the Witch of Edgehill series...

For the last several months, Amber Blackwood has done her best to balance her life as a witch with her non-magical life. In the past few months alone, Amber has had to cope with the death of her best friend Melanie Cole; the discovery that Neil Penhallow had killed her parents; and assisting in the search that finds Chloe Deidrick, the daughter of Edgehill's mayor, safe and sound after being kidnapped. On the plus side, life is certainly more interesting now that both her close friend Kimberly Jones and Edgehill's Chief of Police, Owen Brown, know her secret. But now Jack Terrence, Amber's romantic interest, knows it, too. Her Aunt Gretchen had wiped Jack's memory after he witnessed the violent use of magic and realized that he didn't have the ability to protect Amber from the dangers in her world. But after his memories settled back into place, he knew his desire to be with her was his priority. Amber is nervous about letting yet another non-witch into her magical life, but she's grateful to have Jack back by her side.

The happiness of being reunited with Jack is dampened by the fact that Mayor Deidrick has teamed up with Mayor Sable of Marbleglen, Edgehill's neighboring rival town, in announcing that the Here and Meow Festival Committee will be working alongside the Floral Frenzy Flower Festival Committee on a joint parade to kick off festival season. To make matters worse, the committee is chaired this year by the always brash and rude Bianca Pace.

When Amber isn't in festival meetings, her cousin Edgar is teaching her how to play Magic Cache—a geocaching game with a magical twist. Even though the game is most popular among witch children from a young age, it's new to Amber. As part of her training, Edgar hides caches for her around town and sends her off to locate them on her own. One such assignment inadvertently leads Amber into Marbleglen. The object she finds is indeed a Magic Cache—but one that Edgar had not left for her. Instead, it's been placed there by someone named Simon Ricinus…which means there's a witch in Marbleglen.

Amber tracks Simon down. She finds the middle-aged witch to be kind and very willing to answer her questions. Simon knows a bit about Amber's magical history, namely what a powerful witch her mother had been. In addition to being a witch, Simon—also an avid member of Marbleglen's safety committee—is deeply concerned about the corrupt leadership of Marbleglen's Mayor Sable and Chief of Police, Eric Jameson. While at Simon Ricinus's house, Amber learns that Bianca Pace is his magic-free daughter.

When Chief Jameson is killed in his own home during a dinner party, Simon becomes the number one suspect. After Simon is arrested for the crime that he's adamant he didn't commit, Bianca begs Amber to help her find proof that her father is being framed. Over the course of her investigation, Amber discovers that the murder plot had been orchestrated by four people: Mayor Sable, the newly appointed Chief Daniels, land developer Randy Tillman, and crime lab owner Victoria Sullivan. With Amber's help, the four are arrested, and Simon is cleared of the murder charge.

Meanwhile, as Amber progresses through her Magic Cache lessons, Edgar takes things up a notch to include the search for "dead zones," spots of magical anomalies where magic simply doesn't exist. Amber learns that dead zones are favorite cache places for hardcore players of the game. Edgar suggests that they find a dead zone to hide Amber's parents' grimoires in, and then layer the dead zone with additional spells to create the ultimate hiding place that not even the malevolent Penhallows can find.

With the help of her younger sister, Willow, and their Aunt Gretchen, they find a dead zone in a small town called Quill, a few hours away. They hide the grimoires there. On top of layering the trunk of grimoires with spells, they also add a boomerang spell, assuring them that if someone other than Amber or Willow tries to take the grimoires, the books will immediately be returned to the two Blackwood sisters. The problem with this is that once the boomerang spell is triggered, the cloaking spells on the books will drop, making the books easily trackable by way of their magical signatures.

Though the books are safe, Simon's name has been cleared, and Jack wants to pursue a relationship with Amber, she can't shake her worry that the threat the Penhallows pose is reaching a flash point. Her worry is intensified when Kieran Penhallow calls her from prison. After Amber had lifted his curse, he answered for his crimes, namely the murder of a maid from the Manx Hotel. Kieran tells her that not only has his curse been lifted, but his magic has returned, healed and as it should be. Amber has no idea what this means for herself, the Penhallows as a clan, or the world at large.

CHAPTER 1

Amber reveled in the sound of Jack Terrence's rhythmic breathing. Her head was propped on the crook of his shoulder, and though there was a crick in her neck that would bother her all day, she didn't dare stir. That, and Alley was draped across them both, her head on Amber's side and her body sprawled across Jack's stomach.

As comforting as Jack's presence was, as the last dregs of sleep faded, the events from the day before crept back in. Namely, Kieran Penhallow calling her from his prison cell.

"Something is different now. Before, it almost felt like a rash or like an itch I couldn't scratch, no matter what I did. And even when I did manage to scratch it, it only itched more," he had said. *"What I had before…was a sickness. It was like a poison that slowly kills its host. I think you cut away the parts that were infected. What's in its place now feels…clean. Healed."*

Healed! She had no idea what this meant.

"You didn't take it away, Amber. You gave it back."

She had worried she wouldn't be able to sleep last night, but Jack had shown up unannounced with enough Chinese food for an army, not just four people, and they had all sat around Amber's dining table—herself, younger sister Willow, Aunt Gretchen, and Jack—and had talked about perfectly normal things. They talked about Willow's job as a graphic designer, about Aunt G's garden club, about Jack's plans to expand his business, and about the upcoming Here and Meow Festival. They didn't talk about magic, cursed witches, or Amber's ever-evolving powers.

Amber and Jack had curled up on the couch to try to stay awake long enough to get through the next episode of *Vamp World*. As usual, she awoke once her tiny studio apartment had flooded with early morning sunlight. She woke, feeling grounded, next to Jack. Hearing the soft snores of Aunt G and Willow in the bed on the other side of the apartment had rooted her further.

It was when she was alone that the nightmares pulled her from sleep.

Someone behind her cleared their throat. She rolled over just a fraction and found her sister peering down at her, a wide smile on her face. Willow stood so close to the couch, her knees nearly touched Amber's back. "*You two are so cuuute!*" she mouthed.

Amber's cheeks flamed. She delicately swatted Willow away. It was enough to wake Alley, who in turn woke Jack.

He seemed disoriented at first, then smiled sleepily at her. "Hey."

"Hey," Amber said.

"*Hey,*" Willow drawled.

Jack flinched back, realizing then how close Willow hovered over them.

"Are you staying for breakfast, Jack?" Aunt G called out, then padded for the kitchen. "Growing boys need to eat."

Willow turned toward their aunt. "What a weird thing to say, Aunt G! He's in his thirties. He's not a boy." She peered down at Amber and Jack again. "You *are* in your thirties, right? You have one of those very appealing faces that makes you look like you could be anywhere from twenty to forty. You haven't turned my sister into a cougar, have you?"

"Oh my God," Amber muttered, burying her face in Jack's shoulder. Her forehead bounced as he laughed.

"I'm thirty-five," he said to Willow. Then, louder, he said, "No thanks on the breakfast, Gretchen. I have to get to Purrcolate soon to help Larry open."

Aunt G appeared suddenly at the head of the couch. "Did you want coffee before you go? I suppose you don't want our boring old coffee when you *own* a coffee shop. But Willow and I could go downstairs to start a pot on the little hot plate and kill some time if you two need some alone time to…hmm…what do the kids call it these days?" She glanced over at Willow, who still hovered at Amber's back. "Tonsil hockey?"

Willow snorted. Jack cracked up. Amber wished she had an invisibility spell in her repertoire.

"Oh my God," Amber muttered again. "Get out of here! Both of you!"

Aunt G and Willow, still laughing, headed for the stairs. Amber sat up once she heard the Employee Only door close, signaling that her horrible aunt and sister had shut themselves in the shop below. Jack sat up, too, using the armrest to prop himself up.

"I'm sorry about them …" she started, but he cut her off by brushing a wayward lock of hair—a matted clump, really—out of her face.

"They give you a hard time because they love you," he said. "But, for the record, I'm totally okay with some tonsil hockey before I have to get to work."

She laughed. He cut it off with a kiss.

They broke apart after a minute, but Jack kept a hand pressed to the back of her neck. He rested his forehead against hers. "I really do have to get going, though."

"Boo," she grumbled.

He kissed her forehead. "I agree."

While he used the bathroom and collected his things, Amber fed Tom and Alley. As they munched happily on their breakfast, Amber walked Jack down the steps, across the shop, and to the front door of The Quirky Whisker.

Aunt G and Willow offered wolf whistles when Jack kissed Amber goodbye.

"Have a good day, ladies," he called, then headed out the door.

Amber whirled on her family, hands on hips. "You're both awful."

"I'm glad to see you happy, little mouse," Aunt G said.

Amber flushed. "Thanks."

With that, she hurried back upstairs to change and get ready for the day. She couldn't wipe the smile off her face.

Pawsitively Betrayed

A few hours after opening, Henrietta Bishop walked in. The shop was bustling with customers as usual during the week before the Here and Meow Festival. After helping a little girl decide that she would like the raccoon animated toy instead of the badger, Amber met Henrietta near the counter that ran along the right side of the shop.

Henrietta was a forty-year-old divorcee who had moved to Edgehill, Oregon, several years ago because she wanted to fully embrace the "Crazy Cat Lady" lifestyle. She was a lithe redhead with a mass of curls that hung to her mid-back. The curls never were truly contained, no matter what she did. Amber was always reminded of the young girl from *Brave* when she saw her.

Over the years, Amber had gotten to know Henrietta a little better. Recently, she'd joined the Here and Meow Committee in Marbleglen as a volunteer with the parade floats, and she had joined Amber and her friends during the recent town hall meetings. But Amber had been seeing the woman weekly for over a year, namely because Henrietta was addicted to Amber's signature "sleepy tea" blend. It was a creation Amber made in-house, with a bit of sleep tincture mixed in. Though Amber was abysmal with tinctures, her sleepy tincture was the only one that hadn't ever let her down.

Henrietta swore by it. *"I really wish you'd tell me what you put in this stuff,"* she often said. *"It works like magic!"*

Over the last month, Henrietta had been coming in on an almost daily basis to purchase more tea, and the quantity had gone up, too. Two boxes here, five there. When the purchases of the sleepy tea increased tenfold over a short window of time, and Henrietta's bright green eyes were droopy more often than not, Amber found herself wishing she were better at being a nosier person. She loved gossip just as much as the next Edgehill resident, but as the former reclusive weirdo in town, Amber understood keeping secrets close to the vest.

Henrietta hadn't talked much about her divorce; all Amber knew was that it had been contentious. That had been Henrietta's word, not Amber's. Even the gentlest of pressure to ask more probing questions on the topic often made Henrietta close up like a flower deprived of sunlight, so Amber had stopped asking.

Yet, when Amber met Henrietta at the counter that morning, Amber blurted, "Hen, are you okay?"

Even the woman's signature, vibrant curls looked dejected. The bags under her eyes were more pronounced than they had been a week ago. She wore black leggings, a black tank top, and a slightly ratty oversized green sweater. It reminded Amber of the last day she'd seen Melanie, who had come into her shop looking uncharacteristically like a hot mess.

Henrietta had always given the impression that her divorce settlement had been as good for her financially as it had been bad for her emotionally. She hadn't been the type to flaunt her wealth, but Amber was fairly certain the woman hadn't been employed the entire time she'd been in Edgehill, and yet her attire had always been immaculate.

"I'm hanging in there, I guess," Henrietta said. "Actually, I wanted to ask if you were hiring?"

Amber's brows shot toward her hairline. "I'm not at the moment. Sorry, Hen. I just hired Ben Lydon. I could possibly offer you a seasonal position, but I can't guarantee how long it'll last."

Henrietta sighed, waving away Amber's apology. "Oh, that's okay. What I need to do is dust off my résumé. It's been a while," she said. "Anyway, I'd like three boxes of the sleepy tea again. The stress I'm under right now can only be combated with that tea of yours."

Amber plastered on a strained smile. She excused herself to grab Henrietta's order. She had set it aside for her that morning, anticipating the woman's arrival. After grabbing the boxes for her from one of the cubbies at the base of the apothecary wall behind the counter where Daisy Bowen was ringing up customers, Amber handed the tea over.

Henrietta clutched the boxes to her chest. "Thanks." She started to turn away, as if heading for the checkout line, but then turned back. "Say, I purchased some sleepy tea from the drugstore the other day and that one wasn't nearly as effective as yours. Do you think it's the valerian root in yours that does the trick?"

No, it's the sleep tincture, Amber wanted to say. "You know I don't share my secrets," she said playfully instead, "but yes, the valerian root is essential."

Henrietta nodded, but the usual banter they shared was missing today. "I really appreciate you, Amber. You know that, right?"

Head cocked, Amber said, "Sure, Hen, I know that."

Tapping one of the boxes she held, Henrietta offered a small smile, then walked away to get in line. Amber knew her good friend Kimberly Jones would be able to tease out Henrietta's secrets in a matter of seconds. Betty Harris across the street in Purrfectly Scrumptious would look at Henrietta with her kind brown eyes, cluck her tongue and say something like, "What's got you so down, sugar?" and Henrietta would likely blab all her worries.

Amber, however, merely stood by and stared at Henrietta, frowning. Before she could get up the nerve to ask Henrietta if she needed anything else, another customer came through the door.

Lily Bowen was tending to a couple of customers at the back of the shop, and the other patrons currently seemed to have their browsing under control, which left Amber to attend to the newcomers. She had just rounded one of the freestanding pyramid-shaped bookshelves when she came up short.

Just inside the door stood Connor Declan and Molly Hargrove. Connor worked at *The Edgehill Gazette*, while Molly worked at *The Marbleglen Herald*. Despite being from rival towns, and the fact that Molly was known far and wide for being a snake, Connor and Molly had been working together on stories a lot lately. It still wasn't clear if their continued partnership was strictly professional or if it had spilled over into something else.

"What is *he* doing here?"

Amber flinched. Willow had materialized beside her. Willow and Connor had been close friends in high school, but their friendship had never progressed into anything more. They both clearly still held a torch for each other, but as adults, they still danced around the "what if" of it all.

In another circumstance, Amber might have lovingly shoved Willow in Connor's direction—especially after the teasing Willow had participated in this morning with Jack—but Molly's presence added a new wrinkle.

And by wrinkle, Amber meant napalm thrown on an open flame.

Connor and Molly had moved to the animated toy section on the left-hand side of the shop. Connor held a horse in front of his face, scrutinizing it from every angle. He was speaking to Molly, but she only had murderous eyes for Willow.

Molly Hargrove was five foot nothing, had hair so light blonde it was almost white, and could hold a grown man captive with just her intense focus.

Willow crossed her arms. "That's Molly, right?"

Amber forgot that the two hadn't formally met in person yet. "Yep."

"Let's go say hi," Willow said, and marched toward the couple, but her tone said, "Let's kick Molly in her shins."

Amber scurried after her sister, if only so she could stop a fistfight from breaking out in her shop. "Hi, you two!" she awkwardly called out just before Willow reached them.

Connor glanced up from his examination of the toy horse and visibly swallowed as he realized Willow and

Molly were sizing each other up. "Hey, uh…Amber. Hi. Willow. Hello."

Smooth, Declan.

"Is there something in particular you two were looking for?" Amber asked.

Molly's piercing blue eyes swiveled to Amber. "I realized today that I hadn't been in your shop in a while. Con and I were just about to grab lunch down the street and I thought we should pop in to have a look around. The Quirky Whisker is an Edgehill institution, after all."

Amber's brow creased.

"Right, uh …" Connor put the horse back on the shelf. "I'm also looking for a gift for my mom. She really likes tea. I was wondering if you had any recommendations?"

Willow piped up. "I'd be happy to help you find something for her. Follow me."

Connor smiled weakly at Molly and then followed Willow, leaving Amber alone with the snake.

"And what about you?" Amber asked when Molly just stood there glaring after the retreating pair.

Molly snapped out of it and scanned the shelves around her. "Did you inherit this place from your parents?"

"Uh…no," Amber said. "A woman named Janice Salle owned it before I did and she left the place to me in her will."

Molly's nearly white brows arched. "You must have been very persuasive to convince her to leave it to you."

Amber pursed her lips. She'd only just met Molly recently, when Amber had gotten pulled into a murder investigation in Marbleglen last month. She hadn't come to *like* Molly over that time, per se, but she'd respected the woman's tenacity for finding out the truth. That tenacity was just…a lot when it was aimed directly at you. "I didn't persuade her to do anything; I was just as shocked as anyone when I found out she'd left me the store."

"Did you choose to work here because Janice didn't have any living relatives?" Molly asked, running a finger along one of the pyramid-shaped bookshelves. "Like how young busty women 'fall in love' and marry old rich men with one foot in the grave? Grandpa drops dead and then Candy gets a mansion?"

Amber gaped at her.

A man nearby coughed in an effort to cover up a laugh and quickly walked away.

What on earth did Connor see in her? Amber had to assume Molly had a nice side. Amber had yet to see it.

Amber crossed her arms, taking on a stance that had no doubt mirrored Willow's from earlier. "Is there a destination for this very rude line of questioning?"

Molly shrugged. "Just making conversation. I'm sure your parents would be proud of all you've accomplished over the years." She picked up the horse Connor had been eyeing earlier. "The way you've honed your skills in such a unique way, you know?"

Connor, sans Willow, reappeared then. He held up a bag with The Quirky Whisker logo on the front. The bespectacled top-hat-wearing cat winked at Amber. "Got a really good selection."

Molly put the toy back. "Nice talking to you, Amber."

Connor led the way out the door. Willow joined Amber a few seconds later, and they watched as the pair walked past the front windows of the shop. They were headed in the opposite direction of the restaurants on Russian Blue Avenue, as well as the parking lot. Molly was speaking a mile a minute while Connor listened intently. Neither one glanced back.

"What was that about?" Willow asked once they were out of view.

"I have no clue."

CHAPTER 2

There were only six full days left until the Here and Meow, and even though Amber had participated in this annual festival many times over, it always managed to sneak up on her. One day her feline-obsessed town had only a few tourists wandering its streets, and the next, shops, parks, and hotels were bustling with people who had flocked to the town to participate in the three days of festivities.

As usual during the week before the Here and Meow, Amber was fast at work increasing her inventory of animated toys. The three days of the festival marked her largest sales days of the year. New customers discovered her unique creations at her booth in the fairgrounds, but longtime fans of her toys often dropped by—or placed advanced orders—for one of her new or festival-exclusive models.

This year, the exclusive offering had been inspired by the rustic spring aesthetic of the Hair Ball gala two months ago. Amber planned to craft hundreds of little plastic flower garlands to adorn the heads and necks of the animated cat toys. There would also be a limited number of cats with pastel-colored "fur." The lavender-colored cats were an early favorite; she had yet to find a seafoam green paint that didn't make the poor cat look as if it were suffering from a bout of seasickness.

Seated now around the dining room table in her apartment, Amber, Willow, and Aunt Gretchen were all working on various stages of the cat-making process. Aunt Gretchen used a fine-grain sandpaper to smooth the rough edges of a daunting pile of curved plastic cat tails. Willow, with her tongue caught between her teeth, painstakingly assembled the tiny wreaths of flowers.

And Amber, her grimoire open on the table, enchanted plastic disc after plastic disc with a "sit" spell. The discs were no larger than a dime. They looked like the tiddlywinks she and Willow played with as children. The plastic discs were the heart of Amber's toy operation. It had taken her years to find a way to create moving toys for the children of Edgehill without anyone discovering they were powered by magic instead of wires and electricity.

Once the small discs were enchanted, the disc would be attached to the wall of the animal's body cavity. The cat's various parts would then be fused together, creating a seamless toy that shielded the inner workings of the toys—or lack thereof—from the prying eyes of parents suspicious about how the toys played with their children for hours on end without the need to replace the batteries.

The stack of tiny discs to Amber's left—the unspelled batch—was a few inches tall. The one to her right had at least fifty in it. Her mouth was dry from uttering the "sit" spell so often.

Though the Blackwood women had magic at their disposal, the three witches were limited in how much magic they could use on the toys. Willow was gifted in glamour spells, which altered the appearance of an object. Or, in some instances, altered a viewer's *perceived* image of a thing. She could easily utter a spell to have an assembled, unpainted cat turn any color she wished. The very daunting pile of tiny wreath parts lying on the table in front of her could all be fully assembled and awash in a riot of color with the right series of incantations.

But spells faded eventually, and glamours were often the first to go. Some Edgehill parents were already a little wary of the curious toys that came out of The Quirky Whisker. If the toys suddenly were leached of all their color and their accessories fell to literal pieces in the middle of a play session, Amber would have a hard time explaining that away.

After adding a spell to yet another disc, Amber sat back in her chair and stretched. She excused herself from the table and grabbed a bottle of water from the kitchen, then drank it as she stared out the largest window in her tiny studio apartment. The window overlooked Russian Blue Avenue, and she admired the soft early morning colors of the sunrise. Ever since Amber's altercation with a cursed Penhallow witch a few months back, her ability to sleep through the night had become hit-or-miss. Though it was getting better, some days were harder than others, today being one of them.

Jack hadn't stayed the previous night, so his steady presence hadn't kept the nightmares at bay. She knew she couldn't use Jack as a crutch forever; she'd have to find a way to calm her restless worries on her own.

Until then, there would be lots of insomnia combated with caffeine.

The bonus to so many sleepless nights was that she could work on her toy inventory. And with her family here, they would help make sure it all got done in time. Daisy and Lily Bowen were scheduled to man the shop for the morning, which would help, too. When the ladies' shift ended at noon, Amber would take over to run the shop with Ben—the same Ben who had been awarded the prestigious title of "best designer" in the Best of Edgehill competition at the Hair Ball. He had been selected to design all the swag for this year's Here and Meow, as well as the commemorative pin that attendees could win if they completed a scavenger hunt by the end of the weekend.

Ben had finished his designs weeks ago, and now was waiting anxiously for the swag and pins to arrive so he could see what his art looked like once commercialized. According to Kimberly Jones, the Here and Meow's festival director, a sample box of swag had shown up at her door yesterday. Kim had called Amber late last night to do an over-the-phone unboxing. Amber had tried to explain that a video unboxing would have made more sense, but Kim had been so excited, Amber couldn't get a word in edgewise around all Kim's exclamations of "Shut the front *door*; this is amazing!" and "Oh holy smokes, this Ben kid is a genius!" and just flat-out squealing.

Kim had proven during the preparation for the Hair Ball, she could become…unglued…once faced with stress and pressure. So if she wanted to call to flail about things Amber couldn't even see, Amber wasn't going to rain on her parade. An excited Kim was better than Kim the Galazilla any day.

Amber wrinkled her nose at the thought of parades. Today being Saturday, she would have to head over to the float barn later this afternoon in the mostly odious town of Marbleglen to help with the finishing touches on the floats. The floats were the stars of the Edgehill-Marbleglen parade that would be the kickoff to both towns' festivals in a week.

So much to do. So little time to do it.

With a sigh, she got back to work.

After Aunt Gretchen made sandwiches for Amber and Willow, they had a pleasant lunch together where they only teased Amber about Jack once each. Then Amber hurried downstairs to prep the shop for the afternoon rush.

The Bowen sisters had mostly cleaned up before they'd hurried off to their own lunch, but a small section filled with non-animated toys in the back of the shop was in disarray. Amber was in the middle of straightening up when someone knocked on the front door.

Amber stood and eyed Russian Blue Avenue beyond the glass wall of windows, the street clogged with wandering tourists. Across the street, a long line snaked out the front door of Purrfectly Scrumptious, the bakery run by Betty and Bobby Harris, and continued down the street beyond what Amber could see from her current vantage point. A small cluster of kids were crouched on the sidewalk across the street. Even though Amber couldn't see her, she knew the children were fussing over Savannah, the shop cat who belonged to the Harrises.

Savannah was a gorgeous white and gray Maine coon who was just as much of a fixture of Purrfectly Scrumptious as Betty's legendary cupcakes.

The bakery had won Best of Edgehill in the treat category during the Hair Ball, and as a result, business at the bakery had skyrocketed nearly overnight. Betty was in her sixties and had been apprehensive about even entering the competition, concerned that she was somehow too old for her business to be taken to the next level. Amber couldn't have been happier for the Harrises' well-deserved success.

And, given the two women in Purrfectly Scrumptious aprons who were armed with clipboards and were taking down orders from people in line, it looked like the Harrises had finally hired help, too.

The knock sounded again. Amber found Kimberly Jones at the front door with a large tote bag hung from her shoulder. Smiling, Amber quickly unlocked and pulled open the door, the bell above it tinkling.

"*Are you open yet?*" someone from outside called.

"About fifteen more minutes," Amber said as Kim rushed in.

Once the door was locked again, Kim, who had practically flung herself backward over the counter, said, "Oh my God, Amber, they're like vultures!"

Amber stifled a laugh.

"They practically clawed at me while I stood at your door!" Kim said. "Wait. No. They're not vultures. They're worse than that. They're zombies with a hankering for human flesh!"

Amber snorted.

"Anyway!" Kim said, heaving out a long, loud breath. She plopped the tote bag on the counter. "I have goodies!"

Amber rounded the counter so she stood on the register side, with Kim on the other, and watched as Kim pulled out window decal stickers, lanyard strings, a stack of bingo cards, and a small handful of pins.

"Oh wow," Amber said, picking up the pin. "These turned out great!"

"Right?" Kim said.

The pin was about an inch square and shaped like a cat's face. But instead of mere lines and shapes, the face had been constructed with the names of each Best of Edgehill business and owner. The window decals for the winning businesses were standard postcard size and had twelve hand-drawn buildings running along the length. The detail in each storefront was remarkable, especially in such a small space. Amber had always envied an artist's ability to take something from the world around them and recreate it based on their own unique vision. "Here and Meow Festival" was written on the right side, the words hovering in the sky above the buildings, and a bright yellow starburst, like a sun, hung in the sky on the right, with a "Best of Edgehill Business!" stamped in the middle.

And to top it all off, on sidewalks, in windows, and on roofs were cats. Lounging, sleeping, playing. Ben's designs were so quintessentially Edgehill that Amber had to fight the urge to hug the decal to her chest. She was a little jealous of all the businesses which got to affix one to their shop front windows.

"Are these the final product?" Amber asked.

"Yep. Finally. There have been roughly nine billion printer malfunctions on their end. I can't believe how close they cut it. We can make minor requests for changes, mostly because they're relatively local, but if we *do* want changes, we have to let them know by tonight, especially since they're closed on Sunday. And I'll have to pick up the new materials in person. With less than a week left before the big day," Kim said, then furiously rubbed at her forehead. "It's fine. I'm sure everything is fine. Is Ben going to be here soon?"

The bell above the shop door chimed as Ben let himself in.

"Speak of the devil," Amber said.

Ben had just pulled an earbud out, his brow creased. A question was clearly on the way out of his mouth but then he saw what was on the counter in front of Kim. Voice shaky, he said, "Is that…are those …"

"Sure is! Come look!" Kim said.

As the two gushed over the swag, Amber headed for the front door to flip the sign to "open," giving the ravenous zombies the go-ahead to come inside. As Amber pulled open the door, she smiled at the woman she'd spoken to earlier. A line of tourists poured in after her, the shop's wooden floors creaking underfoot.

Amber had just let the door go, making her way toward a man who attempted to get something off a high shelf, when the door flew open behind her with such force, the bell above it was nearly knocked loose. A woman stood in the doorway, chest heaving. She held fast to the hand of a weeping little boy.

"What kind of racket are you running here, Amber Blackwood?"

Amber blinked at her. She recognized her as a resident of Edgehill, though Amber didn't know her personally. Despite the fact that this was a small town, Amber had kept herself relatively isolated here until recently. Amber was almost positive her name started with an S.

"I'm sorry, Sarah, but—"

"My name is Sally!" Sally snapped, then stomped a foot for good measure. Her crying son wept harder.

Right. That was her name. Sally Long.

Everyone in the shop had stilled. Even Kim and Ben had been shocked out of their gushing over the newly arrived festival goodies.

The only sound came from the soft whimpering of the little boy whose arm was hoisted in the air by his mother. Amber wondered if the weeping was due to how tightly the woman held him.

Quickly glancing around, her face hot, Amber took a step forward. "I'm sorry, but what seems to be the problem?" she asked, keeping her voice low.

"The *problem*?" Sally let the boy go so she could root around in her large brown leather purse and produce a mangled toy bear. She thrust it at Amber.

Startled, Amber instinctively grabbed hold of it. The whole front half of the toy bear was a blackened, melted mess, as if someone had taken an open flame to it. The back half looked perfectly intact, which somehow made the destruction done to the bear's face even more upsetting. Amber turned it so she could see into the gaping hole where the bear's hollow stomach had once been. From what she could tell, all the magic-fueled discs inside the bear had melted along with its face.

Had the spells malfunctioned?

Amber's chest constricted at the thought that this little boy's tears might be *her* fault.

She dropped to her knees in front of him. It took a second, but then she remembered his name. Noah. He had short black hair, brown watery eyes, and a little trail of snot running out of his nose. He had been rubbing the back of his pudgy hand against one eye, then jumped slightly when he realized Amber was in front of him. He stopped whimpering and gave a little sniffle.

"Are you okay, Noah?" she asked, searching those sad eyes. "Did the bear hurt you?"

He sniffed again, then he straightened, resolve sobering him up. Amber got the impression he was pleased to be asked his side of the story. "I was just playing with him in my room, Miss Amber. I wasn't doing anything bad…just playing chase like we always do. He was running after me and then…*boom!*"

Amber flinched.

"Can you fix him, Miss Amber?" he asked, a bit urgently. "Did I do something to break him? I love Toast a lot."

Amber fought a laugh, despite the tension in the room. When children got a new toy, part of the activation process was assigning the toy a name. The act of naming it allowed Amber to tailor the spells so they worked best for the child in question. It added longevity to the spells, too. She remembered how enthusiastically Noah had shouted "Toast!" when she asked him to name something brown.

"I like Toast better than all my other toys. I even like him better than that smelly dog that lives across the street. I just want Toast back." Noah's tears started up again.

"I demand a full refund," Sally said from somewhere behind Amber. Amber ignored her.

She was mildly relieved that the boy was upset because he'd lost his friend, and not because the explosion had wounded or traumatized him. She shivered at the thought of all the possible things that could have gone wrong. A glitchy spell in the hands of a child had always been her biggest fear—which was why she checked and triple-checked that everything was in order before any of her creations graced a shelf.

Had the stress of the last few months made her careless? Her stomach ached.

"Did you hear me?" Sally asked, followed by the stomp of a foot. "A. Full. Refund."

"Yes, of course," Amber said without looking at her. Addressing Noah, Amber said, "I'll work on Toast and get him back into tip-top shape. I promise."

The boy smiled for the first time since his mother had dragged him in here.

"Absolutely not!" Sally said, reaching around Amber to grab hold of the boy, his arm once again hoisted in the air.

Amber quickly got to her feet.

Sally got nose to nose with her. "Your toys are dangerous, Amber." Giving the boy's arm an absentminded shake, she said, "Look at him. You get him to fall in love with these weird toys of yours—he won't play with *anything* else—and then it almost kills him!"

Amber flinched once more.

"You should be ashamed," Sally hissed. "We're never buying another toy from you. I've always known something about this place, about *you*, was…strange. Off. Not right. Now I have proof. I should have listened to my gut. You better believe every parent I know will hear about this."

Noah wailed. "But I want Toast!"

"Don't buy toys from here!" Sally called out, doing her best to make eye contact with every shocked onlooker. "They aren't safe for your children!"

"Listen, Sally," Amber said, hoping that if she lowered her own voice, it would make the woman lower hers, too. "I'm sure there was just a—"

"I don't want to hear it!" Sally said, taking a step back. "You'll be hearing from my lawyer. I'm leaving." She yanked her son toward the door, then whirled to address the other patrons again. "I suggest you all leave, too."

Then she was out the door, pulling her son after her. Noah looked back forlornly over his shoulder, stumbling over his own little feet because he only had eyes for the shop where he'd abandoned his friend Toast. Amber still held the mangled bear.

The tension in the shop was nearly tangible. When she turned away from the retreating boy and his mother, she spotted Willow and Aunt G standing in the doorway of the Employee Only door. Kim and Ben still stood wide-eyed on the right side of the shop. Movement to her left caught her eye just as a pair of women delicately put down the toys they'd been holding. They gave Amber a wide berth and hurried out of the shop with their eyes downcast.

The bell above the door sounded more like a gong.

Amber felt sick.

Slowly, the shoppers resumed perusing, but they did so while casting worried looks over at Amber every few seconds.

In high-stress situations, Kim either went totally mute or talked non-stop. Her being quiet through all this somehow only added to the tension.

Amber had only made it halfway across the shop—intending to duck behind the counter and never come out—when the bell above the door chimed again. She half expected Sally to have returned with her lawyer already.

Instead, Chief Brown stood there.

The look on his face made her stomach drop. He was in full-on cop mode.

"Hello, uhh…Miss Blackwood," the chief said a little awkwardly. "We have a bit of a situation and I think it would be best if you come down to the station."

Kim, still silent, detached herself from the counter to stand beside Amber. A silent guard.

"Is this because of Sally and the exploding toy bear, because—"

"What? Exploding…what? No," he said, shaking his head. His gaze briefly drifted to the ruined plastic bear she clutched to her chest. "Like I said, it's a…*situation*."

Amber figured the situation was magic-related, as he was one of the few people in town who knew she was a witch, but she was still so rattled from her run-in with Sally Long that she wasn't thinking clearly. "What kind of situation?"

He pursed his lips, then gave a quick scan of the patrons—as well as Willow and Aunt G who presumably still stood at the back of the shop—before taking a step toward her. "It would be best that we get your statement now before this gets out of hand."

Her nerves were frayed. "Before *what* gets out of hand?"

Letting out a huff of resignation, he said, "It's about Henrietta Bishop."

The image of the forty-something divorcée popped into Amber's head, with her wild mop of red hair. She'd been in the shop only yesterday. Amber was almost too scared to ask. "What about her?"

He quickly scanned the shop again, then cast a furtive glance at Kim who stood with her arm flush with Amber's. Amber had to assume the brunette's eyes were as wide as dinner plates. "As of this morning," the chief said, "she's in a coma."

Kim gasped. "Shut the front door!"

CHAPTER 3

Amber stared slack-jawed at the chief. "*What?*"

He bent so low, his mouth was practically on her ear. He urgently whispered, "Like I *said*, it's a sensitive matter and I need you to come down to the station."

Huffing out a breath after he took a step back, she nodded. "Fine."

Without another word, he went out the door, knowing, apparently, that she'd follow him.

Amber turned to Kim, whose eyes were still wide, and said, "I promise I'll tell you everything when I get back."

"What if—"

"No, you can't come with me."

"I could—"

"He's not going to let you in on this conversation, Kim," Amber said.

"Maybe I could—"

"Who knows how long this will take," Amber said. "You have to get back to work. I'll call you. I promise."

Kim groaned. "The second you get out—"

"First person I call," Amber said.

Begrudgingly, Kim nodded.

Shifting her attention to Willow and Aunt G, Amber said, "You'll be the second call."

"I've only been back in Edgehill for a few days and you're already getting arrested, little mouse?" Aunt G asked. "It usually takes at least two weeks."

A patron somewhere to Amber's left let out a little gasp. The rumor mill was going to have a field day with this one.

Amber managed a chuckle, which helped loosen the knot of anxiety in her chest. She quickly grabbed her purse from behind the counter, feeling the eyes of the still-remaining customers on her the whole way, and then hurried out the front door after calling out an awkward goodbye.

The chief waited in his cruiser directly outside The Quirky Whisker. She wasn't sure if she was still allowed to ride shotgun. She eyed the back seat, which had a hatched partition that protected the officer from any delinquents being escorted to the station. She remembered the day the chief had found her snooping around the coroner's office in the days after Melanie's death, and had made Amber ride in the back like a criminal.

He seemed to sense her hesitation and reached across the passenger seat to open the door for her. "C'mon, Amber. No need to be dramatic."

Her nostrils flared in annoyance and she climbed into the car. "I think I have every right to be dramatic. Am I under arrest?" She closed the door a little harder than necessary.

"Do you see any handcuffs?" he asked.

She honestly wasn't sure if that was rhetorical or not, so she didn't reply. What had happened to Henrietta?

The chief pulled out onto Russian Blue. It wasn't until The Quirky Whisker was out of sight in the rear-view that he said anything. "This is all preemptive. I got a call from Thea Bishop, Henrietta's sister, early this morning. According to her, last night Henrietta called Thea in a mild panic, saying she didn't feel right and that her deteriorating condition was scaring her. She told Thea about doubling up on your 'sleepy tea.' Apparently half a cup is enough to get her to sleep, but she told Thea that the tea wasn't as effective lately. She had finished her second cup just before she started to feel really off, called her sister, and then collapsed while she was on the phone."

"Oh my God," Amber breathed.

"Thea is the one who called an ambulance. Henrietta had been breathing but unresponsive when she reached the hospital. By late this morning, she was in a coma." He paused a bit too long, and Amber's stomach tightened again. "Thea said she was going to get on the first available flight here from Ohio."

While all of this sounded terrible on its own, Amber was twice as horrified because this was all so similar to what had happened to her close friend, Melanie Cole, just months before. Something from Amber's shop had, initially, been treated as the reason for Melanie's death. While it was later proven that nothing toxic was in the vial of headache tonic Melanie had supposedly ingested just before she died, Amber had still been under scrutiny simply because of the reputation of her "weird" products.

In the end, it had been discovered that ethylene glycol had been added to Melanie's tea, slowly making her sick.

Was this all a coincidence?

"Oh, and I should add that Thea is both furious…and a lawyer."

It took Amber a moment to process this. "So…Thea thinks that my tea poisoned Henrietta?"

"Yes," the chief said simply. "Thea went online to look up the ingredients in your tea, as Henrietta has a few known allergies, but Thea couldn't find your store listed anywhere. She wants to be in Edgehill to care for her sister, but she also made it very clear she wants to talk to you in person to learn what's in your products."

Amber stared out the window, not really seeing anything.

After a minute of silence, he asked, "Did you say something earlier about a toy bear?"

Amber had almost forgotten. She told him about the altercation she'd had with Sally Long just minutes before the chief had arrived.

"Is this just really bad timing or is there something…*else* going on here?" the chief asked when she was done. "Have you ever had problems like this before?"

"Never," she said. "I mean, I've had toys malfunction on me countless times, but I work all those kinks out a million times over before I put a toy on the market. A toy exploding while a child is playing with it, or one of my tinctures making someone sick …" She shook her head, her stomach queasy again. "Those are pretty much my worst nightmares. It's why I've never wanted to expand the toy-making operation. I need it to be small and contained so I can make sure that everything that leaves my shop is safe. Too much could go wrong if production is scaled up. Too many corners would be cut for the sake of time, money, or both."

The chief pulled into one of the diagonally aligned parking spots in front of the station. Neither made a move to get out.

"I'm not one to jump to conclusions," he said, "but we likely need to consider the possibility that a Penhallow is behind both instances."

Amber had thought the same thing but hadn't wanted to voice it out loud.

"What would a Penhallow have to gain from under-mining your business?" he asked.

"To keep me off-kilter," she said. "To find ways to introduce even more variables into my life to increase their chances of being able to trick me into telling them where I hid my parents' grimoires."

Last month, Amber, Willow, and Aunt G had driven several hours away to the small, remote town of Quill where a dead zone was located. From Amber's brief foray into Magic Cache with her cousin Edgar, she had learned that there were unexplainable spots of varying sizes scattered across the earth where magic simply didn't exist. These particular spots were difficult to locate, making them well-loved challenges for the most hardcore Magic Cachers.

The trunk holding Amber's parents' grimoires was now hidden in one such dead zone, and the hard-to-trace spot had been layered with ten spells. If a Penhallow was somehow able to find the location, he or she would then need to break through the wall of spells—which got more complicated and powerful the closer one got to the grimoires. And even then, the trunk had been layered in a powerful boomerang spell. If the books were threatened in any way, or if someone other than Amber or Willow tried to take them, the spell would be triggered and would send the trunk of books back to Amber.

The problem with that was that the books would also simultaneously lose their cloaking spells, making them easily traceable. The magic that came off the Henbane book, her mother's book in particular, was not only strong, but unique. And then Penhallows, desperate for the highly coveted time-reversal spell inside the grimoire, would come flocking to Edgehill. Assuming some weren't already here.

If the books were ever unexpectedly returned, Amber would have to drop everything and run. Anything to keep the books, her family, and her beloved town of Edgehill safe.

Amber supposed it was no wonder that she had such a hard time sleeping lately.

The chief, with his gaze locked on some spot ahead of him, finally said, "A Penhallow can take on the identity of anyone they choose. And it sounds like they can change that appearance often. With the town filling with tourists, that means they could both hide in plain sight as well as become dozens of different people. You're going to need to devise a way to tell who's friend and who's foe."

That knot of anxiety tightened again. "What, like a safe word?"

"Maybe," he said, not acknowledging her sarcastic tone. "You cast truth spells on everyone you came into contact with when Kieran was in town, didn't you? You can't do that now. There are too many people."

As he said that, a large group of tourists stopped in front of the chief's cruiser, their guide pointing to the building.

"You can't cast a truth spell on each new person who comes into your shop," he reiterated. "Nor can you cast one on every stranger you meet on the street. And from what you said happened a few days ago, Damien and Devra were in town for a while without you even knowing it. So you can't use their magical signature as a way to know they're here."

Amber stared at his profile for a moment, likely as shocked as he was that over the course of a few short months, they had gone from being leery of each other to him casually discussing details about the cursed Penhallow clan. Somehow his casual, practical tone made her sense of dread even more acute.

She looked away. "Hinklebert."

His head cocked in her peripheral vision. "Excuse me?"

"That's our code word," she said. "If I get suspicious about your behavior, I'll ask for the word."

"Right. Hinklebert," he said flatly. "Life was a lot less weird before I met you. You know that, right?"

She didn't say anything. She watched out the windshield as the backward-walking tour guide continued down the sidewalk to some other destination. On this stretch of sidewalk, the nearest shop was Paws 4 Tea. It was the tea shop where Susie Paulson had worked—the woman who had helped Whitney Sadler poison Melanie's tea for weeks.

If Henrietta's coma and Noah's exploding bear were both the work of a Penhallow doing their level best to unsettle her, she was disgusted that someone would stoop this low. But it made sense that a Penhallow would take something that Amber feared most and use it against her, and to use the raw memories of Melanie's demise and throw them back in Amber's face.

Without a word, she let herself out of the cruiser and made her way inside the station.

As usual, Dolores, a.k.a. Sour Face, was behind her wooden box of a desk, clacking away at the keyboard. Amber didn't even bother to acknowledge her; it wasn't as if she'd speak to Amber anyway.

The chief came up behind Amber and said, "Right this way, Miss Blackwood."

Instead of taking her left, toward his office like he had been doing for months, he directed her to the right and into the tiny closet-like interrogation room he had taken her to when she'd been under suspicion for Melanie's murder.

She silently took a seat at the tiny table and clutched her purse to her chest.

The chief excused himself for a minute, closing the door behind him. She could feel the eyes of the two cameras in the corners watching her. Thankfully, instead of the chief leaving her alone for ages as he had before, the door opened again a minute later.

"Hiya, Amber!"

She looked up to see the gangly form of Carl, the chief's youngest officer. A small smile broke out across her face involuntarily. Carl was the human equivalent of a golden retriever puppy. Excitable, goofy, and eager to please.

"I haven't seen you in a while," he said, flopping into the only other available chair. "Chief Brown's got me doing so much paperwork my hands are more papercut than skin." He held up a long-fingered hand decorated in several Band-Aids—one covered in Superman symbols—as evidence. "How you been?" Then he winced and slapped a Band-Aid-covered hand over his face. "Dumb question! You're in here. What're you in for?"

The door opened again and the chief came up short. "Carl, what on earth are you doing in here? There's a huge pile of work on your desk."

Carl slouched in his chair and let out a whimper that seemed better suited to a little kid having a tantrum. "I just wanted to say hi to Amber."

The chief wordlessly pointed toward the door.

"Fiiiine." Carl dramatically pushed himself out of his chair and stood. Just before he left the room, he said, "Hope it all works out, Amber."

The chief muttered to himself as he sat down, dropping a legal pad on the table. He offered Amber a bottle of water. She waved it away.

"Okay, Miss Blackwood, what I need from you is a statement of what ingredients are in your 'sleepy tea,'" he said.

She knew the formal tone was for the sake of the cameras recording this conversation, but it still irked her. She did as he asked.

"You create your own tea blends in-house, correct?" he asked.

"Yes."

"Does the tea have an official recipe anywhere to prove that these are the only ingredients that are ever found in the blends?" he asked. "Has anyone recently observed you make the tea to help corroborate that this is how it's made? Do you have a license for selling things like tea blends?"

Amber flushed. "Well, no. I'm technically an herbalist and we aren't required to get any kind of licensing. The ingredients are printed on every box and vial; as long as I let clients know what's in the remedies, herbs, and tinctures, as far as I know, that's enough. First amendment rights…or something." She awkwardly cleared her throat. "Is that going to be a problem?"

"I honestly don't know," he said. "Technically, only physicians can legally prescribe cures and treatments for diseases and illnesses. I think as an…*herbalist*…you're operating in a gray area and run the risk of being sued if you make a claim about the effectiveness of a treatment that then causes harm to the customer."

Amber groaned and buried her face in her hands.

"I suggest you start compiling as many records as you can," the chief said. "Write down when you made your last batch, if anyone helped with any part of the process, when Henrietta bought the most recent batch, and how much she purchased. You'll also need to figure out if it was you who handed the tea over, or if one of your employees did."

"Her last batch was purchased yesterday and I'm the one who prepared her order and handed it to her," Amber said. "The order was sitting in one of the cubbies behind the counter for a while before Henrietta came in, but I highly doubt Ben or the Bowen sisters would have done anything to tamper with it. Who's to say the tea wasn't tampered with after it left my store?"

"Which is exactly why this compilation of information will be helpful," he said. "Make it as clear as possible what your business practices are in case someone comes asking questions."

"Someone as in a lawyer convinced my products put her sister in a coma," Amber grumbled.

He held up a hand to placate her. "I just want to help you get ahead of this before Thea arrives. She already implied she thinks you need to have the book thrown at you for selling consumable products that haven't been evaluated by the FDA. She may have used the term 'snake-oil salesman.'"

"This makes me scared to sell *anything*," she muttered.

"We're only investigating whether someone committed a crime. We aren't here to flesh out civil litigation claims."

Whatever the heck *that* meant.

"Remember …" he said very slowly and deliberately. "The fear you're experiencing now very well might be the reason for this. *Someone* might be trying to undermine your business …"

Right. The Penhallows. She needed to keep her spiraling worries in check.

"Do *I* need a lawyer?" she asked after a moment.

"It might be worth it to make a few phone calls," he said. "But we don't know how much of Thea's threats are those of a woman scared about the well-being of her sister, how much is posturing, and how much she's truly hell-bent on going after your products. My guess is, the state of Henrietta's health will guide Thea's actions more than anything."

Amber had just seen Henrietta yesterday. She hadn't been her usual immaculate self, and she'd asked for a job, but Amber hadn't thought anything about Henrietta's appearance or behavior was alarming so much as out of character. Amber would never forgive herself if Henrietta didn't wake up.

"I think that's all I need for now, Miss Blackwood," the chief said, picking up his legal pad and pen. "We'll be in touch if I have any more questions."

Amber nodded absently, then followed him out of the interrogation room.

When Amber got back to The Quirky Whisker, she didn't immediately go in. Instead, she loitered in the parking lot beside the building and called Kim as promised, but the call went to voicemail. She left Kim a long message detailing what had happened at the station, and also apologized for needing to bail on the float decorating that evening in Marbleglen. The idea of maintaining a cheery outward demeanor while surrounded by people like Bianca Pace and Harlo sounded like too much to deal with today. Bianca was getting easier to tolerate, but Amber currently didn't have the energy to even entertain the idea of participating.

Once she finally entered the shop, she found both Aunt G and Willow bustling about helping customers, while Ben effortlessly worked the cash register, winning the customers over with his awkward charm. Amber was relieved to see that Sally's outburst earlier hadn't cut her profits for the day off at the knees, but she also wondered how soon news of the exploding bear would make its way through Edgehill.

What would happen if news of Toast the Bear's demise reached Thea Bishop? The exploding toy could potentially be even more of a problem than whatever had happened to Henrietta.

The rest of the day passed by in a blur. Amber flinched every time a new customer walked into the shop. Any one of these unfamiliar faces could be the mask of a Penhallow. Any one of them could be a customer coming in to complain about a malfunctioning purchase. Both her aunt and sister attempted to catch Amber's attention throughout the day, no doubt wanting an update on what had happened at the station, but Amber didn't want to talk about it.

That evening, when the door was finally locked behind the last customer of the day, Amber was tempted to bewitch her chalkboard welcome sign to say, "Sorry, we're closed for the rest of time!" Instead, she merely flipped it over.

Then she beelined for the section where she kept all the animated toys and grabbed the three remaining bears off the shelf. One woman had already tried to buy a bear today and Amber had gently eased her in the direction of a non-animated cat instead. Amber wanted to believe the chief's assessment of the situation. She wanted to put the blame on a Penhallow lurking in town. But a bigger part of her was terrified her magic had glitched in some horrific way and had put young Noah in danger.

All the same fears she'd faced when Melanie had died were resurfacing now. Grief she thought she'd been managing was now swelling up like a tidal wave she hadn't seen coming.

Without a word, Amber carried her purse and armful of toy bears up the stairs. She had just dropped them on the table and was about to tend to the cats' dinner when Aunt G stopped in front of her, hands on her hips. Amber came up short.

Aunt G was a little shorter than Amber and tipped her head back to look up into her face. "I'll take care of the cats, little mouse. You and Willow try to figure out what happened to that toy."

Amber frowned.

"You can give us the silent treatment if you want, but I know you, little mouse. You retreat into yourself when you're upset. And I know you're worried about what could have happened to that sweet boy if the toy had exploded in his hands."

Without warning, Amber's eyes welled with tears.

"Just as I thought," Aunt G said in her no-nonsense way. Even when she was being sympathetic, she still sounded practical. "Figure out what happened, hmm? I'll join you two when I'm done."

Amber nodded.

Tom jumped onto Amber's bed then and let out a yowl. Aunt G turned to him. "Oh, relax, Tom Cat. You won't croak in a matter of a few minutes."

He yowled in reply as if to say, "*You can't possibly know that, human.*"

Last month, Amber learned that a now-abandoned neighborhood in southern Edgehill had once been home to witches. When the ley lines—veins of magic that crisscross the entire globe—below the neighborhood had erupted several decades ago, expelling cursed magic into the air, it had first scared off the animals, and then had sent the witches packing so they wouldn't be overcome with magic sickness. But even after the poisoned magic had sunk back into the earth and the cat familiars returned, their witches had not. Now it was speculated that the abundant cat population of Edgehill was made up of descendants of cat familiars. If that was true, Amber thought the regal, calmer Alley was likely a more direct descendant than scaredy-cat, food-obsessed Tom. The pressure of being a cat familiar would probably give the poor boy an aneurysm.

Currently, while Tom yowled as if he would expire at any moment from starvation, Alley was curled up on the bench seat in a ball. One black ear swiveled this way and that as she took it all in even while acting like she didn't care.

Gently shaking her head, Amber turned to face Willow behind her, who already rooted around in Amber's purse for the mangled bear. Once she grabbed it, she examined it from several angles to inspect the damage.

"Do you remember which spells this one had?" Willow asked.

"The bears all had 'walk,' 'run,' 'lick paw,' and 'roar,'" Amber said. "The last one is the one that gave me the most trouble, since I had to add a noise dampening spell on top of the sound spell to make sure it wasn't so loud that it rattled the windows—which happened the first time."

With her focus still squared on the bear, Willow nodded. "Well, I'm not sure if this is good news or not, but I can't detect any Penhallow magic on this. That could mean the signature has already faded, or it could mean—"

"It was never there to begin with," Amber said, her shoulders slumping.

Picking up the three unscathed bears, Amber lined them up in a row on the floor. On Amber's long list for checking the safety of a toy, the last test involved activating spell after spell in rapid succession to help mimic the ever-changing desires of a child. If the toy was able to switch actions seamlessly for an hour without anything going haywire, the toy had passed inspection. Often if a toy malfunctioned, it happened in the first half hour of rapid play.

Amber stood before the bears with her arms crossed and waited for the cats to finish eating. Tom was already growling while he ate, sensing immediately that the toys he so despised had been placed nearby. Once he gulped down his food in record time, he darted under the bed. Alley slithered under it shortly after.

Blowing out a slow breath, Amber said, "Chocolate, Mocha, and…uhh…Potato…walk."

All three bears started to move, wandering aimlessly near her feet. She commanded them to lick their paws. She told one to roar, while the others were instructed to walk again. She cycled through each movement, save for "run," several more times, before she got up the nerve to issue the command that had been connected to Toast's demise.

The bears started throwing their heads back and offering muted, but still mildly threatening roars. One stopped just beside the dust ruffle, stomped one front paw, and let loose a roar loud enough to cause Tom to sprint out the other side a second later, hissing and spitting. He scrabbled across the hardwood floor of the studio and almost ran headlong into another bear slowly making his way across the apartment. Tom made a quick last-minute decision and dug his claws into the wood to stop himself long enough to change course and dash into the kitchen. A moment later, he sat on top of the counter. His chest heaved and his pupils were dilated. Alley had made it safely onto the bed and was hunkered down low on the comforter, her black-and-white ears pinned to the sides of her head.

Aunt G stood near the top of the staircase, her arms crossed as she watched the bears. "You've improved so much over the years, little mouse. I know you think of these toys as parlor tricks, but the precision needed to get these to react as quickly as they do is really remarkable."

Amber and Willow both gaped at her. It wasn't that Aunt G wasn't one to issue compliments, or even that she was a mean-spirited person, but Aunt G was the type to show you she cared through actions more than words. So when kind words were offered, it was a bit of a shock.

"Thanks, Aunt G," Amber said, her face flushing.

After letting the bears roam around for another minute, Amber switched the command to "walk." Eventually they were all in view and, one by one, she issued the "run" command.

And, one by one, like fireworks, the bears exploded.

Willow shrieked and clapped her hands over her mouth. Aunt G cursed. Amber's mouth fell open.

Boom, boom, boom. One after the other, the mangled bears, now robbed of their magic-given life, collapsed onto their sides, their faces blown away. Little bits of melted plastic marred Amber's floor. The edge of her rug, where one bear now lay, was charred black.

At a loss, Amber looked at her aunt and sister, then glanced over at the pile of newly magicked discs lying on the table. If the "run" spell was the one that was malfunctioning, *all* the cats she'd been working on for the festival were in jeopardy, too. Did she have to test every toy she'd made in the last few months to make sure it was safe? Did she need to toss this batch and start over completely? Almost every toy she made had a "run" spell. How many had she sold today that might encounter the same fate as the bears? How many in the past few weeks?

A pair of hands grasped either of Amber's elbows. She looked into her sister's concerned face.

"Stop it," Willow said gently. "Whatever that panicked brain of yours is telling you, don't listen. We'll figure this out. We'll start by testing one of each toy that has the 'run' spell. If only the bears were affected, that means we have a smaller number to worry about."

"Do you have a record of how many toys have been sold in the last few weeks—the bears especially?" Aunt G asked from behind them.

"I have a ledger under the counter downstairs," Amber said.

Without a word, Aunt G descended the steps.

"Let's go get one of each," Willow said. "You test them, and I'll check your grimoire to see if I can find anything immediately obvious about the language of the spell."

Then Willow headed for the stairs too.

Amber followed her but turned back toward her apartment. From here, she could only see the ruined bodies of two of the three bears. All of them had exploded the exact same way Toast had. It had to be her own faulty magic that did this.

She descended into The Quirky Whisker, wondering how someone who had been called a "legendary witch" just days ago could also be someone who couldn't even correctly bewitch a toy bear. If Amber and her magic were somehow the cure to the Penhallow curse, she thought the Penhallows were in even more trouble than they had been before.

The next couple of hours were spent testing the lions, tigers, leopards, panthers, ocelots, hippos, elephants, horses, and the like. None of the others exploded, though Amber was filled with unmitigated panic every time she commanded one to run. The floor of her apartment was nearly covered in various plastic animals. But they were all still intact. Only the bears had been compromised.

According to Amber's ledger, three bears had been sold to residents of Edgehill in the past week, including Sally. Amber would call the other two in the morning and ask for the toys to be brought back. She wasn't sure if lying about the need for the recall was the best course of action, as she had to assume that by tomorrow, every parent who had ever purchased a toy from her would know what had happened to Toast the Bear. But being upfront that the toys had a tendency to turn into mini plastic bombs would likely cause the rumor mill to spiral out of control.

Willow checked and rechecked the run spell Amber had written in her grimoire. She didn't find anything amiss.

They even worked to quickly get three more bears created—one with the run spell activated by each of the Blackwood women.

Not one of them exploded.

When the last of the new bears had been deactivated, Amber sat in the middle of the floor of her studio apartment and worried at a frayed end of the scorched rug. The reality of her findings had settled over her now. She couldn't deny it: someone had sabotaged the toys. Another Penhallow—if not several—was in town.

Someone had put innocent children in danger because of her.

Willow and Aunt G, without discussing it, layered the apartment in sound-dampening spells while Amber sat listlessly on the floor. The spells they cast felt the same as the one Zelda had used in Sorrel Garden when she'd wanted to keep the discussion between herself, Amber, and Edgar from being overheard. Once they finished, they sat at the table silently. Amber could feel their eyes on her.

Eventually, Amber said, "What do I do now? Those two other toys were sold over a week ago, so it could have been Damien and Devra. But…what if it wasn't?"

Neither one replied for a while.

"To start, I think we need to come up with another alarm spell to put on the shop," Aunt G said. "Something that will either specifically keep Penhallows out—regardless of whose face they're wearing—or at least warn us if one of them is nearby. We lucked out with Kieran if only because he was so sloppy. Though I suppose he always *wanted* us to know he was around. The Penhallows are either getting craftier, or Kieran just wasn't that careful."

The idea of dozens of face-changing Penhallows being in town, slowly driving Amber mad was…well…maddening.

"We'll also need detection and protection tinctures so we're not caught unawares when we're beyond the walls of this building," Aunt G said. "Something that's tailored specifically to Penhallows would be the most useful."

"That awful-tasting protection tincture you made us drink when Kieran was here …" Willow said. "Wasn't that one made to work against Penhallow attacks?"

Aunt G wrinkled her nose. "I may have fibbed. It was the most powerful tincture I had that protects against a magical attack, but it wasn't Penhallow-specific. The fib kept you girls from being more worried than you already were."

Amber grumbled to herself but didn't say anything. It was all such an Aunt G-like thing to do, it wasn't even worth the energy to be upset about it.

"I have a few witch friends in Maine I can call to see if they have any ideas," Aunt G said. "Do you think Zelda Rockrose might be able to help?"

"Maybe," Amber said. After a moment, she voiced the thing that had been weighing on her since the moment she'd realized the reality of the situation. It just made her a little nauseated to say out loud. "Should I keep the shop closed until we know it's okay to let anyone back in?"

It was the safest option, even if this was the absolute worst time of the year to do it.

"Probably," Willow said softly.

Amber slowly stood, found her cell phone, and sent texts to Ben and the Bowen sisters, letting them know that due to an emergency, the shop would be closed until further notice. She assured them that she would still pay them for the days they'd been scheduled.

"We'll figure this out, little mouse," Aunt G said after Amber just stood rooted to the spot, staring at nothing. "For now, we should get some sleep. Goodness knows what tomorrow will bring."

CHAPTER 4

At the crack of dawn Sunday morning, Amber found herself back inside The Quirky Whisker. She had been awake since four. Her usual Penhallow nightmares had been replaced by ones about Melanie, her face ghostly pale as she begged Amber not to let the same thing that had happened to her happen to Henrietta.

The shop looked just as she'd left it. Aunt G and Willow had placed three layers of alarm spells over the doors and windows before bed last night. A bell would have gone off in their heads had the alarm been tripped, so Amber knew everything was likely okay, but it took a sweep of the shop before the knot of tension in her chest would fully unfurl.

Reluctantly, Amber walked to the front door and stared at the chalkboard sign hanging there. The board was one of the few ways Amber flexed her magic muscles on a daily basis—aside from the toys, of course. The logo was a bespectacled, top-hat-wearing cat who always had a cheery expression on his whiskered face. With a quick often-used incantation and the swipe of her hand, Amber could change the message and the expression of the cat to provide a unique welcome message for her customers each day.

She plucked the board off the door, then turned her back to Russian Blue Avenue to shield her actions from view. The cat looked his jolly self as he gripped the brim of his top hat in two claws and winked out at his audience.

With a resigned sigh, she uttered the spell and swiped a palm over the board. The cat went from jolly to forlorn. His eyes were downcast, and his hat slipped a little low over his brow. Next to him were the words: "Sorry. We're closed for the rest of the week."

Amber hung the sign back up, her heart heavy.

Around seven, she gave Zelda Rockrose a call, hoping the woman could offer some suggestions on how to create Penhallow-specific spells. Zelda didn't answer, so Amber left her a quick message.

At opening time, Amber made calls to both of the parents who had purchased the toy bears and let them know that the toy may be defective and that she would like to issue a refund.

The first parent arrived half an hour later. Russian Blue Avenue was already bustling with people, many of whom were carrying bags adorned with the logos of other shops nearby. The sight panged her. She glanced across the street and marveled at how the line outside Purrfectly Scrumptious seemed to get longer every day, even this early in the morning.

While Amber tended to the parents today, Aunt G and Willow would remain upstairs. They had told her that they didn't want to be in the way since this was such an emotionally charged time, but Amber suspected they were using skills both magic and non-magic alike to rid the studio apartment of the evidence of the exploding bears.

Amber unlocked the door for the woman waiting outside and hurriedly ushered her in.

"*I thought you were closed!*" someone called out. "*Is the sign wrong?*"

"Still closed!" Amber said. "Sorry." She quickly locked the door after the woman.

Claire Petrie had moved to Edgehill about a year ago, from what Amber could remember. She'd first bought one of Amber's toys during the festival the year she and her family had moved here, and she'd been buying a new one for her daughter every few months since then.

"Thank you so much for coming by," Amber said. "Did you bring the toy with you?"

Claire fished the bear out of her purse. "What kind of defect does it have? I…uhh…heard Sally Long claim her bear *exploded*?"

Amber took the unmarred bear from Claire and gave his little plastic snout an absentminded pat. "Well, sort of. I believe some of the wiring got too hot and then most of the bear…uh…melted."

Claire winced. "Sally likes to exaggerate, so I figured 'exploding' had to be hyperbole. I really appreciate you offering a refund on the off chance something might be wrong with this one. Wendy loves these toys; she'll be sad we had to return this one."

Amber rounded the counter and made her way to the cash register. "Better safe than sorry. We're actually going to be closed for the next few days while I assess *all* of the toys. I'm a little nervous about so many out-of-town folks possibly picking up a defective toy. They won't be as easy to recall if they leave Edgehill."

Claire nodded, but Amber could tell by her creased brow that she thought Amber's decision was a touch dramatic. Amber didn't want to get into the whole "and a Penhallow might be trying to destroy my business from the inside" thing.

After Amber had issued the refund, she said, "I'm working on some Here-and-Meow-exclusive toy cats this year. I'd like to gift one to Wendy when they're ready. What's her favorite color?"

"Oh, that's so sweet," Claire said as they made their way to the door. "Green."

Amber definitely needed to find a better shade than "seasickness." "Green it is."

An hour after Amber had seen Claire out, the second parent arrived. The interaction went much the same as the first. Paul was a bit grumpier about the whole thing than Claire had been—clearly Sally had gotten to him, too—but he was more upset about how much his son Kyle had screamed his head off when Paul had explained that the toy had to be returned.

While she held open the door for a retreating Paul, a few more customers asked Amber why the store wasn't open. It hurt to turn away so much potential business during the busiest part of the year, but as soon as she reminded herself that any one of these curious potential shoppers could be a Penhallow trying to gain access to her shop, she no longer felt bad about closing and locking the door.

She'd just heaved out a long, weary sigh when her cell phone rang. Fishing it out of her back pocket, she hoped she'd see Jack's smiling face staring up at her. He'd be able to calm her down. Instead, it was an unfamiliar, out-of-state phone number that scrolled across her screen.

"Hello?" she said.

"Hello, dear." It took Amber only a moment to recognize the voice as Zelda's.

"Sorry it took me so long to call you back this morning," Zelda said. "I'm guessing you've already heard, though. It can't be a coincidence, given the hubbub."

Amber stilled. "Hubbub?"

"Oh," Zelda said, then cleared her throat. "Kieran Penhallow escaped from prison late Friday night."

The day after he'd called her. "*Escaped*?"

"Yes. My daughter said the witch community is in full panic mode," Zelda said. "There are a few witch guards at the prison, and since my daughter is in law enforcement herself, she's friends with a few of the guards. From what the guards have been able to glean, a witch got him out."

Amber didn't know what to say. "He just called me the other day."

Zelda hmmed. "Did he now?"

Amber couldn't put a finger on what it was about Zelda that sent off little trilling bells of alarm for her. While Amber wanted nothing more than to have more witches she could confide in, she knew that confiding in the *wrong* witch could spell untold trouble. Perhaps Amber just had trust issues in general these days. What Amber really needed was to get Zelda Rockrose and Gretchen Blackwood in the same room—Aunt G would have Zelda figured out in a hot second.

"You don't have to tell me what he phoned you about," Zelda said after the silence stretched on. "From what I hear, it was a big to-do. All the electricity in the place shut off at once and the backup generators never kicked on. Staff and prisoners alike were placed under sleep spells, which started to wear off while the electricity was still out, so when staff came to, they had to navigate the place in the dark. They didn't know if any of the prisoners had escaped."

Amber swallowed. "Did they? Other than Kieran, I mean?"

"Just him," Zelda said. "And the spells on the staff wore off before the ones on the prisoners did. Little bits of glass were found in various rooms, so it's believed the witch or witches threw vials of sleep tinctures. If crafted and then thrown just right, sleep tinctures can be used like smoke bombs. One smashed vial could knock out several people within seconds of the tincture making contact with the air. Anyway, by the time they got the electricity up and running again, all the cells were checked. Every door was still closed and locked—including Kieran's. But he was gone."

When Kieran had called Amber three days before, he had dropped the bombshell that his powers had come back. His powers were changed, though. His magic was no longer the tainted, cursed thing that had warped his mind and turned him into a monster with an unquenchable thirst for more power. He'd said that his powers felt cleaner now. He'd said that Amber, when she had severed his connection to magic, hadn't stolen away his magic so much as healed him.

Kieran had been careful not to use words like "witch" and "magic" on the phone call with her, as calls were recorded. But if there were witches on staff at the prison, who knows who could have heard what he'd said—or what he may have blabbed freely to someone else—causing that information to result in a prison break.

"Do they have any idea who got him out?" Amber asked. "Is it possible he got *himself* out?"

"I'm not sure how he could have gotten himself out of a locked cell when he'd been stripped of his magic." Zelda's tone implied she was worried about Amber's mental state.

So the news about Kieran's magic being healed hadn't become widespread knowledge. Amber decided to keep this information to herself for now.

"As far as I know…uh…Neil Penhallow is his closest living family member," Zelda said.

Amber bristled at the name of the man who had killed her parents.

"But anyone even loosely related to his immediate family would want him out," Zelda said. "News has gotten around about how you cured him of his curse. Perhaps it wasn't a Penhallow who had an interest in him. He went from being a very powerful witch to being a relatively normal magic-free human—this is a first. Kieran is a curiosity for many right now."

Amber felt deeply unsettled by all of this.

After a brief bout of silence, Zelda said, "So I gather there's a *different* reason why you called me?"

Putting aside her reservations, Amber told Zelda about what had happened recently both with the toy bears and with Henrietta.

"Oh my," Zelda said, drawing the last word out. "Honestly what troubles me most is that this is all coinciding with Kieran's escape. The Penhallows are no doubt making their play."

Amber just wished she knew what that play was. "Do you have any idea how we could craft spells or tinctures that would be Penhallow-specific? My business is effectively shut down until I can find a way to screen who comes and goes, and who I interact with in town. I don't think anyone would *keep* sabotaging items from my shop; I believe they wanted my attention more than anything. Which they have. But now I need a way to know who's a Penhallow wearing a false face."

"They could be wandering town with their own faces, too," Zelda said. "If their natural form is a stranger to you, a mask isn't necessary."

Amber groaned.

"I have an idea, though," Zelda said. "A spell for clarity should work, but it would need to be tailored. Unfortunately, the only way to assess whether or not the spell worked would be to test it on a Penhallow."

Amber sighed. "I can get my sister started on something. She's not as skilled as the Penhallows are at glamours, but she's pretty good."

A little part of Amber hoped Kieran would call her back soon. While he'd been cursed, he'd tried to kill her. She still had nightmares about that encounter on a weekly basis. And yet, the intellectual part of her knew that the Kieran who had called her three nights ago, trying both to thank her and to use careful language, had been the *real* Kieran. Not the crazed, power-hungry man who had terrorized herself and Edgehill.

If he could somehow be a buffer between herself and the rest of his cursed family, she would welcome him back to Edgehill without question.

But if his cursed family had already gotten to him, was it possible that they could undo the work Amber had done? Could they reignite the curse in Kieran—like a once-dormant ember, stoked back into a raging fire?

"That sounds like a good start," Zelda said. "I'll put out my own feelers here and check in with my daughter as often as I can. If I hear anything, I'll let you know."

"Thank you," Amber said. "Oh! Think of a code word we can use so I know it's you the next time we talk."

"Butterscotch toffee," Zelda said without hesitation. "It's my favorite."

"Perfect."

"Stay safe, dear."

As Amber hung up, she wondered if it was already too late for that.

CHAPTER 5

For the next few hours, Amber and Aunt G worked on Amber's Here-and-Meow-exclusive toys while Willow scoured all their grimoires for a suitable clarity spell. She would then use that as a starting point for a more complicated spell geared specifically toward witches wearing a glamour. Given how often Willow uttered profanities and then paced the small studio apartment while pulling at one—or both—of her long braids, Amber guessed it wasn't going well.

When Amber's phone rang just before noon, the grin that spread across her face as she saw who it was was both embarrassing and involuntary.

"Ohh, it looks like the baker is calling …" Aunt G said, waggling her eyebrows suggestively.

Amber snatched up her phone, stuck her tongue out at her aunt with all the maturity of a teenager, and then made her way to the stairs.

"Tell Jack I say hi!" Willow called out from behind her.

Amber answered the call just as she reached the Employee Only door at the base of the steps. "Hey, Jack."

Sound-dampening spells had become a permanent fixture on the building at this point, so she at least felt comfortable talking freely.

"Hey, Amber," he said, his voice hushed. She pictured him huddled in a corner of Purrcolate, trying to avoid being overheard by his brother Larry, or their newest employee, Sabrina, who had developed a pastime of embarrassing Jack about Amber at every opportunity.

"*Are you talking to your giiiirlfriend?*" she could imagine Sabrina asking, causing Jack's cheeks to turn as red as the raspberries baked into his scones.

Amber didn't hear much in the background, so maybe he was hiding in a quiet section of the parking lot.

"I'm hearing all kinds of Quirky Whisker rumors today," he said. "What's going on over there? Is it true you had to shut the place down because the whole toy section caught on fire?"

"Good grief," Amber muttered, then told him about the exploding bears, Henrietta's coma, and Kieran's prison escape.

"Wow," he heaved when she was done. "How is your life this exciting? And what are you doing with boring old me?"

Amber flushed. "First of all, you're not boring. Second of all, if you actually *are* boring, then boring is very attractive."

"Oh stop, you flirt," he said, laughing softly. Then he lowered his voice a little more as he said, "So, uh, do you think Kieran is on his way…*here?*"

Amber hated how quickly worry overtook his tone. A big part of why Jack had asked Aunt G to wipe his memory a few months ago was because Jack had witnessed what Kieran was capable of. With only the aid of his magic, Kieran had nearly choked Amber to death. Jack had felt so powerless in the wake of it, that in his terror, he'd requested to have it all purged from his mind. Instinctively, Jack wanted to be able to protect Amber from people like Kieran. When he realized he couldn't, he took the chicken's way out by making himself forget his own non-witch shortcomings.

"I don't know what Kieran's plan is," Amber said after a moment. "No one knows how he got out either. He either magicked his way out or someone else did. It could have been someone who knew his magic has been healed. It could have been someone who broke him out *because* it was healed. It could be a fellow Penhallow…or it could be someone else entirely."

"And it could be someone who is connected to what's happening with your shop," Jack said, "or it could be a coincidence."

"Exactly," Amber said. "And until I know, I'll feel better keeping the shop closed. It's the one thing I can control right now. We're working on a way to figure out who's a Penhallow and who isn't. I'm just trapped here until then."

"I'm really sorry this is happening," Jack said. "Especially on the eve of the Here and Meow."

Amber sighed.

"Tell you what…I've got dinner covered," he said. "Text me what you guys want and I'll drop it off tonight. And don't protest. If you do, I'll bring you ten olive, pineapple, and anchovy pizzas. Don't make me waste food, Amber."

She laughed. "Fine. And thank you."

"Of course," he said, quickly followed by a grunt. "Ugh, I gotta go. Larry is waving me down. I think the Dungeons & Dragons group is back. Those nerds eat a *lot* of scones."

Amber was still smiling softly to herself as she hung up, then let out a startled yelp when the mental alarm in her head went off. Someone was trying to get into the shop without permission. Quickly glancing up, she rapidly scrolled through a list of things she could use as a weapon. But she immediately relaxed when she saw the wild-eyed brunette at her door.

"It's okay!" Amber called out, hoping her aunt and sister could hear her. "It's just Kim!"

With a quick incantation, Amber dropped the spell on the front door and went to pull it open, only to hesitate with her fingers on the deadbolt. If the Penhallows were doing their best to work past Amber's defenses and wear her down, showing up wearing Kim's face was a good way to do it.

Amber opened the door, but only a crack, and peered out at her friend. The scent of food—most likely sand-wiches—hit Amber's nose and her stomach rumbled. Kim held up a large white paper bag with the words "Catty Melt" stamped on the front.

A glamour changed the way someone looked, not the way they thought. So even if this *were* a Penhallow who looked like Kim, they wouldn't have the same memories as Kim.

"What did you get me?" Amber asked in a way that she hoped was casual and not accusatory.

Kim's brow creased. "A turkey on rye with no mustard. The usual. Why?"

Amber let her in. Once the door was locked behind her friend, Amber filled Kim in on what she'd missed since this morning.

"Holy mackerel," Kim said. "I've been trying to keep out of your hair since that voicemail you left yesterday, but then I heard the shop was closed down! That's why I came over with sympathy sandwiches. I just didn't think things could have gotten this bad this fast."

"The worst part of all this," Amber said, "is that I don't know how Henrietta is doing. I just wish I knew if her tea had been tampered with the same way the toys had been, or if what happened to her really was my fault."

"I don't believe for a second that it was anything you did," Kim said. "But it's giving me the worst flashbacks of what happened to Melanie. If Whitney and Susie weren't already in jail, I would say it was them." Then Kim gasped. "What if it's not a Penhallow at all, but a copycat!"

Amber doubted that was the case.

Kim placed the large bag of sandwiches on the counter and pulled out one wrapped in brown paper. It was held closed with a strip of masking tape, and Amber's name was written on it in black marker. Kim pointed the sandwich at Amber like it was a fencing foil. "This is not just a sympathy sandwich, but a bribery sandwich."

Cocking a brow, Amber said, "Oh?"

"I'm friends with Terri over at Edgehill General. I was there this morning talking to her about Henrietta. I bring the nurses doughnuts and coffee once a week, so they all love me.

Anyway, she said we could go in to see Henrietta this afternoon! I know she's in a coma and all, but Terri said it helps coma patients sometimes to hear familiar voices, you know?"

Amber did know, but she wondered if it was protocol to let non-family members in so soon. After all, not even Henrietta's sister had been in to see her yet. At least Amber didn't think so.

"I was also thinking…that if this Thea person is as much of a hardnose as she sounds, this may be your only chance to see Henrietta before Thea gets here. Be proud of me! I bribed nurses instead of bugging you yesterday when you clearly needed to be with your family. I showed incredible restraint," Kim said.

Amber laughed. "I'm quite proud."

Kim grinned. "Also…maybe…oh, I don't know, you could try to figure out what happened to Hen like you did with Melanie?"

Amber chewed on her bottom lip. As much as she wanted to go, if only to see Henrietta and to see for herself that she was alive, the idea of walking into a place full of unfamiliar faces made Amber uneasy.

"I'll be your bodyguard," Kim said, waving the wrapped sandwich around as if she were going to stab unseen assailants with it. "No one will talk to you if you don't want them to. I'm the festival director of the Here-and-flippin'-Meow. I can handle anything."

Smiling, Amber said, "Okay, but on one condition: let's see if Willow has made any progress yet."

"I got them sympathy-slash-bribery sandwiches, too. Well, I got Willow two of them since she eats like a linebacker," Kim said, depositing Amber's sandwich back in the bag and then following Amber up the stairs.

Willow was sitting cross-legged on Amber's bed, a pen caught between her teeth as she stared down at the yellow legal pad on the comforter.

Stopping at the foot of the bed, Amber asked Willow, "How's it going?"

Willow flinched. "Oh! Hi. Hi, Kim. I didn't hear you guys come in." She sniffed the air suddenly. "Are those Catty Melt sandwiches?"

"Yes, and you can have one after you tell me about the spell."

"Oh, right," Willow said, then climbed off the bed with her legal pad. "I think I've got one working for at least a basic glamour. Let's test it out. That's the spell there," she said, pointing to a circled piece of scribbled text at the bottom of the page. "I'll glamour myself. You read the spell, and then we'll see if it works."

Shrugging, Amber read over the spell a few times to get comfortable with the words. Her own magic felt a bit reluctant every time she read it. As always, her intention was the most important part of casting a spell. *I want to detect glamours so I can protect my family from the Penhallows.*

Her magic remained sluggish.

Okay, so that wasn't quite right. Often, one's intention was far more selfish than one wanted to believe.

I want to detect glamours so I'm not caught by surprise.

Her magic thrummed.

Amber looked up when Kim gasped. Standing before Amber wasn't Willow, but the redheaded Sienna Tate. It was the persona Amber herself had taken on last month when she had been trying to ferret out who had killed the police chief of Marbleglen.

"That is *so* cool!" Kim said.

Amber ignored her, if only to help keep herself focused. With her intention true and alive in her mind, she mentally uttered the spell. The glamour didn't peel off Willow so much as turn it translucent. *Aura* came to mind. Or even the way ghosts were often represented on TV. There was a see-through version of Sienna that lay on top of Willow's natural form.

"What do you two see?" Amber asked Kim and Aunt G.

"Pretty redheaded girl," Aunt G said.

"Anything else?" Amber asked.

Aunt G and Kim shared a look, then shrugged.

"This is a really good start, Will," Amber told her sister.

"Cool. I'll keep working on it," Willow said, both Sienna's translucent mouth and Willow's own solid one talking at once. "I don't know how long this one will last. I'm guessing the more times it has to reveal someone's true face to you, the quicker it'll wear off."

Full of apprehension, Amber followed Kim back down the stairs.

Edgehill General was located on the east side of town, where a large portion of the town's population lived—including Kim. The town's biggest grocery store, the closest thing

Edgehill had to a mall, and Edgehill High were all also on this side of town.

Amber had brought her grimoire with her, and on the drive to the hospital, she worked on crafting a spell she could use on Henrietta. It would be similar to the one she used on Melanie in the morgue. While Amber had had no idea how a memory reveal spell might work on a person after they'd passed, she also had no idea how it would work on someone in a coma.

She had initially tried to explain her plan to Kim, but Kim was so enthralled by it all that they almost got into several accidents each time she slammed on the brakes whenever a detail was especially exciting. So Amber decided to keep the rest of it to herself. Otherwise, they might arrive at the hospital as patients, rather than visitors.

The hospital looked more like a high school than a sprawling complex found in large cities. A large, peaked awning sat above the entrance of the one-story building, the façade made up of brick and tan stucco. The sliding glass doors were flanked by floor-to-ceiling windows on either side.

Amber had written the spell she needed on a scrap of paper she'd stuffed into her pocket, but had decided to keep her grimoire in her purse. Leaving it behind in Kim's car felt dangerous, but so did carrying it with her. This Penhallow threat had turned Amber into a skittish rabbit and she didn't like it one bit. All of her progress over the last few months felt like it was unraveling, like a moth-eaten sweater. As Amber walked with Kim along the shade-dappled sidewalk, she tried to relax her racing heart.

This hospital isn't swarming with Penhallows, she assured herself. What business would any of them have here? Of course, if Henrietta's current state had been the result of the Penhallows, then perhaps one of them was loitering at the hospital, like a murderer who revisits the scene of a crime.

The door to the hospital whispered open, letting out a wave of too-cold air. Kim marched over the threshold with no hesitation and headed down the threadbare navy blue carpet that lined the walkway. A few photographs lined one side of the hall in random intervals—mostly benign landscapes in old-fashioned, faux-silver frames. The only décor on the other side was a sad-looking Ficus tree in a wicker pot, a few pieces of loose fake Spanish moss littering the ground at its base.

Straight ahead sat a U-shaped nurse's station where two women were busy with work, their heads bowed. They each had a head of short, curly brown hair and were wearing green scrubs. Amber and Kim were a few feet from the station when one of the women looked up and grinned.

"Well, hey there, Kimmy!" the middle-aged woman said, waving enthusiastically. She quickly let herself out of the back of the U and hurried around the desk so she could give Kim a hug. The woman was just barely five feet tall and was a bit portly. Once she broke the embrace, she said, "Two visits in one day? I hope you didn't bring any more doughnuts." She patted her stomach. "I'm going to have to start walking ten miles a day instead of five if you keep this up!"

Kim laughed. "No more doughnuts until next week, I promise."

The woman smiled; it lit up the room.

"Terri, you know Amber, right?" Kim asked.

Amber held out a hand when Terri turned her bright smile toward her. "Nice to meet you."

Terri shook it, then patted the back of Amber's hand. "You as well, sweets. And, for the record, I don't believe a word about what they say about you."

Uh …

Kim offered a short, hysterical laugh that caused Amber, Terri, and the other nurse at the station to all flinch. "Can we still see Henrietta? We both don't have much of a lunch break left …"

"Oh!" Terri said and tapped herself on the nose twice with a pointer finger. "You bet. Follow me."

They headed down another hallway straight back from the nurse's station, then took a quick right into another hallway. This one was lined with closed doors, reminding Amber of a quiet hotel more than a hospital. But then Amber remembered that the noisier surgery and emergency section of the hospital had a separate entrance. And if the surgery needed was extensive or the emergency was truly dire, patients often had to be transported to a bigger city nearby.

Terri stopped halfway down the hall and knocked on a door to her left. She smiled sheepishly over her shoulder at Kim and Amber. "I know she can't give me permission to enter, but I like giving her the chance anyway. She's been here two full days now." Terri waited a moment, heard nothing, and then opened the door.

It was a tiny room with a single bed. A boxy TV was mounted on the wall across from it, the screen off. A set of heavy curtains on the wall opposite the door were pulled open to reveal a small courtyard. Beyond the window, an older man sat on a stone bench in a bathrobe.

Henrietta lay unconscious in the small bed. She was neatly tucked under the cream-colored blanket, her arms lying by her sides. A monitor on a stand stood by the bed, the screen awash with blinking lights and pulsing lines. A few wires snaked from one hand and arm, and into the monitor displaying Henrietta's vital signs.

The woman's signature wild mop of curly red hair was splayed out across the white pillowcase. The vibrant red made Henrietta's pale skin look even paler. Though the beeping screen beside her prone form implied Henrietta was still alive, her ghostly pallor and stillness spoke to something much worse.

Oh, Henrietta …

"I'll leave you two here to have a private chat, hm?" Terri said. "Just talk to her as you would normally. It truly does help brain function."

With that, Terri ducked out of the room and softly closed the door behind her.

"Okay!" Kim said in her best "we're on a clandestine mission!" voice, and immediately began creeping around the room.

After a few long seconds of watching Kim move around the room like she was in a spy movie, Amber said, "*What are you doing?*"

"Looking for cameras!" Kim said. "We need to make sure we're not being watched."

Amber rolled her eyes, but she did a quick search, too. After they decided they weren't under surveillance, Amber dropped her purse onto the lone chair in the room and took the scribbled spell out of her pocket.

She studied it for a moment, double-checked her intention, and then approached Henrietta's bedside. Blowing out a breath, she grabbed hold of Henrietta's hand, this one without anything attached to her pale skin. Unlike Melanie's hand, which had been cold and stiff, Henrietta's hand was warm. This bolstered Amber's hope more than the rhythmic beeping of the monitor on the other side of the bed.

Closing her eyes, Amber spoke the words of the spell, willing Henrietta to find a way to let Amber know what her last memory had been. Amber knew Henrietta had been on the phone with Thea when she'd collapsed, but if Henrietta hadn't been met with foul play in the way Melanie had been, it was very likely that Henrietta's last memory would reveal nothing.

A time spell was too risky at the moment, especially when Amber didn't have a solid time when this phone call had taken place, or how soon after that second cup of tea Henrietta had started to feel somewhat off. Not to mention the fact that Henrietta was currently lost, in a way, in her own mind. What happened just before she fell ill could feel like it had happened years ago, while something that happened when she was ten could feel like yesterday.

Amber imagined Henrietta trapped in her body, slipping below the surface of her own memories like they were dark, turbulent waves trying to carry her under. She envisioned Henrietta's hand above the surface, grasping for someone or something to pull her to safety.

Usually, when Amber used her time or memory magic, a bright burst of light tore through her vision. This time, it was a muted flash, like the last dying pulse of a flashlight before the batteries went dead.

Amber's mind filled with a familiar view of Russian Blue Avenue, not the inside of Henrietta's house, as Amber had expected. Henrietta walked down the sidewalk with a purchase from The Quirky Whisker, given the brief glances of the bag Amber could make out in her peripheral vision. She soon made a left around the side of the building toward the parking lot. Amber realized then that there was no sound in this memory. Or, rather, the sound was as muted as the light had been earlier. A low hum of voices, like a TV kept at a low volume, was all she could hear despite the sidewalks being packed with people. Which spoke to this potentially being a recent memory, as Edgehill was busiest during the Here and Meow, summer, and the winter holidays. People's attire implied spring more than summer, but Amber couldn't be sure of that.

Henrietta had just reached her car when a slight uptick in sound made her turn. Molly Hargrove stood a few feet away, her face contorted. She pointed a finger at Henrietta and shouted something. Henrietta said something back, then hurried to unlock the door. Molly reached her before Henrietta could get the car door open and yanked Henrietta back by the elbow. The two women shouted at each other. Amber tried to read Molly's lips, but the argument was too frantic, and over too soon, for Amber to grasp much of anything beyond the fact that it had been an emotional exchange.

Henrietta eventually got herself into her car, tossed her bag into the passenger seat, and then took off out of the parking lot, leaving Molly standing there alone, her chest heaving.

The muted flash of white signified the end of the memory, and Amber was kicked back out into the present, disoriented. She quickly let go of Henrietta's hand and placed her own on her forehead. The room spun.

The monitor beside the bed gave a shrill whine and then the beeps sped up at an alarming rate. Henrietta's forehead creased slightly. Was she waking up?

Terri hurried into the room a moment later, followed by two other nurses. Amber wondered if she'd heard the beeping or if she'd gotten an alert at her desk. Either way, she urged Kim and Amber to leave while they tended to Henrietta.

Amber didn't say anything until she and Kim were back in Kim's car, the scent of their uneaten sandwiches filling the space. Amber hardly remembered leaving Henrietta's room, much less getting into Kim's car. What could Molly Hargrove and Henrietta have been arguing about?

"Oh my God, Amber!" Kim finally chirped. "You have to tell me what you saw."

Amber snapped out of it and explained what the memory had shown her. "The thing is, I don't know when that memory happened."

Kim reached into the back seat to pluck a sandwich out of the bag. "Eat this. Maybe it'll help you come up with an idea of what to do next."

With that, Kim pulled out of the parking lot and headed back toward The Quirky Whisker. While Amber ate, she ran through all the possible reasons why Henrietta and Molly would have been arguing. Amber cursed herself once again for not being nosier. She knew so little about Henrietta.

"Do you think Molly was doing a follow-up story on Henrietta and her divorce or something?" Kim asked. "Hen's divorce was movie-level coo-coo town, after all."

Amber swallowed her bite of sandwich. Of course Kim would have the scoop. "What made it so coo-coo?"

Kim turned to look at her askance and the car swerved. Kim yelped as she righted it. "It's criminal how little gossip you hear, you know that?"

Amber winced as she peered down the side of her seat where a knocked-loose pickle had fallen during Kim's near miss with a parked car. Amber swiped at the corner of her mouth with the back of her hand. "Why do I need to keep up with gossip when I have you?"

"True, true," Kim said, thankfully keeping her eyes on the road this time. "Okay, so Hen's ex was a financial guy at some big company. He had been siphoning cash out of their accounts for years, apparently. He was funding his and Hen's lavish lifestyle with all the stolen money. A few years ago, just before she moved here, a woman contacted Hen and said she knew 'exactly what her husband was up to,' then hung up."

"Oh gosh!"

"I know! So, of course, Hen immediately thinks he's having an affair and starts snooping. Hen was blindsided by the call, but she also had enough little suspicions over the years that it piqued her curiosity enough to make her go digging. She eventually found all this evidence that her husband was actually a high-level crook."

"Dang," Amber said. "Then what?"

"Well, this woman ended up being the wife of another man at this company, and she had just stumbled on all this evidence that her husband and Hen's husband were running a scheme to rob this company to fund an even shadier operation that had something to do with drugs. Or was it money laundering? I can't remember. It was bad, whatever it was," Kim said. "She and Hen banded together to take down their husbands before their husbands took *them* down as collateral damage.

"They sold their story to a newspaper for a pretty penny, then on the same day, they left their husbands and fled the town they were living in. Hen moved here, and the other lady moved to the east coast. Apparently, the story broke a few days later and both men ended up in jail. I think the company paid Hen and the other lady hush money in exchange for not doing more interviews. The company folded pretty recently, though. I think Hen's money from the whole debacle is running out."

"Wow," Amber said. "Why would Molly want to do a follow-up story on it now unless it was an anniversary or something?"

"No clue. It's just a theory," Kim said. "None of it explains how or why Hen is in a coma though, right? That's still the Penhallows."

The bite of sandwich in her mouth suddenly tasted like sawdust, and she grimaced as she swallowed it down. She placed the rest of the sandwich on the paper laid out across her lap, her appetite gone. She could give the rest to Willow.

When they pulled up outside The Quirky Whisker, Amber wrapped up the rest of her lunch and stuck it in her purse.

"Feel free to say no, given everything," Kim said, a bit hesitantly after a brief pause. People milled about the sidewalk on either side of the car. "But do you think you can make it to the float-decorating session tonight? It's the last, last one to put the final touches on the float before the parade on Friday. Harlo and Bianca were both total nightmares yesterday. I can't wait until this is over."

Amber didn't like the idea of being around so many people without having a proper clarity spell in place, but she also knew how stressed out Kim was with all her Here and Meow Festival director duties. And despite all that, Kim still found ways to make sure everyone else was doing okay, as evidenced by the sandwich in Amber's lap, and the weekly doughnuts delivered to the hospital.

A woman holding the hands of two small boys hurried across Russian Blue Avenue. One of the boys broke free just as they reached the sidewalk in front of Purrfectly Scrumptious and he dropped to his knees before Savannah the Maine coon, who was sprawled on her back while two little girls cooed over her. Savannah's eyes were squinted closed as she basked in the attention. The Here and Meow season was no doubt Savannah's favorite.

"I'll be there," Amber said, not realizing that was going to be her answer until it was out of her mouth. "I may bring Willow with me though. You know, as magical backup."

Kim beamed. "The more the merrier! And it'll be good to have a bigger buffer. I may strangle Bianca otherwise."

"She wants to have a spa day or a girl's night out when all this festival madness is over, by the way," Amber said.

"Oh my God. Amber, she is the *least* relaxing person on this planet!" Kim said. "A spa day with Bianca Pace! Now I've heard everything."

Amber laughed. "We'll meet you over at the float barn in a few hours, okay?"

Kim nodded. "Sounds good."

"And thanks for lunch."

"Of course," Kim said. "Now get out of here. I have like ten minutes to get back to the bank and I have to scarf *my* sandwich on the way."

Stepping out onto the sidewalk, Amber only allowed herself to stand there for a moment before she hurried inside the shop. Even with the clarity spell in place, Amber didn't trust her eyes.

She quickly closed and locked the door behind her, peering out the glass at the bustling world happening beyond the quiet walls of her shop. Amber had come so far in the last few months—actually venturing out to meet new people, strengthening her friendships, and trying new things. And now she was locked up again like the recluse she'd once been. The Penhallows had taken her parents and now they were taking her sense of safety in her beloved town.

How long would it be before they took something else?

CHAPTER 6

Amber and Willow headed out for Marbleglen a little before 4 PM. They both had cast Willow's latest version of the clarity spell before they'd left.

"Do I get to meet the infamous Bianca Pace?" Willow asked from the passenger seat just as Sphynx Way turned into Buttercup Road.

"She should be there. When Bianca and I were caught up in trying to free Simon, Harlo got a taste of what it would be like to be the head of the Floral Frenzy Festival. I think most people like working with Harlo better, and Bianca senses that. So now she's trying to insert herself back into the leadership position so Harlo doesn't snatch it away from her," Amber said.

"Who I really want to meet is Simon," Willow said. "It would be nice to get to know a witch we aren't related to."

After the ordeal Simon Ricinus had gone through last month—being framed for the murder of Marbleglen's Chief of Police—Amber hoped Simon was able to bounce back. Amber had no clue what jail was like to begin with, but to be there when you weren't guilty of the crime had to be ten times worse. Simon was a witch, so he had magic at his disposal, but he also couldn't have used it so brazenly that someone would have realized he was…different. That was a can of worms no witch living in a magic-free area wanted to open.

She hoped he was back in his garden that he loved so much, and was as busy making wreaths for the Floral Frenzy as Amber was at making her toy cats for the Here and Meow. She hoped his sleep wasn't plagued by nightmares.

Willow oohed and ahhed at the beauty of Marbleglen as Amber drove the now-familiar path to the float barn tucked behind the gates of Magnolia Estates. When Amber drove past the house on Sweetbay Court where Randy Tillman had been staying last month, she gave a little shudder. Tillman, along with the new chief of police and the mayor of Marbleglen, had been caught up in the murder plot of the former chief of police, Eric Jameson. Unraveling the plot had, at one point, involved Amber conducting multiple stakeouts on this very road while she was disguised as the redheaded Sienna Tate. Amber had spent three long days as Sienna, waiting for Tillman to do something nefarious and show his hand.

The gravel lot to the right of the float barn was packed with cars, so Amber and Willow had to make a trek up the road on foot. Since float decorating was messy business, she and Willow were both dressed in old jeans and oversized shirts. Willow's had the logo of her company on the breast pocket of her grungy shirt. Amber's jeans were still speckled with spots of black from all the times she'd absently rubbed her dirty fingers on her pants during the process of placing an endless number of black onion seeds on the Edgehill cat float. Amber had her brown mid-back length hair in its usual braid, while Willow's was tied up in a wild bun on top of her head that still managed to look chic.

Mid-to-late spring was Amber's favorite time of the year, where it was some perfect mix of not-too-hot and not-too-cold. The sound of voices hummed in the slight breeze. The buzz of the insects in the air seemed to be in sync with Amber's own buzzing anticipation of seeing the floats again. The Blackwood sisters both had artistic sides—Amber with her toys, and Willow with her graphic design—which they'd learned a few months ago was something they'd inherited from their mother. The Henbane grimoire was filled with detailed drawings of herbs and plants. Amber knew Willow would appreciate the design of the floats with the eyes of an artist.

When Willow finally had a full view of the barn, she stopped in her tracks and gasped.

The leftmost float was the one designed like a vibrant garden. The top of the giant willow tree that was the star of the float still hadn't been attached to the trunk yet; the cap of the tree adorned in long, droopy branches was being worked on just outside the barn by a cluster of teenage volunteers. At the front of the float sat the giant white mushroom with large red circles decorating its cap, and an all-black, dog-sized beetle perched on top. A giant ladybug now crawled its way up the bark-covered trunk of the tree. Beyond the willow was a garden of wildflowers, some being visited by insects propped up on wires to help mimic flight. The whole thing was just as much a celebration of the beauty and vibrancy of spring as Kim's Hair Ball gala had been.

The rightmost float was Edgehill's. From what Amber could tell, the float was mostly complete. The cat at the head of the float reminded Amber of her Alley. Its body was nearly all black, but a white triangle-shaped patch covered the cat's nose and half of one cheek. Just behind him, Amber could make out the cat who sat on its haunches and licked a paw. The pads of the cat's raised foot were lined with the soft petals of pink roses.

As much as Amber loved the cat float, and admired the beauty of the garden float, it was the float in the middle that nearly took her breath away. The meadow of marbled rhododendrons was complete now, their unique navy blue-and-white marbled pattern on display. If this float was even half as beautiful as the meadow the founder of Marbleglen had discovered—the meadow that had made him fall to his knees and weep at the sight of the "glen of marbled flowers"—Amber understood what had stirred such emotion in the man. The back half of the float was covered in blue flower pieces of varying shades to represent the water of Lake Myrtle.

The design team had truly outdone themselves.

"Oh my God!" someone said.

Kim had materialized behind them, but her attention was focused on the floats. She had a hand pressed to either side of her face like a shocked cartoon character. "They got so much work done on the garden float after I left yesterday. I'm still on the fence about how much we're allowed to hate Marbleglen as a rival, but holy smokes they make a pretty float."

Willow laughed her tinkling bell laugh and Amber smiled.

Kim dropped her hands. "Hi, Willow. So nice that you could join us! I'm not sure what's left to do today. Bianca and Harlo apparently got into a heated argument over the rhododendron float just after I left. Nathan and Jolene said it got so intense that several people left only halfway into the evening shift, just to get away from them. An entire bucket of tapioca pearls got dumped on someone's head. That might just be a rumor, but I hope it was Bianca."

It took less than a minute to reach the barn, but somehow Kim and Willow had already launched into a squee-filled conversation about John Huntley and his impending arrival in Edgehill. He wasn't due to arrive until the second-to-last day of the festival, but Kim kept hinting that *maybe* he'd grace the town a little sooner, since, despite being a heartthrob television actor and Grammy Award-winning country star, he was also "positively giddy" about cats. John's people had been in contact with Kim and the mayor on numerous occasions recently to make sure the celebrity would have a trouble-free visit.

Kim and Willow were so caught up in their conversation that they didn't see Amber hang back. The pair joined the small group of Edgehill volunteers while Amber stood alone, scanning the assembled crowd. The clarity spell didn't reveal anyone was wearing a glamour, but it was also possible that Willow's spell wasn't strong enough to detect a Penhallow-level glamour. And, as Zelda had said, it was possible a Penhallow could be wandering around with his or her true face. In that instance, a clarity spell would be even less useful.

Chloe, Ann Marie, Nathan, and his wife Jolene welcomed Kim and Willow. Chloe and Willow squealed before wrapping each other in a hug. Willow had sometimes tagged along when Amber had babysat Chloe, and they clearly remembered each other.

Amber's mind filled with the image of Henrietta lying on that hospital bed. Last week, Henrietta had been here, too. Even she and Bianca had gotten along relatively well. Guilt was like a lead weight in Amber's stomach. No matter what had put Henrietta into a coma, it tied back to Amber somehow.

"Get over here, Blackwood!"

Snapping out of her thoughts, she found Nathan smiling at her, while the rest of the Edgehill group waved her over. Smiling softly to herself, she joined them. They spoke of Henrietta and wished her well, but there was no malice thrown Amber's way. The only person blaming her was herself.

Harlo approached the group. The fifty-year-old man wore grubby jeans and a stained shirt, as did everyone else, but like Willow, was able to make it look chic. He had bright green eyes and he was rocking salt-and-pepper stubble. He was equal parts easy on the eyes and intimidating. Harlo doled out assignments for the Edgehill group and then everyone scattered amongst the floats.

Amber had been assigned to the rhododendron float with Willow, working on the lake section. The float designer had apparently been "deeply unhappy" with the way the flowers' petals were reflected in the water. Amber had a feeling that his unhappiness had been at the heart of the argument between Harlo and Bianca yesterday, each snipping at the other for failing to do a job worthy of the designer's approval. A large swatch of flower parts had been entirely removed last night, according to Harlo, and now a substantial number of volunteers were frantically filling the space back in.

Though Amber did her best to get lost in her task—as Willow was doing beside her, bopping along to whatever was piping out of her earbuds—she was distracted by a group of people on the other side of the float. It was a trio of unknown twenty-something Marbleglen residents: two young women and a man. Her first, largely irrational worry was that they were Penhallows sent here to stare at her in intermittent bursts, solely to drive her batty.

After catching the trio quickly looking away for the sixth time, Amber's already frayed nerves made her snap, "Can I help you?"

The two young ladies sucked in a breath.

The boy straightened his shoulders and looked Amber square in the eye. She noted, though, that his pale face had turned an alarming shade of red. "We're just wondering what you're doing in Marbleglen. We assumed your absence yesterday meant you were licking your wounds."

"Jesse!" the girl next to him hissed, slapping him on the arm. "Rude."

"Well, if we're being honest, all *three* of you are rude."

Amber, a little shocked, glanced over to see Willow had her earbuds out and was glaring daggers at the trio across from them.

"You've been whispering like little kids about my sister for the past half hour," Willow said, none of her usual easygoing charm evident now. "So out with it. Licking *what* wounds?"

The boy, Jesse, visibly swallowed. "You know, that scathing article in Friday's *Herald*."

"What article?" Amber asked, though she truly didn't want to know the answer.

"It was about the top five businesses in Edgehill that Marbleglen residents should visit during the festival season," Jesse said. Then in a tone that suggested he thought both Blackwood sisters were a little slow, he added, "Don't you read the *Gazette*? That Declan guy wrote one just like it about Marbleglen. Hargrove's was more cutting than Declan's, though."

Willow stiffened beside Amber at Connor's last name.

"And?" Amber prodded.

"*And*," one of the girls chimed in on Jesse's behalf, "Molly mentioned five businesses that won that contest you guys do, which was a little lazy on Molly's part, if you ask me. But she also mentioned toward the end of the article that normally she would recommend The Quirky Whisker too, since you have really unique gifts, but this year she said she couldn't do it in good conscience. She listed a bunch of odd events that have happened in Edgehill over the last few months and how most of them could be tied back to you." She awkwardly cleared her throat, likely from the death glare Willow was shooting her way. "She said your products are unsafe for both kids *and* adults."

Amber clenched her jaw. "And this article came out on Friday?"

"Yeah," the girl said.

Henrietta had slipped into her coma on Friday evening. The exploding bear incident happened Saturday morning. Which meant Molly's article had come out *before* Amber's wares malfunctioned.

The irrational worry Amber had aimed at this trio now shifted to someone else. Molly Hargrove had returned to Marbleglen a year ago after a failed stint at a big city tabloid. As much as Molly was disliked for her sketchy journalistic tactics, Amber had gotten the impression that even though the tabloid had gone under, many were surprised Molly had come back to Marbleglen. Molly the snake had been destined for bigger and better things. But what if the Molly running around town causing trouble wasn't a Hargrove at all?

That argument between Molly and Henrietta replayed in Amber's head and she wished even more now that her memory-retrieval spell had come with volume control.

Could Molly have had something to do with both Henrietta's current condition and the malfunctioning toys that resulted in Amber shuttering her shop during the busiest season of the year? Or did Molly have a paranormal source?

Amber did her best to concentrate on her float-decorating duties after that, but it was hard to calm her racing thoughts. Bianca and her father Simon showed up within the hour. Amber knew only because one of the young ladies beside Jesse had muttered a very dramatic, *"She has arrived."*

The Marbleglen half of the group in the float barn seemed to collectively take on a markedly "more work, less play" mentality, and the chatter went down a few notches almost instantly.

Harlo and Bianca shared air kisses that they both clearly found equal parts necessary and revolting. It didn't take long before the conversation got a bit heated, as Simon who stood behind Bianca wore a wide-eyed expression. Perhaps he wanted to hightail it like half of the volunteers had done last night in the wake of Harlo and Bianca's arguing.

"Oh dear," Amber said. "Will, come with me. We need to diffuse."

Willow followed her without question.

Harlo, with his back to Amber, said, "We managed just fine without you when you had—" he gave Simon a very obvious head-to-toe scan, "personal matters to attend to. If you have other obligations, *love*, I don't have a problem keeping this operation…afloat." He laughed at his own terrible joke.

Bianca's nostrils flared. Color had risen in her perfectly sculpted cheeks, making her jet-black hair look even darker somehow. "Oh, you would love that, Harlo, wouldn't you? I'm sorry to break it to you, *love*, but I'm not going anywhere."

"Hi, Bianca!" Amber said in a too-loud voice that startled Harlo and Bianca both. Simon beamed at Amber from behind Bianca, whether due to being happy to see her, or just glad someone had broken the tension, she couldn't be sure. Amber turned to Harlo and said, "Sorry to interrupt, but I wanted Bianca to meet my sister."

Harlo offered a small smile. "Of course. I'll leave you all to it."

Bianca was still glaring after Harlo even as he disappeared around the back of the garden float. "Ugh. That odious man."

Amber was no more interested now in Bianca's feud with Harlo than she had been last month, so she gestured to Willow instead. "This is my little sister Willow."

Bianca appraised Willow and then smiled. A real, genuine smile. "Well, aren't you a doll!" Then her gaze drifted to the logo on Willow's shirt. "Do you work at Hamish & Nicols?"

"I do!" said Willow. "I work in the art department."

As Bianca and Willow fell into an easy conversation about design, Simon caught Amber's attention and jerked his head behind him. She followed after him. Once they were halfway down the road, he stopped and turned to face her.

"I haven't been able to thank you in person for what you did for me," Simon said. "I know I sort of forced it on you, but I needed another witch on my side. Imagining the rest of my life in prison—for murder, no less—" He shook his head. "I wasn't thinking clearly. I was so dang scared. I—"

Amber briefly placed a hand on his arm, which had its intended effect of cutting off his rambled apology. "I'm glad I could help."

"I also know Bianca can be…a lot," he said. "But I can't thank you enough for helping her, too. Her life as a non-witch in a hybrid town scarred her in ways I didn't even know about until recently. Most people give up on her. I'm just grateful you hung in there—for both of us."

Amber flushed at the praise. "Like you said…us witches have to stick together, right?"

With a warm smile, he nodded. "Absolutely. If you ever need anything, anything at all, don't hesitate to ask, okay?"

Amber's list of people she could trust was very short, and the constant threat of being blindsided by a Penhallow wasn't helping. "Well…I did have a question …"

He laughed. "Wasting no time, huh? I like it. What's up?"

She gave him a quick rundown of the events that led to her shutting down her shop. "Any ideas on how to craft a stronger clarity spell?"

His expression turned thoughtful as he stared off into space a moment. "A tincture might actually work better than a spell. Tinctures often last longer. We Ricinuses usually lean in the kitchen witch direction. Let me see what I can throw together and I'll give you a call."

"That would be great. Thanks."

Simon nodded, started to say something, and then stopped. He stared at Amber for a long moment. She realized then that she'd never considered the possibility that the Simon she currently spoke to now could be a Penhallow. Bianca would have no way of detecting a Penhallow or a magical signature. And there Amber had gone, blabbing away. The clarity spell she'd used before leaving gave her a level of security she possibly shouldn't trust. It seemed unlikely that a Penhallow would have learned this much about Simon by now, including his intonation and mannerisms, but she also knew that she and her family had underestimated the Penhallows thus far. Damien and Devra sneaking around undetected for some time was proof enough of that.

"Can I ask *you* a question?" he asked, cutting into her thoughts.

She hesitated a moment. "Sure?"

"It's actually why I tagged along with Bianca today. She said you'd be here." He looked around; no one was in earshot. Still, he moved a ways farther down the road. "I told you my wife had been a detective, right?"

Amber nodded, immediately sensing where this line of questioning was headed.

"Well, there's a rumor going around that Kieran Penhallow—the witch *you* supposedly cured of his curse—escaped prison Friday night," he said, scanning her face, clearly searching for a sign of whether or not any part of his statement shocked her.

"I heard that, too."

His eyes doubled in diameter and he took a small, involuntary step back. "So it's true? You really cured him?"

"That's what he told me when he called from prison a few days ago."

Simon whistled in disbelief, then laughed. "You mean to tell me that the same nervous woman who didn't know the first thing about Magic Cache—a *children's* game—is the same woman who was able to lift a curse that's been plaguing the witch community for decades?"

Her doubts about this being the real Simon mostly faded away and she shrugged helplessly. "I'm just as confused by it all as you are, believe me."

He laughed again. "This is wild!" After he pulled himself together, he asked, "Do you have any idea where he is now?"

"Nope," she said. "It sounds like he had help getting out. No one knows who that help is."

"Wow," he said. "Well, I'll keep my ear to the ground and let you know if I hear anything."

"Hey, uh …" she said, "the next time we talk, let's have a code word to use. Just to help me make sure you're you."

Simon nodded at this, as if it were a perfectly reasonable request. "Jasper's folly."

It was almost as weird as the word she'd given Chief Brown.

They headed back toward the float barn then, Simon casting periodic, disbelieving looks Amber's way. It made Amber recall what Aunt Gretchen had said after she'd found out that Amber had transported Damien and Devra Penhallow into a memory—and had left them there—with the aid of the ley lines below the abandoned neighborhood in the southern end of Edgehill. "*I guess you just might be a legendary witch after all, little mouse.*"

Simon cast another look her way, laughed softly, and muttered, "This is so wild …"

For someone who was supposedly equipped to end a legendary curse, Amber had never felt so inadequately suited for a task in her life.

CHAPTER 7

Amber and Willow made it back to The Quirky Whisker just after eight in the evening. Though this usually would be around closing time, sometimes during the hoopla before the Here and Meow Amber would keep the shop open a little longer. People still milled the streets late into the evening during festival week, and Purrfectly Scrumptious often stayed open until they were completely wiped out of inventory. There was still a line of a couple dozen people snaking out the door across the street.

Amber sat on the counter of the dark shop and alternated between peering outside and watching Willow angrily pace the shop. Occasionally someone would approach the windows and cup their hands around their eyes to better see inside. It was often children. Children who stared longingly at the toys she had on display.

When she saw a little girl get dragged away by her father, Amber sighed dejectedly and returned her focus to her sister. On the drive back from Marbleglen, Willow had mostly talked about how fascinating and intelligent Bianca was, so Amber wasn't sure what Willow was currently so worked up about.

"You're going to wear a hole in the floor," Amber eventually said.

Willow came to an abrupt halt and whirled to face her. Amber wondered if this was about the trio of young people who had informed them of Molly's article—Willow's current venomous expression was the same as the one she'd worn earlier.

"Am I a complete idiot to be upset about Connor ghosting me?" Willow finally asked.

Oh. "When did you last hear from him?"

"Not since I was last here," she said. "So…two months, I guess? Things were going well, I thought. We went out to eat a few times and it was like high school all over again, you know? We get along really well—annoyingly well—and I thought he was feeling what I was feeling. Then I got that phone call that had actually been stupid Kieran Penhallow *pretending* to be Connor. When I called the real Connor, all happy about our supposed date, things got weird very quickly. And by weird, I mean nonexistent. I totally scared him off." Willow huffed out a dramatic breath and gave her arms a little flail. "Is he actually dating Molly? She's the worst."

Amber shrugged. "I honestly don't know. Molly hinted that they're close, but Molly is…well, she's Molly. She likes saying things solely to get a rise out of people. But they *are* working together a lot lately. Maybe it's all professional."

"But maybe it's not." Willow threw her head back and groaned. The gesture seemed to run in the family; Edgar employed it often.

"Have you tried calling him?" Amber asked.

"Obviously!" Willow snapped. Then she sagged and frowned in Amber's direction. "Sorry. I'm just frustrated. It was like this in high school, too. We'd flirt and hang out and just when I'd think it was going somewhere, he'd ghost me, and soon after, I'd find out he'd started dating some other girl. Red flag city, right? He's just not that into me. He likes having me in his back pocket when he needs some womanly attention. I know all this. I do, I swear. But I can't seem to get over the guy."

Amber had briefly been interested in Connor herself, but Jack had always had more of a hold on her even when she was doing her best to deny it. Amber wasn't sure if Connor was in denial about Willow in the same way Amber had been about Jack. Even Amber could see Connor still had a thing for her sister, but he couldn't seem to commit to going from friendship to something more.

"Maybe it's time for an ultimatum," Amber said. "He needs to tell you where you two stand and if he really *is* with Molly. If this pattern of behavior is mirroring how he treated you in the past, it's likely the same thing is happening again. His feelings for you freak him out and then he jumps into a relationship with someone else. Maybe his answer will give you closure or at least nudge you in that direction."

Willow's shoulders somehow sagged further, and she trudged across the shop to hop up on the counter beside

Amber. Their feet hung a few inches above the floor—Willow's closer to the ground than Amber's. Willow gently leaned against her, so their sides were pressed together. "I know you're right. I just don't want the answer. I don't want confirmation that the one guy I've been hung up on for over ten years never wanted to be with me as much as I wanted to be with him."

"It definitely sucks," Amber said. "But it's better to know than to wonder about it forever. You don't want the 'what if' of Connor Declan hovering over every future relationship, do you?"

Willow sighed. "He kind of already does."

"Right. You need answers either way," Amber said.

After a few quiet minutes, Willow hopped back off the counter and grabbed her phone. Seconds later, it was pressed to her ear. Amber wasn't sure if she should scurry upstairs to give her some privacy. When Connor presumably answered, Willow shuffled off to a far end of the shop. Amber did her best not to overhear.

"I'd rather it just be us," Willow said, voice rising in volume and easily carrying across the shop. "Nothing against Molly, but you and I need to talk. Yeah, noon is perfect."

Willow kept her cool during the short conversation, but she remained firm. After she'd ended the call, she slowly made her way back to Amber. Between snapping at the trio who had been rude to Amber, and this emotional roller-coaster she was on with Connor, Willow looked drained.

"Want to watch that episode of *Vamp World* where John Huntley is shirtless for, like, ninety percent of it?" Amber asked.

When Willow looked up, she was smiling. "So, what, all of season three?"

"Yes. The shop is closed; we're basically on vacation."

"Deal," Willow said, and headed for the stairs. "It's just sad that you have the smallest screen in the history of the universe."

She sounded like Edgar. She briefly wondered what her grumpy recluse of a cousin was up to at the moment. He'd come over for a family hangout a couple of days ago, but he hadn't answered any texts since. He was likely caught up in another of his days-long gaming binges.

Amber and Willow watched *Vamp World* late into the evening. Even Aunt G joined, though she interrupted nearly every scene with, "Wait, who is that again?" or "Ugh! So much blood!"

Once her aunt and sister went to bed, curled up on Amber's bed with the cats, Amber lay on the couch and stared at the dark ceiling. Tomorrow at noon, Willow and Connor would be having lunch. Amber didn't know if Connor and Molly had a standing lunch date, or if they'd had something special planned, but Amber thought it would be best if she called up Molly Hargrove in the morning to offer her own lunch invitation. It was for Willow's sake, Amber told herself. If Molly was the jealous type, would she disrupt this lunch between Connor and Willow? Willow and Molly both would benefit from Connor finally making a decision about who he wanted.

And if Amber just so happened to see "Molly's" real face hiding underneath her Molly-disguise, Amber would at least know the identity of the Penhallow in town.

Willow was a nervous wreck for most of the morning. She'd run through the talking points she wanted to cover with Connor during their lunch date so many times that Aunt G finally let out a muted scream and told Amber and Willow to take their "boy drama" downstairs so she could work on the toy inventory in peace.

It was like high school all over again.

Before they descended the steps, Amber said, "I just realized that I haven't had you two pick a code word yet."

Willow grabbed her shoes and purse and said, "Hmm. Logomark."

Amber shrugged. "And you Aunt G?"

Casting her gaze to the ceiling for a few long seconds, Aunt G tapped her chin. "Ah! Voodoo lily. They're gorgeous and striking. Like me. Now get out of here."

Amber and Willow laughed as they hurried down the steps.

After Willow left for her date around 11:30, Amber went over her own talking points that she wanted to discuss with Molly Hargrove—namely, where Molly was getting her information, and what had she been arguing with Henrietta Bishop about.

A quick search online of *The Marbleglen Herald* site revealed the office phone number. The receptionist quickly patched Amber through to Molly's desk.

"Molly Hargrove speaking."

"Hi, Molly. This is Amber Blackwood."

Amber could almost hear Molly's eyebrow raise in curiosity.

"Hi, Amber. What can I do for you?"

"I was wondering if you'd like to meet me for lunch," Amber said.

Molly let out a short little laugh. "You trying to keep me occupied so I don't crash Connor's lunch with your sister? If this is the best plan you two can come up with, I have to admit it's a little pathetic. What Connor and I have can't be broken in one afternoon."

Amber was tempted to hang up. "To be fair, what Connor and Willow have has lasted a lot longer than a few months. History trumps a flash in the pan." She chastised herself for sinking to Molly's level. It would be hard to get Molly to agree to get lunch with her if she started the conversation with insults. Willing herself to remain civil, she calmly added, "I'm calling about the article in Friday's paper."

The silence stretched on for long enough that Amber knew she'd piqued Molly's curiosity. "Okay," Molly said. "Where would you like to meet?"

Connor and Willow were having lunch in Edgehill, so despite Molly's assurance that she wouldn't cause problems for the pair, Amber figured keeping Molly occupied in Marbleglen wasn't a bad call. "What's your favorite place in Marbleglen?"

"There's a great Mexican place on Dahlia Drive," Molly said. "Give me your number and I'll text you the address."

Amber hurried back upstairs to change and to tame her hair into something more respectable. She called a goodbye to Aunt G, who seemed more than happy to be working on the cat toys in the quiet, and with only Tom and Alley for company, and darted out the door.

As she mentally cast the alarm spell to lay over the entrance, and then manually locked the door, someone said, "Good afternoon, Miss Blackwood."

Amber spun around and eyed the pair of people standing behind her. One man and one woman, both in crisp black suits. They were both about five-foot-seven and wore identical impassive expressions. The woman was in her forties and had short black hair cut in a bob, and the man was a bit younger with a head of wavy blond hair. His face was clean-shaven.

Her clarity spell told her that there was no detectable glamour here.

"Do you plan to stab us with that, Miss Blackwood?" the woman asked.

Amber realized then that she held her keys in her fist, her car key poking between her pointer and middle finger. Then she looked back up at the pair standing before her. A couple of months ago, Amber had spotted a man watching her while she ate breakfast with Edgar. With one look, Edgar had pegged him as a cop. Or, rather, a private investigator. There had been something about Alan Peterson that had stuck out to Amber immediately, though she hadn't been able to pinpoint it until Edgar had slapped the cop label on him. She got that feeling again now. These two didn't feel threatening, necessarily, so much as wildly out of place on the street before her curiosity shop while dozens of happy feline-obsessed tourists milled about.

Just beyond the pair, Amber spotted Betty Harris standing on the sidewalk watching them. One dark brow was raised in question. Amber knew if she gave Betty a signal that she was in trouble here, she'd come running across the street armed with a rolling pin to whack these two over the head. Amber was sure spry old Bobby would help, too.

Instead, Amber nodded at her and smiled softly, letting her know she was okay. Reluctantly, Betty headed back into her busy bakery.

Refocusing on the pair, Amber said, "Can I help you with something? The shop is closed for the foreseeable future."

The man's gaze briefly swept back and forth along her shop front, as if he were cataloging everything that lay beyond the windows. "We have no interest in your store, Miss Blackwood. But we would like to speak with you."

"About what?" she asked. "I have somewhere I need to be."

"Cancel whatever it is," the woman said. "What we need to discuss with you will take a while. And considering that your shop is closed, you have the time."

Amber's face heated. Who the heck did this lady think she was? "Look, I don't *have* to do anything. I have no idea who you people are. Tell me what you want or I'm leaving." She clutched her keys a little tighter.

Tourists were starting to give them a wide berth. Amber imagined her expression was somewhere in the realm of "terrified rabbit." Betty was inside Purrfectly Scrumptious now, but was watching Amber with her nose practically pressed to the glass wall.

The woman in front of Amber flared her nostrils just slightly, the first sign that she actually possessed human emotions. So, that ruled out this pair being aliens or robots from another planet. Hopefully.

"We're from the WBI," the man said. "The Witch Bureau of Investigation."

Amber worried her eyes would fall right out of her skull, given how wide they grew.

"I'm Agent Barker," the man said. "And this is Agent Howe."

The woman, Agent Howe, nodded once. "We know Kieran Penhallow called you three nights ago."

Now Amber's mouth hung open.

Agent Barker angled a look at Agent Howe and said, "We're really buying into the rumor that *she* is going to solve the Penhallow problem?"

"Hey!" Amber said, brain catching up enough to be offended.

"We'll buy you lunch," Agent Howe said, then turned and walked away, presumably headed for the parking lot.

"And maybe even dessert if you behave," Agent Barker said, following her.

Amber glared after him. She wasn't sure why either of them had to be so rude. She knew she didn't have to follow them, though. Amber supposed the tools the WBI possessed would blow the FBI's out of the water. They were witches, and likely very powerful. Granted, Amber knew nothing about the organization, but the image in her head was dang impressive.

She could walk the other way. She could call a cab. She could just lock herself inside her shop until they went away.

It had been a full minute since the pair of suit-clad grumps had rounded the corner of her building. She was fairly certain Betty still had her nose pressed to the glass.

Amber's curiosity, as always, got the better of her.

Heaving out a breath, she followed them. When she emerged into the parking area, the two agents had their backsides resting against the hood of a black sedan, their arms crossed. When they spotted Amber, Agent Barker held out a hand to Agent Howe, palm out. Agent Howe grumbled, reached into her pocket to pull something out, and then slapped what looked like a few dollar bills into the man's hand.

Amber clenched her jaw. She should just turn around right now.

But she trudged forward anyway. Agent Barker held open the back door of the SUV and Amber climbed into its spacious interior, which was pristine and smelled new. Amber wondered where the WBI's headquarters was located, and if there were smaller branches scattered across the country, like with the FBI.

As the eerily silent SUV pulled out onto Russian Blue Avenue, Amber stared out the black-tinted windows. She needed to tell her family that she'd been peacefully kidnapped. She pulled out her cell phone. "Where are we going?"

"The Manx Hotel," Agent Barker said. "It's quiet this time of day, and we're also meeting someone there."

Amber texted her aunt and sister to let them know where she'd be, giving them her location, but staying light on the details. Considering that she didn't have any yet.

Even though her gut told her these people had been truthful about who they were, Amber remembered how thoroughly duped her own mother had been by a Penhallow who had taken his glamour to a level so extreme, he'd assumed the identity of someone else. Who was to say these two weren't Penhallows conducting an elaborate ruse?

Blowing out a steadying breath, she called on her magic, which had been buzzing anxiously under her skin since these two had materialized out of nowhere. Her intention was to find out the truth of their visit, but she also wanted proof that she wasn't being tricked like a kid being lured into a creepy van by a nefarious man offering candy.

She called on the fear she'd felt when she worried her magic had put little Noah in danger. She called on her worry that somehow her sleepy tea had harmed Henrietta. And she called on her paranoia that every new face she encountered in Edgehill was someone who wished *her* harm. Her magic responded in kind, as if it were bubbling lava waiting to erupt from an angry volcano.

She took all that built-up feeling and poured it into her words. "Agent Barker, Agent Howe, what are you doing in Edgehill?"

Her magic practically sang as she unleashed it, happy to be used in such a direct and forceful way. Forceful enough that the car swerved. Amber pressed a hand against the door to keep herself from bumping into it. The agents let out twin grunts of discomfort.

Robotically, Agent Barker said, "I have been sent here to question Amber Blackwood on the spell she used to cure Kieran Penhallow of his curse."

A moment later, Agent Howe said, "I've been sent here to make sure Agent Barker doesn't botch the assignment."

Amber's magic immediately settled. They were telling the truth.

Agent Howe's gaze snapped to the rear-view mirror to glare at her.

Agent Barker however was shooting daggers at Agent Howe in the driver's seat. "You're my babysitter?"

Agent Howe unleashed a dramatic sigh. "Yes, Barker. But it also means they're going to start giving you your own cases soon, assuming you don't screw it up."

"Maybe they put you with me to help you work on your people skills," Agent Barker snapped, "since you don't have any."

An awkward tension settled over the car. Amber envisioned opening the car door and rolling out onto the street.

Agent Barker seemed to remember then that there was someone else with them, and he turned in his seat to glare at Amber. "A simple question would have sufficed, by the way. We're both layered in protections that keep witches from using truth spells on us. It's difficult to do your job when criminals force you to show your hand. When those spells get bypassed—which you shouldn't have been able to do—it *hurts*."

A sense of smug pride washed over Amber despite the precarious situation she was in.

"Probably more information than you needed to give her," Agent Howe hissed.

Amber crossed her arms and offered Agent Barker her own glare. She squashed the urge in her to apologize. "Yeah, well, if you two weren't so cryptic and downright mean, I wouldn't have had to do it."

Agent Barker grumbled and turned back in his seat.

"Don't do that again," Agent Howe said.

Amber didn't appreciate being scolded.

Then she added, "But it's good to see the rumors about you actually hold the possibility of being true."

The feeling of inadequacy slammed back into Amber, exhausting her. She kept quiet for the rest of the ride, wondering who on earth would be meeting them at the hotel.

CHAPTER 8

The Manx Hotel was the most lavish hotel in Edgehill. The exterior was more reminiscent of a Victorian-era mansion than a typical hotel complex. Kim had said she had it on good authority that John Huntley would be staying there in the coming days. Security was no doubt going to be beefed up to keep the diehard fans from trying to storm the guy's hotel room.

As the SUV pulled up in front of the building, Amber craned her neck to study her favorite part of the hotel— the elegant black cat statues that were scattered around the property, several of which were perched on the corners of the roof like gargoyles. The last time she'd been to this hotel had been when Kieran was in town and, while he'd been prowling around, had murdered an innocent maid.

Had the agents chosen this hotel because of its loose connection to Kieran, or were they clueless? Could it be *Kieran* who was meeting them here? Had the WBI been the ones to free him from prison because of the change in his magic?

Silently, the agents stepped out of the SUV and headed for the entrance. Perhaps Chief Brown had gone through the same training program as these two. They just wandered off, knowing somehow Amber would follow them. Then she flashed back to Agent Howe slapping cash into Agent Barker's awaiting palm.

This was Amber's danged curiosity's fault. Maybe she gave off a pheromone that let everyone around her know that if they provided the smallest amount of interesting information, Amber would trot along behind like a sheep. She let herself out of the back seat, then made her way through the small black gate and up the steps.

She only allowed herself a moment to marvel at the oval-shaped window resting in the center of the front door—and the cat paws, whiskers, and pointed ears etched into the glass—before she stepped in after the agents.

Though the interior of the hotel was as elaborate and sprawling as the outside, the dark colors of the lobby made the space seem smaller than it was. The walls and floor were made of a rich, dark wood, the elegant black-and-white photographs on the walls were encased in thick black frames, and the few plants in the room were in massive black pots. The wide staircase rose behind the C-shaped registration desk that sat in the middle of the room. An open doorway stood on either side of the lobby.

A few months ago, from the rightmost doorway, Amber had heard the sound of Connor and his friends talking and laughing on the eve of Connor's birthday celebration. Today, the agents hardly stopped in the lobby long enough to acknowledge the receptionist before heading for the left doorway.

Amber trudged after them. The room they walked through was a lounging area furnished with a few forest green sofas, a handful of armchairs, small tables, and a flat-screen television sitting atop a dark wood stand toward the back of the room. The agents didn't stop here either; they moved through yet another open doorway into a swanky in-house restaurant.

Small, intimate tables were positioned on the left side of the room, while the right side was taken up by a curved, glass-fronted bar. Expensive bottles of liquor lined the mirror-covered wall behind the pair of bartenders, one of whom was busily chatting up two women who sat before him. Elegant silver lamps hung from the ceiling.

The agents strolled along as if they owned the place. Amber was mostly only aware of how underdressed she felt. Her black ballet flats were scuffed and filthy when compared to the gleaming floor beneath her.

After following the curve of the bar, the space opened up into a large dining area. Plush black booths flanked shiny dark tables. A large, square brick fireplace took up a chunk of space in the middle of the room, the wide shaft disappearing into the ceiling. A fire roared behind a metal grate, but Amber was fairly certain it was actually a looping video of a crackling fire. When a woman in black slacks and a white top, a large tray balanced on her hand, came bustling out of a black door to the right, Amber caught a brief glimpse of busy kitchen activity.

As Amber and the agents rounded the fireplace, Amber spotted the only occupied booth in the back corner of the room. In the next second, she realized it was her cousin Edgar.

What in the world was *he* doing here? And how had the agents gotten him to agree to show up? She often couldn't get the man out of the house—and she was family.

When Edgar saw her, he practically sprung from his seat, looking both relieved and desperately uncomfortable. Which meant he had no idea what this little meeting was about either. He said nothing to her when she reached him, just visibly swallowed and nodded a hello. They slid into the booth together on one side, and the agents took their seats on the other.

A waiter showed up to deposit four ice waters on the table and then hurried off again without taking their orders.

Amber gave the room a quick once-over and noted that no one was seated near them within earshot. She crossed her arms on the table and leveled a stare at Agent Howe across from her. Amber needed straightforward answers before her myriad theories about why they were here gave her a stress-induced ulcer.

Edgar spoke before Amber could think of what to say. "So what's this all about? I was just about to start a dungeon raid when you called."

Agent Barker looked like he was seconds away from neutralizing Edgar as if he'd just admitted that he made bombs in his spare time.

"It's a video game thing," Amber said quickly. Then she jerked her head Edgar's way. "He's a total nerd."

Agent Barker relaxed.

Agent Howe looked mildly disgusted, but that seemed to be the woman's default expression. "Is it true that you cured Kieran Penhallow of his curse by severing his connection to magic, Amber?"

"Yes."

"And how did you accomplish that?" she asked.

Amber's gaze flicked back and forth between the agents, nervous about confessing this out loud while also knowing these people likely already knew the answer and were only seeking confirmation. There had been a warning written by her mother in the margins of her grimoire, stating that she hoped Amber and Willow never needed a magic-severing spell. Which likely meant that Amber's mother had figured out that the most viable way to end the curse was to take magic away from the cursed witch altogether. Amber's mother never had the chance to find out if her spell worked.

"A spell I found in my mother's grimoire."

The agents exchanged a look.

"The same grimoire that has the fabled time-travel spell in it?" Agent Barker asked.

"Yes," Amber said. "And it's not fabled. I've seen it."

Agent Barker leveled his gaze on Edgar, who stiffened beside her. "And you were the keeper of the book since the deaths of Annabelle Henbane and Theodore Blackwood?"

Amber's heart constricted at the mention of her parents.

"That's right," Edgar said, then a bit reluctantly told them about his altercation with Neil Penhallow—the man who had killed Amber's parents and was Kieran's older brother—the night of the fatal fire. At the beginning of his story, Edgar balled his hands into fists on the table. By the middle, he had one of those fists pressed to his forehead. And by the end, as he explained how Neil had used his magic as a weapon against him, Edgar could hardly get the words out. Not from emotional pain, but mental. His eyes were squeezed shut. Neil was no doubt trying to get Edgar to stop talking, to keep his secrets from the WBI.

Edgar let out a guttural cry and slammed a fist onto the table, making the glasses of water jump. Amber caught hers before it tipped over. The couple on the other side of the dining area looked over to see what the fuss was about. Agent Howe quickly waved away a concerned-looking waiter.

Amber took over the story then, explaining that Neil had infected Edgar with a small dose of cursed magic. "We don't know how, but Neil's magic and Edgar's have fused. Neil's voice lives in Edgar's head. Neil either is able to see through Edgar's eyes, or he can read Edgar's mind enough that he's able to deduce things about Edgar's surroundings."

"So does that mean Neil Penhallow knows where the Henbane book is?" Agent Howe asked, alarmed.

Agent Barker eyed Edgar as if were Neil himself—a threat.

"No. Only I know where it is," Amber said. "It's safe."

"The book is of great interest to the WBI," Agent Howe said. "If you could—"

"No," Amber said.

Agent Howe's nostrils flared. "Our resources are more extensive than yours. That book cannot fall into Penhallow hands."

"I know," Amber said. "And it won't," she added with more conviction than she felt.

"That's all you want it for?" Edgar asked, his voice low. He seemed to have pushed Neil back down in his mind, but he was clearly still struggling. The bags under his eyes were pronounced; Amber wondered how he'd been sleeping lately.

They were both involuntary members of the insomnia club.

The look the agents shared didn't sit well with Amber. Agent Howe was the harder one to read, so Amber focused on Agent Barker. Despite the lecture she got in the car, she had to know the truth. She was banking on the fact that they likely hadn't taken the time to refortify their protection spells between the ride over here and now. And if they had, maybe she had enough magical juice to mow down their protections again.

She called on her magic, still as bouncy and anxious as she felt, and funneled it into a truth spell. "Agent Barker—

"Amber Blackwood, don't you—" Agent Howe started, but Edgar cast a wind spell that was so strong, the agent tumbled to the ground.

"Agent Barker," Amber said, "why does the WBI want my mother's time-reversal spell?" Then she hurled her magic at him.

He clearly fought the magic, wincing as he held onto the lip of the table. Amber felt the resistance, like two magnets repelling each other. It felt like an oncoming sinus headache, the pressure making her eyes water. But Amber's magic eventually pushed her way past his defenses. The mental dam burst open and she sucked in a gulp of air as the pressure in her mind released.

Glaring at her the whole time, he said, "Annabelle didn't know what she created. The Henbanes and Blackwoods immediately labeled the spell as a danger that should be kept from the world and hidden away. The WBI knows the spell's true potential and the benefits it could have for humankind—witch and non-witches alike. Yet, every time the WBI has tried to gain access to the spell, they've been outmaneuvered."

Amber cocked her head at that. How many times had the WBI tried to get the book over the years? Had her parents not just been hiding the book from the Penhallows, but from the WBI, too?

Agent Howe got to her feet, brushed herself off, and slid back into the booth. Her expression made it explicitly clear that she would murder everyone at this table if she wouldn't get punished for it. And even then, she might risk it.

Agent Barker, jaw clenched as if that would keep the words inside his mouth, said, "We have the intel, firepower, and knowledge of hindsight on our side. Where the council failed, the WBI will succeed. One of the final pieces of solving the Penhallow problem is Annabelle Henbane's spell."

He sagged and Amber's magic retreated. Amber wasn't sure which version of history Agent Barker believed or had been taught to embrace—that the council created the Penhallow curse through no fault of their own, or that the curse had been borne out of actions so reckless, the council was just as guilty as the Penhallows. Either way, as far as Amber's magic was concerned, Agent Barker had spoken his truth.

Agent Howe glowered at Amber. "I've had quite enough of you. Amber Blackwood, where is the Henbane grimoire?"

No! her magic instinctively screamed, and shoved hard against the agent's probing magic. The sudden sinus pressure in her head made Amber's eyes water. The hint of an image of a deserted town started to form in her mind, and even that was too much information. *No!* her magic yelled again, slamming a door on the prowling, foreign magic. *No, no, no.* "I won't tell you," she ground out.

The magic retreated.

Agent Howe's jaw was tight. "Truth spells aren't fool-proof, Amber. As you just demonstrated, if the recipient of the spell has a strong enough desire to keep the truth hidden, they can fight it. Or they can outright lie."

A sound spell immediately went up around the agents and the pair launched into a heated discussion that neither Amber nor Edgar could hear. There was quite a bit of pointing in Amber and Edgar's direction and Agent Barker was turning a rather stunning shade of red as Agent Howe laid into him. Amber was glad there wasn't any silverware on the table, otherwise Agent Barker would have a fork in his eye by now.

"Do we bolt now or …?" Edgar whispered, attention focused on the muted argument.

"Problem is, they'd find us," Amber said, equally engrossed in the scene as her cousin. Her sinus headache was fading at least. "And we just royally ticked off two members of the flipping WBI."

"They had it coming," Edgar said, folding his arms on the table. "I don't like either one of them."

Zelda had told Amber and Edgar that the history they'd always been taught had been wrong. It was no secret that the power-hungry Penhallows had been a problem well before their curse took hold, and that the council, at its wit's end, had needed a way to control the clan. But that was where stories diverged.

Growing up, Amber had always been told that the now-defunct witch council had stripped a Penhallow of his power, and when that Penhallow later retaliated by murdering a council member, the magic from the murdered man transferred into the Penhallow. But that transferred magic had been corrupted—cursed. A witch without magic was like a butterfly without wings; one needed the other. So when the councilmember died, his magic filled in the missing places in the Penhallow even if that magic didn't belong there.

In Zelda's version of history, however, the council had forcibly taken a Penhallow to a great ley line convergence in Sedona, Arizona. The council, hands clasped, used the Penhallow as a conduit, and had cast a severing spell that they then poured into the convergence at once. The goal had been to strip all Penhallows of their powers simultaneously, using the ley lines—ribbons of magic that span the world—to reach every Penhallow on earth. What happened was an overloading of the ley lines that then short-circuited the entire magical grid. Not only had the council *caused* the Penhallow curse, but they'd also created six pockets of unsteady magic across the world. One of those pockets was on the outskirts of Edgehill.

Amber didn't know how two wildly different versions of history existed simultaneously, especially when the history wasn't that old.

Zelda had shared a memory with Amber from Zelda's childhood when one of those unsteady pockets of magic erupted without warning. Zelda's entire community had had to flee at the drop of a hat when the lines exploded, releasing tainted magic into the air that would have killed everyone had they stayed. *"Do you see now that anything more done to the ley lines could cause untold effects?"* Zelda had asked. *"What if another blast to the ley lines causes them to splinter even more?"*

"Where the council failed, the WBI will succeed," Agent Barker had said. Was he suggesting that the WBI planned to use the time-reversal spell to go back to that moment in Sedona and not reverse it…but do it better? Who knew what kind of destruction that could cause? Their grand plan might result in something even worse than what had happened to the Penhallows.

Amber was so lost in thought, she hadn't registered when the sound-canceling spell around the agents dropped. When Agent Howe spoke, Amber flinched.

"We have the authority to effectively arrest you both and bring you in for formal interrogation at our headquarters," Agent Howe said. "Pull another stunt like that—either one of you—and we'll haul you out of here unconscious. By admitting you know the location of an object we consider to be a threat to national security, and then refusing to hand over said object, we could label you as terrorists."

It was such a ludicrous statement that Amber almost laughed. Neither agent looked remotely amused. She sobered quickly.

"We want to work with you, Miss Blackwood," Agent Barker said. "Not against you. This can be a relationship beneficial to us all, but you need to cut us a little slack. We're on the same side here."

Alan Peterson the PI had used the same line on her. She'd grown to trust him, but the jury was still out on these two.

Agent Howe let out a slow fortifying breath. "Records show that you were the last person Kieran called, and it happened the night before his escape. Is that correct?"

Edgar stiffened. "Wait, *what*?" He furiously tapped the side of his head, his gaze focused on something in the middle distance. "And what about you? Your brother escapes prison and you didn't say anything?" He tossed his hands in the air and slumped in the booth. "Great. Now he's cackling like a madman."

The agents stared at Edgar with twin expressions of mild concern.

"No, you know what?" Edgar sat up straight and turned forcefully in the booth to glare at Amber head-on. She rocked back an inch. "I expected this much from him, but *you*? When were you planning on telling me any of this—when Kieran shows up trying to kill us both again?"

An irrational swell of anger made Amber offer him her own glare. "My plate's been a *little* full. I can't keep you informed every step of the way." She instantly regretted the words.

Amber knew her long sleepless nights were catching up with her. She was exhausted. One of her animated toys almost gravely injured a child, Henrietta was in a coma, a Penhallow was possibly in her town again, and these two nightmare people from the WBI were calling *her* and her mother's grimoire a threat to national freaking security.

She didn't need her grumpy cousin making her feel any worse than she already did.

"Ohh, *sor-ry*, Miss Legendary Witch," Edgar snapped. "I'm just dealing with a psychotic witch in my head day and night. I haven't slept in forty-eight hours. Have you called? No. You only call me when you need something."

She knew she shouldn't engage him. They both were sleep-deprived and were very good at getting under each other's skin. Edgar had become a big part of her life very quickly over the last few months. Despite everything he was going through, he always did what he could to help her, whether that was teaching her Magic Cache or giving her magic lessons. He was grouchy more often than not, but at least recently, he had been doing his best to make time for her. And, yeah, maybe she could have called him. Maybe some part of her even felt guilty that she hadn't.

But to say she only called him when she needed something? *Low blow, Henbane.*

Amber turned in her seat and it was Edgar's turn to instinctively scooch back. "Don't. You. Dare. I tried for *years* to get you to at least talk to me and that was *only* to make sure you were all right. If you're upset now because I haven't called in a few days, sorry, okay? But phone lines go two ways. You haven't called me either. Did you know I had to shut down my shop?"

He said nothing, but color rose in his cheeks, letting her know her words had hit their mark. She felt badly, but barreled on anyway.

"There are better ways to let me know your feelings are hurt than to give me a guilt trip. I worry about you every day. I want Neil out of your head too and I feel horrible that you've basically had your life ruined because of what my family has directly or indirectly done to you."

Edgar now looked downright furious, but she knew him well enough now to know that he wasn't mad at her in this moment, but himself. "I've never blamed you. Or your parents. This is all the Penhallows' fault. Always has been." He worked his jaw and his eyes grew a little glassy. If she hadn't known better, she would have said he was near tears. "Never say you ruined my life. *Never.* Got that? You're one of the few things that's made it bearable."

Amber's eyes welled up and her bottom lip shook a little. Oh goodness, was *she* going to cry? After a moment, she croaked out, "Love you too, cousin."

"Yeah, yeah," he said, sniffing and quickly looking away. "Same."

Agent Howe let out a soft groan as if she couldn't imagine who she'd ticked off in a past life to be sitting in this exact place at this moment.

In a stage whisper, Agent Barker said, "The whole terrorist thing feels a bit much now, right? She's the least terror-inducing terrorist I've ever met."

Amber flushed.

"Do you know anything about Kieran's escape?" Agent Howe asked, ignoring her partner.

"Nothing," Amber said, trying to reel in her emotions. "He called that night and I haven't heard from him since."

"What was the nature of his call?"

Amber chewed on her lip. Given Agent Howe's barely contained annoyance, Amber figured it would be in her best interest to be honest here. Maybe the information would buy Amber back into her good graces a little. This was something she hadn't even told Zelda, Simon, or Edgar. "His magic is back. Healed, I mean. The way it was supposed to be."

Neither agent seemed surprised by this, but Amber didn't know if that was because they'd already known, or because they had unshakeable poker faces.

Edgar let out a low whistle.

"When was the last time you were in contact with your father, Mr. Henbane?" Agent Howe asked.

Edgar choked mid-whistle, gasped, then started to cough. Amber patted his back.

"I'll take that as not recently," Agent Howe said. "It was actually the movements of your sister, Amber, that put Raphael Henbane back on our radar. The timing of it all struck our offices as interesting, given everything else. Is it safe to assume that you haven't been to the facility to see him then, Mr. Henbane?"

Edgar sputtered again. "He's…alive? You found him?"

Agent Howe raised a brow in Amber's direction, silently asking, "Should I tell him, or should you?"

Sighing, Amber recounted what Willow had told Amber just a couple of weeks ago: that Willow had tracked Raphael to a psychiatric institution in upstate Washington and that his memory had either been completely wiped or heavily tampered with. Reluctantly, she also added that Raphael was afflicted with a condition similar to Edgar's own, but in Raphael's head, it was a female voice taunting him to find the coveted grimoire.

Edgar had turned his mashed-together brows and pursed lips toward the direction of the table about halfway through Amber's story. Perhaps he was so angry now, he didn't even have the strength to maintain eye contact. If he didn't tear her a new one now, he surely would later.

"Willow doesn't know who the female voice belongs to," Amber told the agents. "We assume it's a Penhallow, obviously, but Willow didn't get a name out of him or anything."

"Well, that's at the heart of why we're here," Agent Barker said. "We need your help. Clearly Kieran feels a connection to you. Whether he values you as a person or feels indebted to you because of how you helped him, it doesn't matter. We need to use that to our advantage before he tries to use it for his."

Amber cocked her head, wondering why Kieran's name had been brought back into this. "What do you mean?"

"Our belief is that Kieran's secret got out," Agent Howe said. "Even though his magic is healed, we don't believe this will change the Penhallows' long-standing mission. The Penhallows don't want a fresh start, they want to go back to the height of their power."

"Which means they still want the spell," Edgar ground out, though he still kept his gaze focused on the table. "They still want to stop the curse from ever happening in the first place."

"Exactly," Agent Barker said. "Kieran is now saner and has a connection to the infamous Amber Blackwood. You're known not as the witch with the cure to the curse, but the witch with the location to the Henbane grimoire. Kieran will be seen as the perfect poster child for their cause. He's rational, he can blend in better than a glamoured Penhallow because *his* magical use won't have a signature, and he has access to you and your family. We believe the Penhallows are working now to manipulate him to do their bidding. And then he'll be headed straight back here. To you."

Amber swallowed. As much as she wanted to believe that Kieran had changed—*truly* changed—she could never fully disassociate the new Kieran from the old, cursed Kieran who had not only murdered an innocent, but had threatened her town, and had nearly killed her.

"What does any of this have to do with my father?" Edgar asked, looking up.

Amber glanced over at him briefly, glad his boiling rage of an expression was pointed at someone other than herself.

"Our intel suggests that Raphael Henbane had been up to something that spooked the Penhallows," Agent Howe said. "He posed a threat of some kind, and he was hit with a blast of cursed magic, just as they did to you, Mr. Henbane. We don't know how much Annabelle shared with her family in Delin Springs before they scattered to different parts of the country and effectively became fugitives. Your grandparents passed away years ago; Raphael is the last living member of Annabelle's immediate family who knows the truth of what happened while Annabelle was on the run.

"The fact that Raphael lived here in Edgehill for a while implies that Raphael and Annabelle remained in contact most of their adult lives. We believe Annabelle confided in her brother about something that eventually led to his run-in with the Penhallows. He then learned something about the Penhallows that they didn't want him to remember. Perhaps they tried to kill him and failed, and Raphael's current condition is the result. We believe when he left Edgar here in Edgehill shortly after Annabelle's death, he had every intention of coming back—a Penhallow just got to him first."

Edgar let out a soft, pained sound that Amber wasn't sure anyone else heard.

Amber had always assumed her grandparents had passed on, but to have it confirmed so casually by Agent Howe somehow made it sting even more. Her small family seemed to grow smaller by the day.

"We don't know how he ended up in this particular institution," Agent Barker said. "It's an exclusive and extremely remote place, and has no ties to witches whatsoever. He must have had close friends who felt it necessary to get him off the grid, so to speak. Someone close to him likely worried that the Penhallows would finish the job if they got a second chance."

"Valuable information is locked up in Raphael's head. We're sure of it," Agent Howe said. "Your memory magic should allow you to witness what happened to Raphael the day he was hit with that blast. That, or you can sever his tie to the female witch inside his mind, similar to what you did with Kieran."

Amber gaped at her. She had no clue how to do this without her mother's spell, which was hidden three hours away.

Softer, and with more emotion than Amber thought she was capable of possessing, Agent Howe added, "You have an opportunity here to heal your uncle just as you healed Kieran."

A little voice in the back of her mind told her she was being manipulated, but a louder voice was cheering. If Amber found a way to heal her uncle, it meant Amber would be that much closer to healing Edgar. She could put what was left of her family back together.

"Consider this a compromise," Agent Barker said. "Raphael has intel the WBI desperately needs to help us combat this incoming threat. Get us this, and we'll give you more time to willingly turn over the book to authorities."

What exactly did they think was in Raphael's head that was valuable enough that they'd temporarily give up the fight to get their hands on an "object of national security"?

"What do you need *me* for?" Edgar asked.

"Your father is still in there," Agent Howe said. "If there is anyone on this earth who could help jog Raphael's memories, it would be his son. You are to join Amber to jumpstart his mind. Amber's job is recon."

Over the course of a few short months, Amber had been labeled a psychic, a private investigator, a detective, and now…what…a government spy? What had happened to her quiet days of being a toymaker?

Noah's crying face popped up in her mind and she frowned. Her quiet days of being a toymaker were in jeopardy until the Penhallow problem was solved.

"I'm not saying I agree to any of this," Amber said, "but when do you expect this *recon mission* to happen?"

"As soon as possible," Agent Howe said. "The Penhallows are planning…something. If what's locked away in Raphael's brain can help us defeat the Penhallows once and for all, we needed it yesterday."

"Can you give me a week?" Amber didn't only need the time to help Kim and the others through the Here and Meow, but she also needed to talk to her aunt and sister.

Agent Howe's nostrils flared again. "Tentatively, I will say yes. But if things progress, we'll call on you sooner. You can try to say no, but we're very persuasive when necessary."

Amber couldn't wait to be rid of them both.

Agent Howe produced a business card and slid it across the table. "Call me if anything comes up—especially if Kieran makes contact again."

Amber managed a faint nod.

Without a word, the pair slid out of their side of the booth. They adjusted their suit jackets; Agent Barker rebuttoned his.

"Enjoy your lunch," Agent Howe said.

A waiter rounded the fireplace in the middle of the room. He carried two plates—one with a pasta dish and one with a massive salad, as well as two boxes. He nodded once to Agent Barker, who was already striding out of the room. Agent Howe threw several bills onto the waiter's tray, bid him a good day, and then she was on her way across the restaurant, too.

The waiter placed the pasta before Edgar and the chicken Caesar salad in front of Amber—it was one of her favorite dishes. Then the waiter placed the two boxes with clear covers on the table. One had "Willow" written in black marker, and the other said "Gretchen."

The waiter left without a word.

"This is all *really* weird, right?" Amber stared down at her salad. "Are they trying to scare us even more with intuitive food orders?"

In a soft, faraway voice, Edgar said, "I can't believe he's really alive."

Amber turned to him. "Edgar, look, I'm sorry that we didn't—"

He held up a hand to stop her. "I'm too angry to talk about it yet. Just eat your plate of plants."

She was just about to do so—Edgar had already shoveled three very large forkfuls of Alfredo pasta in his mouth— when, all at once, she remembered who she'd originally been scheduled to have lunch with. Cursing under her breath, she frantically searched her purse for her phone.

It was forty-five minutes past the time she was supposed to have met Molly. There were two missed texts and three missed calls. All from Molly.

Is this payback for the article? Marbleglen residents deserve to know the truth about how dangerous your products are. This passive-aggressive tantrum isn't a good look on you.

Ten minutes later, she received:

Now I know how you treat people you don't like.

As Amber stared at her phone, wondering what to tell Molly to assure her it had been an accident to stand her up, another message from her came in, sent fifteen minutes after the previous one.

Consider this bridge burned.

Amber groaned and dropped her phone back into her purse. She wondered which was worse: having a Penhallow as an enemy…or Molly Hargrove.

CHAPTER 9

Amber, sitting in the passenger seat of Edgar's truck, was in the process of organizing her belongings—her purse and two boxes of food—when Edgar said, "Who is that?"

She looked up just as Edgar pulled in front of The Quirky Whisker and found a woman in a black skirt suit standing in front of the shop. Her back was to Amber, and as she peered in through the front door, a cell phone was pressed to her ear.

The woman's red hair was pulled back into a bun. Though nothing about her was immediately familiar, the color of her hair alone put Amber on high alert. In the chaos of this morning alone, Amber had managed to forget about the non-magical problems in her life. When the woman turned around a moment later, Amber's guess was confirmed.

"Thea Bishop," Amber said. "Henrietta's sister."

The woman was so unmistakably related to Henrietta that Amber briefly wondered if they were twins. Upon closer inspection, the differences in their features became clearer. Amber guessed Thea was younger, but likely only by a year or two.

Amber had told Edgar about the fate of her shop—and the events that had led to her shuttering her doors—over lunch. She'd done most…all…of the talking, as he was still too upset with her to say much.

Thea said something else into her cell, ended the call, and put her phone into her shiny black handbag. Then she cocked a brow at Amber, as if to say, "Are you going to hide in there all day?"

Amber considered it. Even from this distance and with a car door between them, Thea was clearly formidable. She didn't need cursed magic running through her veins to give Amber the willies. All she needed was the poise and confidence of a lawyer—paired with sisterly love that was as powerful as any spell. Willow had worn the same expression in the float barn when the trio from Marbleglen had been rude to Amber. Thea was here as a sister as much as she was here as a lawyer.

Amber swallowed.

A moment later, she grabbed her own phone out of her purse and quickly sent a text to Chief Brown. *Just a heads-up that Thea is in town and she's at The Quirky Whisker. Hopefully we don't get into a brawl and end up at the station.*

He replied almost immediately. I'm not amused, Amber.

Oh, he was never amused! Didn't he realize how funny she was?

"Hey, I have an idea!" Amber told Edgar as she dropped her phone back into her purse. He was eyeing the redhead with an air of trepidation. "What if you take me back to your house and I move into that old shed in the back until this lady goes away?"

"Nope," he said. "I think dealing with her is a fit punishment for…everything."

She frowned as she stared at his profile. "I really am sorry for not telling you about your dad."

He sighed, and when he looked at her, a little of the earlier venom had dissipated. "I know. I'll get over that. It's just easier to be mad at you right now than being mad about everything else. I know no matter how mad I get at you, you'll still have my back when I need it."

She desperately wanted to hug him, but she knew if she tried, it would take him even longer to forgive her. "I'll take it. Talk to you later."

Once she was out of the truck, Edgar honked the horn once in goodbye. Amber watched him go. Maybe she could sprint after him and launch herself into the bed of his truck. She glanced across the street at Purrfectly Scrumptious and spotted Betty inside. Bobby was out front chatting and laughing with the couple at the door. The line snaked down the sidewalk again. He didn't see Amber. The Harrises wouldn't be able to rescue her either.

Reluctantly, Amber turned to face Thea. Amber's sidewalk was decidedly less busy.

"Are you Amber Blackwood?" Thea asked as she took a step toward her with her hand outstretched. She was the same height as Amber, and a light smattering of freckles lined her cheekbones. Her eyes were a startling green behind her glasses. "I'm Thea Bishop, Henrietta's sister."

Amber plastered on her best smile and shook her hand. Thea's nails were painted a bright red. "That's me. It's nice to meet you."

Once Thea let her hand go, she gave Amber an appraising elevator scan. "I was hoping we could have a chat. Inside, perhaps?"

Amber hesitated, still searching for an escape from this conversation.

When the silence stretched on for an awkward length of time, Thea, in a volume louder than necessary, said, "My sister is in a coma after purchasing something from your store."

A pair of women who had been on the sidewalk nearby quickly crossed the street. Good grief.

"Sure, let's go in," Amber said, and quickly bustled past Thea so she could unlock the door. She mentally uttered the alarm deactivation spell in her head, feeling the magic dissipate. As she stepped inside, she called a loud hello to her aunt and sister but got no response. Amber wondered if Willow and Connor were still at lunch. Would Molly have been so upset with Amber that she'd crash Willow's lunch? Perhaps it would be Molly and Willow who ended up at the police station for having a brawl.

Amber flipped on the lights and deposited her purse behind the counter before turning to address Thea. The woman was busily scanning the room, taking in Amber's wares with big sweeping motions of those green eyes. When her gaze finally settled on Amber, Thea's lip curled just slightly, like she'd just gotten a whiff of something foul.

Oh boy.

Amber headed for her apothecary wall behind the counter and scanned the labels on the drawers until she landed on the one for "sleep." She trundled it open and pulled out a package of her sleepy tea blend. The round circle on the package featured Amber's cheeky top-hat-wearing logo, as well as the ingredients for the tea.

Stopping before Thea, the counter between them, Amber slid the package across the worn wood. "That's the blend Henrietta has been buying for a year. I make it in-house and have been making it the same way for years. That's the kind Hen last purchased."

Thea picked the package up very carefully, as if it were set to explode. Amber expected her to at least open the package to sniff the contents. But she supposed if the woman thought it was laced with arsenic or something equally as toxic, she wouldn't risk harming herself. Instead, she slipped the package into her purse, unopened.

Over the next several minutes, Thea questioned Amber about her business—how long she'd been in operation, how she learned to create tea blends, and if anyone else who had purchased her teas had ever issued a complaint. Based on her line of questioning, Amber assumed Thea hadn't yet caught wind of the Toast the Bear debacle and decided it best to keep that part to herself.

Then Thea abruptly changed the subject. "I heard you visited Henrietta at the hospital yesterday."

"Yes," Amber said. "My friend Kim and I went to see her."

"Why?"

Amber cocked her head. What kind of question was that? "Because she's my friend and I wanted to see how she was doing."

"You see, that's very interesting, because the nurses today told me that shortly after your visit, Henrietta's vitals went haywire. The phrase they used to describe her condition was 'acute distress.' They'd never seen anything like it," Thea said. "Can you explain what happened?"

Amber stared at her. "I have no idea what happened. Is she okay?"

Thea said nothing for several seconds. "They were able to stabilize her again, yes."

"Do they have any idea what may have caused her condition?" Amber asked. "The coma, I mean. Not the acute distress."

"A toxicology report should be in soon." After a brief stint of very intense eye contact, Thea said, "You know, Henrietta has mentioned your shop many times. Toys that have more functionality than even the most complex robotic ones. *Fluid* was the word she used—as if they were alive. On that wall behind you, you have everything from headache tonics to memory supplements, if the labels are to be believed. Henrietta swore by your tea. She said you'd make a killing if you sold the stuff online…that it's more effective than melatonin."

Amber had heard Henrietta say as much.

"Why haven't you tried to expand your business if you have a seemingly miraculous item on your hands?" Thea asked.

Swallowing, Amber said, "It's not something I wish to pursue at this time."

"I see," Thea said rather unconvincingly. "Did you notice that her purchases of the tea have increased lately?"

"In the last month or so, yes," Amber said.

"And did you think that was strange?"

Amber cocked her head. If this was how lawyers usually were in court, Amber could see how some people might crack on the stand out of sheer exhaustion caused by a relentless line of questioning. She didn't want to deal with any of this right now. She also didn't know where Thea was going and wanted to get to the destination quicker. So without giving it much thought, Amber hurled a truth spell at her. "Why would Henrietta buying more of my products be strange, Thea Bishop?"

A sense of calm washed over Thea. "Because it *was* strange. Henrietta was trying to recreate your tea blend. Since you wouldn't offer the tea on the market, Henrietta was going to try to do it herself. She has an online shop set up and even has a couple of interested investors."

Amber lightly shook her head. But Henrietta had asked about the recipe again the other day. Amber had thought it had been part of their usual banter, but perhaps it had been more than that.

"*I purchased some sleepy tea from the drug store the other day and that one wasn't nearly as effective as yours,*" Henrietta had said. "*Do you think it's the valerian root in yours that does the trick?*"

Thea floundered a little as the magic faded. "I'm…I'm not really sure why I said that. Uh." She cleared her throat.

"Henrietta's been struggling to find a business venture since her divorce."

As if this was information she'd had for a while, and not only a day, Amber said, "She's been looking for something that could match the income she had when her husband was funding their indulgent lifestyle."

Thea gave her head a little shake, like shucking off the last dregs of a dream. She eyed Amber warily, and bit by bit, a different kind of calm washed over her. Understanding, maybe.

"I see," Thea said again, then walked away from the counter, running her fingers along the edges of the pyramid-shaped bookshelf nearest her, then wandering farther into the store. "You have dreamcatchers that actually catch dreams. Just over there, there's an 'ever-burning candle,'" she said, pointing off to the left. Amber didn't look; she kept watching Thea. "I explored the town a bit this morning before I came here. It's so quaint, Edgehill. A town built around its cats. And a town with a resident who everyone seems to have an opinion about. Every time I brought up your name to a shop owner or resident, you know what word came up?"

Amber pursed her lips but remained silently standing behind the counter. She wondered if Thea was this theatrical in court.

"*Weird,*" Thea said after a beat. "*Odd* was used quite a bit, too. Your toys get mentioned the most. The way children can play with the things for hours and hours and the batteries never die. The way the toys interact with the children as if the toys are powered by breath and a beating heart."

She headed back toward the counter. "When I couldn't do research on your ingredients, I researched you instead. My profession has trained me to look at something from as many angles as possible. And no matter what angle I chose, quite a few odd events cropped up. Your parents died in a mysterious house fire. A swarm of exotic insects materialized out of nowhere, stung multiple people, and then disappeared again. Several people claimed that when the insects were wreaking their havoc and people were fleeing the building, you ran farther *into* the building. A maid was killed in a way that defies scientific explanation—a maid who had been cleaning the room of *your* aunt. Two cars on your cousin's property were torched with a fire so hot, the vehicles melted as if they'd been made of wax instead of metal."

Thea folded her hands on the worn wooden counter and stared Amber dead in the eye. The silence stretched on for long enough that Amber's palms started to sweat.

"I'm a believer in what's real and tangible," Thea said. "There's always a logical explanation as long as you keep digging. I'm exceedingly good at digging, Amber. It's why I'm so successful at my job. No question is too big for me to find the answer to. Usually the answer is simplest and most obvious. Sometimes the answer is much more complicated than one first thinks." She paused and gave Amber another of her appraising elevator scans. "And, rarely, the most obvious answer is the…*weirdest* one."

This pause was so long, Amber was nearly driven mad. She broke the silence with, "I'm not sure what you're getting at."

"I have a very weird theory, though I will admit that Henrietta is the one who first put the possibility in my head," Thea said. "But I must ask…are you a witch, Amber Blackwood?"

Amber froze. Admitting the truth could go one of two ways. Thea could react the way Kim had, and nearly burst out of her own skin in excitement. Or she could react the way Jack had initially: abject fear.

What damage could this cause Amber's already "weird" reputation if a woman like Thea Bishop knew her secret? Amber imagined being on trial, a jury box full of her "peers" gaping at her in horror over using her magic on unsuspecting non-witches.

The bell above the door chimed, jarring both women out of their staring contest. Amber had forgotten to lock the door. Had the WBI agents returned, had Molly Hargrove come to clock Amber in the face, or had another of her wares gone rogue, and a customer was here to demand an explanation?

She relaxed when she saw that it was only Chief Brown.

At least she hoped so.

He must have read the wild-eyed look of concern on her face, because the first thing out of his mouth was a loud, confident, "Hinklebert."

Amber sagged in relief.

The chief strode across the shop with a hand extended. He was in full uniform. "You must be Thea Bishop. We spoke on the phone Saturday. I'm Owen Brown, the police chief. I didn't realize you were in town already."

Thea seemed a bit dazed, her theatrical assessment of Amber interrupted before it had reached its conclusion. "Ah, yes. Hello, Chief Brown. I arrived early Sunday afternoon."

So she'd been wandering the streets of Edgehill for nearly a full day. Goodness knew how many gossip-hounds she'd talked to.

Now that there was another person in the room, Thea didn't seem as keen to get back to their earlier conversation. But she did offer an over-the-top laugh, and said, "How curious that you should show up when you did, chief. It's almost as if she conjured you here by magic!"

Amber's laugh was both too loud and shrill.

The chief's blond brows bunched up as he eyed Amber curiously. Then he refocused on Thea. "The only magic that brought me over here is the scent of Betty Harris's cakes from across the street. I should have figured there would still be a line. When I saw the lights on here, I came over to make sure everything was okay since Amber had shut the shop down for a few days after the incident with the toy bear."

Amber almost chucked the entire cash register at his head.

"Ah, so *that's* why you've closed up shop," Thea said, attention swiveling back to Amber. "Was there a problem with one of your toys? And on the heels of my sister's condition as well?" She pulled her cell phone out of her purse as she spoke. "I think it might be time to call for an inspection of your shop, Miss Blackwood. I worry your products are unsafe."

Unsafe. The same word used in Molly Hargrove's article.

Amber shot a panicked look at the chief, who shot a panicked look back. While Thea scrolled through her contacts, the chief started to mime a complicated series of movements. As she watched him in dismay, she decided then and there that if there were ever a chance for them to be on a charades team together, she would pick someone else to be paired with. Anyone else. A potted plant, even!

He seemed to be mimicking a chimpanzee now. Perhaps she should heave the cash register at his head just to put him out of his own misery.

Clearly her mouthing "*What?*" at him every other second had finally frustrated him beyond measure because he finally shouted, "Memory wipe!"

Thea abruptly stopped her endless swiping and whirled toward the chief. "You know she's a witch?"

"*You* know she's a witch?"

"I speculated but you just confirmed it," Thea said. "Not only is Miss Blackwood selling dangerous items to people who have no idea what they're really buying, but the chief of police is complicit in this town-wide deceit?"

Before Amber's jaw could hit the counter, the shop lights went out, Thea's eyes rolled back in her head, and the woman slumped to the floor. Chief Brown yelped, followed by a series of curses. He spun to look out the windows of the shop, clearly concerned someone had witnessed the whole thing. The lights being off would help throw things into shadow, but it was still the middle of the day.

"Why on *earth* did you let that woman carry on like that!" Aunt Gretchen said, standing outside the open

Employee Only door. Her chest heaved slightly. "Chief Brown is right. We need to wipe her memory."

"How much of it?" Amber asked, still behind the counter as if her feet were rooted to the floor.

"From the moment she stepped in here, I'd say," Aunt G said, hurrying over to crouch by the woman's prone form.

Amber instantly lost sight of her when she dropped to her knees, finally giving Amber the impetus to get moving. She rushed around the counter to join her aunt.

The chief still stood by the door, lightly wringing his hands. "She's already suspicious of you. How are you going to explain away her lost chunk of time?"

Amber and Aunt G shared a "beats me" look that did nothing to calm the chief's nerves. They stood once they were sure Thea was out cold, evidenced by the loud snoring, and was comfortably sprawled out on her back.

Amber began to pace. "Okay, so given that she wants to get an inspection, we can assume that the whole 'magic is real' bombshell is probably not going to go over well with her. We can wipe her memory of everything that we just discussed, but, like Owen says, she'll probably be aware of the gap in time—"

"Do you know if Henrietta has any other family?" Aunt G asked. "Parents, other siblings, nosy cousins …"

Amber cocked her head. "I'm not sure. Why?"

"Just wondering who might come looking for her if she disappears," Aunt G said.

Amber knew her aunt was a problem solver through and through, and that she would do anything for Amber and Willow, but Amber never would have thought she'd have to worry about her aunt being…murderous.

"Mrs. Blackwood …" the chief said slowly, taking a step toward her aunt with a hand out. Clearly he was just as distressed by the implication of Aunt G's words as Amber was. "Let's not do anything rash."

Aunt G ignored them both, turned toward the snoring body on the floor, and aimed both of her palms toward Thea. She quickly spoke the words of a spell. Amber didn't recognize the incantation for what it was until the last few words. When the realization hit, her cry of, "Aunt G, no!" was too late.

In the next instant, Thea Bishop—a redheaded sleeping woman—turned into a rust-colored hamster.

"Oh my God!" Amber yelped.

Chief Brown let out a high-pitched scream one would normally hear on a playground populated by small children. "You said the hamster spell was just a joke!"

And then he fainted dead away.

"Oh my God!" Amber yelped again.

The crash of his large body on the floor startled the already quaking hamster, and the tiny furry creature took off like a shot.

"Oh, poo!" Aunt G said, then scurried after the hamster, who had run along the edge of the counter, rounded it, and then disappeared somewhere behind.

"Oh my God, Aunt G!" Amber said, running after her, realizing she sounded like Kim. "What did you do!"

"We needed a solution more permanent than a sleep spell!" Aunt G said, now on her hands and knees behind the counter, searching for the terrified rodent.

"*Permanent*?" Amber shrieked, on her hands and knees now, too. "Is that what you meant by Thea 'disappearing'?"

"Good grief, little mouse, no. Ha. My little mouse is looking for a little hamster," Aunt G said, clearly amused with herself. Amber assumed she was smiling ruefully, but she currently only had a view of her aunt's backside clad in black stretchy pants covered in cat hair. "A spell like this will last a good twenty-four hours, as opposed to only one or two with a sleep spell that we'd need to keep reinforcing. This one will buy us some more time."

"Is she going to *remember* being a hamster?" Amber asked. A small gap in time in Thea's memory would have been strange, but memories of being a rodent for twenty-four hours surely would be harder for Thea to reconcile. And harder for Amber to explain away.

For being a practical woman, this decision was decidedly the least practical one her aunt had ever come up with.

"You know, I'm not sure," Aunt G said, poking around near the base of the apothecary wall where the supplies for packaging the tea blends were stored—boxes filled with logo stickers, plastic bags, and small containers. "I panicked, truthfully. This Thea woman makes me nervous, and with a Penhallow already in town, it seemed like an additional problem we didn't need."

As if turning a human into a hamster wasn't an "additional problem."

Amber hadn't even told her aunt about the WBI's visit yet.

A small squeak sounded to Amber's right where her purse was stored. A tiny rust-colored face poked over the lip of her bag. The wealth of whiskers and tiny black nose twitched nervously when one of its beady black eyes locked with Amber's.

"Hey, Thea," Amber said softly.

The hamster let out another squeak and dove farther into the purse. Amber quickly snatched the bag out of its hiding place and zipped the top closed. There was a small gap on the right-hand side that Thea could still wriggle out of if she tried hard enough, but this way Amber could at least keep Thea secured until they found a better place to keep her. Amber stood, purse in hand.

Aunt G was on her feet now, too, brushing off her knees. "I'll head over to a pet shop and see if we can find a cage for her. You stay here and keep Thea occupied."

Clutching her purse to her chest as if it were made of glass, Amber silently watched her aunt squeeze past her and walk up the stairs.

A groan from the other side of the room reminded Amber that the chief was still here. He pushed himself into a seated position, using the front door as a backrest as he rubbed one of his temples. All at once, he seemed to remember where he was and quickly scrambled to his feet. He swayed a bit as he did so and propped a hand on the door to steady himself.

When he shot her an incredulous look, as if silently demanding that she confirm he hadn't actually seen what he'd seen, she held up her purse. Even though there was muted chatter from outside, and the faint creaking of Aunt G moving around upstairs—presumably getting her things together for her trip to the pet store—even Chief Brown heard the angry squeaks and rummaging coming from inside her handbag. His eyes widened. "My God."

Amber imagined Thea was fully aware that she was a human who was now a hamster and was furious. There was no doubt in Amber's mind that Thea was chewing holes in all Amber's credit cards and was revenge-peeing on everything else.

"What was she thinking?" the chief hissed and speed-walked over to her, shooting panicked looks over his shoulder as he did. "Is she stuck like that?"

"I don't know! Aunt G said it'll last at least a day," Amber said, then flinched when the furious scratching inside her purse grew more frantic.

"My God," he muttered again.

Amber swallowed. "Aunt G is going to the store to pick up a cage."

"A *cage*? Amber. This…you can't…I mean—" the chief stammered, only to be cut off by his cell phone ringing. He fished the phone out of his pocket, stared down at the screen, and then cursed. "I have to take this. I'll call you later. Just…I…my God, I don't even know what to say."

With that, he headed for the door. The bell chimed, signaling his departure just as he answered the call.

Thea offered another very angry series of squeaks, followed by what sounded like gnawing. Face screwed up in horror, Amber held her purse out in front of her as if it were about to detonate and headed for the stairs. She passed Aunt G who was on the way down, jangling Amber's spare car keys as she went.

"Be back soon!" Aunt G shouted at the purse. "I'll get you some nice fluffy bedding and a few chew toys to keep you busy! This'll be like a relaxing vacation, just you wait and see."

Amber blinked at her aunt in shock. Perhaps the stress of everything had finally made the woman snap.

Squeak! said Thea.

Amber had to agree.

CHAPTER 10

For the next several hours, Amber busied herself in her shop. She had tried working with Aunt Gretchen on the next set of toy orders, but the two had gotten into a snippy fight over the state of Amber's kitchen. Instead of either one being a levelheaded adult and calling the other out for being upset over something bigger than dirty dishes, Amber had stormed downstairs with the hamster cage, and then decided to deep clean the shop.

Thea was in her cage on the counter now while Amber used a citrus-scented wood polish on her shelves. Amber was growing laughably behind on her toy orders, but she couldn't stay cooped up with her aunt right now.

For as long as Amber could remember, Aunt Gretchen had been consistently consistent. She had her core rules and convictions and stuck by them no matter what. When Aunt G made a promise, she kept it. When she made a decision, she stuck with it. When she put forth a rule, she expected you to always follow it.

One such rule when Amber and Willow were growing up had been, "No flashy magic." Magic used to defend yourself or others when things were dire was the one exception. And even then, Aunt G chose spells that would cause the least amount of ripple effect. Amber and Aunt G had gotten into countless fights when Amber was a teenager. Most had been about the death of Amber's parents and her theory that Penhallows had been behind it. But the others had been about the use of magic itself. Aunt G had held so steadfastly to the rule that magic needed to be suppressed that Amber and Willow would push the issue solely to see their aunt get riled up.

The suppression of magic had been beaten into Amber's head for so long, that now even using a simple tincture or sleep spell made her anxious.

A scrabbling sound drew her focus across the shop at the cage. Thea was running around, knocking bits of bedding out onto the counter.

No flashy magic.

Aunt G had turned an innocent woman into a *rodent*. It was such an antithesis to Aunt G's usual behavior that it scared Amber. Scared her so much, she would rather ignore her piling responsibilities and scrub her shelves than face what might really be going on.

It was cowardly of her, she knew, but the fact that Aunt G wasn't forcing Amber to talk about any of it spoke volumes, too. Something was very amiss here.

When the ward on the front door dropped, Amber nearly yelped, so lost she'd been in her thoughts. She turned just as the jangle of the bell above the door sounded and in walked Willow.

Amber wiped her hands on a rag as she approached her sister, ready to chastise her for leaving her alone so long with their aunt who was clearly going through something, but Amber came up short when Willow looked at her. Her eyes were red-rimmed and her face splotchy.

"Oh, Will …" Amber said and tossed the rag over her shoulder so she could take her sister's hands. "What did that awful Connor Declan do?"

Willow shook her head, gaze diverted. She tried to pull her hands from Amber's grasp, but Amber held firm. "Did you get a new pet?"

When Amber had finished telling Willow about who the hamster was and how she got that way, Willow's mouth hung open. "What happened to 'no flashy magic'?"

"Exactly," Amber said. "We can talk about Aunt G later. What happened with Connor? Do you want me to turn *him* into a hamster? He can keep Thea company."

Thea issued a squeak at this—whether she was excited or horrified by the idea, Amber couldn't tell.

Willow managed a watery laugh, then sniffed. "I'm such an idiot, Amber."

Frowning, Amber said, "Hang on a second." She went to her cooking nook to start the hot plate to make them some hot chocolate. Then she moved Thea off the counter and encouraged Willow to hop up onto it. They sat side by side, Thea's cage on the floor directly in front of them a few feet away. "Okay, lay it on me."

It took Willow a few long seconds to start talking. "Lunch was actually really nice at first," she said. "We just talked about old times for a while before I got up the nerve to ask him about *us*, you know?"

Amber nodded.

"He said he and Molly are just 'casual,' whatever that means," Willow said, sniffing again. "He said they've been together a lot working on some big, secret story and that's why he's been MIA. But, I mean, even if you're busy with work, you can at least answer a *couple of* messages. Even if it's just to say you're too busy to talk."

When she fell silent for a while, Amber waited her out. Eventually Amber hopped off the counter long enough to make their hot chocolate—a caramel drizzle for Willow, and a sprinkle of cayenne pepper for Amber. She had drained half her mug before Willow started talking again. She just held hers, staring into the mug while the whipped cream on top melted.

"After we ate, we got some ice cream," Willow said. "We ate it in Balinese Park and talked. He got flirty, and talked about the good old days, and he said I look really pretty today—his usual flirty thing. I…I got so frustrated with him that I used a truth spell on him."

Growing up, truth spells had been on the "no flashy magic" list. It was the kind of spell that always had a consequence—whether it was ticking off the WBI, inadvertently getting a woman turned into a rodent, or opening a can of worms that was better left closed.

Willow finally took a sip of her hot chocolate, and after wiping her mouth with the back of her hand, she said, "I asked him how he truly felt about me." She let out a long sigh. "He said he's always been in love with me but was too scared to pursue it because he didn't want to ruin what we had."

Amber thought that sounded great, but Willow's devastated expression told Amber something else must have come with that confession.

"He also said that part of the reason why he's been so weird with me isn't because of Molly, but because that big, secret story he's been working on could destroy your business," Willow said, wincing.

"What?" Amber asked in a rush. "*Connor* had something to do with—" she gestured to her shop at large, "this?"

"As soon as he confessed that part of it, the truth spell wore off. Then, like what usually happens with truth spells, he was all freaked out that he'd told me any of that—more so the love confession part than the destroying your business part."

Could Connor somehow know about Amber's magic? A couple of months ago, while Edgehill had still been in knots over the kidnapping of Chloe Deidrick, Amber had run into Connor outside The Quirky Whisker early one morning. Amber had just magically changed the welcome sign on her chalkboard minutes before and realized it was possible that Connor had seen it happen.

While looking at the chalkboard hanging in the window, Connor had asked if Amber majored in art in college.

When Amber said she had inherited her artistic side from her mother, Connor's response had been strange.

"I wonder what else you might have inherited from your mother," he said, taking a slow sip of his coffee without taking his eyes off her.

She swallowed. "Meaning?"

He shrugged nonchalantly. "You Blackwood women seem to have so many more layers than I first thought. Just curious what else there is to know about you."

How much did Connor Declan know about the "layers" the Blackwood women possessed? And if he knew about the magic layer, how had he come by that information? Run-of-the-mill journalistic research, or something else?

"Did you find out why he's targeting my shop?" Amber asked.

"Not really," she said. "And the weird thing? Just after the magic faded, he sounded really bummed out when he said, 'You and your sister are more alike than I realized.' I think he knows we're witches."

Amber took another sip of her hot chocolate.

"I can't explain it—maybe it's just because I know the guy, but my guess is, he didn't come to his suspicions of us naturally," Willow said. "I'm willing to bet someone got him started on this path."

"Who?"

"I don't know," she said. "I don't think Edgehill and the surrounding areas are as magic-free as we once thought. I think we—you—have been on someone's radar for a while, maybe years, and they got to Connor somehow."

If that were the case, it meant Amber hadn't been living life off the magical grid after all. If the Penhallows had known for a while that Amber was still in the same town where her parents had been killed, and they suspected that Amber had access to the Henbane grimoire, then why had it taken them fourteen years to come crawling out of the woodwork?

Amber supposed many things could have factored into the Penhallows' hiatus, one of which was that the time-travel spell had been so well hidden that it had vanished off the magical map when Amber's parents had been killed. But even magic as powerful as Annabelle Henbane's—a cloaking spell so strong that it survived even after her death—faded eventually. Perhaps the Penhallows had needed to come up with a new game plan for solving their curse problem in the wake of the Henbane grimoire's disappearance.

And then once the powerful cloaking magic on it started to dissolve, the Penhallows had been able to sense it even if they hadn't known where the magic came from—and the old plan was back on: getting the Henbane grimoire into their possession so they could turn back time and reverse the clan-wide curse.

"I have a theory though," Willow said. "As much as I started to like Kieran *after* he was healed, we don't know the full extent of what he was up to before he got here, and what he was doing when he wasn't harassing us."

Amber flashed back to the day she'd been outside their old family home. After finding her father's beloved watch under the porch of 523 Ocicat Lane, Amber's memory magic had been activated. When she came out of the memory of

Neil Penhallow murdering her parents by fire, somehow Connor had been there to comfort her. It wasn't until later that Amber discovered Connor hadn't been there at all; it had been Kieran wearing Connor's face.

Amber had assumed then that Kieran had chosen Connor based on the perception that Connor was special to her. But what if Connor and Kieran had been the ones in contact?

One day several months ago, Amber had literally bumped into Connor on her way out of Clawsome Coffee after an upsetting conversation with the always-awful Paulette Newsome. When Amber had accidentally barreled into him, he'd dropped his book. It had been a fantasy novel with a witch on the cover—a book which he then claimed he reread every year.

With Connor's love of fantasy and his inquisitive nature, maybe all Kieran had needed to do was plant a few enticing seeds to get Connor going.

Amber asked, "Do you think Connor's curiosity has overridden everything else at this point?"

"I think so," Willow said. "But…I get the impression he's doing this because he thinks you're dangerous."

"*Me?*"

Willow sniffed. "I think he's doing this in part to protect me. Like he needs to prove that you're up to something terrible so he can save me from you. But he seems to have the same suspicions about me, so I don't know what he thinks he's going to accomplish."

Amber opened her mouth, then shut it again. She had no idea what to say to that. When she thought about

Connor asking her to join him at the Sippin' Siamese for his birthday celebration, she'd genuinely thought, at least for a short window of time, that Connor had been *interested* in her. She wondered if this fascination with her and her supposedly dangerous ways had come before or after the invitation to the bar. If it had come after, had a conversation with the cursed Kieran Penhallow been what had caused the shift?

"We more or less got into a screaming fight after that," Willow said. "I've been wandering around town for a while. He can't really think taking you down would put me in his good graces, can he? If I somehow indirectly ruined your business because I can't get over Connor Declan, I'll never forgive myself."

Amber hugged Willow to her side, who dropped her head onto Amber's shoulder. "Will, c'mon. There's no way any of this is your fault. I would never blame you for any of it." After a moment, she asked, "Does he have an opinion on Aunt G?"

"I don't know," she said. "All his focus is on you."

Amber held Willow to her side while Willow cried. She wasn't sobbing or gasping for breath. She just sniffed occasionally and swiped at her eyes. It was the kind of crying that came from being deeply sad and unable to feel much else.

Amber's mind had drifted to Kieran again. Why had *he* ended up in Edgehill? Aunt G, via her tincture-induced premonition, had only seen one Penhallow heading their way three months ago. Once the cloak on the hidden grimoires started to fade, had Kieran been able to track the magical traces faster than anyone else? Amber would have thought that Edgehill—the current home of the Blackwoods' eldest daughter—would be the first place the Penhallows would look. Yet, Kieran had come alone.

He'd been reckless, using "flashy magic" and leaving his sticky, molasses-thick magical signature all over town. Maybe Kieran had gone rogue—a crazed lone wolf. But what if her assumptions about Kieran—and Penhallows in general—had been wrong? What if there had been a grander plan all along and Kieran had been sent in like a scout onto a battlefield to test the ground for land mines? The question was: had Kieran been sent in as collateral damage by someone more calculating—or had Kieran willingly come to Edgehill in search of the book while someone else waited in the wings to see what happened?

Amber wished she knew where Kieran was now and who had orchestrated his escape, an escape that could very well be another piece of the plan. She'd thought that she and her family were on top of it, that they were one step ahead of the cursed witches who sounded disorganized, wild, and scattered across the globe.

But perhaps they'd been operating together underground this whole time. They'd made themselves known only because they'd wanted to be found. And now the WBI was in town, trying to recruit Amber.

Just last week, after Willow had confessed that she'd found their uncle, she'd said, *"I just keep thinking that the Penhallows are picking off our family. First Mom and Dad. Then they went after Edgar. One of them threatened to go after Aunt G. One tried to kill you. And now it sounds like they got to Uncle Raph, too. What if, even though they're cursed, they're too powerful for us to outrun forever? We'll hide the book, sure, then what? What if they find it? Then it won't just be our family that's in danger, it's…everyone."*

What if Amber and her family were already too late to stop whatever was coming?

CHAPTER 11

Instead of Penhallow-filled nightmares being the source of Amber's insomnia, now it was due to the animals inhabiting her apartment. Amber had no way of knowing if Thea retained her human mind while trapped in that furry little body, but the rodent sure seemed ticked off.

Between the hamster making a ruckus in her wheel, and Amber's need to shoo the cats away from the cage, Amber hardly slept a wink. The cats found that watching the hamster offered a level of entertainment that stretched beyond their wildest imaginations. Entertainment that paled, however, to the harrowing hour when the cats had gotten onto the counter in the middle of the night—during the brief window Amber had been asleep—and had managed to knock the cage over. Bedding, the hamster's beloved wheel, and the hamster herself had been dumped on the counter. How the hamster had managed to not only get to the floor, but to do so unscathed had been a small miracle. Tom and Alley had taken turns chasing the poor rodent all over the apartment. If the crash of the cage onto the kitchen counter hadn't woken Amber and her family up, the shrieks of the hamster as she dashed around the apartment trying to escape the cats definitely would have.

Tom seemed delighted that for once, he was the one doing the chasing.

Once the hamster had been safely deposited back in her cage—not before nipping Amber on the thumb—Amber had locked her in the bathroom. The cats sat outside the door and yowled as if they were being tortured within an inch of their nine lives. So Amber put the cage on the coffee table next to the couch where she tried to sleep. She had managed to fall asleep for all of a few minutes before she'd woken herself up, her heart racing, to find a wild-eyed Tom perched on top of the hamster cage, gnawing on the rubber-wrapped handle. One would think the hamster had been doused in *eau de catnip*, given how crazed her presence made the cats.

When the sky outside her window finally started to lighten, Amber was so relieved, she nearly cried. After feeding the cats—Tom's first true love still remained food— Amber sent Kim a text, asking if she needed any help today with Here and Meow duties. Kim had abruptly stopped giving Amber assignments a few days ago, which Amber had secretly appreciated. But now? Now Amber needed to get out of this apartment before she lost what shred of sanity she had left.

She debated who the hamster would be safest with. If left unattended, the hamster might find a way to escape. If left in the vicinity of the cats unsupervised, Amber would have to break the news to Henrietta when she woke up that her sister had been eaten by a house cat. If left in the possession of her aunt or sister, who knew what would happen. Edgar was likely still too angry to even take her call.

Aunt G had said the spell would last for twenty-four hours, meaning it would wear off around noon today. That gave Amber four or five hours to figure out what in the world to do about…everything…before Thea turned back into a human who likely would have even more questions than she had before her transformation.

Amber's cell phone rang and Kim's smiling face popped up on the screen. Aunt G was still fast asleep, but Willow stirred. Amber quickly answered the call, grabbed the hamster cage's handle, and then hustled down the steps, shooing the cats away with her foot as she went, which made descending the steps rather difficult.

"Amber?" Kim said. "Are you okay? What's happening? Why are you breathing so hard?"

Amber somehow managed to get herself and the hamster into the shop, and the door closed between herself and her lunatic felines. She heaved out a breath. "Oh my God, Kim! I've had the most bonkers couple of days—which is saying a lot."

Kim paused and Amber could imagine her narrowing her eyes as she assessed the situation.

"You asked if I need help," Kim said slowly. "Are you sure you're up for helping? You sound exhausted."

The hamster was back in her wheel. It must have gotten warped during the tumble onto the counter, because it offered the most annoying creaking sound now. Amber was reminded of a wonky shopping cart wheel. *Creak, creak, creak.* Pause. *Creak, creak, creak.*

Amber's eye started to twitch. "I'm so tired I could scream, but if I don't get out of here, Chief Brown is going to have to arrest me for a crime I *actually* committed this time."

"I am intrigued and very worried," Kim said. "But I also have a million things to do today. It's Kids Day!"

Ah, Kids Day. Tons of kid-friendly events were scheduled a couple of days before the festival as a way to jumpstart their parents' spending. Amber had tentatively been scheduled to do a toy demonstration today—she'd supplied the demo toys weeks ago—but since Kim hadn't brought it up, Amber wasn't going to either. It was too precarious a time to demonstrate her toys right now.

"The committee is trying to get as much done as possible this morning because we're going to need all hands on deck for Kids Day. So, yes, I'd love the help, but don't you want to be with your family—"

Creak, creak, creak.

"*No.*"

"Yikes," Kim said.

"I'll be ready in twenty," Amber said. "Oh, and I'll explain later, but I'm bringing a hamster."

Kim arrived in front of The Quirky Whisker in Ann Marie's minivan. The back seats—save for one—had been laid flat so Kim could fill the vehicle with various boxes of supplies and decorations. The hamster was safely strapped into the only available back seat. For the next two hours while they ran errands, Amber filled Kim in on her conversation with the WBI.

They picked up several boxes of black headbands—which had been outfitted with cat ears—from Letty Ortiz at Angora Threads. Then they dropped the boxes off at the community center. Participants of the Saturday 5K could pick up their running bibs, T-shirts, and extra goodies—including the cat-ear headbands—from the center on Friday.

The center was filled with volunteers putting the bags together, and boxes of all sizes were stacked around the room. Some had yet to be opened, while others lay empty and dumped on their sides, packing paper spilling out onto the floor. Amber watched as a volunteer opened a box and took out a baby blue T-shirt, Ben's design of the twelve Best of Edgehill businesses running horizontally across the front. Behind the volunteer, several others sorted the shirts on a long table, presumably arranging them by size. Other tables were stacked with what looked like postcards—most likely coupons from the various Edgehill businesses doing all they could to take advantage of the influx of tourists eager to spend money. The restaurants especially got an extra boost on Saturday after the race, when sweaty runners went in search of a meal or a cool drink.

No sooner had Amber and Kim dropped off the boxes and Kim had thanked Ann Marie, the volunteer coordinator, and Chloe Deidrick, her assistant, for being rock stars, then they were on their way again.

When they got back into the minivan, Amber was relieved Thea was still safely inside her cage. Amber had yet to go into detail about the hamster, as Kim nearly had a conniption over the fact that the Witch Bureau of Investigation not only existed, but that they'd given Amber a mission.

"My best friend is a freaking *spy*!" Kim had happily chirped.

Their next task was to drop off window decals to the winners of the Best of Edgehill competition, as well as rubber stamps for the scavenger hunt bingo cards. Halfway down the list—after they'd dropped off the materials to Grace Williams at Hiss and Hers—Kim finally got over her excitement about Amber being an "undercover operative" and asked where the hamster had come from.

Steeling herself, Amber told Kim about Thea Bishop and how she'd come to the correct conclusion that Amber was a witch. Kim pulled into a parking spot outside Patch's Pizza and turned abruptly in her seat to face Amber.

"Shut the front door!" Kim said. "She must really be a good lawyer to have pieced all that together. What did you *say* to her?"

Amber swallowed, debated the best way to diplomatically say this sentence out loud, then went with the blunt approach. "Aunt Gretchen turned her into a hamster."

Kim stared at her for a few long seconds, then threw her head back and laughed until she was in tears. "Oh my God, Amber! That was a good one. Hoo boy, I needed that. But really, what did you tell Thea? Her blabbing your secret all over town when a Penhallow is on the loose can't be good. What if the WBI agents find out? Would they wipe her memory with those flashlight things like in that alien FBI movie?"

Amber had no idea what Kim was talking about.

It took a few more seconds for Kim to realize that Amber hadn't been joking. She let out a soft screech, then unhooked her seatbelt and whirled in her seat. With her knees on the cushion, she gripped the sides of her seat and peered over the headrest at the hamster. Amber glanced back too and spotted the rust-colored rodent sitting at the gate of the cage, staring at Amber and Kim as if she'd been listening to the conversation the entire time.

"That …" Kim said, "is Henrietta's *sister*?"

The hamster squeaked, then started running around her cage at an alarming speed, sending pieces of her bedding out of the cage's slats and onto the seat.

Amber winced. "Yes. She's supposed to turn back into a human around noon, but I didn't trust my cats *or* my aunt around her, so I brought her with us."

"Holy smokes," Kim muttered. It took her a while to finally sit properly in her seat. "What are you going to do when she turns back?"

"I really don't know. I can't let her tell everyone in town—and possibly beyond—that I'm a witch," Amber said. "Can you imagine what parents like Sally Long would do if they found out the toys they've been buying for their kids all these years are magic-powered? She was livid when she thought it was a normal toy that had exploded. If she finds out that it was otherworldly, she'll go postal. It won't just be my business in danger if *that* rumor catches fire."

Kim pursed her lips, then shot a quick look over her shoulder at the hamster who was now munching on a carrot-shaped piece of wood. Amber couldn't be sure, but the hamster seemed to be glaring at Amber while she gnawed away. "What if you guys keep her as a hamster until all this nonsense with the Penhallows is sorted out, or until Henrietta wakes up—whichever happens first. Would she get stuck like that?"

Amber shrugged, surprised Kim was even suggesting this. "I don't know."

"I'd be happy to pet sit tonight to help you get some sleep," Kim said. "I'm sure Jack would help, too. We can rotate who has her until you figure out what to do…and so Tom and Alley don't eat her."

Squeak!

"I'm sorry to dump all this on you," Amber said after a moment. "This is almost too much for *me* to handle. But I can't tell you how much it helps to talk about this stuff with someone who isn't my family. Well, I can talk to the chief about it, but he literally fainted when Thea turned into a hamster."

Kim cackled. "Lightweight."

Amber grinned at her.

They got back to The Quirky Whisker just before noon. Amber and Kim were both rather terrified that they wouldn't get the hamster to Aunt G in time and that

Thea would snap back into her human form while still in the cage. Thea was currently covered by the bedding so completely that the only evidence of her presence was the movement of the shavings as she rooted around underneath them.

Once the door was unlocked, Kim hauled tail up the steps while Amber locked up and reset the alarm. A shriek from upstairs sent Amber tearing off across the shop and into her studio apartment.

Kim had Tom, who was wriggling in Kim's grasp as if all his bones had turned liquid, clutched in her arms. Alley sat primly in a chair, her eyes wide and fixed on the hamster cage on the dining room table.

Aunt G and Willow stood on either side of the cage, and Aunt G was already well into the incantation of the spell that would add at least another twenty-four hours to Thea's hamster sentence. Thea was flat on her back, her four feet in the air. She wasn't moving.

"Oh my God," Amber yelped, squatting by the cage. "What happened to her?"

Willow had a paintbrush's handle poked between the slats of the cage and was gently jostling the bedding near Thea's unmoving body. "I don't know, but I'm too scared to open the cage yet."

"What are we going to tell Henrietta?" Kim asked. "Ow! Tom! Stop biting me!"

Aunt G finished her spell and slowly lowered her hands to her sides. There was no sound in the room as they all stared at Thea. Well, no sound other than Kim and Tom's battle of wills.

Amber sat in a chair opposite Alley and leaned so close to the cage that the tip of her nose practically poked between the slats. "Thea?" she whispered, heart in her throat. Had all this excitement and spell-use been too much for the hamster's little heart? Even if Thea's consciousness was still alive in the rodent, she couldn't have weighed more than two ounces. Amber couldn't imagine that a hamster's nervous system was resilient enough to handle all this.

Thea's little feet were still pointing to the roof of her cage, her mouth was slightly open—revealing her large yellow teeth—and her rounded ears lay flat against the bedding. A full minute went by with no movement from inside the cage. As Amber stared at the stiff-looking rodent body, she wondered how Aunt G was going to cope with the reality that she'd just murdered someone.

And then one beady little black eye opened—the one pointed in Amber's direction. The other eye remained closed. When Thea's gaze met Amber's, she quickly shut her eye again.

Amber sat up and gasped. "She's faking!"

The hamster suddenly wriggled and got herself upright, then darted to the side of the cage where Amber was crouched and used those large teeth to start chewing on the bars.

Aunt G, Willow, and Kim heaved out a collective breath of relief.

Amber put her face to the cage again so she could be level with Thea's tiny face. "I don't like this any more than you do, but you have to understand why we had to do something drastic, don't you? This is the worst time for you to be here. You don't know what trouble your investigation could cause."

Thea chewed even harder on the bars, grunting and squeaking as she did. She clearly didn't care about Amber's reasons. Amber couldn't say she blamed her.

"That wasn't very nice, Thea!" Kim snapped, still doing her best to keep Tom in her arms. "We could let the cats have you as a snack, you know!"

Thea dove under the bedding.

While Aunt G, Willow, and Kim discussed the best place to keep Thea for the night, Amber found her attention pulled toward her window. The noise from Russian Blue Avenue was a steady hum during Here and Meow week, so she was used to that, but the sound was more intense than usual. She took a squirming Tom from Kim and then walked over to the window to peer outside.

Amber could clearly see the line outside Purrfectly Scrumptious, snaking even farther down the sidewalk now that Betty had her Best of Edgehill sticker affixed to her shop front window. But there seemed to be activity on Amber's side now, too.

People in the Purrfectly Scrumptious line were focused more on what was happening outside The Quirky Whisker. Amber couldn't angle her neck just right to see what was happening below her. People aimed their phones toward the shop, while others got out of the line in front of the bakery and ran across the street.

The mental alarm bell triggered by uninvited shop guests went off. All three Blackwood women winced in unison.

Without saying anything to her family or Kim, Amber deposited Tom on the window bench seat, hurried across the apartment, grabbed the hamster cage's handle, and then nearly flew down the stairs, terrified of what she might find waiting for her at her shop's door.

CHAPTER 12

Peering out the Employee Only door, Amber half expected to find the windows smashed and her store looted. She hadn't heard the shatter of glass to accompany the mental alarm, but that didn't stop her from assuming the worst.

The shop itself looked fine, though. It was quiet and dark: the shop's usual, now. The swarm of people outside it, however, was new. They weren't huddled against the windows with their faces cupped to the glass. There were no pounding fists or contorted faces. And, blessedly, no pitchforks.

Their focus wasn't on the shop itself, but on the figure whose back was pressed against the glass door. The person had several people standing in front of him, shielding the person from the mob holding up their cameras and phones.

Then the person turned and faced Amber, a wild look in his eye. The recessed doorway of the shop, plus him being crowded into a small space, cast him into shadow despite it being the middle of the afternoon with the sun high in the sky. Something like recognition tickled her memory.

Someone behind her screamed. Then someone else did. But it wasn't a scream of terror.

It was more of a squeal, really.

"Is that *John Huntley*?" Willow and Kim yelped in unison.

And then the semi-shadowed face peering in at her solidified in Amber's mind. It *was* John Huntley. Heartthrob and county music phenom. Here. At her shop.

And about to be torn apart by rabid fans.

Amber quickly deposited Thea on the counter—even as a hamster, she seemed to have recognized him and had gone silent—and then rushed to the front door, fumbling with the lock. The spell on the door dropped just as she reached it and Amber silently thanked Aunt G for her help. Once the door was open, John Huntley and three men who must have been bodyguards flooded inside. A swell of excited shouts and screams poured in after them. Amber just barely got the door closed again before two wild-eyed teenage girls flung themselves at the door. One cursed at Amber as she locked the door again, while the other burst into tears.

The alarm spell went up a second later. Amber winced when the cursing girl shoved hard on the locked door and the metal alarm buzzed in Amber's brain.

She turned to face her new guests.

All three bodyguards looked like they'd been purchased from a catalog and shared the same model number. They were about six feet tall, had dark, short-cropped hair, brown eyes, bulky physiques, and wore all black. They looked more like a cross between Secret Service and special ops agents than the bodyguards of a celebrity, but when one was as famous as John Huntley, maybe this was the level of protection one needed.

One bodyguard moved toward the door; Amber scurried out of his way. He turned to face the door, his stance wide and his hands clasped in front of him. He didn't appear remotely fazed by the pair of emotional teenage girls whaling on the door. One still sobbed while the angry one had switched tack and was attempting to negotiate now. Amber figured the guard wore a flat expression and stared past the pleading girls, never breaking his expression, much like the guards outside Buckingham Palace.

John Huntley stood in the middle of the room, glancing around appreciatively at the shop. Somehow he was even more handsome in person. He wore faded well-loved jeans, a black T-shirt with a breast pocket, and red Converse sneakers. He had a blue baseball cap on, which Amber guessed had been used to help shield his identity. Often celebrities were much shorter in person than they appeared on TV, she'd heard, but John was a good six feet.

When Amber realized she'd been staring at him open-mouthed for what felt like hours, she glanced across the shop to find Kim, Willow, and Aunt G all huddled together by the Employee Only door. They, too, stared at John with their mouths agape.

A moment later, she realized that the door behind the trio was open. And a moment after that, a commotion sounded to her right. She looked over just as she spotted Tom on top of the hamster cage. The cage tipped, and feline and hamster alike gave a shriek. While the cage pitched forward, Tom jumped the other way, doing what he could to save himself from crashing to the floor. The cage hit the counter and the door popped open, sending the hamster on a death drop toward the hardwood floor.

John moved before anyone could react and managed to get to the counter in two strides of his long legs, dropped to his knees, and caught Thea in his large hands just before she hit the ground. He closed his fingers around her and slowly stood, his attention focused on the rodent. As he stood, he slowly opened his hands and brought them close to his face. "You okay? You almost took quite the spill, little one." He had the faintest hint of a southern drawl.

Amber watched as Thea nuzzled her little face against one of John's thumbs. Then, quick as a snake, she ran across his forearm, jumped onto his shirt, and then dove into his front pocket. After some wiggling, she righted herself and poked her head out, gazing up at John. Her nose gave a little twitch.

He petted her head with the tip of his finger and Thea gently closed her eyes.

John laughed, then turned to Amber. "I promise I'm not trying to steal your pet, but she's mighty cute."

Thea squeaked.

Amber cautiously approached the man, gaze affixed on his pocket. "I…uhh …" Her face was so hot, her skin would surely burst into flames. "I'm really sorry about her. That rescue was very impressive. We've had a real problem getting the cats acclimated to having her here." She tentatively reached for Thea, only for the hamster to snap her teeth at Amber's approaching hand. Then she ducked back into his pocket.

Great.

A soft mew sounded and Amber glanced down to find Alley rubbing her face against one of John's pant legs. This was getting ridiculous. What, did this man give off pheromones that affected all living creatures, regardless of species?

"It's no problem," he said. "I love animals. I had hamsters when I was a kid. It's kind of comforting having her around. I don't mind her riding around with me while I'm here."

As if by magic that she didn't possess, Kim was by Amber's side. She held a hand out to John. "Hello! I am Kimberly Jones, the director of the Here and Meow. I've been talking to your people all week."

"Nice to meet you," he said, not fazed by the fact that Kim had said all of that so fast, it had sounded like one long word, and shook her hand.

Kim gazed at him longingly, the handshake lasting much longer than was polite. John seemed unfazed by this, too. Amber wanted to pull her friend's hand loose before she embarrassed herself.

"Why *are* you here?" came Willow's voice. Then she awkwardly coughed, taking a few steps forward. "I mean…I thought you weren't due to arrive for two more days—on Thursday."

John's attention shifted to Willow, and he froze for a moment. Then a slow smile inched onto his face. "Hi."

Willow took a few more steps forward. "Hi."

They stared at each other for a long moment. Now it was Kim who awkwardly cleared her throat, mostly because John was still shaking Kim's hand while he was homed in on Willow. He quickly let Kim's hand go. "It might sound strange, but I've been wanting to come to the Here and Meow for years. An interview I had scheduled for today got canceled, so I thought I'd pop in early to see the town. I was hoping this little place was small enough that no one would recognize me. But …" He shrugged.

Willow was standing in front of him now, somehow edging out Amber and Kim without Amber understanding how it happened. "You thought no one would recognize *you*?"

John's smile, even though it was meant for Willow and Willow only, made Amber a little weak in the knees. Kim gave Amber's forearm a squeeze, as if she needed the extra support too. Thea chirped once from his pocket. "Wishful thinking, I guess. If only I had a magic spell that could disguise my face for a while."

The series of high-pitched, semi-hysterical laughs that erupted out of all the women in the room—and the squeaks of one woman-turned-hamster—was apparently such an alarming sound that all three bodyguards moved toward a visibly confused John Huntley.

The outburst of noise also seemed to have broken the non-magical spell that had overcome John and Willow. John turned toward Amber, lightly rubbing his neck. "So the reason for my visit is that my sister follows Letty Ortiz on Instagram. Crystal wants to be a designer too," he said. "Anyway, the other day, Crystal sent me a link for one of Letty's menswear lines, and clicking that led me down a wormhole to Sydney Sadler's account. Do you know Sydney?"

Amber in fact did know Sydney. She was a young prodigy who had participated in a junior fashion show a few months ago—a show that had caught the attention of Olaf Betzen, the host of a long-running reality design show. The show had been interrupted during Sydney's fashion debut by Kieran Penhallow—wearing Olaf's face—throwing bursts of cursed magic at innocent bystanders.

Sydney Sadler was also the daughter of Whitney and Derrick Sadler. After Whitney had found out about an affair between Derrick and Amber's good friend Melanie Cole, Whitney had embarked on a twisted path that resulted in Melanie's death.

Amber still felt sick when she thought about Sydney getting caught in the middle of her parents' messy lives. There was no small amount of guilt, too, at the fact that the biggest day of Sydney's young life had been completely derailed because of Amber's kooky magical past.

"Yes, I know Sydney," Amber said.

"Well, in one of her videos, she had a gorgeous peacock toy walking around on the table behind her. Enough people asked her about it that she told everyone about you and The Quirky Whisker," he said. "Her comment section was flooded with people saying they wanted one of their own. When I saw all the interest, the fact that you don't have a website, *and* that you're located in Edgehill, I figured my best chance of getting one of your creations would be to get one in person before the festival rush. I was surprised to find the place closed."

Amber was both deeply touched that Sydney would still give Amber and her shop an honorable mention despite the role she had played in her mother's arrest, and angry with the Penhallows all over again that her shop had to be shuttered. Sydney had given her free publicity so effective that even someone like *John Huntley* had seen it, and Amber wasn't able to put it to use.

"We've had a few…uh…issues with inventory lately," Amber said, hoping he wouldn't ask too many more questions.

"Dang," he said. "Sold out already?"

"Sort of!" Willow quickly chimed in. "All the toys in here are currently claimed, but Amber's been working hard to replenish her stock for the festival. She's making some exclusive ones. Maybe she can save one for you."

"I bet if you asked really nicely," Kim said, "she'd even make you a custom design!"

John perked up at this.

Amber wanted to stomp on Willow's and Kim's toes. She couldn't promise a toy to John-freaking-Huntley until this mess with the Penhallows was sorted out. The last thing she needed was for a Penhallow to sabotage one of her wares and then be responsible for horribly maiming America's heartthrob. But she plastered on a smile anyway. "Is there an animal you prefer?"

"I love cats, obviously," he said with a chuckle. "But do you ever make fantasy creatures?"

"She made a dragon once!" Kim offered.

Ah, yes, the dragon who set her curtains on fire. That malfunction had entirely been her own though.

"How about you surprise me," John said. "Favorite color is blue, if you want to work that in somehow."

Amber hesitated. "We've got a ton of orders already lined up so I might not—"

She winced when Kim elbowed her in the side.

"I'll see what I can do," Amber amended.

"Excellent," he said, then fished a protesting Thea out of his pocket and handed her over to Amber. Kim righted the cage on the counter, and after Amber was bitten *four* times, she managed to get Thea back inside the cage with the latch secured. When they were finished, and Kim and Aunt G scoured the shop for the cats, John said, "Where's your back door? Does it lead out into an alley?"

The teenage pair was still at the front door, alternating between taking pictures with their phones and attempting to negotiate with the bodyguard.

Amber wrinkled her nose. "There's actually no back door. One way in and out."

One of the girls pounded her fist against the glass and Amber's eye twitched when the mental alarm bell went off.

A slam made Amber whirl around; she found Aunt G and Kim heaving, their backs pressed to the now-closed Employees Only door. They'd presumably gotten Amber's looney cats back upstairs.

"I was thinking ..." Aunt G said. "Willow...you're so good at...*glamorous* makeup. I bet you could alter Mr. Huntley's appearance enough that no one would recognize him."

Now Aunt G was encouraging glamour spells to be used on celebrities? Amber was about to protest, but Willow brightened.

"Great idea! Would you…uh…like to come upstairs, John?" Willow's face went crimson. "All my makeup supplies are up there."

"She's really good!" Kim added. "Missed her calling as a makeup artist on movies."

John's gaze flicked between all the women present, then he arched a brow at the nearest bodyguard, silently asking his opinion on this very strange development.

The man considered it a moment, then said, "Take Troy with you. Todd and I will stay down here."

"Tad, if I get kidnapped," John said, "you'll have to be the one to inform my mother. She likes you best." John didn't seem all that concerned for his safety as he followed Willow.

"Can you keep an eye on the hamster?" Amber asked Tad. "I promise she's not much trouble."

Tad nodded once but didn't seem remotely comfortable with any of this.

Amber headed up the stairs next, but before she was even three steps up, someone grabbed her by the elbow. With the door closed, Amber huddled near it with Kim and Aunt G. Amber heard muffled conversation from upstairs.

"What is it, Aunt G?" Amber asked, leery of the calculating look in the woman's eye.

"It's all well and good to glamour John, but if a man of his height and build leaves here, won't his fans just assume it's him in a disguise?" Aunt G asked.

"You're saying we need a diversion!" Kim whispered excitedly.

"I don't know if—" Amber started, only to be cut off by Aunt G.

"Exactly," she said. "We need to come up with something that will distract the group outside to give Willow enough time to get John out."

Amber eyed her aunt warily.

When her aunt noticed, she turned to Amber, hands on hips. "What is it, little mouse? I would have thought you'd be all over this idea."

"Yes, but *you* wouldn't normally even suggest it." Amber crossed her arms. "What's going on with you?"

Her aunt rolled her eyes as if their roles had just been reversed and now Aunt Gretchen was the annoyed teenager dealing with her rigid guardian. "Nothing is *going on* with me."

Amber narrowed her eyes further.

"Time is of the essence, little mouse!" Aunt G hissed.

"Then explain what's going on," Amber said. "I'm not going to be blindsided by bad news again. The last time you started acting weird—granted, not turning-women-into-hamsters weird—you'd just found out Kieran was on his way to Edgehill." Her stomach flipped. "Is that it? Did you get more bad news from a premonition tincture?"

When Aunt G defiantly kept her lips pursed, Amber's stomach sank further.

"Oh, Aunt G," Amber said softly. "What did you see?"

"Not now, okay? We have to deal with this issue first," Aunt G said. "I promise I'll talk to you girls about it tonight.

We need to be able to discuss this openly without others around to possibly overhear."

"Fine," Amber said, then shot a look up the stairs to make sure the coast was clear. "Okay, I have an idea. Can you keep Tad and Todd distracted, Aunt G?"

"I thought Tad was upstairs," Kim said.

"No, that was Troy," said Aunt G.

"Are you sure?" Amber asked.

"Well, no …" Aunt G said. "But leave it to me. Feeble old lady in need of assistance coming right up."

Amber fought a laugh, then opened the Employee Only door and cautiously peered out. One of the guards was at the door—Todd, Amber guessed—while Tad stood near the hamster cage. Once Amber, Kim, and Aunt G had entered the shop again, Amber closed the door to make sure Tom didn't make another attempt at rodenticide.

"Your hamster is…strange," Tad said in greeting.

Amber didn't want details. "Thank you for looking after her."

Aunt G approached Tad and said, "Excuse me, young man by the door?"

Todd, eyebrow raised, turned around. "Yes, ma'am?"

"Can I ask you two a question? It's a bit of a delicate situation," Aunt G said, her voice wavering slightly. She hobbled toward the counter and put a hand on the worn wood. Then she stumbled so dramatically that Tad had to grab her by the elbow to keep her from slipping to the floor. "Sorry, dears, my knees just aren't what they used to be."

Reluctantly, Todd moved closer to Aunt G and Tad.

Aunt G's forehead was creased as she leaned a little more heavily on the counter. Amber knew her aunt had to be mentally uttering a spell at that moment, even if on the outside she appeared to be working through a pain flare-up. Amber felt when the magic was hurled at the two men. Voice now strong and posture straight, Aunt G said, "Tell me about your favorite hobby and spare me no detail."

All at once, the gruff men started rambling. Todd, it turned out, was an avid fisherman and started down a sure-to-be-riveting path about the various types of lures he liked best and why. Tad, however, was a horror movie buff and started in on why *The Exorcist* was the most perfect film ever created.

Amber looked at her aunt in dismay, feeling terrible about leaving her here with these two men talking over each other, but Aunt G, her eyes slightly glazed over already, discreetly waved a hand in her direction. *Go*, the gesture said. *Leave me here to suffocate under the weight of sheer boredom.*

Amber and Kim then faced the front door and the awaiting mass of John Huntley fans.

"His fans are called Hunters, you know," Kim said ominously. She held up her large purse with both hands. "I'll use this as a shield to get us out."

Amber dropped the ward on the front door, unlocked it, and with Kim crowded in behind her, quickly shoved her way out into the throng.

"Back it up!" Kim yelled in a voice Amber hadn't known she possessed. "Move aside. John will be out eventually, but you need to let us out!"

"Why is he here?"

"How do you know him, Amber?"

Kim shoved her way past Amber, and as promised, shielded Amber so she could quickly lock the door and reset the spell.

"He'll be out in the next ten minutes," Amber said. Several in the group squealed. "Just wait here and you'll get to see him. Kim and I have to go run a few errands for the Here and Meow. Hold tight, okay?"

As Amber and Kim made their way through the crowd, several strangers patted her arms and back as if Amber had just promised them a sack of cash each. She hoped the possibility of John Huntley coming out the front door would make the eager fans stay put.

As she and Kim rounded the corner of the building toward the parking lot, Amber was relieved both to find it empty and that no one had immediately followed them outside.

"Let's get into the back of the minivan," Amber said. "I have an idea."

"Ooh, this is so exciting," Kim said.

After rolling the door shut and sealing them inside, Amber said, "I think one of us should be glamoured to look like John so that we can keep the crowd occupied while real John and Willow sneak away."

Kim's eyes widened. Then she rattled off an impressive series of stats about John. "Oh my God, Amber! I'm a walking, talking John Huntley encyclopedia. You *have* to glamour me to look like that hunk! 1. It will help me live out my dream of being a celebrity, and 2. I've always wanted to know what it feels like to be six feet tall."

"Are you going to be able to keep it together when you get swarmed by all those Hunters, though?" Amber asked. "You sort of…break down when under pressure."

"I turn into Galazilla *one* time …" Kim laughed. "I can handle it. I'll swagger a little. I'll schmooze for pictures. Give diplomatic answers about not being allowed to discuss details of the next season. It's like a dream come true for me, honest."

Amber still wasn't fully convinced, but Amber pretending to be John Huntley would be a million times worse. She knew his height, eye color, and that he was a talented actor and singer. That was the extent of it. "Okay, I'll be Sienna again. I can be, I don't know, your publicist or something. We'll walk out of the parking lot as if there's a side door."

Kim beamed.

Amber sent Willow a text that said:

Operation Diversion is underway. I'll text you when the coast is clear.

Amber was quite adept at turning herself into Sienna Tate, so that didn't take long. And even though Amber had never used a John Huntley glamour before, it didn't take much effort to recall the details of his perfectly sculpted face.

Kim yelped when her glamour took hold, warming her skin to near scalding for a moment. Amber knew the feeling all too well. She'd done such a good job of transforming Kim that Amber's face flushed a little when that disarming John Huntley smile made an appearance.

"Don't look at me like that!" Kim said. "It's creeping me out. Oh wow, I have an incredibly sexy voice now." She started to sing one of John's recent hit singles, but quickly stopped. Clearly John's singing talent hadn't come with the glamour. "Oh, *no*."

Wincing, Amber said, "If anyone asks you to sing, say you have a sore throat."

Amber and Kim peered out of the minivan's windshield. A few people milled near the open space made by Amber's building and the one beside it, but no one currently looked their way.

"Okay, go," Amber hissed and they piled out of the van, hunching low, then headed for Russian Blue Avenue.

Kim walked with swagger, as promised, but it was borderline too much swagger. It was closer to a sashay. "Who wants to meet John Huntley?" she called out, arms wide, with all the bravado of a circus ringmaster.

A shout of "Was that John?" sounded just seconds before several people hurried to the mouth of the parking lot.

"It is I," Kim said, arms still outstretched as if she were a divine entity here on earth to bless the masses. "I am John."

Oh, good grief.

Amber quickly texted Willow to let her know the distraction had begun. In the short time her gaze was off Kim, she had been surrounded by adoring Hunters hurling questions at her. One woman squeezed Kim's bicep, then giggled. The pair of teenage girls who had the prime spot at the door, thinking John was coming out the front, shrieked. One of them burst into tears again.

"Ech!" Amber said loudly, trying to get closer to Kim. "One question at a time, lasses!"

Ah, her panic-induced Scottish accent had returned.

No matter how much Amber tried to calm down the Hunters, and no matter how often Kim assured them that she would get a picture with everyone, Kim was being grabbed at and prodded and had cameras shoved in her face. Even with Kim's back to her, Amber could tell Kim was starting to freak out.

"Ech, keep it together, Johnny boy!" Amber called out, still two body lengths away from Kim, unable to get close enough to grab her.

Amber worried more than anything that the aggressively excited Hunters would push and poke at Kim so hard that the glamour would be shaken loose. As Amber tried to figure out what to do, she saw Willow and an unfamiliar man quickly cross the street and then head down the sidewalk in the opposite direction. All the tourists crowding the sidewalks on both sides were so preoccupied with the commotion that no one seemed to have noticed it but Amber.

Kim let loose a roar that startled everyone so much, the group jumped away from her in unison. And then Kim just...*took off*. She sprinted down the sidewalk away from Willow and the real John, her arms flailing as if she were warding off a swarm of bees.

"Oi!" Amber called after her.

It took only a moment, but then several Hunters took off running after her, cheering as they went. Though she was in shoes not suitable for running, Kim was hauling some serious tail. Amber knew Kim had been training for the 5K, but this was Olympic track-and-field speeds.

Soon the crowd dispersed, and from what Amber could glean from conversations around her, several Hunters were going to fetch their cars so they could chase John Huntley down by vehicle.

Ugh.

Amber whirled to head back into The Quirky Whisker to get her car keys—the ones for the minivan were in Kim's pocket—when she almost slammed headlong into someone.

Not just any someone.

It was Molly Hargrove.

CHAPTER 13

"Oh, my giddy aunt!" Amber yelped. "I'm right sorry."

When Amber tried to sidestep her, Molly mirrored her efforts.

"Your name is Sienna, right?" Molly asked. "Sienna Tate?"

Amber blinked at her. "Aye, that's me. Do I know ye? I don't think we've met."

"I'm a reporter at *The Marbleglen Herald*," Molly said. "Could I ask you a few questions?"

"Oh, I'm sorry, lass," she said, trying to sidestep her again. "But I really must be getting on after my—"

"It'll only take a few minutes," Molly said.

Sighing, Amber said, "I'm not sure what ye would like ta talk to me about. I'm not even from this area."

"That's exactly what I wanted to ask you about," Molly said.

Amber glanced behind her, in the direction that Kim had sprinted. "Okay, but can we talk while I search for my, uhh…client?"

Molly narrowed her eyes at Amber, then nodded. "I'll drive so you can keep an eye out."

Molly's car—a little white four-door—was parked on the street several buildings down from The Quirky Whisker. Once inside Molly's car, while she watched for pedestrians and oncoming traffic, Amber checked her phone, hoping to have a message from Kim. But nothing had come in yet from her *or* Willow.

As Molly pulled out onto Russian Blue Avenue, she said, "So, Sienna, how do you know Amber Blackwood?"

Amber swallowed. "That's tha owner of tha shop we were just outside of."

"Right. But how do you know her *personally*?" Molly asked. "And don't bother lying to me. Just last month you were seen driving a car Amber had been renting. Not only were you seen driving it, but you were using it to spy on residents of Marbleglen."

Amber had been doing surveillance on Randy Tillman, but he hadn't been a resident of Marbleglen. He'd been visiting because of his role in a land development deal. Amber decided not to correct her though, as that was the easiest way to implicate herself. Instead, she said nothing while she scanned the streets for any sign of Kim—either as John or as herself.

"I've done what research I can on you and came up with nothing," Molly said. "You're like a ghost. Is Sienna even your real name?"

Amber squirmed in her seat. Molly was direct and unflinching. She was either made for this job, or the job had trained her to become comfortable with asking strangers probing questions.

Amber knew Connor and Molly were working on a "big" story about her. Likely whatever opinions Molly had about Amber were in line with the wild theories Connor had recently divulged to Willow. What better way to find out about the article than from Molly herself? Especially since she'd already declared that the bridge with Amber had been burned.

Flashing back to all the conversations she'd had with Alan Peterson, Amber did her best to channel him. Not only was Alan Peterson not his name, but the way he carried himself was even more unflinching than Molly.

Dropping the accent and taking on one slightly deeper than her own, Amber said, "No, Sienna isn't my real name. I'm a private investigator."

"I knew it!" Molly said, hitting the heel of her palm on her steering wheel once for emphasis. "Hired by whom?"

Amber chucked in a way that she hoped was more amused bewilderment than amused cartoony villain. "You know I'm not going to tell you that." Then she went out on a limb and said, "But I can tell you that I've been hired to keep an eye on Amber Blackwood."

Molly nodded as if this made perfect sense. "I've been keeping tabs on her myself. I know you can't give up too much without jeopardizing your investigation, but if you'd be willing to float some information my way, I would compensate you for it."

"What's your interest in her?" Amber asked.

Molly was silent for long enough that Amber wondered if she wasn't going to answer at all. She continued to scan the streets while she waited. She didn't see a line of people running down the sidewalk, so she assumed Kim had either ducked into a building or had run down another street. Amber discreetly turned her phone over to check the screen. No new messages.

"I don't know if you've uncovered anything…unusual about Amber," Molly said slowly, "but I'm concerned she's not who everyone thinks she is. Bad things seem to happen when she's around. And now her products are putting people in comas and exploding in people's hands."

Amber nodded. "Well, we're on the same page. Amber is clearly dangerous."

"That's an understatement. I can't tell you how I know, but she's planning something very sinister," Molly said, her voice flat. "She's angry about what happened to her parents. She's never believed the fire was just a horrible accident. She thinks someone *murdered* them. No one would listen to her. She had a hard time in high school after their death. Her grades suffered. Her family moved away from her the second her sister turned eighteen. I'm guessing Amber was hard to be around, as obsessed with conspiracy theories as she is."

Amber wondered how Molly would change her tune if she knew that all Amber's "theories" had been right. "She's rude, too. I finally set up a one-on-one lunch with her and she stood me up."

Molly gasped. "Me too! Ugh. The nerve of that woman. She's a recluse who's kept to herself for most of her adult life so she's awkward at best. I could almost excuse her odd behavior if it was social ineptitude, but she's passive-aggressive. There's a calculation there. Once she finally started emerging out of her little hidey-hole, destruction followed. Melanie Cole was one of the few people in town who wanted much to do with Amber, and in less than three years of living here, Melanie winds up dead. Not that I think Amber had anything to do with her death, but what happened to Melanie reopened Amber's old wound about the supposed injustice of what had happened to her parents.

"Mark my words, but that resident slipping into a coma and the little boy who almost had his hand blasted off are just the beginning of what Amber has in store. I mean, this is the busiest time of year in Edgehill and she's closed her shop? Those creepy toys of hers sell like hotcakes at the festival. What business owner would willingly shoot herself in the proverbial foot during peak tourist season? Who knows what she's working on now behind closed doors. She wants people gossiping about her behavior so they're distracted. She wants people blindsided to what she's really up to."

"Which is what?" Amber asked, not sure she wanted to hear anymore.

"Revenge on Edgehill and everyone in it."

Amber involuntarily swallowed. If someone like Molly, who wasn't even from Edgehill, could think such things, what opinions did Amber's fellow residents hold? Thea Bishop had said the residents here had called Amber "weird" and "odd." Had Thea watered that down, or was Molly making it sound worse?

The more Molly talked, the more Amber believed the possibility that Kieran had been supplying Connor with information. Connor had either passed it on to Molly, or Kieran had been chatting Molly up, too. Which was a move that felt far more calculated than the over-the-top whimsies of a madman. Ambushing the fashion show to "sew chaos" while wearing the face of a beloved reality TV show host was the work of a narcissistic lunatic. Planting ideas in the head of a man like Connor months ago took forethought. Kieran knew it would take time for Connor to witness enough weird events to hook him on the story, and also knew that once the hooks were in, Connor wouldn't let up until he had his story, no matter the consequences. That was twice as true for Molly.

It meant someone was in this for the long game. Amber just didn't know if the narcissistic lunatic and the manipulative, patient informant were one and the same.

"It's clear to me," Amber said, "that Amber assumes someone in town knows who murdered her parents and that she's angry no one will confess. Do you think she stayed in Edgehill all this time so she could eventually punish those who took her parents from her?"

"Bingo," Molly said. "She's gotten close to the police chief so she can get access to his files, I'm sure of it. I know you haven't been in town for long, but she and the chief used to despise each other. He looked at her like she was something sticky he found under his shoe. Then all of a sudden, over the course of a few months, the two are buddy-buddy."

"Maybe they're having an affair," Amber said, easily picturing Chief Brown's appalled expression. "I haven't found any evidence of it yet, but they'll slip up eventually."

But Molly was already shaking her head. "I don't buy that. My theory? She's a psychopath. Sure, she might act like she cares *so much* about this town, but psychopaths know how to blend in. They're human chameleons. She used her charms to win the chief over, which couldn't be too hard because he's not that bright. But she needs him for something. He's only been here for three years. New blood. He didn't live through the Blackwood fire saga. She's controlling the narrative with him, I'm sure of it."

Amber couldn't say that sitting through the evisceration of her character was remotely enjoyable.

"Amber thinks there's a conspiracy happening here and wants to uncover what the police are hiding from her," Molly said. "But regardless of what she finds out, she's on the brink of trying to tear this place apart from the inside out. I can't tell you how I know that, but I do. We're on the precipice of something big here."

"And you think she's capable of doing all this by herself?"

Molly laughed. It was a sharp, derisive sound. "Are you saying you haven't met her family? There's something very…off…about all three of them. And don't even get me started on her cousin. He's one of the most unpleasant people you'll ever meet."

Amber knew for a fact that Molly Hargrove had never talked to Edgar. Even if he was angry with her for one reason or another, if a reporter from Marbleglen had tried to pump him for information, he would have mentioned it.

What concerned Amber most of all was the undercurrent of venom in Molly's tone. "You seem emotionally attached to this story," she said.

Molly adjusted her posture to something a bit more relaxed. Had Molly already been a step away from furious before Amber stood her up for lunch, and Amber's oversight had pushed her over the edge? "Let's just say she's putting someone in danger who I care about very much. Her *and* her weird family. He might be in denial, but I'm not. I won't let him get caught up in their schemes. I refuse. All we know is that their grand revenge plan is going to happen during the Here and Meow this year. We have to stop them before then. The fact that Amber has pulled Kimberly Jones into her web doesn't bode well."

"Ah, yes, the head of the festival," Amber said. "Do you think Kimberly is in on it, or is she being taken for a ride? I can't get a read on her. She's very protective of Amber."

"Oh, Kim has no idea," Molly said. "Poor thing is clueless. She's even dumber than Chief Brown. She's always followed Amber around like a puppy dog and now they're joined at the hip. Kim needs to feel like she belongs, so I'm sure Amber has indoctrinated her by now."

Indoctrinated?

"I'm impressed that you've gotten a source here in Edgehill who is willing to share this much insight with you," Amber said. "We both know how reclusive Amber is, so your source isn't someone in her inner circle."

Molly laughed good-naturedly. "If you won't tell me whose payroll you're on, I'm not giving up my source."

But Amber was almost positive Willow was right: Connor's, and thereby Molly's, source had been Kieran Penhallow. The question was, was he *still* their source?

Where are you, Kieran, and whose side are you on now that you're out?

Amber and Molly had been driving in awkward silence for the better part of two minutes, Amber scanning the streets while Molly glared ahead, when Amber's phone buzzed in her hand.

It was a message from Kim. I'm still John and I'm locked in the men's bathroom in Ma and Paw's. They're outside. I can hear them. They're scratching at the door.

Ma and Paw's was almost a mile and a half from The Quirky Whisker. Kim had moved quickly.

"Can you drop me off at Ma and Paw's?" Amber asked.

Molly didn't immediately reply. "What's your connection to John, by the way? You said he was your…client?"

Crap. Amber had forgotten about that part. She made something up on the fly. "Yes, he has an obsessive fan who's been following him across the country for about a year now and he thinks her behavior is starting to escalate. I'm well-known for what I do, but not just anyone can find me. I was hired to figure out what I could while he was in town. Edgehill is small enough that we thought it would be easier to flush the stalker out."

"Is that why he ran off like his butt was on fire?" Molly asked.

"Yes. She must have been in that crowd outside Amber's shop," Amber said.

Molly seemed to accept this. Amber was glad, because she wasn't sure how long she could keep up this lie. Molly remained silent while Amber gave her directions to Ma and Paw's, the biggest grocery store on this side of town. When she pulled up directly outside the store, Amber made a move to get out, only to have Molly stop her with an "I meant what I said about compensating you for information about Amber Blackwood."

"Oh, I believed you."

"How do I get in contact with you?"

With a smile that she hoped was suitable for the spy persona Kim thought Amber had, she said, "I'll find you."

With that, she got out of the car and headed for the store without looking back.

The inside of Ma and Paw's was always a little too warm and stuffy for Amber's tastes. It gave the place a lingering earthy smell. The front of the store was devoted to produce, which was currently filled with people picking over the selection. The bank of cash registers was to the right, and to the left were the aisles for frozen food, dry goods, and everyday essentials. It was also the direction of the bathrooms.

A shout went up in the leftmost corner and Amber headed that way. A harried-looking grocery store employee was on the move, too. She was a short, heavyset woman who wore a determined scowl that made it clear she wouldn't be above knocking people's heads together if they caused trouble in her store. Amber was happy to follow her.

The restrooms' entrance was wedged into a corner between the small deli counter and a cold storage area for single containers of soda, water, and energy drinks. The area was crowded with mostly teenage girls idling in a cluster.

As Amber slowed her approach, wondering if these girls were going to let her pass, one of them recognized her.

"You're the lady who was with John earlier!" the girl accused, then took a picture of Amber with her phone.

Amber tried to get her hand up to shield her face but wasn't sure if she succeeded. She assumed that within hours—if it hadn't happened already—Sienna's face would be plastered all over John Huntley's fan sites. *"Does anyone know this lady, Hunters?"*

Amber knew they would come up with no information on who she was. She was a ghost, as Molly had said. She sent a silent apology to John.

The grocery store employee Amber had been following eyed her. "You know John Huntley?" she whispered.

"I work for him, yes," Amber said, worried this woman was going to ask for a favor she couldn't grant.

The woman nodded. Then, in a loud, commanding voice, she addressed the loitering teens. "Out of the way! Let this woman through!"

The girls standing in the mouth of the hallway that led to the restrooms smashed themselves against the wall as the woman marched forward, Amber close behind. Once they reached the restroom doors—a small hallway space that gave way to the storage area behind thick black rubber doors—the grocery store employee used her barking, no-nonsense voice to herd the girls out of the hallway and back toward the deli counter. Now the woman stood at the mouth of the restroom's hallway, arms crossed, blocking the teens' path.

As she used her body as a shield just as Tad—Todd?—had done back in The Quirky Whisker, the woman patiently listened to one girl wail that she actually needed to use the restroom and it wasn't fair that she was being denied access.

Someone further back called out, "Don't lie, Tammy! You used it like ten minutes ago!"

A squabble broke out between several of the girls and colorful insults were exchanged.

With the Hunters distracted, Amber turned her attention to the men's restroom, blew out a breath, and knocked. "John? It's me, Sienna."

The "occupied" label immediately flipped to "vacant," and the door flew open. Amber jumped back, but a manly hand reached out to grab her by the shirt, and then yanked her into the musky-scented men's restroom. It all happened in a matter of seconds. Kim flipped the lock on the door again and then started to pace. It was meant for only one occupant, so Kim didn't get far before she had to turn around and head in the other direction.

"Monsters!" she hissed. "All of them are *monsters!*"

Amber blurted, "I think Connor and Molly are onto me."

That stopped Kim's pacing. "What do you mean?"

Amber forgot for just a moment that the gorgeous man standing in the foul-smelling men's restroom wasn't *actually* the world-famous John Huntley, but her very overwhelmed friend. She shook her head quickly to refocus herself, then recounted the conversation she'd just had with Molly. "The thing is, even if Kieran is her source for a lot of this stuff—"

"It doesn't explain how she knew about your products malfunctioning a day before it happened," Kim finished. "Kieran got out Thursday night and Molly's article was out Friday morning."

"Exactly," she said. "She's talking to someone else with magical intel, even if she doesn't know it. The thing with Henrietta's coma is that if it's magic-induced like I think it is, magic is the only way to reverse it. I would need a lot of time with Hen to work through a bunch of spells to find one to wake her up. Assuming I could come up with the right spell in the first place. Magic that affects the mind is the trickiest and experimenting on Hen when I don't know the nature of the spell could actually make things worse. We need to find the Penhallow who did it so we can get him or her to reverse the spell, or at least tell us which one they used."

Kim frowned. "How are we supposed to do that? They don't seem like the type to willingly give up information."

"I don't know yet," Amber said. "And I don't know what Aunt G saw after she used the premonition tincture either. I think Molly was right that we're on the precipice of something, but obviously *I'm* not the mastermind. The Penhallows are."

"And we know for sure that Kieran didn't also make a call to Molly the night he called you?" Kim asked. "I know you said he changed once the curse was lifted, but what if he was faking it?"

Amber hadn't thought of that. "We'll worry about that later. We need to get you out of here."

Kim's eyes went wide. "Don't make me go back out there. I've had my butt pinched so many times. Those girls are even scarier than the tourist-zombies. These ones are *fast* zombies. Everyone knows those are the worst ones!"

Amber tried not to laugh. John Huntley wearing Kim's worry made it hard to take him seriously. "I think our best bet is to go out through the storage area. The doors are to the left of the bathroom. I'm guessing a few girls will be on the other side waiting, but the main crowd is being held back."

Kim nodded. "Okay."

"When I say go, follow me. Don't stop running."

Amber flipped the lock and opened the door so she could peer out. The hallway was still clear. A shout went up from the group when the door opened, but it petered out when they saw that it was Sienna's head poking out of the bathroom and not John's. Looking right, Amber confirmed that the Hunters were still being managed by the grocery worker. The irate girl, Tammy, was now threatening the woman with legal action from her lawyer uncle if she kept being denied her rights to use the facilities.

"If I suffer from a bladder infection because of you," Tammy said, "you don't really think you'd be able to pay my medical bills on a grocery store employee wage, do you?"

The woman didn't reply. Nerves of steel, that one.

Looking left, Amber watched as a man with a pallet of plastic-wrapped boxes emerged from the black rubber doors. As the door flapped open, she saw a large opening at the other end of the small warehouse, a hint of blue sky evident before the doors closed again. Amber had seen the light of freedom.

Without looking back at Kim, Amber said, "Go!" She threw open the door the rest of the way and then bolted for the warehouse area. Kim was fast on her heels.

A series of shrieks erupted behind them. The grocery store guard started barking orders and demands, but Amber feared the woman had been overpowered. Amber sent up a silent prayer for the woman's likely bruised shins. Not all heroes wear capes.

Pushing their way into the warehouse, Amber quickly realized that there wasn't a clear path to the door on the other side. Wrapped pallets, loose boxes, and warehouse workers were all in their way. What seemed like seconds later, one of the excitable teenagers burst through the doors behind them. Kim wasn't wrong: the Hunters were quick. The only thing on Amber and Kim's side was that the warehouse's lighting was dim.

Amber grabbed hold of Kim's elbow and yanked her to the right, where they slipped between a massive stack of boxes filled with toilet paper on one side and a pallet of crackers on the other. Amber then pulled Kim into a crouching position.

"*Where did they go?*" one of the girls screeched.

"What are you all doing in here?" a masculine gruff voice replied. "Hey! You don't belong in here!"

"Oh my God, Amber," Kim hissed urgently in John's voice. "Don't let them find me!"

"I'm sorry," Amber said, and before Kim could ask for what, Amber slapped her across the face.

"Ow!" Kim yelped, holding her cheek. Then her eyes widened; her voice was her own again. Without warning, Kim slapped Amber back.

Amber toppled onto her side, narrowly avoiding whacking her head on the corner of a wooden pallet. Her head spun. "*Kim!*"

"Oh my God, Amber, I'm so sorry!" Kim said, helping Amber back to her feet. "I was so caught up in the moment. I forget my own strength."

Once Amber got her bearings, she motioned for Kim to follow her, and they crept back the way they'd come. When Amber peered around several open-topped boxes of tomatoes stacked near the doors, she found a dozen wild-eyed girls creeping about the warehouse despite the fact that several annoyed men were threatening to call security.

"There he goes!" Amber cried, pointing to the open door before taking off for it, weaving around boxes and leaping over packing supplies as she went.

She was relieved to see the girls were giving chase, their sights back on the prize. They leaped over boxes and crates with all the agility of hurdlers. It wasn't long before they bypassed her and Kim, and were running out into the open loading area behind Ma and Paw's. A few confused workers stood on the fringes, watching as the heaving teenage Hunters scanned the area.

"Someone on Scuttle says they saw him near the library!" one of the girls called out and off they went, running out the open gate that surrounded the loading area.

Amber and Kim slowly followed, but instead of turning left when they reached the sidewalk as the horde of teenage girls had, they went right. It would take a good twenty minutes for them to walk back the way they'd come, but at least they could do it at a leisurely pace now. Amber's face stung and she rubbed her cheek.

"Sorry about your face," Kim said.

"Sorry about yours."

Kim managed a chuckle. "If John has to deal with this nonsense on a regular basis, I'm surprised he's as nice as he is. The adoration was only fun for like, two minutes tops, then it got…bizarre."

Amber let Kim ramble on about her traumatic experience, but she was only half listening. Everything Molly had said only made her that much more concerned about her aunt's premonition, and that Henrietta might not wake up.

Once they got back to The Quirky Whisker, Amber could tell how exhausted Kim was. The adrenaline likely had slowly ebbed away during their walk.

"Do you have a lot more things on your agenda today?" Amber asked. "Other than Kids Day, that is."

"Ugh! Kids Day …" Kim blew out a weary sigh. She checked her phone. "The main events don't start for another couple hours."

"Can you take a nap?" Amber asked. "Just for an hour. You'll need it if you have to deal with that many kids hopped up on sugar." Last year, Kids Day had gotten completely out of control when a cotton candy vendor decided to have a cotton candy eating contest. Nearly every kid participated and ten of them had gotten very sick. One had thrown up in Anne Marie's lap.

Kim shuddered. "I was going to go on a run this evening for my 5K training, but I think I can skip that, no?"

Amber laughed. "If you run the 5K as if you're being chased by Hunters, you'll finish it in ten minutes flat."

Kim cackled. "I'll call you later."

Even after Kim drove out of the lot, Amber still didn't go inside her shop. Her aunt was upstairs holding onto information that was so upsetting, it altered her behavior, and Willow was presumably still out on the town with a superstar, so Amber didn't want to bother her. Especially not after the lunch date she'd had with Connor yesterday. An outing with John Huntley hopefully was making up for that tenfold.

Amber leaned against the wall of her building, well out of view of The Quirky Whisker's front windows, and watched the milling tourists. Though they streamed down both sides of the sidewalk, she focused on the ones across the street.

Of all the questions bouncing around in her head right now, two had moved to the fore. One, how was she supposed to identify who was a Penhallow and who wasn't? Even if she managed to uncover the best way to combat the cursed clan without losing her mind, her life, or both, it wouldn't matter if she couldn't track the cursed witches down. It was hard to pinpoint your enemy when their face kept changing.

Two, had Kieran's plan to come to Edgehill been his own or someone else's?

Both questions kept leading her back to the same answer—an answer absolutely no one in her life would think was a good idea. So she pulled her phone out of her back pocket and called the one person who was sure to back this idea even if it were awful.

"What?" he said in greeting.

"Are you *still* mad at me?" she asked.

"It's safe to assume I'm always a little mad at you about something," Edgar said. "What do you want? Have any more earth-shattering family revelations you forgot to share with me?"

Yeah, it was going to take him a while to get over this one.

"Wanna take a trip to the abandoned neighborhood?" she asked.

She could practically hear his scowl. "I don't even have details and I already think this sounds terrible."

"It sounds terrible to me, too," Amber said. "But there are a couple of people there who might be able to answer several of my questions at once."

"This idea keeps sounding worse, cousin," he said. "I'll see you in twenty minutes."

CHAPTER 14

Amber headed into The Quirky Whisker, unsure of what she might find. The ward on the door was down, but the door was locked. She let herself in and peered around the space, finding it empty. Thea's cage wasn't immediately visible either.

Locking the door behind her, she made her way across the shop and up the stairs, only to stop halfway up at the sound of laughter. Her aunt's laughter. Amber took the remaining steps two at a time to reach the top landing.

Sitting at the dining room table on one end was Thea's cage. Thea crunched her way through a piece of lettuce two times the size of her body. Aunt G and one of the bodyguards sat across from each other, each nursing a mug of what smelled like cinnamon tea.

"Oh, hi, little mouse," Aunt G said, turning in her seat to smile at Amber.

"Uh…where is everyone?" Amber asked.

"Willow and John are sightseeing. Tad and Todd are keeping an eye on him," Aunt G said.

"And you?" Amber asked Troy, an eyebrow raised.

"Well," Troy said, his voice as nondescript as the rest of him, "Tad and Todd don't actually know where they are. They're scouring the town for them. I stayed here in case they came back. Your aunt was kind enough to offer me refreshments."

Eyeing the hamster cage, Amber said, "And our…pet…is doing okay?" It wasn't until then that Amber noticed Tom Cat and Alley were sitting side by side on one of the chairs, watching the hamster diligently, but keeping their distance.

"Indeed," Aunt G said. "I gave her the latest dose of medicine already. She'll be good until tomorrow."

"I'm going to meet Edgar in a few minutes," Amber said, then moved to her window bench seat. Underneath it was a cabinet where she kept her witchy materials, namely her grimoire and a few crystals. She took the spell book out of its hiding place. "I just came to get a few things."

Aunt G eyed the book. "Troy, dear?"

"Yes, ma'am?" he asked.

Oh no, Amber thought just as her aunt said, "Sleep."

Troy's head immediately pitched forward, his chin resting against his chest.

Aunt G was on her feet in a second and stalking toward Amber. "What are you up to?"

"I need to figure out what's going on," she said, bypassing her aunt so she could stuff her grimoire into the purse she'd left hanging off the back of a chair. "Damien and Devra might know what the Penhallows have planned. Maybe they'll cough up information if I promise to let them out." She slung her purse over her shoulder, then headed for the stairs. "Hopefully you'll be willing to talk about whatever the heck is going on with *you* once Willow is back later."

Amber was a moment away from her foot hitting the top step when her aunt blurted, "The vision changes every night."

She turned and crossed her arms, waiting.

"One night you get run off the road," Aunt G said. "The next night, Willow gets kidnapped. The night after that, The Quirky Whisker burns to the ground. Willow gets cursed. You get arrested. You're both sacrificed on an altar. But every single night, something horrible happens to one or both of you."

Amber frowned.

In a softer tone, Aunt G said, "I'm scared, little mouse. You girls are in danger and I don't know how to stop it. There are so many variables being added every day that not even the future can keep up. All I know is that something is coming and I fear I can't save you from it."

"Oh, Aunt G …" Amber said, her earlier anger dissolving instantly. She searched her aunt's brown eyes, searching for some lie or manipulation. But all she saw was her aunt's worry—worry that mirrored Amber's own.

Just as Edgar had said yesterday, it was easy to get angry at those closest to you. Amber and Aunt G seemed to butt heads often, both frustrating each other in ways few others could, but Amber knew deep down that Aunt G would do anything for her. Sure, she'd taken on the responsibility of raising Amber and Willow due to necessity, but there was nothing forced in the concern in her aunt's eyes now.

Her aunt loved Amber and Willow as if they were her own children.

Amber pulled her aunt into a tight hug. One that startled a little sob out of Aunt G, who hugged Amber around the middle, her temple resting on Amber's shoulder. As they stood like that, Amber explained her plan for visiting the abandoned neighborhood.

"How do you even know they're still there?" Aunt G asked, still holding tight to Amber.

"I don't," she said. "But if we want any chance of finding Penhallow-specific spells, we need Penhallows, right? We've got two trapped in 1971."

Aunt G finally let Amber go and took a step back. "What if they're wreaking havoc on 1971 and rewriting history right now? What if that's what's making my premonitions change so wildly every night?"

Well, that was a new horrifying possibility. It had only been a week, but two ticked-off Penhallows could do a lot of damage in a week. "All the more reason to go."

Aunt G nodded. "Okay, well, I'm going with you. We need to get a hold of Willow and tell her what we're doing. I suggest you call Simon as well. We'll need all the magical backup we can get."

Amber opened her mouth to protest, but snapped it shut again when Aunt G sent her a look that clearly said, *If you argue with me, I'll turn you into a hamster.*

While Aunt G tried to get a hold of Willow, Amber called Simon. It was midday on a Tuesday, and though Amber knew he made wreaths, she didn't know if that was part of his business, or merely a hobby. She really didn't know much about the guy.

"Hey, Amber!" he said after the first ring. "Jasper's folly."

Laughing, glad that he remembered her request to use code words, she said, "Hi, Simon. So…uh…are you busy?"

"Cashing in a second favor so soon?" he asked with a chuckle. "I'm still working on that first favor. I think I've got a decent clarity spell worked up. I started another tincture last night. The tincture is supposed to be a milky orange color, but every time I used the spell, it just brought clarity to the tincture itself and turned it from orange to clear. Tastes like water, too. I think I might use that instead of my filtration pitcher. It was utterly useless for your purposes, though. So far, the new one is maintaining its color, but I haven't had a chance to test it out yet. What's up?"

That all sounded promising, at least. "Remember that story you told me about magic veins under the ground in Edgehill?"

Simon was silent for a moment. "Sure. The legend about Edgehill once being a magic town."

"It's not a legend," Amber said, then told him the version of history she'd learned from Zelda.

Simon whooshed out a breath. "That version of history was never taught in any hybrid town I know of. How strange …"

She wondered again how these two very different histories existed in the minds of people who were either old enough to experience part of it—like Zelda—or knew people who had. Wouldn't Simon's parents or grandparents have heard this version?

"Uhh…not to be rude," Simon said, "but how did *you* find this out?"

"I met a witch who was there when the ley lines exploded in the 1970s," Amber said. "She showed me the day they all had to abandon the neighborhood. She also had family who lived through the day the council short-circuited magic. The council, even after it disbanded, did a good job of controlling the narrative, but the witches who lived through it remember what really happened."

"From what little I know about the council, it makes sense they were the ones behind it, to be honest. But I wonder if they had help controlling that narrative," Simon said.

Men and women in black suits popped into Amber's mind.

"So…is this related to why you asked if I was busy?" Simon asked.

"Just hear me out, okay?" Amber said, knowing that this next part would sound next-level bonkers. She then explained the connection she felt to the ley lines in the abandoned neighborhood, and how, with the help of the magic there, Amber had sent two Penhallows back in time.

Simon was silent for so long, Amber pulled the phone away from her face to make sure the call hadn't dropped. "And since the only way to be sure a glamour-detecting clarity spell works on a Penhallow is to test it *on* a Penhallow, you were thinking you could use these two as guinea pigs?"

"More or less, yeah," Amber said. "You down for some time travel?"

"You could take me *with* you?" he asked, his voice a little reverent.

"If you hold onto me when I cast the spell, you should technically be able to travel with me," she said. "I think. I'm not totally sure if I left this time and went into another one, or if I had just been transported to a memory. I went somewhere…I just don't know where. Or when. Time travel literally and figuratively makes my head hurt."

"There's no way this is a good idea," he said. "Where do I meet you?"

Amber smiled to herself. She was lucky to be surrounded by people who were willing to put themselves in compromising situations. "Meet us here and then we can caravan over."

Disconnecting the call, she found Aunt G sitting on the end of the bed, waiting for her. She was idling petting Alley's head, which rested on Aunt G's leg. Tom was still wholly focused on Thea at the table.

"Willow didn't answer, but I left her a very ominous voicemail," Aunt G said.

Glancing toward the still-dozing Troy, Amber jutted her chin at him. "What do we do with him?"

"Leave that to me," Aunt G said.

Amber frowned but went about collecting her belongings all the same. She grabbed the handle of the hamster cage and her purse, then descended the stairs.

Edgar idled at the curb. He warily eyed the cage that she put on one of the small back seats of his truck. Amber was in the middle of catching Edgar up on everything when Troy went sprinting out the door and down the sidewalk. Aunt G followed a few moments later, locking up the shop and resetting the ward as she did.

Aunt G took the seat beside Thea in the back, while Amber rode shotgun.

"Do I want to know what you did to Troy?" Amber asked.

"Nope," Aunt G said.

Within a few minutes, Simon arrived in his vehicle, and then Edgar led the way to the abandoned neighborhood. It wasn't until Edgar made a right on Korat Road that anyone spoke.

"So what exactly is the plan?" Edgar asked. "The last time we used magic here, you got your butt thoroughly kicked, Amber."

Amber's ankle still throbbed some mornings. A little twinge of pain went through it now as if it, too, were reminding Amber that the magic here wasn't something to fool around with. Not to mention the fact that the two Penhallows who were potentially trapped there would be livid.

Instead of answering him, Amber called Simon, putting the phone on speaker.

"Hi, Simon," she said when he answered. "So, first, we should pool together our best defensive spells. I don't have many of my own. When I used magic against Damien and Devra a few days ago, I was channeling the magic in the ley lines. I was a…I don't know…vessel, and the ley lines worked through me more than anything else."

"The rest of us likely won't be able to rely on that," Edgar said as he made a slow left turn onto the unmarked road that led into the neighborhood. "I tried the last time we were here and the magic wouldn't respond to me."

"I tried a couple of times myself," Aunt G said from the back.

"And I don't even know if it'll work for *me* again," Amber said. "So we need to go in as armed as we can. Simon, the house we'll stop in front of is about halfway up the street. I don't know if the connection I felt to it was because it used to belong to that friend of mine or because of something else."

"Do we have any idea if Damien and Devra are even still alive?" Simon asked.

"No," Amber said. "They were unconscious when I last saw them."

Simon didn't reply to that.

Once they pulled up outside Zelda's old house, Amber disconnected the call and climbed out. They left Thea inside.

Armed with their grimoires, they met behind Edgar's truck. He pulled open the tailgate and laid his book down. Amber did the same with hers.

For the next half hour, they brainstormed the best spells to take with them when they went into the memory. The Ricinus clan, like the Blackwoods, were skilled kitchen witches. Tinctures were one of Simon's specialties. Amber knew now that the right tincture could be thrown or consumed in the heat of an altercation and be just as effective as tossing a bomb or instantaneously donning a full suit of armor. But a witch had to anticipate what he would need and have said tincture at the ready.

Simon had two sleep tinctures, two confusion, and four shield vials. The shields, he said, erected a temporary wall in front of the thrower, hopefully giving them enough time to escape. Aunt G had brought four vials of the protection tincture she, Amber, and Willow had been drinking every twelve hours a few months ago, when Kieran was in town. The tincture was easily the most foul-tasting thing Amber had ever consumed, but it very well had saved Aunt G's and Willow's lives when they'd both been hit by a dose of Kieran's cursed magic that had been powerful enough to lift them off their feet.

"For a Penhallow-specific protection tincture, what would you guys need?" Amber asked.

"Hair," Simon said.

"Or blood." Aunt G patted her fanny pack strapped to her waist. "I brought a few syringes with me."

Amber didn't even want to ask why her aunt had spare syringes.

While Simon, Aunt G, and Edgar debated the difference between a blowback spell and a wind spell, Amber studied the locator one she'd written while in this very spot not that long ago. She'd written it to reveal a hidden object—which at the time had been the cache Zelda had placed in a fountain back in 1971, just before the ley lines under the neighborhood had erupted and sent everyone packing. But now, Amber wondered if she could repurpose it to show her the hidden Penhallows. If they were still alive, they were hidden from sight because they were stuck in the past, just as the cache had been.

Even though she was sure she could touch the ground and tap into the ley lines that were already making her head feel woozy, she—and her ankle—remembered all too well what happened when she tried to harness that much magic. She would like to avoid that if she could. An indirect route into the past felt like a less traumatic trip than diving into it headfirst.

Starting the spell on a fresh sheet of paper, Amber tweaked it until the language was more specific to a person than a thing. When the words on the page glowed gold, she knew the spell was complete.

Twenty minutes later, each witch had the spells they wanted to use. They stood in a circle behind Edgar's truck, each holding a vial of Aunt G's horrendous protection tincture.

Uncorking the tiny bottles, they clinked them together, then knocked them back. Amber tried plugging her nose as she drank, but it didn't help. Her eyes and nose immediately started to water and her tongue felt like it was coated in thick pond scum. She gagged. Somehow it was even worse than she remembered.

Simon had his hands on his knees while he coughed violently. Edgar had his head tipped to the sky as he shouted a few choice words at the canopy of leaves above them.

Aunt G shuddered, but otherwise didn't make a fuss. "Oh, you're all so dramatic!"

Once they'd all more or less recovered, Simon handed Amber and Edgar a sleep tincture, and handed a confusion one to Aunt G, keeping the other for himself. They each got a shield tincture, the liquid inside a dark blue. With their vials pocketed and their defense spells either memorized or scribbled on loose pieces of paper—no one wanted to lose his or her grimoire in the past—they moved to the middle of the dirt road.

Before Amber recited her spell, she dropped to one knee. She swayed a bit, even though she didn't have any skin directly in contact with the ground. The magic below this neighborhood was not only powerful, but felt alive. One of the theories about why the ley lines short-circuited was because magic itself had been angry and retaliated. As much as magic felt like a physical thing, Amber had had a hard time buying into that theory. Until she'd been here, that is. Until she'd experienced the magic here and felt like it understood her and vice versa.

She'd asked magic for help when she didn't know what to do with Damien and Devra, and magic had responded. It had taken their unconscious bodies back in time, and then spit Amber back out into the present.

She placed her hands on the ground now and nearly toppled over. She sat back on her haunches to keep herself from collapsing.

I'm back, she thought, hoping the magic here could still sense her. *We're here to speak to Damien and Devra, if they're still here. We think the Penhallows are planning something, and these two might have answers. The Penhallows still want to reverse the curse. There's no way to know how much damage that could do to the witches alive now—or to you.*

It felt strange speaking to magic directly, as if it were a singular being, but she didn't know how else to address it. When nothing happened other than a slight rumble beneath her palms, Amber shakily got to her feet.

The group formed a circle, holding hands—Simon on one side of her and Edgar on the other—and Amber recited the hidden-person spell out loud. She kept her eyes closed, hoping it would heighten her other senses. On the surface, it was a simple spell. It used the same framework as the spell she'd perfected over the years when she needed to find her cell phone.

Once the last word left her lips, she cracked open an eye, half expecting the Penhallow siblings to be standing in front of her wearing twin sinister smiles. But nothing immediately looked different.

Then the ground beneath her rumbled—more of a vibration, really. The others opened their eyes too and looked down, as if they all expected Damien and Devra to come crawling out of the earth like mutated sandworms.

Amber wasn't sure if anyone else noticed the bright burst of white light, but her yelp of alarm was cut off before she'd made a sound. Moments later, the light faded and Amber was in the neighborhood from decades before. It was the same scene, too. Doors to houses stood open, a suitcase lay overturned on someone's lawn, and the woman's laundry from across the street still hung from the line, flapping slightly in the light breeze. Not a person was in sight.

The last time this had happened, Amber had been alone; Willow and Aunt G had been left behind.

This time, Aunt G, Edgar, and Simon had made the journey with her. They all tentatively let go of each other's hands. The spell held firm.

"This. Is. *Wild*," Simon said, looking around. "So this is what this place looked like in the 70s?"

"Yeah," Amber said, scanning the area just as the others were, but Amber was on the lookout for Damien and Devra. She had no idea how this all worked. If they'd truly traveled back in time and it had been nearly a week since she was last here, the Penhallow siblings could be anywhere. If this was merely a memory, were they trapped within the confines of this single neighborhood during this one day?

A door slammed behind her. Damien and Devra stalked down the front walk of a house two buildings over. Just like Neil and Kieran, these siblings had jet-black hair. They looked remarkably similar—twins, possibly, if not close in age. They were both about 5'7", Damien perhaps an inch taller. Damien kept his hair cut short to his scalp, while Devra's fell around her shoulders in loose waves.

From what Amber could tell, they were wearing the same clothing they had been a week ago. Jeans and a dark blue T-shirt for Damien, and skinny jeans and a black tank top for Devra. She wore knee-high rubber-soled chunky boots. The line of silver buckles on the sides of them glinted dully as the pair marched toward them.

Without discussing it, Amber and her group formed a horizontal line along the width of the dirt road. A united force ready to take these two on if they decided to attack. Amber had a hand in her right pocket, where she had placed her shield tincture.

"Couldn't stay away?" Damien called out from behind Devra. He had an apple in one hand and took a final bite of it, tossing it over his shoulder as they continued forward. Once they reached the street, they walked side by side toward Amber's group. "The good thing about being stuck here, at least," he said, "is that every house is newly abandoned. Food in every fridge and pantry."

"You here to reverse whatever this is?" Devra asked as the pair stopped a few feet away. She crossed her arms and glared at Amber. "If not, I'll be on my way. I left the oven on."

"I wanted to ask you a few questions," Amber said, her palm growing sweaty around the vial.

"And why exactly would we help you, time witch?" Damien asked.

"Because I'm your way out," Amber said. "I'm guessing you wouldn't still be here if you could get out. You're both powerful witches. A week would have given you plenty of time to work through your arsenal of spells."

The siblings simultaneously paled.

"A *week*?" Devra asked. "I was awake when you vanished. We weren't able to move until you were gone. The sun hasn't set since we've been here. All the clocks are stuck at the same time ..."

Damien eyed Amber warily, some of his earlier bravado gone. "What is this place, then? A memory?"

"That's the theory," Edgar chimed in.

Devra snorted derisively. "You don't even know?"

Simon fidgeted next to her. "So you've *tried* to leave here?"

Damien assessed him, then refocused on Amber. "Is this your new plan for dealing with our clan? The council's plan to sever our magic didn't work—clearly—so now you're going to lock us away in pockets of memories so we couldn't even use our magic if we wanted to?"

Aunt G cocked her head. "You can't use your magic?"

"Didn't I just say that, old lady?" Damien snapped.

"Watch it," Amber snapped back.

Devra rolled her eyes. "We still *have* it. We just can't use it. It's…dampened here. It's like an itch I can't scratch."

Damien worked his jaw. Amber could tell he was angry, but he was scared, too. Scared that Amber would leave them here indefinitely, forever trapped in the memory of a single day until they ran out of food in these abandoned houses.

"Why did Kieran come to Edgehill?" Amber asked.

While Damien was equal parts rage and fear, Devra was all calculating assessment. "Oh, I get it. This is an interrogation tactic. You get recruited by the WBI or something?"

Amber's cheeks heated, embarrassed almost. "What do you mean?"

Damien cocked his head. "This is the kind of thing the WBI does. Large-scale memory wipes. Imprisoning witches in creative new ways. This—trapping someone in a time loop—sounds like something right up their alley. What did they offer you to get you to do some of their dirty work for them?"

Amber couldn't say she liked the agents from the WBI either, but could she trust an assessment from a pair of cursed witches?

Devra stalked up to Amber, nose to nose. Amber could see Simon tense on one side of her, and she had to grab hold of Edgar's forearm on her other side to keep him from intervening. Amber held her ground, though her heart raced. She knew the Penhallows could have been lying about their dampened magic, and had been biding their time while they lured Amber into a false sense of security, but threatening either Amber or her companions would be a stupid move on Devra's part and they all knew it.

Because at the end of the day, only Amber could get the Penhallows out of this memory. Hurting her or infuriating her would do them no favors.

"Is that the plan? Throw us in a memory like a jail cell and make us wait it out?" Devra asked, her breath warm on Amber's face. Devra turned her head this way and that, like a snake. "Are you waiting for us to go mad in here so that by the time you bother to come back, we'll be so desperate to get out of here that we'll tell you anything?"

Amber didn't flinch, though she squeezed Edgar's arm a little tighter. "Something like that. We can leave if you don't want to talk. I can come back when the food runs out."

"There's a lot of food, time witch," Damien said.

"Yes, but you thought you were only here for a few hours," Amber said. "It's been a week. Now you know you can't tell time here. The sun doesn't set. The clocks don't work. So you might think you have plenty of resources—and you might—but what if it takes me ten years to come back and you think it's only been a day? Sounds like enough to drive a person a little loopy."

Devra's lip twitched a fraction.

"What do you want to know about Kieran?" Damien blurted.

Devra whipped around to glare at him. Damien glared back.

"I want to know why he came to Edgehill," Amber said. "I know he was here for the grimoire—but what made him come looking for it after all this time?"

Damien and Devra had a silent conversation. Eventually Devra groaned loudly in what sounded like defeat, took a few steps back both from her brother and Amber's group, crossed her arms, and glowered.

Damien refocused on Amber, but he didn't speak. He worked his jaw.

"If you want any chance of getting out of here," Edgar said, "I suggest you talk."

Damien said, "Kieran was sent here to do reconnaissance."

"Sent by whom?" Amber asked.

"I don't know," Damien said. When Amber started to protest, he held up a hand. "Honestly. There's a network of us online. We mostly keep it anonymous."

"Is everyone in the network a Penhallow?" Simon asked.

"Nope," Devra said, wearing a sly grin now. "There are quite a few witches from other clans who are sympathetic to our cause. Reversing what the council did will heal magic *and* places like this. This—" she said, waving her hands around the memory they were in, "shouldn't exist."

Amber couldn't argue with her on that point.

"The Henbane grimoire, about five months ago, started giving off little pulses of magic," Damien said. "The witches in the area sensed it and informed the network that there must have been a cloak on the book this whole time. We didn't know if it was a cloak Annabelle had put there, or you, but now it was traceable. Rumors about Annabelle Henbane's children have been circulating for a while, but the witches assigned to check up on you over the years had never witnessed either you or Willow using magic for more than basics."

Witches assigned to check up on them? She shuddered at the idea. She supposed she had her parents and Aunt

G to thank for forcing Amber and Willow to bury their magic. It had kept them safe all these years.

"Kieran volunteered to come to Edgehill, thinking it would be easy to scare you into giving up the book since you're so unskilled at magic," Damien said. "But somehow you not only fought him off, you hid the book again and its trace vanished. Then you stripped Kieran of his magic."

"Sounds like you all underestimated her," Aunt G said, and Amber tried not to puff up at the pride she heard in her aunt's voice.

Devra's lip curled.

"How many of you are coming to Edgehill?" Amber asked.

"A dozen had confirmed they were on their way before we got here," Damien said. "We were the second wave of the reconnaissance."

"Who broke Kieran out of jail?" Amber asked.

Devra froze; Damien's jaw dropped. "*What?*" they asked in unison.

Then Amber remembered they'd been trapped here while Kieran had escaped.

Before she could think to ask anything else, Edgar let out a cry and pressed the heels of his hands against his temples. He sank to one knee.

Amber, momentarily forgetting about the Penhallow siblings, dropped in front of him. She gently took his face in her hands and angled it up to force him to look at her. But his eyes were squeezed shut. "Edgar," she said softly. "What is it? Is it Neil?"

Edgar nodded. "He's…cackling. He said …" Then Edgar's eyes flew open, and they frantically searched Amber's. "Someone broke him out, too."

"Of the mental institution?" Amber asked.

Now it was Devra who was laughing. "Neil's connection to Annabelle will guarantee that grimoire is ours. Just you wait."

When Edgar seemed to have a handle on his episode, Amber asked, "Did someone in the network mention this? Getting Neil out of the institution?"

Aunt G and Simon helped Edgar to his feet.

Damien started to answer, but Devra clapped a hand over his mouth. "That's enough," she snapped. Shoving her brother behind her, she addressed Amber. "Now you need to give *us* something. Let us out of here and we'll tell you anything else you need to know. Being stuck here isn't worth any of this."

Damien nodded. "We'll go underground. Leave town immediately. The network will just think we were compromised."

Amber didn't believe either one of them. "In order to consider letting you out," she said, addressing them in turn, "I need something else."

Devra narrowed her eyes.

"What?" Damien asked.

"A few locks of your hair," Amber said.

The Penhallows both took involuntary steps back.

"What for?" Devra looked truly worried for the first time. "You're planning to bind us here, aren't you?" She took another step back. "Nuh uh. I'm not giving up something like that. Come back when you want to talk, time witch." She grabbed hold of Damien's elbow and started to drag him back with her.

"Now," Amber said, and thankfully her companions sensed what she meant. All four of them threw their vials at the retreating pair.

Simon called out an activation spell just as the small glass vials smashed on the ground at their feet. Devra had realized what was happening a second before Damien did, and had taken off at a fast clip, leaving her brother behind. Damien got the full dose of the vials. One of the sleep ones took him out first. His eyes rolled back in his head and he collapsed to the dirt road.

Simon and Aunt G hurried to his prone form, Aunt G producing a syringe and a pair of scissors from her bag. Simon pulled a few empty vials from his other pocket and he and Aunt G quickly collected what they needed. Amber and Edgar stood watching Devra, who had made it halfway down the street before she spun around. She screamed at them from a distance, calling them foul names and promising that when the witches from the network found out about this, that the network would hunt them down.

Once Aunt G and Simon were done, Amber dropped to her knees a few feet from Damien's prone form. She instructed the others to keep contact with her—a hand on a shoulder, arm, or back—and then she placed her hands on the earth and asked the ley lines to return them to their timeline.

Amber swayed from the surge of magic that slammed into her as the ley lines granted her request. As the world around her was enveloped in white light, Amber could make out the sound of rapid footfalls as Devra barreled back toward them, realizing what was about to happen.

"You can't leave us here!" Devra cried out. "You call us monsters, but what does this make you?"

When the light faded, Amber, Aunt G, Edgar, and Simon were back in the ruined abandoned neighborhood. Their cars waited nearby. There was no Penhallow lying unconscious on the street. Amber shakily got to her feet and stared in the direction of where Devra had been a moment before—where she likely still was in a different, simultaneous moment.

"This is the kind of thing the WBI does," Damien had said. *"Large-scale memory wipes. Imprisoning witches in creative new ways. This—trapping someone in a time loop—sounds like something right up their alley. What did they offer you to get you to do some of their dirty work for them?"*

It couldn't be true, could it? Did the WBI somehow operate in a moral area even grayer than the nefarious Penhallows?

Devra's words echoed in Amber's head. *You call us monsters, but what does this make you?*

Amber didn't know.

CHAPTER 15

Simon and Aunt G conferred on the types of recipes they were considering for the Penhallow-specific tinctures. Amber had given up on her tincture-making skills a while ago—she was just bad at it. She had never been the greatest cook or baker, and that seemed to have spilled over into tincture concoctions, too. At least with her tea blends, she had a very precise recipe to work from and never needed to stray from that. Tinctures needed too much nuance.

A kitchen witch she was not.

She turned to Edgar. "What's happening with Neil now?"

His arms were crossed and his thick black brows were smashed together. To an outsider, he would look livid—either at his present company or at the world at large. Amber knew he was being introspective and didn't like what he found there. "He stopped cackling. But…something is different. It's been different since this morning, but I couldn't put a finger on it. He's more…animated? Excited, hopeful…I don't know. If it's true that they got him out, maybe he's just happy to be in the world again."

The murderer of her parents loose in society. It wasn't a thought that set well with Amber. "Do you know where he is?"

"No," Edgar said. "I don't know where the institution is either. I've tried tracking him down a bunch of times, but patient information isn't easy to find. It's that way by design."

Maybe she should put Willow on the case, since she'd been able to find Uncle Raph when not even the WBI could.

"And as much as he's able to pick up on things about my surroundings," Edgar added, "I don't know if it works going the other way. Until now, he's always been in the same place, so I haven't had to try."

As much as Amber feared coming face-to-face with Neil Penhallow, she figured what Devra had said held some truth. If they'd been able to get him out all this time and hadn't, it meant they had a use for him now. When Neil had taken her father's watch out of the burned rubble of 523 Ocicat Lane, had he taken something of her mother's, too? Is that what Neil would use to find the book? Neil's supposed connection to her mother would likely be tested now, using him like a metal detector to find the grimoire.

"Any idea what this network is they were talking about?" Amber asked.

Edgar frowned. "I can poke around online. I'd guess they're using the back channels of the internet to keep in touch. The Penhallows are all over the globe."

The dark web sounded even scarier when she thought of Penhallows using it to discuss plans to alter time and history.

Amber chewed on her bottom lip. The WBI agents had asked her to alert them if Kieran showed up. Did that also extend to his older brother? Neil being released was potentially even more alarming. She supposed they'd already know, since, like the non-witch FBI, the WBI likely knew things about yourself before you did.

Her mind told her to trust the WBI, but her gut told her maybe the Penhallow siblings had reason to be leery of the organization.

"Do you think we need to tell the WBI about this?" Edgar asked, echoing her thoughts. "I think we're in over our heads already. If Neil finds the books, or if Kieran comes here, or if someone finds out that you banished two of their own in a memory …" He shook his head. "I think we need help. Legendary or not, you can't take on a dozen or more cursed witches, cousin. You've got me, Simon, Willow, Gretchen, and maybe even that Zelda lady. But we need more than that."

Amber knew he was right. Even if the WBI was sketchy, she had to believe siding with them was the lesser of two evils. She gave Edgar's arm a squeeze—leaving him standing with Aunt G and Simon, who pored over their grimoires that were laid out on the bed of Edgar's truck—and went rummaging in her purse. She found Agent Howe's business card in her wallet.

She answered on the first ring. "I didn't expect to hear from you so soon, Miss Blackwood."

"Did you hear about Neil Penhallow?" Amber asked.

The beat of silence indicated Amber had surprised her. "What about him?"

"He was released from his facility just like Kieran was," she said. "They'll try to use him to find the grimoire."

"Tell me where it is and we'll get it into custody," she said.

"I can't do that," Amber said without hesitation. Lesser of two evils, yes, but her gut still told her that both groups had plans for the grimoire that would do irreparable harm to magic itself. As long as the time-travel spell was stashed, *no* one could use it.

It was what her parents had spent their lives doing— keeping the books out of reach. Even if Amber and Willow had been shut away from this part of their lives, Amber's parents had been fully aware of magic and the hidden world that lay over the non-magical one. Her parents could have turned the time-travel spell over to the WBI at any time, couldn't they? Amber knew, thanks to Zelda, that law enforcement from the witch world had looked into the case of the murders fourteen years ago. Amber had to assume that law enforcement had tried to get the spell from her parents well before their deaths.

Her parents had *chosen* to shoulder the burden of keeping the book hidden. There had to be a reason for that.

Agent Howe huffed a breath into the phone. "How did you find out about this? The news is just now coming in ..."

"Edgar has a direct line to Neil, remember?" Amber asked, deciding to keep the whole "and I have two Penhallows trapped in a memory" thing to herself for now. "He thinks Neil is going to try to use his connection to my mother. We don't know how that would work, though."

Agent Howe cursed. "I have an idea. Thank you for the call, Miss Blackwood. I'll be in touch."

The call disconnected.

Edgar had just pulled up in front of The Quirky Whisker when Amber's phone began to ring. She fished it out of her bag, hoping to see Willow's smiling face on the screen, but saw Kim's instead. Amber hopped out of the car and helped her aunt out of the back before she answered the phone.

"Oh my God, Amber, hi!" Kim said in greeting, but her voice was shaking. "I slept too long! Disaster struck Kids Day while I was drooling all over my pillow. A *disaster*, Amber. Can you do me the biggest favor in the history of the entire world and do your toy demo?"

Ugh. Amber really had hoped Kim had forgotten about that.

Amber's silence made Kim's shaky voice get even shakier. The words came out in a rush that only had a few gulps of air in the middle. Kim was on the verge of a meltdown. If Amber said they should cancel, Kim would likely start screaming and not stop for a solid five minutes.

"I wouldn't ask but the entire shadow puppet troupe has food poisoning. Like, all of them. *Eight* people. Marcy had to be admitted to the hospital for severe dehydration. Want to know where they all ate last night? Plants N Things in *Marbleglen*. What a dumb name!"

"Kim, I—"

"The cat toys have been in a locked storage room in the community center for like two solid weeks," Kim said, talking over Amber. Her voice seemed to go up an extra octave with every sentence. "I'm sure the toys are fine. And only the bears were sabotaged, right? There are at least twenty families planning to attend. They're all out-of-towners since the sign-up sheet was in the tourist center, so probably most of them don't even *know* about the exploding bear. Happy kids mean happy parents and happy parents spend money. We need them all happy, Amber. Ann Marie said there was a group of over fifty people waiting for the shadow puppet show when she got the news about the whole troupe *vomiting* and she had to cancel on their behalf. The toy demo would help make the parents less upset," Kim said. "*Please?*"

Criminy. "Fine."

"Yes!" Kim said.

Amber jumped when a car honked three times in rapid succession. She took a few steps back to glance down the street. Kim was parked at the curb. Her friend, with her phone still pressed to her ear, waved enthusiastically.

"Give me your grimoire, little mouse," Aunt G said, "and go take care of whatever you need to."

Flustered, Amber disconnected the call with Kim, and then handed her spell book to her aunt. When Aunt G grabbed it, Amber didn't immediately let go, causing her aunt to hike a brow. "Be nice to Thea."

Her aunt scoffed. "I don't want to harm her. We just needed her out of the way."

Edgar, who was still in the driver's seat of his truck, laughed. "Spoken like a woman on a quick slide into the Dark Side."

"Pah," Aunt G said, successfully taking the grimoire from Amber. "Everyone is so dramatic lately." With the grimoire under her arm, Aunt G ducked back into the truck to take Thea's cage off the back seat. "Come now, little hamster. I'll get you some nice lettuce to munch on."

Thea squeaked.

Amber watched her aunt let herself into The Quirky Whisker, then turned back to her cousin. "Will you be okay?" The question had many layers to it and she knew he couldn't answer it fully in the time they had.

Amber flinched when a car honked three more times.

"I think I should be asking *you* that," Edgar said.

"Want to come with us?" Amber asked. "Maybe your presence will calm Kim down."

Edgar went beet red. "Nothing doing. I have a horde of undead to shoot at home."

Sighing, Amber nodded. "Fine. Bye, nerd."

"Bye, noob."

She rolled her eyes good-naturedly at him, shut the door, and then headed for Kim's waiting car. Kim waved frantically when she saw Amber walking her way, as if Amber didn't already know she was there.

Edgar drove away just as Amber climbed into the passenger seat of Kim's car. The back seat was piled with all manner of things Here and Meow related. Kim's brown hair was up in a messy chic bun that was on the wrong side of messy, her eyeliner was a bit smudgy, and when she smiled, Amber noted the red lipstick on her front teeth.

"What?" Kim asked. "What happened? Is something on my face?" She flipped down her sun visor and shrieked. She slapped it closed again. "Oh my God, Amber! You have to drive. I need to do damage control on my face, stat."

Amber happily obliged, as Kim driving in her current state couldn't be good for anyone—namely every pedestrian within the town limits. Kim was so worked up, talking a million miles an hour about the "absolute calamity" Kids Day had been so far, that Amber figured it would be better not to discuss the evolving Penhallow situation until later.

When they arrived at Balinese Park, Kim insisted that she carry the box of Amber's demonstration materials. While they walked, Amber marveled at the transformation that had taken place in the park so far.

The 5K race would end here, and the setup was already well underway. White canopy pop tents had been erected to the right of the picnic area. The makeshift booths would feature local businesses offering discounts and exclusive offers to the racers. There would be prizes, raffles, and free samples galore.

Off in the distance, on the other end of the park, Amber could see workers tending to the rose garden. The revamped garden was going to be named after Melanie Cole. The official memorial unveiling was scheduled for Sunday morning.

Though it was still four days until Saturday's race, there were already several banners hung from tables in the pop tents, and from the large gazebo that stood over the picnic area. Ben's design looked especially beautiful on such a large scale.

For Kids Day, the park also had a large bouncy house shaped like an oversized cat. The thing was slightly horrifying, if Amber was honest. Its giant head bobbed erratically as children screamed in glee, bouncing around in its innards. A few of the pop tents had been set up there as well, where various artists and entertainers were working booths. Face painting, caricature drawings, and a clown who rapidly made cat balloon animals were the attractions with the most activity, but even Amber could tell that the group as a whole—parents and kids alike—were restless. A few food trucks were parked near the pond and long lines of tired parents stood outside. Children were chasing each other all over the area, while others harassed the ducks, and another pair on the other side of the pond were trying unsuccessfully to scale a tree. The whole scene was chaotic enough that Amber wanted to run back in the direction from which they'd come.

Kim must have recognized the look on Amber's face for what it was, because she'd nudged Amber with the box of cat toys. "Don't you dare abandon me in my time of need, Blackwood."

Maybe Aunt G was right about everyone being dramatic. Wrinkling her nose, Amber jutted her chin toward the picnic area. "I can set up over there and maybe you can try to round up the demons?"

Kim nodded vigorously, her wild eyes taking in the scene. Even though she'd fixed her makeup, the hair was still…a mess. If nothing else, Kim's crazed energy likely would scare the children, and a good number of parents, into submission.

After depositing the box on a table, Kim marched off again, leaving Amber alone. Inside the box was a sampling of the most popular toy cats she sold at The Quirky Whisker. House cats, lions, cheetahs, pumas. Back before she'd needed to shutter her doors, Amber's plan for this demonstration had been to use only one or two toys to show what they could do, and to have the others laid out in hopes of enticing parents to buy them.

Now Amber wasn't sure encouraging purchases was a good idea. Though Kim swore these particular toys had been kept in a locked storage room for weeks, that didn't mean a Penhallow couldn't still have sabotaged them. Normally she would have discounted an idea like that as paranoid, that the cursed-magic-addled minds of the Penhallows weren't capable of devising something that needed that much planning. But now Amber knew better. The Penhallows were in it for the long haul.

She had just taken out the last of the cats and had set the box on the bench beside her when someone said, "Fancy meeting you here."

Recognizing the voice instantly, she turned and grinned at Jack. "Hi!" she said and flung her arms around him. Amber was not a flingy type of person, but given the madness of the day, she couldn't have been happier to see a friendly face.

Then she froze. At least she hoped it was friendly. She and Jack didn't have a code word yet.

Jack wrapped his arms around her, laughing. "It's nice to see you, too."

She pulled back just enough to be able to look into his eyes without breaking the embrace. "What season of *Vamp World* are we on?"

He cocked his head at her, then straightened a moment later. "Oh, you're testing me to make sure I'm me, aren't you? We're still on season three, episode two because we're old and can't stay awake through more than five minutes before we pass out."

Grinning again, she kissed him lightly. "Good work. You passed. I need a code word."

"Merry Pawpins," he said.

She smiled. It was what he'd ordered from Mews and Brews on their last official date a few months ago. "Got it," she said, pulling away. "So, what are you doing here?"

"I got roped into Kids Day by your lovely high-strung friend over there," he said.

They both glanced toward the food trucks, and Amber spotted Kim in a very heated argument with a nine-year-old. The child appeared to be winning.

"I tried to tell her that scones weren't the most kid-friendly," Jack said, redirecting Amber's attention. "She said she would have preferred Betty's cupcakes, but Betty was too swamped. I promise I'm not bitter that I didn't win Best of Edgehill at the Hair Ball, but Kim could have at least made it less obvious that I was her second—possibly third—choice for Kids Day."

Amber laughed. "She's slipping into Galazilla mode again."

"Would it be Festizilla now?" Jack asked. "Oh, that's terrible."

Amber wrinkled her nose in agreement.

"Anyway," he said, eyeing her toys laid out in two neat rows. "I decided not to fight the Festizilla and made a boatload of cat-shaped sugar cookies as a compromise. I set up a cookie-decorating booth and made Larry and Sabrina work it with me. They left a little bit ago; I told them I would clean up." A pair of children screamed at the top of their lungs and then went racing across the park. "It may be my fault that they're all out of their minds now."

"Out of control sugar highs seems to be the annual tradition for Kids Day," Amber said, sighing. "Maybe I'll make it a quick demo …"

"Everyone, we're about to begin! Make your way to Miss Amber for a demonstration of her renowned animated toys!" Kim called out from her spot near the food trucks. No one immediately moved toward Amber, even after she raised an arm and waved. "*NOW!*" Kim bellowed.

A gaggle of children slowly meandered in Amber's direction.

"Don't keep Miss Amber waiting," Kim singsonged. "Move your keisters! Chop chop!"

The children moved faster.

"A really, *really* quick demo," Amber whispered to Jack, who stifled a laugh.

Once most of the group had assembled in front of her, she had the youngest kids sit on the bench that faced the toy cats, and the older children and a smattering of parents lined up behind them. Kim, wild hair and all, stood to Amber's right, likely shooting death glares at the children to keep them in line, and Jack stood to her left. A cluster of parents remained at the food trucks or standing in huddles. Amber imagined they were all delighted to have their kids focused on something else for a while.

"Hi, everyone. I'm Amber Blackwood," she said. "How many of you are from Edgehill?"

Only a couple of kids raised their hands.

"Welcome to all of you who have never been here before," she said. "As you know, Edgehill loves its cats. What I do here is make toys. But these aren't just any toys. These cats can move and meow and play with you like real cats."

A pair of little boys sitting on the bench opposite her turned to each other and rolled their eyes.

Amber laughed. "Oh, so you two don't believe me?" She took a seat on the bench to be at eye level with them. "Want me to prove it to you?" she asked, her attention darting between the little boys.

They both nodded.

"Okay, each of you pick out one of the cats," Amber said.

Twin looks of determination passed over their faces. The dark-skinned boy with the missing front tooth picked a black-and-white house cat, and the light-skinned boy picked a puma. Once they'd selected the toys they wanted, Amber asked Kim and Jack to help her clear the area so the remaining toys were out of the way. They did as asked, then stepped back.

"Place your toys on the table in front of you," Amber told them. "Now, pick a name. A name that matches their coloring works best."

The kids sitting on the bench on either side of the boys leaned forward. One girl in particular looked rather miffed that she hadn't been selected to pick one. The parents and older children stood on tiptoe to get a better view.

"Milkshake," the dark-skinned boy said. The "s" whistled through his missing tooth. "Like an Oreo milkshake."

"Fred," said the other boy.

Amber tried not to laugh. "Both of those are perfect." Looking up to address more of the crowd, she said, "The toys are all programmed for voice command. Once a name is chosen, I can update the programming to respond to that name. Currently, they know how to walk, sit, run, roar, and sleep." Returning her attention to the boys, she instructed them both on how to get the cats to respond.

As they debated on which command to start with, Amber mentally cast the activation spells on each cat and, with her hands below the table, gave a flick of her wrist toward each one.

"Milkshake, walk," the dark-skinned boy said.

Instantly, the black-and-white cat's plastic rigidity melted away and it started to move. The boy gasped, as well as a few of the watching children and adults.

The light-skinned boy had been watching the cat in awe, then seemed to remember it was his turn and focused on his puma. "Fred, roar."

The rigidity of the mountain lion vanished at the command, then it stood, and with its four paws flat on the table, the cat tipped its head back and let loose a roar that was loud enough that the kids in the immediate vicinity jumped.

The pair of boys grinned at each other, then both commanded that their toys should run. The animated cats darted from one side of the long picnic table—where their unmoving counterparts resided—and then back again. Kids whirled on their bench seats to call for their parents, begging them for one of the toys.

Shouts of "Miss Amber! Miss Amber, can I try too?" rose up to match the enthusiasm and volume of the requests to buy one of their own. Though Amber knew it wasn't a safe time to have any of these toys leave her care, she was filled with overwhelming pride not only in her craft abilities, but in her magical ones. The awe on the kids' faces was the reason she decided to use her magic in this way—she wanted children filled with wonder at what beautiful things magic could do.

A hand landed on her left shoulder, where Jack had been standing. He gave her a gentle squeeze, but then his grip tightened slightly. When she looked up at him, his gaze wasn't on her, but rather on the toys on his side of the table. All ten of them were moving.

What the …

Then Kim yelped to her right. The eight toys on that end were moving, too. It was slow at first, like they'd all been dozing and were waking from a deep sleep.

The crowd had quieted again, as they'd all noticed the movement, too. While they looked excited about this apparent finale of Amber's show, Amber was filled with dread. She disentangled herself from the bench seat so she had a higher vantage point and scanned the crowd. Any time she left her home, she used Willow's clarity spell in hopes it was strong enough to pick out a Penhallow wearing a glamour, but the spell wasn't showing her anything.

She hoped that Simon and/or Aunt G came up with a Penhallow-specific tincture soon. It would be the only way to spot a Penhallow glamour.

The shouts of glee from the onlookers grew as the animals all started to roam the table. Tiny tigers roared, and house cats curled into balls to sleep, and lions ran along the surface of the table, their manes flapping about their faces as if they were made of hair instead of plastic.

Amber's gaze kept scanning the crowd, both directly in front of her and out in the grassy area beyond. And then her attention snagged on a woman standing on her own near a young sapling. Her attention was squared on Amber. A small, slow smile crossed her face. She had jet-black hair, which was a common Penhallow trait, but it was a common enough trait in people in general that it wasn't enough to definitively peg her as a cursed witch.

A scream yanked Amber's focus away from the black-haired woman and back down at the rogue toys on the table. Amber's stomach bottomed out. The toys had formed a single line, shoulder to shoulder, and faced the onlooking children. All the toys hunched low to the table, and the hackles were up on their backs. Black, white, beige, spotted, and striped tails were hoisted in the air. It was a predatory stance if Amber had ever seen one.

She quickly mentally cast a deactivation spell and discreetly swiped a hand through the air. No reaction from the cats. She tried to direct the spell at just one of them. Nothing.

Oh crap.

Then, in unison, the cats spoke in a woman's voice. The voice didn't sound like Amber's per se, but it was close enough that it even gave Amber pause. "Get out of Edgehill while you can. Saturday is your last day to get to safety. I will tear this place apart to get what I want. But first, I will tear *you* apart."

The cats leaped.

They landed on children's hair, their clothes, their arms. They scratched and bit and snarled. Amber had been bitten by a rogue toy once herself and knew firsthand how much it could hurt, even if it never drew blood. Getting shot by a paintball couldn't kill you, but it sure as heck could leave a bruise.

Chaos erupted.

Kids and parents screamed. Toys were knocked off shirts and pants and fingers. Some were stomped underfoot. The toys chased terrified screaming kids. Parents scooped up their children and bolted for safety.

"Oh my God, oh my God, oh my God!" Amber and Kim said in unison.

"We have to smash them!" Amber said. "I tried to, you know, dismantle them and it didn't work."

"On it!" Jack said and took off.

Amber and Kim ran after him, but they soon realized they needed to split up to cover more ground. Amber bolted for a little boy who was in the fetal position by one of the pop tents. He had a cheetah running around him at a lightning pace, nipping at him any time he tried to get away. On her mad dash toward him, Amber had found a rock that she'd snatched up on the move.

"You okay, kid?" she called out.

He poked his head up a little to look at her, but then the cheetah leaped up to nip him on the elbow and he curled up again. Amber watched in dismay as the toy started running laps around the little boy again, moving at a speed that would make its real-life counterparts proud. With the rock held firmly in her hand, Amber watched for a few more seconds.

"Okay, kid, when I tell you to, I need you to kick out a leg."

"I'm scared!"

"I know, but I need you to be brave for me, okay?"

"'Kay ..."

Amber watched the cheetah circle and circle and…"Now!"

The boy's leg shot out. The toy saw it and tried to leap, but one of its paws hit the boy's shoe and sent the cheetah flipping end over end and skidding across the grass. Amber slammed down hard on the toy with the rock and it shattered into several—blissfully unmoving—pieces.

As she got the shaking boy to his feet, a man rounded the edge of the tent. "Arthur! Arthur, where are you?"

"Dad!" the boy called out, then burst into tears.

"Sorry about all this!" Amber shouted, then was on the move again before the man could tell her what he thought of her and her toys.

Kids Day was a calamity indeed.

Amber plucked a growling ocelot off the back of a little girl's shirt, and pulled two vicious, snarling calico cats off the ends of a little girl's pair of pigtails. The girl looked like she'd considered jumping in the murky water of the pond in an attempt to drown the plastic demons hanging from her hair.

The task at hand kept Amber focused to an almost tunnel-like effect. It wasn't until the majority of the screaming had died down that Amber let herself slow. She stood near a food truck, her chest heaving, as she scanned the park. It was mostly deserted now, the grass littered with bits of broken plastic. Amber tried to pretend that the pieces were something innocuous, like the bits of streamers knocked loose from a piñata.

Then she pictured a piñata donkey coming to life as it chased screaming children, smoke billowing from its papier-mâché nostrils. She shook the image loose.

She turned in a slow circle and found an equally exhausted-looking Kim and Jack heading her way from the left. The rock slipped from her hand. She was glad her joints still worked and that her hand hadn't fused to the rock from holding it so tightly.

Movement from her other side pulled her attention to another approaching figure. Though this too was a familiar face, he didn't look particularly happy to see her in this moment.

"Hi, chief," she said when he got closer.

"Amber," he said, then eyed Kim and Jack, who had slowed their approach. "I'm going to need you to come down to the station, uh, Hinklebert."

Amber pursed her lips. "I didn't do this, chief. I swear it. There's a ..." She lowered her voice, her gaze shifting left and right. "There's a Penhallow—at least one, maybe more—in Edgehill. They did this, not me. I saw a woman in the crowd. Maybe she—"

He held up a hand to quiet her panicked rambling. "We can discuss this on the way."

"Are the parents pressing charges?" Kim blurted. "Isn't that what happens on TV?"

Amber eyed her friend and noted the messy bun now had a few branches and leaves stuck in it.

"Yes and no," the chief said.

Amber rubbed her forehead, a sudden headache taking hold. She didn't even know what "pressing charges" meant. She should have looked into hiring a lawyer. She needed help, but the list of people in town aside from her family who she trusted were all standing in this park with her now.

"I will file a police report—which is why I would like Amber to come down to the station with me," the chief said. "I'll then turn those reports over to the district attorney. A lawyer will be assigned to the case. That lawyer is the only one who can decide if charges will be pressed. The parents can cry foul until the cows come home, but if the prosecuting lawyer doesn't think there's a case here, it would be dropped."

"So *another* lawyer will be coming here to look into my products?"

"Another?" Jack asked. "Who was the first one?"

"Thea Bishop," Kim said matter-of-factly. "Gretchen turned her into a hamster."

Amber shot Kim a dangerous look.

"Wait, *what*?" Jack asked.

"She's so cute!" Kim said.

Amber groaned, deciding to focus on the chief instead of Jack and Kim's lively conversation. "Can I call someone first?"

"You're not under arrest, Amber," he said. "I just need to file a report." He eyed Jack and Kim. "Since you two were here during the incident, I'll need to talk to you both, too. I would like a chance to speak to Amber privately, so if you could meet me later today at the station at your earliest convenience, I'd appreciate it."

"No problem," Jack said.

"It's a good thing I know you two aren't actually having an affair, otherwise I would think it's mighty fishy you want her all to yourself," Kim said.

Amber might have considered homicide had one of the people in attendance not been a cop. After apologizing to Jack for…all of it…she went back to the picnic area to get her purse, which she found underneath a table. It was zipped closed, so the contents hadn't spilled out all over the ground. Yet, when she opened it to fish out her phone, she found the decapitated head of a plastic bobcat staring up at her. A string had been tied around one of its ears and attached to that ear was a note.

Give up the book before the festival and maybe Edgehill and Henrietta will be spared.

Amber frantically scanned the park, turning in a circle as she did. She didn't necessarily expect the black-haired woman to be lurking nearby, but *not* seeing anyone somehow made Amber even more paranoid. After dialing the number, she pressed the phone to her ear, slung the bag over her shoulder, and walked back toward the chief, Jack, and Kim.

He answered on the second ring. "Alan Peterson."

"Hi, Alan," she said, unable to keep the quaver from her voice. "I need your help."

CHAPTER 16

"What's wrong?" Alan asked. His straightforward problem-solving tone grounded her.

It also made her want to cry because she wanted to blurt out every little magical detail of her current predicament and couldn't. She liked Alan a lot, but even now, she didn't know how much she trusted him, not to mention how he'd react if he learned magic was real.

"Are you in the area, by any chance?" Amber could see the huddle of Jack, Kim, and the chief up ahead. Kim was currently giving the very bewildered chief a demonstration of smashing something with a rock.

"Uhh…I'm actually at Ann Marie's right now," he said.

Amber grinned despite everything. "Things are going well, are they?"

He coughed awkwardly. The sound of a door sliding closed echoed through the phone. "Yeah. Thanks again for putting in a good word for me. She's…pretty incredible."

Amber never failed to be amused by how much his feelings for Ann Marie stripped that no-nonsense air he wore ninety percent of the time. "Glad to hear it," she said, slowing her pace a little. "So…without getting into too much detail, I think someone is targeting me. My products have been sabotaged on three separate occasions now. I was thinking you could just…keep tabs on me? See if someone has been following me, or if anyone is doing anything shifty near my shop?"

"Sabotage how?" he asked.

Amber did her best to explain.

"You think Henrietta was poisoned?" he asked. "There's a short list of chemicals that could cause a coma …"

She wasn't sure if he was subtly questioning her assessment of the situation or if he was thinking out loud.

"I'll look into it," he said. "I'm sticking around through the end of the Here and Meow. Ann Marie is busy with festival tasks for the rest of the week, so I have some free time. Can't say I'll always be available in the evenings though, if you know what I mean."

"Gross," she said, chuckling. "I'll take any time you can spare. I'm just at a loss about what to do now. My shop is shut down because of this, and yet this person still won't leave me alone. I don't know what they want or why they're out to get me."

Lies upon lies. The decapitated head of the plastic bobcat in her purse told her everything she needed to know about the Penhallows' motives.

"Thanks, Alan. I really appreciate it."

"No sweat," he said.

After she said goodbye to Jack and Kim, Amber followed the chief to his cruiser.

Give up the book before the festival and maybe Edgehill and Henrietta will be spared, the note said. Why had the Penhallows done this to Henrietta?

I'm so sorry, Hen.

Thoughts of Henrietta led Amber back to Molly. How much did Molly's wild theories about Amber's supposed Edgehill-revenge plans actually line up with the Penhallows' plans?

She hated how scattered and distracted she felt. Her lack of decent sleep over the last few weeks wasn't helping, either. It felt like it was all unraveling and she didn't know how to stop it. This was likely how the ever-changing premonitions made Aunt G feel. So many options, possibilities, theories—and yet no clear solution.

The festival started in three days. How was she supposed to figure this all out by then?

"Amber."

She startled and glanced over at the chief. Somehow they were already in his car and on the move. She'd been on autopilot while her thoughts ran amok.

"There's a reason I wanted to talk to you alone," he said. "I wasn't sure how much Jack and Kim have been told."

A pit formed in Amber's stomach. "What happened?"

"I got a very strange phone call earlier today from an Agent Howe," he said.

Amber groaned.

"She claims she's with the WBI and that sometimes they confer with non-witch law enforcement when their cases overlap with ours," he said in a casual enough tone, but when he briefly made eye contact with her, she could see the whites of his eyes. "The *Witch* Bureau of Investigation, Amber? You people have whole government bodies?"

"You people?" she shot back.

He huffed. "Sorry. I don't mean it like that. This is just a lot to process."

"Well, if it makes you feel any better, I didn't know they existed until recently either." Sighing, she asked, "So what did she want to *confer* about?"

"At first, she was trying to confirm I knew you were a witch. I was scared to admit that, honestly. What if she showed up with one of those metal wands to erase my memory?" the chief asked.

Amber needed to ask Jack to watch this movie with her so she was in the loop.

"Agent Howe said she believes you're in danger here in Edgehill and that you'd be a whole heck of a lot safer if you turned over the Henbane grimoire to authorities." As if sensing her rising anger, he said, "I told her that even if I knew where the grimoire was, I wouldn't betray your trust by giving up the location. Even if it meant you'd be safer if I did."

Her rage dissipated.

"Mostly because I would be in a world of trouble once you found out and I know now that you really *can* turn people into hamsters," he said. "Sammy and Izzy would love to have a new pet, but I'm not sure Jessica would ever recover."

Amber laughed.

"She also said that you'd be leaving in the morning with your cousin and she wanted someone from my department to keep an eye on your shop while you're away," he said. "You're planning a trip on the eve of the Here and Meow when Kimberly Jones is the director? That sounds both out of character for you, and unwise."

Amber was equal parts annoyed with Agent Howe for going back on her word that Amber didn't have to go on this WBI recon mission for another two weeks, and relieved that her own absence in Edgehill might disrupt the Penhallows' plans. Maybe the Penhallows would follow Amber and Edgar, and then they'd have to contend with the WBI as a result.

She just hoped that her absence didn't *help* the Penhallows somehow.

"This is news to me." She filled in the gaps in the chief's knowledge about Edgar's father and the WBI. "I still don't know what they expect me to find in his memory, but the WBI seems to think that whatever it is can turn the tide."

The chief was quiet for a moment, clearly lost in thought. "And you're sure you can trust them?"

"The number of people I fully trust can be counted on six fingers," she said. "But this also might be the only chance we have to visit Uncle Raphael. Edgar's needed closure on that for over a decade. Even if nothing comes of it, at least Edgar will get to see him."

"Fair enough," he said. "I'll add your shop to as many of my officers' routes as possible. Not sure what non-witch cops can do against cursed witches, but I didn't want to argue with that lady. She gives me the creeps."

Once they were at the station, the chief's light interrogation was similar to the discussion they'd had before Thea's visit. He asked her twice as many questions, though, and she did her best to answer truthfully without giving herself away. Garcia drove her back home. He didn't say a word to her for the entire drive, which wasn't unusual for him, but he did assure her that he would keep an eye on things while she was gone.

While she was gone.

She wondered when the agents had been planning on informing *her.* Did Edgar already know? Amber had a sneaking suspicion that crowded airports and being airborne in a metal tube were not things on Edgar Henbane's favorites list. Perhaps she could get him drunk.

Though a drunk Edgar was likely a handful, too.

Just as she unlocked the front door of the shop, someone behind her asked, "Are you open yet?"

"Sorry, no," Amber said hurriedly, then closed herself inside again. She watched as the woman put a hand on her daughter's shoulder and guided the disappointed little girl away.

At least the news of the rogue toys in Balinese Park hadn't reached this far yet.

It wasn't until Amber was halfway up the stairs that she heard voices. Willow had returned. Steeling herself, she crested the top of the steps and found Aunt G, Willow, and Agent Howe sitting around the dining room table. Thea's cage sat on the far end. Amber wondered if Agent

Barker was with Edgar. If so, it was brave of Agent Howe to send the guy to Edgar's without backup.

"Informing my family about my trip?" Amber asked, unable to tamp down the snark.

Agent Howe eyed Amber from head to foot. "What on earth happened to you?"

"Oh, you know, a Penhallow harassing me in public. What else is new?" She dropped her purse on the table, fished out the decapitated plastic bobcat head, and rolled it across the table to Agent Howe like it was a billiard ball.

The agent picked up the offending object in one hand and held the end of the attached note with the other. Then she focused on Amber. "Tell me what happened."

Amber did, still standing at the head of the table. If she sat down, sheer exhaustion would take over and she wouldn't be able to get up again.

"If this prosecuting lawyer proves to be a problem," Agent Howe said, "we have ways of taking care of it that don't involve turning said human into a rodent." She cocked a brow at Aunt G, who remained stone-faced. "Though I do have an idea …"

The spell was cast so quickly, none of the Blackwoods had a chance to react. Thea disappeared out of her cage at the end of the table and then reappeared a moment later on the floor to Amber's right. With a flick of the agent's wrist, Thea had been restored to her human form.

Luckily, Thea was still clothed, but said clothes smelled heavily of rodent urine. Amber tried to cough discreetly. Bits of bedding were caught in Thea's tangled red hair. Her wild eyes darted between the people assembled and her chest heaved. Amber didn't dare make any sudden movements.

Then Thea screamed—roared, really. Hands balled at her sides, head thrown back, mouth stretched wide. Amber flinched and took a few steps away, rounding the side of the chair before her. "How dare you!" Thea finally screeched, finger pointed at Aunt G. "*A hamster*?"

Well, that answered the question of how aware Thea had been.

"Listen, Thea—" Amber started.

"No, *you* listen," Thea said. "I listened to as much of your conversations as possible and now I'm fairly certain that *all* of you, including your cousin, are witches. Is that right?"

Amber swallowed and nodded. "Yes."

"And you didn't actually poison my sister. Some evil witch did?"

She nodded again.

Thea balled her fists once more. "If I promise to keep your secrets, will you promise not to turn me back into that horrible little creature?" A mew sounded and Thea looked down, shrieked, and shuffled back so quickly that her back hit the wall. Tom had been giving her shoe a sniff.

Amber snatched him off the ground and held him to her chest. She wasn't sure if Tom's desire to eat Thea would still be a problem. Either way, Amber worried that Thea now had a phobia of cats—while in a town devoted to them.

"On one condition," Agent Howe said, getting to her feet. She crossed the space to stand before Thea, who was more or less cowering against the wall. Agent Howe put a fist to her mouth and coughed once, then gave her head a shake. "I looked into your history and you're quite the accomplished lawyer—for a non-witch."

Thea straightened a little. "Thank you. I think."

"I'm going to need you to represent Amber here," Agent Howe said. "If this prosecuting lawyer decides this case is worth investigating, your task is to make sure it gets dropped. Magical intervention in non-witch relations isn't always the best move, so if we had someone like you on our side, it would help a great deal."

Thea's gaze shifted from Agent Howe to Amber and back again. Her nose twitched involuntarily. "What about my sister?"

"The coma wasn't induced by anything Henrietta ingested," Agent Howe said. "It was a spell placed on her by a Penhallow. They're currently doing all they can to unbalance Amber's place here in Edgehill. They want Amber to succumb to the harassment and give up her mother's grimoire. They're using both magical and non-magical means to make her life a living hell. Help us take care of the non-magical problems plaguing her and you have my word that we'll use every resource at our disposal to make sure your sister wakes up."

Thea was still more or less smashed against the wall as her wild gaze darted about the room. As traumatized as Thea likely was, she was exceptional at evaluating a situation. Saying or doing anything to upset the witches in attendance—who wielded magic capable of rearranging her molecules—wasn't in her best interest, and she knew it. "I'm guessing giving them the grimoire isn't an option?"

"Under no circumstances," Agent Howe said.

"Okay," Thea said, swallowing hard. "I'll be your non-witch lawyer as long as I don't end up back in that tiny cage." Her nose wiggled vigorously again.

"Can I ask *you* something?" Amber asked.

Thea eyed her warily.

"Did Henrietta ever mention being in contact with a Molly Hargrove?"

"Ugh. Yeah. The reporter from Marbleglen," Thea said. "Molly found out about Henrietta's tea-making venture and pretended she wanted to be one of the backers for the company. When they finally met to talk details, Molly revealed who she actually was. Henrietta was upset, obviously, because Molly had duped her into thinking she had an investor. Molly claimed she was trying to find out all she could about you, and she was hoping Hen had some insight into the secret ingredient in your tea. Once Henrietta realized how this whole thing was getting out of control, she pulled the plug. But Molly kept harassing her, threatening to tell you that Hen had been trying to steal your recipe."

Perhaps that was the argument Amber had witnessed during the memory-retrieval spell she'd cast on Henrietta in the hospital.

Thea gave the air a sniff then, nose hiked high in the air. "Do you smell that?" she asked. "Is that me?"

"It's truly horrendous," Agent Howe said.

"I thought so," said Thea. "Can I get a ride back to my hotel? I don't know how I'll react when I get out there, to be honest. The cars. The people …"

"Don't worry about any of that. I've been in this business long enough that I know what treatment plans to get you started on if you're having a hard time coping. Human to rodent, oddly, doesn't have that many lasting effects. I once had to deal with a human who had been an ostrich for a week. That guy was a *mess*," Agent Howe said.

Thea didn't look remotely comforted by this information.

Agent Howe turned to Amber. "Take care of whatever you need to; you leave at four tomorrow morning with Agent Barker. You'll be escorted back to Edgehill by Friday afternoon, in time for the parade. You have roughly two days to break into Raphael Henbane's mind. You'll be back here before the festival, because success or not, whatever the Penhallows have planned will take place this weekend and you're currently one of our best defenses against them. We're guessing they chose this weekend in large part because of the festival—they're big on creating chaos in a crowd, as I'm sure you know. And that parade will be jam-packed with people. I'll stay here to assist in any way I can to make sure your family stays safe while you're gone."

With that, Agent Howe headed down the steps after Thea.

"Let's get to work, little mouse," Aunt G said, getting to her feet. "You and Willow work on the mind-cracking spell. I'll keep working on the Penhallow-specific clarity spell. Sounds like we're going to need it by the time you get back."

"Shouldn't the WBI have stuff like this already?" Willow asked. "I would think Penhallows would be experimented on by the WBI like alien cadavers are in Area 51."

"I asked Agent Howe that before you got here," Aunt G said. "She said they've tried for decades to create defensive spells tailored to work against Penhallows, but their blood is too volatile. No spell will hold. Apparently whole facilities have blown up during their attempts to experiment on Penhallow blood."

"And you're still going to work on these spells *in my kitchen*?" Amber asked, eyes wide.

Aunt G waved this away.

Willow stood, smiling. "I know this is all very scary, but it's kind of exciting, too, don't you think?"

Amber grabbed her grimoire off her nightstand table. "You're just saying that because you got to spend the afternoon with a celebrity."

"I have so much to tell you!" Willow said.

Aunt G groaned. "I'll be in the kitchen. Too much gushing happened while you were out, Amber. My old ears can't take any more. Unfortunately, since you live in a postage stamp, I'll hear it all again anyway."

"Oh, you know you love it," Willow said. "Did you prefer 'dreamy' or 'sensual' when I described his eyes?"

Aunt G groaned even louder, then started slamming kitchen cabinets and drawers. Willow grinned and winked at Amber.

Amber knew they were being extra dramatic to help distract her.

She loved them all the more for it.

CHAPTER 17

When Agent Barker pulled up in front of The Quirky Whisker at 4:00 AM, Edgar was already inside the dark SUV. Most of the trip from Edgehill to the airport to being airborne happened in a blur. Edgar's fidgeting in the airport and on the plane gave Amber something to focus on. They reflected on their favorite memories of Raphael, and Amber did her best to convince Edgar that he should attend the Here and Meow for the first time in his life. Edgar had yet to be swayed.

Even Agent Barker took notice of how tightly wound Edgar was, and halfway through the flight, wedged between Amber and Edgar, he encased them in a noise-canceling bubble and regaled them with stories of weird cases from his first year in the WBI. Amber was sure to have nightmares about the probably-a-werewolf story. She decided it would be best not to recount any of these tales to Chief Brown, who likely would faint dead away. Edgar was almost relaxed by the time the plane landed in Seattle, Washington.

They'd only just stepped out of the baggage claim area when a black SUV with tinted windows pulled up. If this had been a thriller movie, someone would have jumped out, thrown a pillowcase over her head, and then tossed her into the back of the vehicle before speeding away. Agent Barker wasn't remotely alarmed by the vehicle's sudden arrival. Instead, he strolled up to the SUV and pulled open the passenger-side door. The man seated in the driver's seat looked like he could be Tad, Todd, or Troy's long-lost brother. He talked even less than Garcia did. At Agent Barker's insistence, Amber and Edgar clamored into the back with their duffel bags.

Two hours out from the airport, Agent Barker began to lay out details. He explained that the facility where Raphael was being held was magic-free and privately owned, which was part of the reason why it had stayed off the WBI's radar. Their intel so far had turned up that Raphael had been admitted to Peaceful Meadows thanks to a hefty anonymous donation made on his behalf.

"And you don't know who made the donation?" Amber asked.

"Not yet," Agent Barker said. "But during your two days here, I'll find out what I can. Truth spells and the like can be used in a pinch, but it's very likely that not even the staff knows who sent the money. It's called an anonymous donation for a reason."

For some time, Silent Agent had been driving on a tree-lined two-lane road populated with more switchbacks than Amber's stomach cared for. Suddenly, he made a smooth, yet unexpected turn onto an unmarked road. It wove slowly uphill into a pine-laden area. Ages later, as the SUV came over a slight hill, a stone manor appeared in the distance. It initially gave Amber the willies; it would have made the perfect setting for a gothic ghost story.

If it hadn't been for the handful of cars parked in a weed-and-gravel field a few hundred yards from Peaceful Meadows' entrance, and the few large pots filled with healthy red, purple, and pink flowers flanking the front door, Amber would have thought the place was abandoned.

Silent Agent pulled into the field-slash-parking lot and killed the engine. When Agent Barker told him that they'd be back "soon," Silent Agent merely grunted in response. He fetched a sudoku book and a pencil from the glove box, then settled into his seat.

As Amber and Edgar piled out of the SUV, she shook out her hands to release some of the tension. She was excited for Edgar—after all these years, he'd finally get to see his father. She was preemptively heartbroken for him, too. After all, unless Amber could "crack" the man's mind, Raphael would never look at his son with recognition. Willow had told Amber that when she came here a month or so ago, Raphael hadn't remembered her, nor basic details about his own life. What if Amber couldn't do what the agents needed her to?

The feel of an arm wrapping around her shoulder startled her out of her thoughts. She glanced over to find Edgar there, offering one of his strained smiles. "We're good, okay? Whatever happens is fine."

Amber could only nod. Edgar let her go. The loss of his warmth made her hug her purse close to her side instead. She and Edgar had left their duffel bags under the care of Silent Agent.

Upon closer inspection of the building, Amber saw that the towering stone walls of the manor weren't as grimy as she originally thought. The windows gleamed in the weak afternoon light. The place was well cared for. That fact made her feel a little better about Raphael being way out here all these years.

The front door of the manor was peaked at the top, reminiscent of a door on a medieval castle, and was coated in black lacquer paint. Agent Barker tested the latch of the heavy bronze lock, and with little effort, it popped open.

Amber followed Edgar and the agent into a small entryway boxed in on all four sides by wooden walls. The leftmost wall had a heavy Plexiglas window in the middle, behind which sat a woman in blue scrubs who had her attention focused on the countertop in front of her. The wall straight ahead had a metal door embedded in it that looked like its first life had been spent in a prison or dungeon. Amber guessed *that* door wasn't unlocked. A bench rested against the rightmost wall, and a painting of a meadow full of delicate yellow flowers hung above it. A bright blue house was out in the distance, and a red rocking chair sat on its rundown porch.

Agent Barker approached the Plexiglas window and the woman behind it hit a button to activate a hidden microphone and speaker system. Once the agent provided his necessary credentials, all three of them signed liability forms, and both Amber and Edgar were asked several questions each. After all that was done, a series of heavy clicks sounded from the metal door and a man in white scrubs stepped into the waiting area. The orderly gave them a run-through of protocols and rules. They were patted down to check for weapons, Amber's purse was rummaged through, and only after they'd verbally agreed they'd understood what would get them kicked out of here in a hot second, did the man let them through the metal door and into the facility.

Amber had transferred the spells she needed into a smaller notebook; one the orderly thankfully hadn't opened and leafed through.

She had hoped Aunt G would have a Penhallow-specific tincture for them to take before they left, but she still hadn't come up with a recipe that she deemed suitable. A phone call to Simon last night had revealed he hadn't had any luck yet either. Willow's clarity spell was still the best they had.

Despite the nearly claustrophobic waiting room and the rather extensive screening process, the facility itself, to Amber's relief, felt warm and inviting. The walls were painted a light blue, the floors were made of light-colored wood, and the room just outside the menacing door was full of plush, comfortable furniture. A hallway ran straight ahead into what looked like a dining area, the floor lined with a blue-and-white runner.

The orderly headed for a hallway to the left, made a right, and then headed up an enclosed staircase. He explained that the patients—who were called guests—stayed upstairs. Guests had a wide range of conditions. Some were patients with terminal illnesses who had stopped treatment and wanted to live out the rest of their days in a peaceful, resort-like setting. Some needed a place to recover from a relapse into alcohol abuse. Others, like Raphael Henbane, were in an almost vegetative state—clearly mentally impaired and unable to function in society. Almost every guest was wealthy or had wealthy families who paid for their time here.

The hallway on the second floor was lined with closed blue doors. Each one had a number hanging from the wood, and most had something decorative outside—either a doormat, a potted plant, or a statue. It felt like a high-end apartment hallway. And yet, Amber noted how many cameras dotted the ceiling. They seemed to be pointed in every possible direction. Though the orderly had assured them that the guests here had no "violent tendencies," the cameras positioned to capture every angle made it clear that security was a priority.

Amber imagined Willow wandering these hallways. Had it unnerved her, being in this place by herself?

Uncle Raph was in Room 9, at the end of the hall on the right-hand side. The only decoration outside his door was a plain brown doormat. It was a stark contrast to Edgar's black doormat, which had "There's No Reason For You To Be Here" written in a cheery red font.

A camera was directly above the door, pointed down. Another one was in the corner opposite, facing the door. Amber wondered if the rooms themselves had cameras, too. She supposed they must. Which could make conducting spells a bit difficult.

The orderly fished a walkie-talkie out of his pocket, hit a button, and said, "This is Johnson. I've arrived at Raphael's room."

A moment later, a click sounded from the door and the orderly let himself in. "Hi, Raphael," he called out. "Those visitors I told you about yesterday are here. You're so popular lately." He held the door open and ushered them inside.

Unit 9 was huge, but aside from the bathroom to the right of the door, Raphael's living space was one giant room—like a loft apartment in a high-rise city building. It was furnished tastefully but minimally; the colors matched the décor downstairs. A few long windows lined the back wall, the scene outside a wash of green pine trees and the blue sky beyond their tops. A hunched figure sat in a wooden chair in front of the windows. His hair was short, mostly gray, and sprinkled with strands of dark brown or black.

Edgar's hand snaked out and grabbed hold of Amber's forearm. She knew he needed something solid to hold onto.

"I'll be just outside if you need anything, Raphael, okay?" the orderly called out.

The shape that was Raphael made no movement to indicate he'd heard him.

"Excuse me…Johnson, was it? Could I ask you a few questions?" Agent Barker asked.

"Stanley is my first name, but everyone here calls me Johnson," the orderly said, then led the way back out.

The door closed on the start of their conversation. Edgar still had Amber's forearm clasped, so she didn't dare move yet. Instead, she scanned the room, her gaze flitting over everything from the mussed sheets on the bed, to his half-eaten bowl of oatmeal on his nightstand, to the packed bookshelves that rested against the wall next to her. A faint layer of dust on the top shelf told her he likely hadn't touched these books in some time. Her attention shifted back to his unmoving shape in the chair. How much of his day was spent sitting there? Even if this place was luxurious by most standards, and even if money was buying these "guests" comforts the average person couldn't hope to afford if they found themselves in similar mental and physical circumstances, this felt like such a sad and lonely way to live.

"D-dad?" Edgar finally managed, his voice cracking. He cleared his throat. "Dad, it's me. Edgar."

No reaction.

Amber took a small step forward, which got Edgar moving, too. As they crossed the room, Amber did another sweep of the wide space and found a camera perched in the corner above a window on the far right. It had a perfect view of Raphael in his chair. Amber wondered if they'd installed a camera there based on Raphael's habits.

Once they finally reached him, they stopped just behind his chair, both clearly nervous about what they'd see. Amber rounded the chair first and peered into a face that was both so familiar and foreign to her, it took her breath away. He was the spitting image of Edgar, just thirty pounds lighter and as many years older.

Edgar rounded Raphael's chair on the other side and let out a shaky breath as he took in his father's haggard appearance. Edgar squatted beside him, one hand tightly gripping the armrest. Raphael's elbows were tucked in by his sides, his hands resting limply in his lap. He wore plain gray sweats, a black T-shirt, and a woolen beige cardigan with a red leaping reindeer on either lapel. His unblinking eyes were still focused out the window.

"It's me, Dad," Edgar tried again. "Can you hear me?"

When he didn't immediately reply, Amber squatted as well, quickly glancing up to see if a camera sat on the wall here, too. No camera. There was a second one above the door that was pointed in this direction, but with Amber's back to the camera behind her, this position put the front half of her in the cameras' blind spots.

"Hi, Uncle Raph," Amber tried. "It's Amber Blackwood. Your niece."

Nothing. Raphael didn't even blink.

Edgar shot Amber a look across Raphael's lap that mirrored the hopelessness she felt. Willow had said that Raphael had talked to her. He'd denied knowing her, and that he'd ever had a sister. Had he slipped even further from reach since Willow was here?

"I don't know you," came a soft, gravelly voice, and Amber and Edgar's gazes both snapped up to Raphael's face. Amber swallowed down a lump in her throat when she found her uncle's brown eyes fixed on her. "You look a bit like that other girl. She said she was my niece, too." Then his head slowly swiveled to Edgar, who hunched into his shoulders as if the weight of his father's gaze were a physical thing pressing him into the floor. "I don't know you either. I don't have a son. I have no family."

"That's not true," Edgar said gently—far gentler than Amber could remember her cousin speaking in years. "You had a wife and a son. Mom's name was Kathleen. She passed away when I was a teenager. Your sister was

Annabelle. She was married to Theodore Blackwood and they had Amber and Willow, your nieces."

Raphael's head started to slowly shake back and forth as Edgar spoke. "You have me confused. You're wasting your time with an old man who means nothing to no one."

Edgar's jaw clenched. "You matter to *me*. I've been trying to find you for almost fourteen years, Dad."

Raphael had settled back into his original posture, his eyes focused out the window again. Seconds ticked by with no further movement.

"Do something," Edgar hissed at Amber. "Try your simplest memory spell first."

Amber's stomach churned. Memory retrieval was the easiest spell of its type. She simply used her magic to pull a person's most recent memory to the surface. Short-term memories were easy to grasp, and it didn't take much energy to snatch one from a person's mind. But the spell was any-thing but simple when memories had been removed in such a thorough way. Even all these years later, the memory wipe—or at the very least an extremely powerful memory burial—had been so extensive that nothing over the course of the last decade had triggered its reversal. What had been done to Uncle Raph's memory could be permanent. Cracking his mind would prove impossible if there was nothing left to crack. If he remembered Willow enough to know what she'd said, and that she and Amber looked alike, it at least meant his short-term memory was still intact.

All spells that involved the mind were tricky for any number of reasons. The recipient of the spell could throw the magic off course if his desire to keep his secrets to himself was strong enough—witch or not. A person's most recent memory could be right on the tip of his tongue, and then before the spell was complete, a bird could fly by, triggering another memory entirely.

And, as Amber had experienced with Henrietta, when someone's mind was in an altered state, what felt like a recent memory to the individual might not be linearly recent at all.

She sighed. Why did the Henbanes have to have a penchant for memory and time magic? The complexity of it made her head hurt.

Still, Amber closed her eyes and called on her magic when Edgar did nothing more than glare at her. First, she'd need to make sure her intention was pure.

I want to know Raphael's most recent memory to make sure his short-term memory is stable.

Her magic was even less responsive than Uncle Raph.

I want to test this simple spell on Uncle Raphael to help me figure out if I can do this at all. If I can't, I want Edgar to know now so he's not filled with false hope.

Her magic ignited, rising up in her like a swarm of butterflies startled into the air.

Then she mentally cast the incantation for the memory-retrieval spell. Moments before she finished, she opened her eyes, then wrapped her hand around one of Uncle Raph's thin wrists. Physical contact always made Amber's spells stronger. They both gasped.

A startling burst of images flicked through Amber's mind. It all happened so fast, it made her dizzy. The point-of-view of the flashes was like one of Edgar's first-person video games.

A leather-bound book with "Henbane" embossed on the cover. *Flash.* Men in dark suits shouting in her face. *Flash.* A twenty-something Edgar glowering at her. *Flash.* The door of Edgar's house slamming shut on a young, confused Edgar. *Flash.* An altercation between men in suits and an elderly couple. *Flash.*

The front of the Pleasant Meadows for a moment, and then a kind woman's face swinging into view. It was the same elderly woman from the flash of memory just before this one. She took Amber's face in her hands and murmured something, then kissed Amber on the forehead. The elderly man from the previous memory was there too, hovering behind, his brow pinched as he muttered to himself, clearly distressed.

Flash.

When the magic abruptly released its hold on her, Amber tumbled away and fell hard on her backside. Edgar was there in an instant, a hand on her elbow as he tried to help her to her feet. But she was too out of sorts to get up just yet. Her equilibrium was off, the world spinning. She was also trying to piece together what she'd seen.

All she knew for certain was that the elderly couple had been her grandparents, Ivy and Miles Henbane. Ivy had been kissing Raphael goodbye, not her. *They'd* been the ones who brought Raphael to Pleasant Meadows. If it hadn't been for the series of memories Amber had seen months ago—thanks to touching her father's watch found under the porch of 523 Ocicat Lane—she wouldn't have known who the couple was.

After a few moments, as her nausea abated and her heart rate slowed, Amber was able to think about the images a little more clearly. The men in suits hadn't been shouting at Amber. They'd been shouting at Raphael. Men in suits that bore a striking resemblance to people like Agents Howe, Barker, and Silent.

She cycled through the memory snippets once more.

Henbane grimoire. WBI. Fighting with Edgar. An argument between the WBI and Raphael's parents. Then Raphael's arrival at Pleasant Meadows with his memory either gone or buried.

Amber allowed herself to be helped to her feet and then she moved back to her uncle's side. He still sat in his chair facing the windows, but his eyes were wild and darting now. His chest heaved. "Uncle Raph?" she asked softly, gasping when his eyes locked on hers.

"She won't go away," he said. "She's always in here, whispering." He tapped his temple. "She says I have a sister who is a witch. She says I can do magic just like my sister but in order to unlock my powers, I have to find where they're hidden."

Amber pursed her lips. "Do you know who she is? The woman in your head?"

Raphael squinted one eye as if a sudden, terrible head-ache had just seized him. It was a pained expression she'd seen on Edgar's face too many times. Softly, he said, "She says I can't tell you. She says you want into my head so you can *steal* my magic. She says not to let you in. She says I should only let her in because she's the only one who cares about me."

Edgar was on Raphael's other side now and he grabbed hold of his father's hand with both of his own. "I have someone in my head, too. Is her last name Penhallow?"

Raphael groaned loudly and hunched forward, his head practically between his knees. He sounded like a wounded animal. "Yes," he ground out. After several long moments, he forced himself to sit up.

"Mine is a Penhallow, too," Edgar said. "They're targeting Henbanes. *You* are a Henbane, like me. Like your sister Annabelle."

Forehead creased, Raphael reached out with his free hand and cupped Edgar's face. It was such a sweet, intimate gesture, it startled Amber. It seemed to startle the two men even more. Raphael dropped his hand and he shook his head, as if he couldn't figure out why he'd felt compelled to touch this stranger as if he knew him.

"How do I know who to believe?" Raphael asked Edgar, then looked at Amber. He sounded like a confused little boy. "I've only just met you and she's been with me the whole time. If you're my family, why did it take you so long to find me?"

A strangled sound reverberated out of Edgar and he sniffed. "I've been trying, Dad. Honest. Someone didn't want you to be found."

Which begged the question: how had *Willow* found him when not even the WBI could?

Raphael let loose an agonized scream then and grabbed hold of his head on either side. He rocked back and forth, eyes screwed shut, while he begged "her" to shut up. "Stop, stop, stop! I don't have a sister!"

A loud buzz sounded, the door to the room flew open, and two orderlies—one of which was Stanley Johnson—hurried into the room.

"Back away!" the other orderly snapped and Amber and Edgar both jumped to their feet and took several steps back. "He's due for his medication and nap. If he's feeling better after dinner, you can come back then. If not, you'll have to try again tomorrow." He was directly in front of Raphael now, doing his best to talk him down.

"But—" Edgar started.

"We'll come back," someone said from the door. Agent Barker stood in the doorway, his hands in the pockets of his black slacks. His casual stance was the antithesis of the tension in the room.

A flash of the WBI memory went through Amber's head again. Two men in suits shouting at Raphael. The image of the Henbane spell book had come just before the one of the agents. Had the WBI tried to get Raphael to turn over the grimoire? Had *that* been what Raphael and Edgar had been arguing about? The books had been entrusted to Edgar on the same day Amber's parents eventually died in a fire. Amber's mother had put a spell on Edgar to force him to hide the books in a safe location and then promptly forget where he'd put them. Edgar couldn't have given up the grimoires' location to his father even if he'd wanted to.

Perhaps Raphael's grief over the death of his sister had made him consider the WBI's demand to turn over the books. Had the WBI threatened him or offered him something in exchange?

Damien and Devra were sure the WBI was a shady organization. *What did they offer you to get you to do some of their dirty work for them?* Damien had asked.

Johnson ushered Amber and Edgar to the door and assured them again that they could come back later if Raphael felt better. After casting a long, worried look at her uncle, Amber followed the men out the door. Edgar and Agent Barker fell into clipped, awkward conversation as they all walked back down the hallway, Johnson leading the way. Amber found herself unable to keep her eyes off the back of Agent Barker's head, her mind whirling.

When Amber's mother was in her twenties, she'd fallen in love with a man named Neil Winters. Amber's mother had been a prodigy of time spells since she'd been a young girl, and Neil had convinced her to craft a time-travel spell, just to see if she could do it. Annabelle had agreed for the sake of a good challenge, but once the thought-to-be-impossible spell had actually been written, Neil had revealed that he had been a Penhallow all along. Though Neil had claimed to love Amber's mother, he also admitted that he'd been assigned the mission of getting her to create the one spell Penhallows had been craving: a spell that would allow them to go back in time and stop the curse from ever infecting their clan. Neil had wanted Annabelle and himself to be a powerful witch couple who would unite the clans, once and for all. Annabelle had been horrified about not only being deceived by a man she'd loved, but having foolishly created a spell that, if used, could cause untold harm to the world at large.

Heartbroken, Annabelle had ended things with him on the spot.

But the desire for the spell couldn't keep him away for long. Soon Neil and his father attacked Annabelle and her own father, Miles, determined to go through them to get the spell if they wouldn't hand it over willingly. The elder Penhallow ended up dead, and Miles Henbane traveled into Neil's mind to bury the memories of Annabelle so deep they could never be found.

Yet they'd resurfaced eventually on their own, like a zombie bursting forth from its grave. And then Neil Penhallow, driven mad by grief, a broken heart, and cursed magic in his veins, had found Amber's parents despite all their efforts to stay hidden.

Miles Henbane had told his daughter that erasing Neil's memories of Annabelle and their time together would have been too complicated to complete under such a time crunch. Miles, in a pinch, had instead buried the memories. The entire Henbane family split off into four directions that night, never to return to their home of Delin Springs.

Amber followed Agent Barker and Edgar down the stairs.

The last image of the final memory snippet had been of Miles Henbane pacing behind his wife, muttering to himself in distress, as they presumably prepared to leave their last living child in this remote facility. But what if the muttering hadn't been distress from the emotionally charged situation, but from the physical strain of casting a complicated spell?

Had Miles Henbane taken away the memories of his own son, so that even if the WBI found him again, Raphael would be unable to tell them anything? Had Miles permanently wiped Raphael's mind clean?

If so, it meant Amber wouldn't be able to crack her uncle's memory no matter how hard she tried. Miles was a Henbane; his memory magic would have been much stronger than her own.

It also meant that the man they were traveling with was part of an organization that had scared her grandparents enough that they were willing to break their own child's mind to assure the grimoire was kept out of the WBI's possession. Perhaps Damien and Devra had been right to be leery of Amber's actions.

The buzz of the metal door jostled Amber out of her thoughts again. Johnson nodded to each of them in turn as they walked into the small claustrophobic waiting area.

"We'll be in touch," Agent Barker told Johnson. The agent waited at the other end of the waiting area, where he held the front door open. He smiled at Amber as she stepped past him.

Despite the warmth of the gesture, Amber shivered.

CHAPTER 18

The drive to the hotel where they'd be staying for the next two days was quiet. Agent Barker was clearly aware that something had happened in Room 9, but he was either biding his time before asking for details, or he just didn't want to do so in front of Silent Agent.

Amber's mind was abuzz. Edgar's leg bounced erratically and he chewed on his cuticles as he stared out the window. She needed to speak to Edgar alone. She also desperately wanted to talk to Willow.

The hotel was actually a rather seedy-looking roadside motel. It was a sprawling one-story facility, and the buildings were all a garish bright pink with mint green accents. A large sign at the entrance told Amber this was the Mermaid Inn. A busty mermaid adorned the sign's front.

"The WBI spares no expense, I see," Edgar said, with an air of distaste, as the SUV pulled into the mostly full lot. A few semis were parked down the road.

"It's best that we not call attention to ourselves," Agent Barker said. "Places like this get a lot of activity from travelers. No one stays here for long. It's a great place to go unnoticed."

After parking, Agent Barker instructed them to wait in the car with Silent Agent. Within a few minutes, Agent Barker was back with a pair of room keys. "You two can stay together in one room, and Windy and I will take the other."

Windy? Amber wanted to ask if that was his first or last name, but decided it was safer not to ask.

Agent Barker did a sweep of their room while they waited outside, then let them in when he deemed the coast clear. He handed the key to Amber. The wide black keychain was adorned with the same busty mermaid as the sign outside. "You two try to get some rest. I'll let you know if we're granted permission to go back. If so, we'll grab an early dinner together to discuss what you learned." It wasn't a question. "I'm sure it was emotionally taxing for you both to see Raphael again after all this time."

Without waiting for a reply, he nodded once, then stepped out, closing the door after him.

"What did you—" Edgar started immediately, but Amber cut him off with a finger to her lips.

She locked the door's two locks and latched the security chain in place. The room was a small, dingy thing whose colors were as garish as the ones on the exterior. Amber supposed they were going for a cheerful beach motif of some kind, but it mostly looked like the 1980s had gotten sick on too much candy and had thrown up everywhere.

Edgar sat on one of the two twin beds covered in mint green comforters, his duffel bag next to him. She tossed her own bag onto the other bed, marched forward, grabbed Edgar by the sleeve of his shirt, and kept moving, dragging him after her. She pulled him into the bathroom. While she flicked on the light, Edgar shut the door. A giant cockroach ran for cover behind the toilet.

Amber turned on both the shower and the sink, then cast a noise-canceling spell. Realizing what was happening, Edgar cast a second one to layer over hers. The sound of the water running in the bathroom abruptly disappeared.

Edgar crossed his arms. She ran through it all quickly, including her theory that the WBI had tried to get information out of Raphael about the grimoire and that their grandparents had been the ones who not only wiped Raphael's mind, but had checked him into Peaceful Meadows.

She pulled out her cell phone and called Willow.

"Hi, Amber!" She'd answered it so quickly, Amber wasn't sure it had rung. "How—"

"Is Agent Howe with you?" Amber asked.

"No, just me and Aunt G."

"Put me on speaker."

"So bossy," Willow said, but did as she asked. "What's going on?"

"Hi, little mouse."

"Tell us everything!" Willow said excitedly. "Have you seen him? Was he—"

"What made you go searching for Uncle Raph, Will?" Amber asked, cutting off her sister's cheerfulness at the knees.

"Uhh …" Willow said. "Well…I'd been having some problems with insomnia because of that really big project at work a month or so ago, you know? So when I couldn't sleep, I was doing a lot of thinking. I wanted to do something for Edgar since he's been helping us so much. I thought finding his dad would be nice."

Amber glanced over at Edgar, who was still staring off into space with his brows mashed together. He had a cuticle between his teeth again. "Right. I know that part. I mean…*how* did you find him? Peaceful Meadows is so remote."

"Scrying spells, mostly," Willow said. "I bought a bunch of maps. I started with the world, then went down to the United States, then scaled it down to Washington. I focused my magic through an old picture I had of Uncle Raph and Mom to pinpoint the location after that."

"I have a very small box of mementos of our family," Aunt G added. "I didn't know what she was up to when she asked if she could have the picture."

Amber had to assume the WBI had tried scrying, too. And likely had vessels for their magic that were more powerful than a photograph. "Was that it? Just scrying while channeling your energy through the picture?"

"Well, no. I found it in a roundabout way, I guess. I was trying sleep and dream spells at the same time," Willow said. "Meadows kept coming up in my dreams, so I worked that into my scrying, too. I was running out of ideas by then, so I ran with it, figuring my magic was out there in the world sniffing out clues while I slept. I eventually got a definite hit on a spot in the middle of the forest. I fussed around on Google Earth to find the exact location. The online listing I found said the place is a residence, so when I called the number, I expected it to be someone's house. They don't make it easy to find the place."

Amber chewed on the inside of her cheek.

"What's with the interrogation?" Willow finally asked.

Amber relayed it all again, ending with her theory that the WBI might not be trustworthy. "The agents said themselves that they had no idea where Uncle Raph was until Willow started poking around. How did Will find him that quickly when they have more resources than we do?"

"So…do you think they were lying and they knew where he was all this time," Aunt G said slowly, "or do you think that hint about meadows was somehow planted in Willow's head?"

"I don't know," Amber said. "Meadow is a very generic, broad clue. And when you think of meadows, you'd think of a state like Montana before you thought of Washington. But, Will, would you have found the place without that clue?"

"I mean, maybe eventually," Willow said. "But it would have taken a lot longer. In my dreams, it wasn't even the generic idea of meadows—it was almost exclusively the *same* meadow. Always a field of yellow wildflowers. And there was a little blue house in the distance."

Amber blinked rapidly. "Was there a red rocking chair on the porch?"

"Yes!" Willow said. "How'd you know that? It was the same meadow and house every time. I'm not sure why I dreamt of that image so often when the manor is surrounded by pine trees."

"You were seeing the framed picture on the wall in the waiting room of Peaceful Meadows," Amber said.

"Really?" Willow asked. "Weird. I don't remember seeing that when I was there. But maybe I wasn't paying close enough attention."

It could have been a new addition, Amber supposed. "Someone was helping you find the place. I just wish we knew who. And why."

For a couple of hours after they'd ended the call, Edgar took a nap. It didn't look like a particularly comfortable nap, as his brows were still pinched. He also slept with his arms and ankles crossed, as if he were a vampire in a coffin. Amber wondered if he always slept like that.

She texted with both Kim and Jack while she lay on her bed, semi-watching a Western kept on low volume on the boxy TV sitting on the set of low drawers against the wall. Kim and Jack had been called into the station to give their statements on what had happened on Kids Day, but neither had any idea what was happening beyond that.

Amber wondered what Agent Barker and Silent were doing in the next room. They shared the wall Amber was currently staring at. She assumed Silent was busy with another sudoku puzzle, but what was Agent Barker doing? And had he found out anything about the anonymous donor who had gotten Raphael into Pleasant Meadows?

Every day her thoughts grew more scattered, pulled in too many directions at once.

Her phone rang, startling her out of her staring contest with the wall beyond the screen where men on horseback raced across open plains. It was Betty Harris.

Amber's heart slammed into her throat. Betty rarely called her. Had something gone horribly wrong at The Quirky Whisker? She pictured her beloved shop in flames. Her hands shook so badly, she almost didn't answer the call in time. "Hi, Betty," she answered urgently, glancing over at her sleeping vampire cousin to make sure she hadn't woken him. "What's wrong?"

"Hi, sugar," she said. "Your aunt, sister, and cats are just fine. Take a deep breath."

Amber did so. "Sorry. Hi. I'm just a little high-strung lately. How are you?"

"I'm good," she said, but her tone was guarded now. "Are you alone?"

That made Amber sit up a little straighter. "Mostly. Why?"

"Is there a possibility that someone you wouldn't want to overhear you could be listening?" Betty asked.

It was a strange question for Betty to ask. Even stranger than her calling Amber in the first place.

Amber's gaze snapped up to the wall across from her. She imagined Agent Barker and Silent Agent on the other side, their ears pressed to the thin walls. She supposed that when Agent Barker made a sweep of the room earlier, he could have been layering the room in magical listening-bugs that had already revealed everything Amber and Edgar had discussed, regardless of their use of noise-canceling spells.

Even still, Amber quickly closed herself in the bathroom again. She turned on the water and mentally cast yet another spell to encase herself in a bubble of privacy. Swallowing hard, she asked, "What's going on, Betty?"

"I need you to know that I've never wanted to keep things from you," she said.

Amber's heart rate increased. "What are you talking about?"

"I know about you," Betty said, her voice hushed. Amber wondered where the woman was. Given how slammed Purrfectly Scrumptious had been, and now with the festival only a couple of days away, Amber couldn't imagine the woman finding much free time. "About you being a witch, I mean."

Amber's mouth went dry. Could this be a Penhallow *pretending* to be Betty? She hadn't had a chance to talk to Betty recently because of how busy she'd been, so they hadn't established a code word.

"I hear distrust in that silence," Betty said, and she lightly clucked her tongue.

Amber couldn't figure out what to say.

"Your favorite cupcake flavor is chocolate, but you're a new fan of the Oreo Cream Dream." It wasn't enough to convince Amber that this wasn't someone trying to deceive her. How in the *world* could Betty know her secret? "You're often up late at night and sit in that window seat of yours with Tom in your lap and Alley at your feet. When you were a kid, you and Willow would come to my shop on your bikes. You on a bright blue one with a white basket and Willow on a green one with a pink basket. On your birthdays, your dad would come in to get your favorite cakes. Chocolate Chocolate Surprise for you, red velvet for Willow, and German chocolate for your mom. When it was *his* birthday, all three of you would come in to get him cupcakes because he wanted—"

"A variety," Amber finished, laughing softly. "He didn't want to have to choose just one flavor so he got a little of everything."

"You girls would argue for half an hour on which ones you thought he'd want that year," Betty said, then fell silent for a moment. Amber frowned, sensing the impending change in tone, even before Betty spoke. "That first year after they died …" She clucked her tongue and Amber could imagine her sadly shaking her head. "I had all your birthdays marked on my calendar, you know. Still do. I remember Gretchen bringing you two in on Willow's sixteenth birthday. I swear it was like the light had gone out of all of you."

As much as Amber was touched by all this, she still couldn't wrap her mind around what Betty had said earlier.

"I don't know if you'd remember this, but back when you girls were really little—when you all first moved here to Edgehill—Bobby and I brought over cupcakes as a welcome gift," Betty said. "We try to do that for newcomers as much as we can. Plus, your parents had just moved into the new development and we wanted to see it. Shame that area never got finished. I guess the developers found it hard to sell off more houses in that area given what happened to yours ...

"Anyway," Betty continued, "your parents were having a barbeque that day and invited us to come eat with you. It's impossible for Bobby to turn down food, so we spent some time out back with you all. Bobby and your dad were manning the grill. You and Willow had been playing in the yard and Willow, who was just getting her walking legs, fell and scraped up her knee pretty bad. Your mom took her inside, leaving you with me. The men weren't paying any attention.

"You came over with a little cat toy and said you wanted to show me something. *One by one let's have some fun, two by two let's turn it blue*," Betty said, speaking the words a bit whimsically.

Amber's mouth dropped open. "I showed you that?"

"Oh yes," Betty said. "Then you told me I couldn't let anyone know you showed me since magic was a secret. I didn't believe it was magic at first, just a fancy toy your mom had gotten you. But when we came by again a few weeks later, you were playing alone on the porch. You told me that you and Willow had gotten into a fight and that you wanted to be alone, but you said it was okay if I stayed. You were playing with sidewalk chalk. I asked if you had any other tricks you could show me and you made the chalk draw a happy face without touching it."

Amber's face flushed. "Were you scared?"

"No, not really," Betty said. "I didn't know if it was only something you could do, or if it was a family trait. Before we left that day after lunch, your mother pulled me aside and said she saw you show me your trick. She said you didn't open up to too many people, even back then. I told her I knew you were special and that your secret was safe with me."

Amber's eyes welled up.

"When you eventually got The Quirky Whisker, I was so happy you'd found a way to keep using your magic," Betty said. "I could tell you *needed* to use yours. Willow wasn't—isn't—that way. It was a muscle you were always trying to flex even though it was clear your mother especially didn't want you to use it. I didn't know why your mother had that rule; it wasn't my place to ask."

Amber chewed on her bottom lip. She remembered something Betty had said to her after Chief Brown had so rudely broken the news to Amber that her close friend Melanie Cole had died.

I've known you since you and Willow were babies. I knew your parents quite well—God rest their souls—and you're one of the last people I'd ever think capable of such a thing.

Even when Amber had shut out almost everyone in Edgehill in the years after her parents' murders, Betty had been one of the constants in Amber's life. They didn't have surrogate family dinners or anything, but Betty had checked in on her over the years—which was more than most people had done. And more than Amber had *allowed* most people to do. They'd seen Amber as weird and reclusive and had left her alone.

Betty had been the one who had come over to gently encourage Amber to come to the potluck lunch in Balinese Park the day the town welcomed Chief Brown three years ago. Betty had been the first person to check up on Amber when news of Melanie's death swept through the town, concerned *for* Amber instead of being concerned about her.

It had been like having a grandparent across the street. A woman who cared enough to ask how she was doing and bring over sweets when she knew Amber needed a little comfort and a sympathetic ear. To think Betty had been that person for her since Amber was five or six blew her mind.

"A few days after your parents died," Betty said, pulling Amber back into the conversation, "I got a call from a woman named Ivy Henbane. She told me she'd been given instructions by her daughter, your mother, that if anything happened to Belle, that Ivy was to get in contact with me. Ivy told me that your parents trusted me completely. I suppose that was because I knew all your secrets and never even considered breaking that confidence. Ivy asked me to keep an eye on you and report back. When Janice took you on as her apprentice across the street, I put in a good word for you. It became even easier to watch over you when you were right across the street."

Amber's mind reeled.

"I call them as often as I can, but especially on your birthdays," Betty said. "I can't always update them on Willow's life, but I can tell them about things I hear indirectly."

Amber's mind slammed to a stop. "Wait. My grandparents are still alive?"

"Oh yes," Betty said. "I don't know all the details about these Penhallow people, but I know enough to know they're dangerous. Your grandparents don't want to risk being in contact with you if it means the Penhallows can either use you as leverage against them, or vice versa. Keeping their distance is the safest for everyone, but they worry about you girls."

Amber had always said Betty had the best gossip, the woman in town who always knew everyone's secrets. But Amber had never considered that Betty had even known *hers*.

"Please don't be upset with me for keeping all this from you, sugar," Betty said. "I promised them I would keep this all to myself. And I'm a woman of my word."

"So…why are you telling me now?" Amber asked. "Did something happen to them?"

"They're fine, they're fine," Betty said. "We've been in contact a lot more the past few months given everything that's been going on. It all sounded like magical happenings to me—the events in Edgehill, I mean—so I wanted them to know about it. When I told them I saw a pair of people in black suits talking to you outside your store a few days ago, they were nervous. When I saw that you left town with one of them at 4:00 AM today, and your family told me you were headed to Washington to visit family, I told your grandparents that too. They figured out you must have found your Uncle Raphael at Pleasant Meadows."

Amber was stunned into silence again.

"Their message to you is not to trust anything these WBI people are saying," Betty said. "Their best guess is that the WBI is telling you there's some key piece of information trapped in your uncle's head and they want you to find it."

"And that's not true?" Amber asked.

"Apparently your uncle has the same magical proclivities that your mother did," Betty said. "They told me to tell you something else. I wrote it down. I'll just read it to you because I don't really understand it." There was a faint rustling before Betty started talking again. "The WBI wants your uncle restored to his old self not to get information out of his head, but to send him back in time to the moment just before your mother created the spell. They want her stopped before she has a chance to write it. When Raphael left Edgehill, he was on his way to solidify a deal with the WBI. We don't know to what extent he was supposed to stop her. He was a very angry, bitter young man back then. They offered him a large sum of money to do this—more money than he'd ever make in his lifetime. He was devastated about the loss of his wife and his sister. He was angry about living so much of his life on the lam because of his sister's actions. He saw this as a way to not only get his sister and wife back, but a way to reset his life.

"We understood his pain, yet the effects of what he planned to do would change history in ways no one would be able to predict. You can't pull the rug out from underneath something as complex as time and not expect consequences. We had to stop him. So we buried his memories *and* his powers."

Amber stared blankly at the dirty white wall of the bathroom. The protective bubble around her felt claustrophobic even though she couldn't see it.

"Did that make sense to you, sugar?" Betty asked, the rustling resuming for a few moments. "I hope I got it all. I wrote it down while Miles dictated it. The paper's been in my back pocket all day. I've been waiting for a good time to call you. I'm sitting in my car in the back of the shop right now. I told Bobby I needed a lunch break by myself because I'm sick of people at the moment. Which isn't a lie, really."

Amber smiled faintly. "It all makes sense, yes. It's just a lot to take in."

"I thought it might be," Betty said. "But they were adamant I get the message to you as soon as I could. I hope I called you in time."

"Perfect timing," Amber assured her. "I was already fairly certain I couldn't trust the WBI. This confirms it. But now I need to figure out what to do."

"I wish I could help more, sugar," Betty said.

"You've helped so much already," Amber said. "And I promise I'm not upset you've been in contact with my grandparents and keeping it from me. My family keeps secrets with good reason."

Betty heaved a little breath, one of relief, Amber thought. "I'm honored they trust me enough with all this. It's felt like a big responsibility. I don't understand much of it and, frankly, I don't need to. I just like knowing I can help keep you girls safe now that your parents are gone, even if I'm just a regular ol' human."

"Oh, I don't know about that," Amber said. "You were the first person outside of my family who I trusted. I was only six years old and I knew you were a safe person to confide in. There's something special about you, Betty, even if it's got nothing to do with magic."

Betty sniffed. "Thank you, sugar. Stay safe and come back soon, okay? Edgehill isn't the same without you."

CHAPTER 19

After her phone call, Amber crept back into the motel room. Edgar was still asleep. She couldn't imagine waking him prematurely would go well, but she wanted to tell him about her conversation with Betty. She inched toward him and stood by his bed. Should she shake his shoulder? Poke his arm? Softly say his name? Leaning over him, she—

His eyes flew open and he roared. Amber screamed and fell backward onto her bed. Except the bed was on wheels for some inexplicable reason and the thing slid away from her. The bed hit the wall and Amber hit the floor. Edgar stood on top of his own bed now, crouched low. He hadn't stopped roaring. He thrust his hands out and Amber dove under the bed just before the blast of wind Edgar hurled her way lifted the bed off two of its wheels. It thudded back to the ground.

"Edgar!" Amber yelped from under the bed. She'd fret later about the horrific state of the threadbare carpet she lay on. "It's me!"

"Amber?" Edgar asked, breathless.

She crawled out from under the bed enough to look up at him.

His shoulders sagged and he jumped down from the bed, then sat on it. He ran a hand through his mussed hair. "What's *wrong* with you? Why were you hovering over me like a clown from my nightmares?"

Before she could answer, the door to the motel room blasted open despite being locked in three places. Amber yelped and scuttled back under the bed. Edgar let out another thundering battle cry, but it was cut off almost immediately. A sickening thud followed.

"What's going on in here?"

That was Agent Barker.

Amber crawled out of her hiding place just as Edgar popped up on the other side of his bed, rubbing his skull. Most of the sheets on the bed appeared to have joined him on his journey. He struggled to disentangle himself from them as he told Agent Barker in very colorful terms just what he thought of him.

Once Amber got to her feet, she found Silent Agent standing just outside of the doorway, his expression blank. Agent Barker, however, looked like an irate parent dealing with two rambunctious kids. Given the way his blond hair stuck up on one side, Amber figured the guy had been sleeping on the job when the commotion started.

"Edgar said I stole his gaming headphones," Amber said, giving the hem of her shirt a straightening tug. "I didn't, of course, because those things are huge and the attached microphone smells like old pizza."

"You *did* steal them," Edgar said, joining in effortlessly. He had just freed himself of his blankets with a kick of his foot. "She wanted to talk to her *precious* boyfriend and she can hear him better with headphones because her phone is a relic of the dinosaurs. Technology and Amber Blackwood absolutely do not mix. A few weeks ago when I was staying with her? She threw away one of my controllers 'on accident,' and stepped on one of my keyboards. Smashed it to heck and back with those clodding feet of hers."

Amber whirled on him. She had done neither of those things. "It's not my fault you left it on the floor, you slob!"

"How *dare* you—" Edgar bellowed, starting for her.

"All right, all right!" Agent Barker snapped. "Putting you two in the same room was apparently a mistake. Do you two always fight like this?"

"Always," Amber and Edgar said in unison.

Agent Barker rubbed his temples. "Well—"

He was caught off guard by the sound of his phone ringing. He snatched it off the holder at his belt and answered it. After a few seconds, he shot a pointed look at Amber and Edgar, raised a finger to signal that they needed to wait there, and then Agent Barker stepped out of the room, phone pressed to his ear. Silent Agent remained standing there watching them from the cement walkway outside. He hadn't moved an inch. Perhaps his mind wasn't on the events at hand, but various number combinations.

"Which one of us do you think is going to get stuck with the mute one?" Edgar whispered, suddenly right next to her. They stood in the middle of the room, staring out the open motel door at Silent. They were far enough away that Silent couldn't hear them, but a guy as quiet as him likely had next-level lipreading skills. "What's his name again? Windy? He's a silent wind …"

Amber snorted and clapped a hand over her mouth for a moment. "Behave!" she hissed at him.

No matter which agent she got stuck with overnight, she couldn't imagine she'd sleep. If Edgar slept like a vampire in a coffin, Silent probably slept like a coat rack—upright and in a corner. She shuddered.

Agent Barker ended his call and headed their way. "All right," he said when he reached the doorway. "Raphael is asking for his son and niece to come back. Something in his memory has been shaken loose. Let's go grab some food, discuss your strategy, then head back over."

They were only given ten minutes to straighten up the room, and themselves, before they were out the door again.

After piling back into the SUV with Silent behind the wheel, Agent Barker struck up a conversation with Edgar about *Undead Carnage*, Edgar's current game of choice. There were few things that could get Edgar going more than his nerdy habits. As Edgar launched into an animated explanation of the various zombie mutations—including ones that evolved to open doors and read signs—Amber's mind drifted.

During this dinner, she would need to give Agent Barker enough information to make him believe they were doing everything in their power to complete the task at hand, while not giving away the fact that the Blackwood/Henbane mission was now running in complete opposition to the WBI-assigned one.

They arrived at a chain-restaurant diner. While the line outside was short, the inside was swarmed with people. It was busy, noisy, a little dingy, and full of strangers. As the no doubt strange-looking foursome stood in the lobby by the "Please wait to be seated!" sign, a haggard-looking waitress bustled by. A few strands of her brown hair had slipped loose from her messy bun, her white apron was splattered with red and brown stains, and her expression was murderous. "I'll be right with you," she practically shouted, the smile she tacked on doing nothing to soften her demeanor. "Malory! What did I tell you about table 7? Your keister will be jobless by midnight if you don't get your act together!"

Amber missed Edgehill desperately in that moment.

The food was better than the service, but the bar was low. Through most of the meal, Agent Barker had been as silent as Windy. He chewed his chicken fried steak with methodical slowness as he kept an eye on Amber and Edgar across from him. Amber thought perhaps Agent Barker was just intrigued by the amount of syrup Edgar had soaked his blueberry pancakes in.

When the din of the diner suddenly disappeared while she'd been swiping a soggy fry through ketchup, her head snapped up and she found Agent Barker staring squarely at her, his arms folded on the table. She swallowed.

"So why don't we start with what happened with Raphael today," he said. "The orderly I spoke to said this was the most lucid the man has been in years. I had my doubts about you, Amber, but it really does seem like the apple didn't fall far from the tree."

Amber was fairly certain she should be offended. "We just talked to him for a while. Told him who we were. Like you thought, seeing Edgar had more of an effect on him than I did. There was a moment he reached out and touched Edgar's face—like for just a moment he might have recognized him?"

Agent Barker and Silent Agent shared an excited look. Well, Agent Barker looked excited.

"As far as magic went, I did a very simple memory-retrieval spell," Amber said, willing her voice to stay steady, as she'd now reached the point where she started lying—to the WBI. "He really only remembered what he had for breakfast. My guess is that he spends most of his time staring out that window, so a little mental stimulus probably went a long way."

Agent Barker seemed pleased by this answer. "Okay, so this time, see if you can go a little deeper." He turned to Edgar. "What's one of your last memories of your father?"

Amber felt him tense beside her. "The day he left, we'd had a really good day, actually. He made us sandwiches and we ate them on the porch. We each had a beer. He said he had some errands to run, that he loved me, and would see me soon. He never came back."

She knew the memory snippet she'd seen of the two Henbane men shouting at each other had been one of the last interactions they'd had. It had been a day filled with angst, not a peaceful lunch.

Agent Barker didn't question this. "Good. Let's see if you can get *that* memory to the fore for him, Amber. Starting with a pleasant memory might help ease him into coming back to himself. If things get dicey, as mind-magic often does, pull out of it immediately so he doesn't get so agitated that the orderlies kick us out. Our window of time to get what we need from Raphael is closing quickly. The Here and Meow Festival is two days away. We've got tonight and tomorrow—that's it."

If what Betty had relayed to Amber was true, it meant that the WBI effectively viewed Raphael as a weapon they hoped to get on their side and use against the Penhallows. Assuming there was even a way to restore her uncle to his past self, could she do so without alerting the WBI to what she'd done? If she were successful, would the WBI immediately whisk her uncle away to do their bidding? Would they leave Amber and Edgehill high and dry on the eve of the festival if they got what they wanted with Raphael?

Agent Barker was still in the process of tracking down the anonymous donor who had gotten Raphael checked into the facility. The WBI was under the impression that her grandparents were dead, and that they'd died before Raphael had been checked in there, so they likely weren't looking into them as a possibility. Ghosts, after all, were rarely able to donate funds.

Half an hour later, they were back in the SUV and headed for Pleasant Meadows. As the car crested the small hill toward the manor, the sun was low in the sky, painting wispy clouds with a bright orange and pink reminder that their first day here was almost over.

As she stepped over the threshold of the prison-like door, she looked over her shoulder at the framed painting of the meadow filled with yellow wildflowers, and the bright blue house in the distance. Who had seen this and shared it with Willow? A WBI agent who wanted to plant the idea in her head to nudge her in the right direction? A Penhallow with the same agenda? Raphael himself?

Once they were back in Raphael's room—with Agent Barker off to scrounge up information from the orderlies—Amber and Edgar stood staring at the man seated in front of the window. They each rounded a side of Raphael's chair and squatted beside it. His posture was the same—his elbows by his sides and his hands resting limply in his lap—but there was a clarity in his expression now.

"Hi, Dad," Edgar said.

Raphael looked over at him. It took him a moment to say, "It's like your name is on the tip of my tongue. I don't recognize you, but I recognize that I should. Does that make any sense?"

"Yes," Edgar said shakily. "Is the voice still there?"

"The woman?" Raphael asked. "Yes. She's more familiar to me than you are, but now that feels wrong. She doesn't like this turn of events, I can tell you that much."

"Can you tell us her name?" Amber asked.

"Patrice," he said, then immediately pitched forward, head in his hands.

Amber bit down on her bottom lip. If the orderlies watching the cameras thought Amber and Edgar were causing their guest too much distress, they'd likely intervene. "Uncle Raphael," she said, her voice firm but her hand gentle on his back. "I need you to tell Patrice to leave you alone. They're watching. You need to make her stop. Sit up straight again or they'll ask us to leave."

Slowly, letting out an agonized groan through his teeth, Raphael sat up while still clutching his skull. As his fingers relaxed, his hands came away from his temples. His eyes, however, were still screwed shut, and his mouth and eyebrows were bunched.

"She won't be quiet," he ground out. "She's trying to tell me something. To show me something …"

"I can help you find ways to deal with her," Edgar said. "Do you know where Patrice is? Physically in the world, I mean."

"Wait. It's starting to come into focus now." Raphael gripped the armrests, his chin tucked against his shoulder. "She doesn't want me to tell you where she is. She says you'll betray me just like my …" He stilled. "Like my parents did."

"They didn't betray you," Amber said. "They made a decision they thought would keep you safe."

Edgar cocked his head at her. This was the part she hadn't been able to share with him yet. Their grandparents had decided that Raphael was not only a danger to himself and his family, but to time and history itself, so they'd stripped him down to a shell and locked him away in this remote location where not even the paranormal government could find him.

Raphael's eyes snapped open and he whirled toward her. Complete lucidity took him over. The glare he aimed her way was all Henbane. "Keep me *safe*? They took my choices away. Them *and* Annabelle. My sister the golden child made the world's biggest mistake and the whole family gets punished for it? We all had to go into hiding because she was stupid enough to fall for a Penhallow's lies. The WBI gave me a chance to have my life back and *my own parents* snatched it away from me."

"If you'd gone back in time to stop my mother, who knows what this future would look like now," Amber said, her own anger mounting. "I might not exist. Your son might not exist. The Penhallows might have found another path to the spell. Maybe—"

"Might, might, might …" Raphael said. "You don't know what would have happened. It's easy to justify that what you all did was the best option for the greater good when there's no way to know it's *actually* better."

"Dad …" Edgar tried.

Raphael quickly got to his feet, spinning around so his back faced the windows. "Patrice showed me the truth. Showed me that my parents betrayed me. You'll betray me too. Once you get whatever you think is up here—" he tapped his temple hard three times, "you'll rip it all away from me again and stick me back in the prison of my own body and mind. Everyone always says the Penhallows are the enemy, but your enemy's goals line up with your government's. The WBI and the Penhallows want the same thing. What do you think will happen when I tell that agent friend of yours that you know more than you're telling him, huh? What'll happen then?"

Amber didn't know what to do. Her uncle's mind had been poisoned for years by Patrice Penhallow, grooming him to reject his own family when the time came. But why?

The WBI and the Penhallows want the same thing.

The Penhallows wanted to use Raphael as a weapon, too? To what end?

Apparently your uncle has the same magical proclivities that your mother did, Betty had said.

The WBI wanted Raphael to go back in time to stop the spell from being written. But the Penhallows still wanted the spell; they didn't want to intervene to stop its creation. What if the Penhallows wanted to go back in time to immediately steal the spell from Annabelle before she'd had a chance to hide it?

It was true that the WBI and the Penhallows wanted the same thing—the time-travel spell. But Amber was willing to bet that neither group actually cared what happened to Raphael once they had what they wanted. He was a weapon for them both, but a disposable one.

Amber lurched forward and grabbed hold of Raphael's forearm. Her magic rose up like a tide at the contact. She didn't have time to perfect her intention; she needed her magic to cooperate, dang it. She pulled up her memories of Edgar. The teenage boy who had never really been a chatty happy-go-lucky kid, but had a lightness to him that was almost entirely gone now. She pushed those memories at her uncle, like they were photographs pushed toward him on a table—physical things he could pick up and hold.

Then came the memories of Edgar during the years after Raphael's disappearance. Edgar going from sad and lonely to furious and antisocial. Edgar disheveled, broken, and lost.

She flipped a page in her mental photo album and shoved snapshots toward her uncle of Edgar venturing out of the house in the last few months, of him doing his best to meet her for breakfast in town on the weekends, and of Edgar and Kim on the dance floor at the Hair Ball. Edgar didn't look particularly happy in any of the most recent memories, but he looked better.

Then she showed her uncle the expression Edgar had worn when he'd seen his father for the first time in years—a memory not more than a few hours old. A bit of that outer shell of hardened anger had chipped away in that moment. A bit of his old light had shown through.

This is your son, she willed him to understand. *He's never stopped missing you, even if he didn't know where you were. Even if your parents betrayed your trust, your son didn't.*

Her magic released its hold and she stumbled away from her uncle. Head woozy, Amber placed a hand on the chair's back to steady herself. Her mouth felt parched, her energy drained. It was a familiar feeling. When Edgar had first started training her on being a better witch, spells zapped her of her energy more often than not.

Edgar quickly darted away, and Amber wondered at first if he was going to flag down an orderly for her, but he came back with a glass of water he'd filled in the bathroom. He handed it to her.

As she quickly drank down the water, she eyed her uncle who sat slumped on the windowsill, the heel of his hand pressed against the middle of his forehead. She didn't know if what she'd shown him would make a difference. Maybe he was too far gone.

He was a very angry, bitter young man back then, her grandparents had told Betty.

That angry, bitter man was still in there. Even if Amber were to heal his mind, how much of that anger would come with his powers?

Edgar stood beside her, his arm flush with hers, as they watched Raphael. The unblinking eyes of the two cameras were boring holes into the sides of her head.

Slowly, Raphael lowered his hand from his face and used it to grip the windowsill. He looked up at Amber. It felt like eons passed in silence. Raphael's expression was as unreadable as Silent Agent's. Any number of things could be going through the man's head—one of which could be more lies fed to him by Patrice Penhallow.

A buzz sounded and the door swung open. Neither Amber nor Edgar turned to see who had arrived.

Raphael didn't seem to notice they had a visitor. As his gaze shifted to Edgar, Amber sagged a little in relief. Being under the intense scrutiny of a Henbane wasn't for the faint of heart.

Finally, his voice a little gravelly, Raphael asked, "What is the name of your Penhallow?"

"Neil," Edgar said.

"Patrice has spoken of him," Raphael said. "I can't remember it all, but my gut tells me I hate Neil Penhallow."

Edgar grabbed hold of Amber's forearm again.

Raphael stood, no longer slouching on the windowsill. He still looked a bit unsteady on his feet, but the determination that came over his features made up for it. His intense gaze swung back to Amber. "I want to remember. Can you help me?"

"She sure as heck is going to try."

Agent Barker stood in the doorway, his smile wide and triumphant. "We'll start in earnest tomorrow morning, Raphael. Get some rest. Tomorrow is a big day!" His eyes slid over to Amber. "We're one step closer. With your skills and my help, we're going to change the course of history."

Which was exactly what she was afraid of.

CHAPTER 20

Back at the Mermaid Inn, all four of them holed up in Amber and Edgar's motel room. Agent Barker must have had a grimoire like any other witch, but he either didn't have one with him, or agents weren't allowed to share their grimoires with civilians. Amber could only imagine the kind of spells Agent Barker and Silent had on hand as members of the WBI.

Silent Agent remained in a chair by the door for the hours-long planning session, busy at work on his sudoku puzzles. He would throw out suggestions on occasion though, so he was clearly paying attention even when he pretended he wasn't.

He was a lot like a cat in that way.

"Doesn't the WBI have some high-level memory spell we could use?" Edgar asked in frustration sometime around hour three.

"A) Don't you think we would have tried that already?" Agent Barker asked, tossing his pen onto the pad of paper he'd been scratching ideas onto and running a hand through his short blond hair. He sat on the end of Amber's bed, one leg bent on the comforter and his other foot on the floor. He'd taken off his suit coat by then, had unbuttoned his white collared shirt, and had his long sleeves rolled up to his elbows. The more casual air had helped Amber feel more comfortable being in a closed space with him. She knew she couldn't trust the WBI as an organization, but the jury was still out on the integrity of individual agents. "And B," he said, "memory and time magic use are highly restricted—especially in the WBI—largely because of Annabelle's spell. Its mere existence threw so many things into question that even dabbling in it can get you into serious trouble. As it is, very few witches can do time and memory magic at all. It was why Annabelle was always such a fascination to people. She was rare because she could do magic like that at all, and then to be a prodigy at it was extraordinary."

Amber recalled something Simon had said to her. Growing up, since his hometown was near Delin Springs, he'd heard about her mother often. *The rumors about your mother being a prodigy with time spells was like hearing a fourteen-year-old just graduated from Harvard with a degree in quantum physics. It wasn't—still isn't—anything most of us were capable of, so a lot of us from that area started to see her as an almost mythical creature.*

Her mother the unicorn.

"Then why are the Penhallows trying so hard to get the spell?" Amber asked after a moment, curious if Agent Barker would ever admit that both the WBI and the Penhallows saw her uncle as the most viable caster of the spell. "Even if they get their hands on it, could any of them *do* the spell?"

Agent Barker pursed his lips, clearly mulling over the best way to answer that. "It's believed that Penhallows and Henbanes have intermingled over the years, so there are at least a few candidates who have the skill set necessary to attempt the spell once they have it. It's unlikely they'd pursue the spell for this long if they didn't have someone in their ranks who they believed could pull it off."

Amber didn't need a truth spell to know that was a diplomatic answer laced with lies. Yet she nodded. "That makes sense."

"I think you were right earlier, Edgar," Agent Barker said, returning the conversation to the task at hand. "Since magic is such a defining trait of a witch, reminding him of his powers might be an even more effective way to get his memories back."

"I know we only have a day left to do this," Amber said, "but I wonder if these really complicated memory-transfer spells are…*too* complicated?"

Agent Barker looked down at the pad of paper in front of him and frowned. He'd been taking notes on every significant date they could think of that might hold a strong memory for Raphael to latch onto. Annabelle and Theodore's wedding, where Edgar was the ring bearer. Edgar's first time riding a bike without training wheels. The time Amber and Edgar had been tasked with looking after Willow while Raphael and Annabelle had been busy with something in the parlor. "Busy" in those days usually meant a screaming match between the siblings before Annabelle stormed off with Amber and Willow in tow, leaving a sad, lonely Edgar behind.

Willow had gotten her head caught in the banister upstairs, and Edgar and Amber had panicked, sure they were going to get torn new ones for letting something like this happen on their watch. They'd tried to get her unstuck using both a tub of mayonnaise and the limited magic Edgar knew how to use. Yet, whatever he'd tried had unexpectedly turned the banister stakes into rubber. Willow had screamed as she slipped through the bars and went careening to the floor. Annabelle and Raphael had come running at the sound of three shrieking children and had used twin bursts of wind to save Willow from falling headfirst onto the hardwood floor.

"What are you thinking of as an alternative?" Agent Barker asked. "I realize that transplanted memories might get rejected just as transplanted organs might, but we don't know how many holes there are. Plugging them up and filling them in might be our only option, depending on how extensive the damage to his mind is."

Amber was exhausted and it felt like they'd been rehashing the same ideas for hours. "His memories are on the tip of his tongue. Even he said that. Memory transfers and transplants would make more sense if his memories were *gone*."

Edgar and Agent Barker both cocked a brow at her.

"Meaning they *aren't* gone?" Agent Barker asked her.

Her face heated. Amber still hadn't told Edgar what she'd learned from Betty. She mentally thunked herself in the forehead, then made a show of rubbing her eyes and stretching. "I guess I'm hoping for the easiest solution because I'm so tired. I'm not the most advanced witch. This much magic use is really wearing me out."

Agent Barker nodded at this. "You are indeed a novice. It's no wonder you're tapped out. We can revisit all this in the morning. Get some sleep, you two."

Amber held her tongue as she watched the two agents collect their things and leave the room. Once they were gone, Amber slunk down against her pillows. She *was* tired.

She wished she had the Henbane grimoire so she could study the magic-severing spell her mother had crafted. The same spell Amber had used to cure Kieran of his curse. What they needed now was the exact opposite of that spell—a magic-reattaching spell. If Amber had her mother's grimoire in front of her, she could work backward to create something of use.

But she was also glad that once she and her family had realized the extent of what was in the Henbane book, they'd shut both grimoires and layered them in cloaking spells. Penhallows had likely been sniffing around Edgehill for months now. If Amber had given into the temptation to open the Henbane grimoire, even for a few moments to take a picture of the spell she needed, that alone might have given away their hiding place.

Deep down, Amber knew the Henbane book was safer out of anyone's hands—even hers.

A flash of white appeared in her peripheral vision, and a moment later, a small paper airplane landed in her lap. Her cousin sat on his bed, legs crossed, and stared at her expectantly.

She unfolded the note.

What aren't you telling me this time?

She grabbed the pen off her grimoire. Our grandparents are still alive and they're the ones who checked your dad in. They didn't erase his memories. They buried them along with his magic.

She sent the paper airplane back. Edgar didn't write back, just stared at the note for a long time. Then he tore it up into tiny pieces and flushed them down the toilet.

What felt like hours later, Edgar interrupted Amber's staring contest with a reddish-brown stain on the ceiling. His tone was thoughtful, missing his usual biting edge. "I can't really remember that last day I had with him. You'd think it would be clear as day. But I blocked out so much of my twenties."

Amber rolled onto her side, her head propped on her hand. He lay flat on his back, his hands by his sides, and his dark eyes focused on nothing in particular. She anticipated his question before he asked it. "Do you want me to try to find it for you?"

Without looking at her, he shrugged. Which meant he very much wanted her to but couldn't bring himself to admit it. Amber climbed off her bed and sat on his. He scooted over a fraction, still keeping his attention on anything but her.

"I can't promise it'll work," she said.

He nodded.

Recalling how this had worked with Zelda when she had shown Amber her memory of 1971, Amber said, "Think of every little detail of that day…what you were wearing, what the weather was like, anything Uncle Raph had said to you."

She gave him a couple of minutes. When he suddenly squeezed his eyes shut, she took that as her cue. She mentally cast the memory-retrieval spell, let out a slow, steady breath, and placed her hand on Edgar's forearm.

A white light tore through her vision.

When the light faded, she found herself standing on Edgar's doorstep, but the mat here was a plain brown one. The paint on the house was a soft baby blue, and the wooden floorboards were clean, strong, and had nary a weed poking between them. Amber had forgotten how nice the house had been before Edgar had been left to his own devices.

The door to the house was open, revealing a cluttered but overall tidy foyer. Sunlight streamed into the house from the windows above the staircase to Amber's left. Her awe at her surroundings was interrupted by the sight of a younger Raphael Henbane walking her way. He had robust dark locks, dark bushy brows, and a scowl marring his face. If it weren't for the fact that Amber was aware that this memory was Edgar's, she would have thought she was looking at her cousin.

"Dad …" Amber said in a voice that wasn't hers. "Can you at least tell me who these people are and what they want?"

"The less you know, the better, E," Raphael said as he stepped over the threshold and playfully ruffled Edgar's hair. He jangled his car keys off one finger and the first hint of a smile graced his face. "No one believes me, but I know this is what we need to turn our lives around. These people can help. I only have to be gone for a little bit and when I get back, everything will be better, I promise. Not everyone gets the chance to start over."

Edgar, his voice strained, asked, "Are you doing this because I can't remember where it is?"

The hint of the smile was gone and Raphael clamped a hand over his once-jangling keys. "Belle never should have put you in this position in the first place. That blast could have killed you. Now you're…different. It's not your fault. It's mine. I never should have moved us here. She warned me. I was an idiot to think I could change her mind." He grunted, his head tipped back to the roof of the patio for a moment while he collected himself. "It was always about her. Always. Even when we were kids. Now she's even screwing up my life from the grave."

"*Dad* …" Edgar said. "You can't mean that."

"I do, E," Raphael said, his jaw set. "Now that she's gone, I can make decisions about *my* life. I'm doing this for you as much as myself. I can get…this—" he gestured to Edgar's entire person, "reversed. All of it. I can fix it all. Just wait for me here, okay? I'll be back before you know it." He started to walk backward, offering his son a salute.

A mounting worry filled Amber's chest then. An ache she recognized as grief, as one of loss. Some part of Edgar had known then that his father wouldn't come back. Whether he thought Raphael was lying to him and didn't actually plan to return, or if Edgar knew his father was in danger, Amber couldn't be sure.

"Don't go!" Edgar said, taking a few steps forward. "You're all I've got left. Doesn't that matter to you?"

"Not as much as fixing this," he said. "Not as much as unraveling all of my sister's mistakes."

"Screw you, then!" Edgar snapped. "I'm practically on my own even when you're here anyway." He turned and stormed toward the house, but he was whipped around. Raphael's face swung back into view, his finger pointed in Edgar's face as his father yelled something about respect. Edgar shoved him, then ran inside and slammed the door in his face. Edgar rested his head against the door.

Don't fret, came a whole other voice. It was *in* Amber's—no, Edgar's—head. It seemed to come from everywhere at once.

"Go away," Edgar growled.

I'm afraid it's too late to make that request, friend, the voice said. *I do suspect it'll just be me and you now.*

Neil, Amber realized.

Oh. Tsk, tsk. You're not supposed to be here, Amber.

Before she could react, she was airborne.

Her startled yelp was cut off when she hit her bed again, sending it sliding several inches on its wheels before it thudded into the wall. She slipped to the floor, her legs stuck out in front of her and her back against the side of the bed. She imagined she looked like a discarded doll.

Edgar was by her side in an instant. "Dang. Are you okay? What happened?"

Amber winced, rubbing her head. "Neil kicked me out. Sort of literally."

"He's a jerk," Edgar said, nodding. A noise-canceling bubble slammed down around them. "What'd you see?"

She recalled the memory as he helped her to her feet. Her head spun. "It's all true. The WBI made him an offer on how to fix it. I honestly think he planned to come back to you. Well, you know, assuming altering time didn't eliminate your existence."

Edgar chuckled darkly as they both sat on the side of her askew bed.

"They told us Uncle Raph had been on an unknown mission when he was attacked by a Penhallow," Amber said. "But it was *their* mission. They've known this whole time what Uncle Raph had been planning to do and they didn't tell us."

"Because they want my dad restored so he can finish what he agreed to do fourteen years ago," Edgar said, sighing.

"I just don't know if they really think a Penhallow intervened," Amber said. "Agent Barker says our grandparents are dead…but who knows if he was lying about that, too."

"You know, in a different life, I think Agent Barker and I could have been friends. But in this one?" Edgar shook his head.

They were quiet for a moment, sitting side by side on Amber's bed. She cleared her throat. "I want to help Uncle Raph, I honestly do. And I know he's your dad but—"

"But it's hard to know whose side he'll be on when he gets his memories back," Edgar said slowly. "Theirs or ours."

"Yeah …" Amber said. "I would hope time and introspection would change his mind, but he's had Patrice in his head for who knows how long. Other than the orderlies, Patrice has been his closest friend for years. He could be even angrier and more determined to go through with this now than he was then."

"Do we abort?" Edgar asked suddenly, turning to study her face. "Can we wait until the middle of the night and just duck out of here?" He winced then, heel of his palm pressed between his eyes. "Neil hates that plan." Edgar fought it as long as he could, but then screwed his eyes shut, grabbed his hair at the temples, and stuck his head between his knees. He let out a roar that was equal parts frustration and heartbreak.

Amber's throat felt tight. She hated seeing him like this, unable to help him. She placed a hand on his bent back, but he bucked away from her touch as if it had scalded him. "We'll stay, okay!" she practically shouted. "We'll stay, Neil! Leave him alone!" She didn't know if Neil could hear her as if he was on the other end of a phone line and Edgar was the mouthpiece.

After a few moments, Edgar settled a little. The roaring had stopped. He let out a shaky breath and slowly sat up. Releasing the hold he had on his hair, he swiped a hand under his nose.

"Edgar, I—"

The noise-canceling bubble abruptly dropped and Edgar stood. His eyes were lined in silver now. He looked so impossibly tired, like that ordeal—like the last two days especially—had shaved years off his life. "I'm going to take a shower." He walked away without looking back, grabbing his bag off the floor in the corner as he went. She wondered if his inevitable tears started the moment he closed the door, or if he would save them until he was under the spray from the shower.

She listened for the sound of the water turning on, and shower curtain rings sliding along the rail, before she let her own tears fall.

Legendary witch? he asked, but it came out almost like a purr, as if he were sharing a quiet, intimate secret. *How can someone as ordinary as you be legendary? You're going to screw it all up, you know. Best to quit now and leave the rest up to fate.*

Amber's eyes shot open.

It took her a moment to reorient herself. She lay on top of the mint green comforter in the Mermaid Inn. The room was dark. She pushed herself up, half expecting to hear that voice again—Neil's voice. But the memory of it faded along with the rest of the dream. Edgar was under the comforter on the other bed. He wasn't in his vampire pose this time, but the fetal position. Amber wasn't sure that was any better.

Tapping the screen of her cell phone on the nightstand revealed that it was just after midnight. A text from Jack had come in ten minutes before.

I'll be awake for a while if a nightmare wakes you up.

The simple message made her eyes well up again. When she called, he answered immediately.

"Hey," he said. "You okay?"

"I would have expected you to be asleep by now, old man," she whispered.

He laughed.

Edgar groaned a little and shifted under the comforter.

"One sec," she said, and eased off the bed. Since she'd fallen asleep in her clothes, she only needed to slip on her shoes. Unlocking the motel room door, she peered outside. The parking lot was quiet, the air cool. Craning her head to the left, she double-checked that Silent Agent wasn't lurking anywhere, then she crept out onto the side-walk, gently closing the door behind her. The lot had at least twenty cars in it, but she didn't see any people other than the figure of a man on the other end near the motel entrance. He leaned against the wall smoking a cigarette while he talked on the phone, if the rectangle of blue light was any indication.

"Okay, hi."

"Hi," Jack said. "What's going on over there?"

She gave him a brief rundown of it all. "I hate that I can't help Edgar. The reason he's suffered with this for so long is *my* family's fault. He's been through so much already."

"I don't know him that well," Jack said, "but I don't think anyone can make Edgar do anything. He wouldn't be there if he didn't want to be. Which means he doesn't blame you for any of this."

She knew Jack was right. Edgar had told her as much. But the guilt was eating away at her. That, and her crushing self-doubt. Her greatest fears about everything had manifested through Neil's voice—the voice of the man who had killed her parents.

"What else is bothering you?" he asked.

She sighed, then tried to explain her mounting worries. Once she got started, she couldn't stop. She told him that she blamed herself not only for Edgar's condition, but for Melanie's death. If she had been honest with Melanie about her abilities, maybe Melanie would have come clean about the affair she'd been having with Derrick Sadler. Maybe Amber could have recognized Susie Paulson's and Whitney Sadler's odd behavior for what it was before Melanie was poisoned. Maybe she could have saved her.

She blamed herself for Wilma Bennett's death—the maid who had been killed as collateral damage by Kieran. He'd wanted the three Blackwood women good and scared so that when he came calling for the grimoire, they'd willingly give it up.

And now Henrietta's life, and Edgehill itself, hung in the balance if Amber didn't do what the Penhallows wanted. She wanted to believe that her raw, untested magic was powerful enough to restore Raphael, but it was possible that even if she were successful, it would help her enemies get closer to their goal. If Amber and Edgar abandoned the mission, Neil would torture Edgar into madness. It was a lose-lose situation.

Silence descended on them after she finally stopped speaking. It went on long enough that she was convinced she'd scared Jack away all over again.

Finally, he said, "What I wouldn't give to be able to hug you right now, Amber. I don't have any answers. I understand why you feel this way. This is…a lot. I don't know how I would deal with this kind of pressure. Heck, I almost had a total system meltdown over serving scones to Olaf Betzen."

Amber managed a little laugh, some of the tension in her chest easing.

"But you have to know that you have people here who are rooting for you," he said. "Kim and I don't have a lick of magic between us, but we'd go up against a Penhallow for you in a heartbeat. Chief Brown is probably as freaked out about this as I am, yet that guy is basically your best friend now. Your aunt and sister would tear the Penhallows apart with their bare hands for you. Edgar has been through heck and back and he's not only still supporting you, he's by your side." She could imagine him shrugging. "That doesn't sound like someone who's the *reason* for all these terrible things. It sounds like someone who is doing her best and who has a ton of people who love her. Win or fail, right choice or not, we'll all still be here."

Amber started crying.

Jack cursed softly, his tone regretful. "Do you have a teleportation spell up your sleeve? 'Cause we really need one right now."

Once she got herself together, she huffed out a long, shaky sigh. "Thanks, Jack. I guess I just needed to purge it all."

"Don't thank me," he said. "This is what boyfriends do."

She fought a grin. "Oh, so it's official now?"

"Definitely," he said. "You're stuck with me."

"Good."

After a moment, he said, "You should probably try to get some sleep. Big day tomorrow."

Amber nodded. Her throat hurt from talking so much, and her eyes itched from crying. At the very least, she should take a hot shower. "Night, Jack."

"Night, Amber."

Though nightmares didn't plague her, her sleep was fitful.

With Jack's words ringing in her head, she felt a little less daunted, at least.

Win or fail, right choice or not, we'll all still be here.

That was the thought that would get her through. That, and the text she received early the next morning from Kim.

I believe in you, friend! Kick butt and get back here ASAP. You'll be here for the parade, right? RIGHT? I may set the floats on fire just so I don't have to answer any more terse emails from the Floral Frenemies. It is my solemn wish that a blight of locusts eats their entire town.

CHAPTER 21

Amber wasn't sure what Agent Barker did at Peaceful Meadows while she and Edgar visited with Raphael. For all she knew, Agent Barker knocked out every orderly in the place with a powerful sleep spell and then holed up in a viewing room to observe the goings-on in Room 9. She pictured him leaned back in a chair, feet propped up on a table with his ankles crossed, as he watched a bank of monitors. Maybe he had a bowl of popcorn, too.

Either way, she and Edgar found themselves alone with Raphael the next morning. He greeted them both by name, which was a good sign. Amber had pretended not to notice Edgar's eyes welling up.

Currently, Raphael lay on his back on his rumpled bed. Amber had positioned his beloved chair beside it. Raphael's gaze was focused on the ceiling, and his hands were balled into fists by his sides. His anxiety was a palpable thing—as was his hope that this would work.

The plan was to show Raphael memories that were tied to magic, hoping that jogging the recovery of one buried thing would help unearth another. Since Raphael couldn't remember anything about his life before Peaceful Meadows, she couldn't ask him to hold details of a particular memory in his mind as she had with Edgar last night. She would have to go rooting through his memory drawers like a burglar.

Raphael assured her that he understood how the process worked. His tone was relaxed enough, but his fingers firmly grasping a handful of his sheets told her otherwise.

She shot a look over her shoulder at Edgar who was busy wearing a hole in the floor, his bushy brows smashed together and his eyes on the ground. She wondered if he was giving himself a pep talk or if he was currently having a mental fight with Neil. Maybe both.

Refocusing on Raphael, she uttered the words of the spell, took a fortifying breath, and then placed her hand on his arm. The first two memories she pushed at him were received with relative ease. She could feel the muscles in his forearm bunch and relax occasionally under her palm, but otherwise the process was moving along more smoothly than the one from yesterday.

She moved onto a third memory—the one where Willow had slipped past the rubber banister stakes—and had just gotten to the part where Amber and Edgar were lathering up Willow's head and hair with mayonnaise when all the players in the scene froze. A glob of mayo hung in the air like an opaque bubble.

Then everything vanished. It was like the color leaking from the abandoned neighborhood, but all at once. She pitched forward into the abyss of black, screaming on the way down but unable to produce a sound.

Besides, one needed a mouth, a throat, and vocal cords to scream and she had none of those now. She couldn't feel the wooden chair she sat on or the warmth of Raphael's forearm beneath her hand. The black was all-encompassing, and she knew on some level that she should be panicking, screaming, begging for help. But now she just…was.

"Am I dead?" she asked and was surprised she had a voice when she didn't have a body.

"No," came the reply, and she recognized it as Raphael's voice, but there didn't appear to be another person here with her. Just two consciousnesses. Was Patrice here as well? "We don't have a lot of time, Amber. I need you to listen to me. The orderly Stanley Johnson isn't who you think he is."

"Who is he?"

"Patrice," Raphael said. "My memory was restored a couple of years ago, but I have to pretend it wasn't. Patrice threatens me on a daily basis that if I don't do as she says, she'll take it all away again. But I can't even share my true lucidity with Patrice."

If Amber had a head, it would have been spinning. "But she's in your mind, isn't she? How can you hide that from her?"

"She isn't in my head the way Neil is for Edgar. If she has eyes on me, she can use her magic to float thoughts into my head. She's the one who got them to install the camera that's aimed at my chair," Raphael said. "What the WBI has told you is likely only part of the truth. I was never hit with cursed magic; I wasn't infected the way Edgar was. I had all my memories and powers buried by my parents, as

I think you figured out. Patrice found me here a few years ago. She's no memory witch like the Henbanes are—like you are. But slowly, bit by bit, Patrice was able to restore my memories. Restoring my powers, however, is beyond her abilities. That's why the Penhallows have done what they can to reunite us. They wanted you to believe that finding me was organic."

"Was Patrice the one who put the meadow image in Willow's dreams?" Amber asked.

"Yes and no," Raphael said. "The Penhallows have been keeping tabs on you and Willow for years, but they started paying closer attention ever since the cloak started to fade on Belle's grimoire. The network of witches—mostly Penhallow, but some from other clans—rotate which witches are assigned to watch you. A few in Seattle have been assigned to Willow and Gretchen. That's how the Penhallows knew your sister started looking for me. They communicated through the network to devise the best way to influence Willow. One of them posed as a barista at Willow's favorite coffee shop and got a dream tincture into her drink that opened her mind to influence. The witch then projected the simple image of the yellow flowers, blue house, and red chair into Willow's mind while she slept."

"Did one of them *break into* her apartment?" Amber asked.

"I believe Patrice said Willow left her second-story window open and the witch climbed in."

Amber wished she had the ability to shudder. Willow had been taking tinctures for sleep and dreams then, she'd said, to help combat her insomnia. Perhaps the concoctions she'd been taking had been so strong that not even a prowler had woken her up. Amber was going to scream "Always lock your windows!" at Willow at her first opportunity. "And they're doing all this just to get my mom's book?"

Though there was nothing to see here, Amber could feel him bristle. "Believe it or not, this has been more about me than my golden child of a sister. They'll use Neil to find the spell; they believe he has a connection that can transcend time and death itself. The night of the fire, he collected both your father's watch and the promise ring Neil had given Belle years ago. The fact that she kept it told Neil that Belle still loved him. As you well know, objects from events of great trauma can hold a person's essence, as well as a bit of their magic. They're convinced that's all Neil needs to find the hidden grimoires."

Mom kept a promise ring from Neil? Amber could hardly process that, so she shoved it to the back of her mind. "How is all this more about *you* than my mother?" she asked.

"Once they find the spell, they need someone to cast the thing. Patrice is proof enough that Penhallows, as powerful as they are, don't have the ability to do memory and time magic—few do," Raphael said. "They want me to take the time-reversal spell Belle wrote and alter it so I don't reverse *all* of time, but rather send a single person back to a *moment* in time. Neil will go back to the moment Belle created the spell and steal it from her."

Neil's younger self was part of that memory, too. Wasn't there a rule about time travel and not meeting yourself, otherwise it could break time itself…or something?

"This will be a trial run for the real thing," Raphael said. "Reversing over a hundred years on the first try is a bit ambitious. If Neil's mission is successful, the Penhallow clan will make the trek to modern-day Sedona, Arizona's ley line convergence. Once there, I'll cast the time-reversal spell to take us back to the day the curse was born. It will be future Penhallows against the council—and the Penhallows are sure to win."

It took Amber a moment to think clearly. "And what about everyone in *this* timeline?"

"They don't care," Raphael said. "They'll be back in a time where Penhallows were at the height of their power. Patrice wants to be the head of the new council made up entirely of her clan. She's even hinted that she wants to use the same spell the council used to strip the magic from enemy clans."

"So she wants to make the same choice the council did, but expect a different result?" Amber asked. "Isn't that the definition of insanity?" She mentally shook her nonexistent head. "None of this matters. You know I can't let you do any of it, right? I can just outright refuse to help you get your magic back and then the whole plan falls apart."

"I'm on your side, Amber," he said. "Why would I risk telling you this if I was sympathetic to the Penhallows?"

"Isn't that exactly what someone who is sympathetic to the Penhallows would say?" she asked.

There might have been a flicker of amusement in the darkness. "I don't plan to send Neil back in time. When my memories came back, so did my bitterness and anger. I've had years, thanks to Patrice, to work through that. I know the Penhallows can't succeed. When it became clear that Patrice, despite all her efforts, wouldn't be able to restore my magic, the network started to panic. I figured as long as my magic was hidden, their plan would fall apart. I just needed to bide my time. But then you and Willow got pulled into it. They see you as the backup plan because they don't know if you have the aptitude for memory and time magic the same way that I do."

Perhaps being an untrained witch with unknown potential wasn't always a bad thing.

"I'm telling you this because I want to help you and Edgar," Raphael said after a moment. "I couldn't do what I needed to for him back then, but maybe I can right things now. But to do that, I need my magic restored. I need Patrice to think their original plan is going off without a hitch. And *you* need to let me betray my son to his face. Once you restore me, I'll use my magic to break out of here. Her instructions are: *Get her to return your magic, exact your revenge as you see fit, and then meet me out front.* She's waiting for me in the parking lot right now."

Amber's gut and her heart were at war. "Was betraying Edgar her idea or yours?" she finally asked.

There was a slight pause in the black. "Mine. She thinks my loyalty is fully with her now that she's returned my memories. I need her to believe that so the network is more focused on me. They underestimate you. Make them regret that."

"Where is Patrice going to take you?" Amber asked, but she already knew.

"Edgehill is the nearest location in the United States with a ley line spillover," he said. "That's where she'll take me. I'll do whatever I can to buy time until you can get back there."

"Get back there to do *what*?" Amber asked, the same feelings from last night rushing back in. Worry, self-doubt, panic, inadequacy.

"You need to gather every witch you know. Every witch your family knows. Call in every last one of your favors and get everyone to Edgehill as fast as possible. You're running low on time. You have to stop them—stop *me*—from succeeding," Raphael said. "But remember: you can't let Edgar know this is a ruse. If you tell him, Neil will know."

Amber wanted to scream. She wasn't cut out for this. She wished more than anything that she could ask Aunt G for help. When she was overwhelmed, she'd complain, whine, and generally be overly dramatic. Aunt G would humor her for a moment, then offer a practical solution. "Did they really have to do this during the tourist season? I get that maximum chaos is their whole thing, but so many innocent people are going to get hurt because they chose to do this on the busiest day of the festival."

There was a ripple of confusion in the darkness.

"What?" Amber asked.

"This has nothing to do with the festival. They're using it to their advantage, sure, but Saturday evening marks the fifty-year anniversary of the spell's creation. *That's* why it's happening now; they see a significance in the number. They have a ritual they plan to conduct on the ley line spillover on Saturday evening. They'll have Penhallows there spe-cifically for the ritual, and others there for defense. We need all the witch power there we can get."

A flare of anger rose up in this not-place at the real-ization that the WBI had kept *this* from her, too. It had been Agent Howe who had lied about this one. "*We're guessing they chose this weekend in large part because of the festival—they're big on creating chaos in a crowd, as I'm sure you know. And that parade will be jam-packed with people.*"

Amber had no idea what she and her ragtag group of family and friends could do against a barrage of Penhallows. This was a plan years in the making and Amber was only now piecing it together with less than two days until her town would be under significant threat. Chief Brown had said that he didn't know what non-witch cops could do against cursed witches…well, Amber wasn't sure what *she* could do either.

Her thoughts flailed around aimlessly for a while. And then they slammed to a halt. "Do you know who Damien and Devra Penhallow are?" Even if Patrice had been grooming Raphael for years, keeping him abreast of the Penhallows' grand plan, Amber didn't know how much information from the outside Patrice was bringing in. Perhaps the lines of communication between Raphael and Patrice were on a need-to-know basis.

"Patrice mentioned them," he said. "All I know is that they disappeared recently. Something about them being volatile and that no one was surprised when they bailed on the mission."

She desperately wanted to trust him, but she didn't know if that was just the pre-teen Amber part of her who missed her uncle. She wanted to trust him for Edgar's sake. "They didn't disappear voluntarily. I'm able to tap into the ley lines. I asked the magic there to help me and somehow I transported them to a memory in 1971. Their magic is suppressed there. What if we could get the other Penhallows into that memory? Then I could heal them the way I healed Kieran."

The silence was long. "I can't say it's any less loopy-sounding than the Penhallow plan."

"Gee, thanks," she muttered.

"What would you need to pull this off?"

"The grimoire," Amber said. "I know the second the cloak drops on the books, even if I get a cloak back on it immediately, Neil could trace the location of the magical signature. So I would need as much magical backup as I could get in case I get ambushed."

"Sounds like you have some phone calls to make," Raphael said. "Can you inform your sister and aunt about this without Edgar finding out? You have roughly twenty-four hours to amass an army and get that book back. If the Penhallows don't get me and that spell, they've got a Plan B. I'm not sure what it is exactly, because Patrice won't tell me, but what I do know is that it involves funneling large quantities of magic into the modern-day, already broken ley lines. It'll be like a bomb; Edgehill will be a crater."

It sounded like Plan B was the very thing Zelda Rockrose had practically begged Amber not to try: using the ley lines to cast another complicated, widespread spell.

There was one thing left to discuss before she made her decision. "How do we get your magic back? The one solid idea we had was based on the assumption that your memory was gone," she said. "At least I know you're a good actor."

"Your presence here stirred my magic," he said. "It feels a bit like when Patrice started her memory work with me. A faraway tingle in the back of my mind. A gentle pressure, almost. I know something is there, but I can't get to it. I think I need a nudge in the right direction. This might sound odd since we don't really have a physical form here—wherever here is—but can you use magic in this space?"

"I don't know," she said, feeling a little self-conscious even though he obviously couldn't see her. She thought of the simplest spell she knew. "*One by one, let's have some fun. Two by two, let's turn it blue.*"

The world of black they were in flashed blue, like a TV screen, then faded to black again. They both let out astonished laughs.

"Man, that brings back memories," he said. "Those rubber cats were sold in every convenience store in Delin Springs. Nothing special about them at all as far as witch kids were concerned. But you and Willow loved those things. You know, there's a whole series of rhymes to change those cats all kinds of colors, but your mother enchanted your cats to only turn blue."

"Aha!" Amber said. "I knew it. We spent hours trying to get them to change other colors."

"Try something else," Raphael urged.

Amber tried thought-reveal, memory-retrieval, and truth spells. Nothing worked. Most of Amber's magic was heightened by touch. She couldn't touch anything here. She tried confusion, sleep, and wind spells. Nothing.

"Ugh!" Her frustration mounted. She tried the one-by-one spell again. The fact that it worked only frustrated her more. All she was good for was parlor tricks, simple spells even children could do. And children were probably more skilled! She had only just learned about Magic Cache, for Pete's sake! "Maybe I need something stronger."

Funneling all her annoyance and worry into where she thought her core might be, she cast a blowback spell. When she pretended that magic itself had a physical form, she pictured it like sentient smoke, snaking and curling in the direction she told it to go. The magic erupted from her not-hands and slammed into a wall.

And shot her straight back. The chair she was in scooted backward and toppled over, tossing her to the wood floor of Raphael's room.

"Amber!" someone called out, and in the next second, she realized it was Edgar.

A loud buzz sounded, followed by a door slamming into a wall.

Out of the corner of her eye, she saw Raphael swing his legs off the bed. Edgar was too focused on her to notice. Raphael made very brief eye contact with her, nodded once, and pursed his lips as he eyed the back of Edgar's head. Then a wholly terrifying look crossed his face.

"They told me you were a gullible idiot," Raphael said. "A silly, untrained witch who is so desperate to believe in the good in people that she gets steamrolled at every opportunity."

Edgar was on his feet in an instant, whirling to face his father. "Dad …"

"I never actually planned to come back that day, you know," Raphael said. "Neil ruined you just as much as he ruined my sister. I found a way to reverse it. Maybe you would have been there in the new future, maybe you wouldn't have been. This version of things is pretty screwed up, if you ask me." He winked at Amber. "Thanks for giving me a chance to try again."

Edgar growled and ran for his father. Raphael shot out a hand and Edgar flew backward, slamming into the wall.

"What the …" one of the newly arrived orderlies said, his wild eyes bouncing from the perfectly lucid Raphael, to Amber on the floor, to Edgar who was struggling back to his feet.

Amber noted that the orderly, Stanley Johnson, wasn't among them.

Raphael turned to the orderlies, his bed between them. "I'm afraid I'm leaving, boys. This place is a peaceful nightmare. Fisher, Hearn…*sleep*."

Both men's eyes rolled back in their heads and their bodies hit the floor.

Raphael bolted. Edgar scrambled after him. Amber, however, ran to the window. The door to the SUV where Silent had been waiting sat in the same place, but two of the doors stood open. If Amber craned her neck just right, she could make out a black sedan idling on the dirt road, facing the exit. Was that really Patrice?

"Good work, Amber!" Agent Barker called out, and she spun to find Raphael and Agent Barker squared off. "I'm going to need you to come with me, Raphael."

"No thanks," Raphael said. "I already have a ride."

"You're going to be hunted by Penhallows if you leave here," Agent Barker said, hands out, placating.

"For an agent in an organization as prestigious as the WBI, I would think you'd be a little smarter," Raphael said. "It's not called hunting if it's voluntary." Then he charged toward Agent Barker.

The agent cast his own spell. In one second, Amber saw Raphael vanish from view, then reappear a moment later directly behind the agent. The wind spell that Agent Barker had intended for Raphael careened into Amber and Edgar, sending a rug, chair, and potted plant into the air, too. The prone bodies of the two orderlies slid a few inches as if they were nothing more than debris, rather than full-grown men. It had been more of a small, contained hurricane than a blast of wind.

Raphael hurled a blowback spell, hitting an unsuspecting Agent Barker, who went sprawling.

"Much appreciated, Amber," Raphael said, then flicked his wrist. The door to Room 9 slammed shut.

It took them all a few seconds to get reoriented and back on their feet. Amber ran after Edgar and Agent Barker. Across the hallway, down the stairs, and out the standing-open, prison-like door. The woman behind the Plexiglas was passed out face down on the counter.

The trio sprinted outside. The two men ran to either side of the SUV. Amber stopped in the middle of the dirt road and stared down the small incline.

Agent Barker reached into the driver's side door. "Wake up, you oaf! How'd you let someone sneak up on you!"

Edgar paced back and forth behind the SUV, his hands in his hair.

Amber's chest heaved as she kept staring down the road as if the black sedan would come back and the two passengers would stick their heads out the window and call out, "Gotcha!"

Patrice and Raphael were gone.

Amber hoped she hadn't just made the worst judgment call in the history of the world.

CHAPTER 22

It took nearly twenty minutes for the sleep spell on Silent Agent to wear off. Agent Barker tore him a new one, shouting that he only had one job and he'd literally fallen asleep on it. Amber did what she could to comfort Edgar, but he had retreated into himself. He'd only had his father back for two days and he'd just abandoned him again.

Amber hoped like heck that Raphael had told her the truth. She'd destroy him otherwise.

As Silent drove them to the airport, they all made phone calls. Agent Barker called Agent Howe first, then called into what Amber assumed was the WBI headquarters. A sound-canceling spell went up around him after he stated his ID number, shielding his conversation. She supposed he was also going to file a report against Silent Agent for allowing himself to be compromised.

Edgar called Aunt Gretchen. What Amber heard of the conversation was short and clipped.

Amber contacted Simon and Zelda, begging them both to call in reinforcements. Amber knew Simon had many connections to the witch community because of his time in

Weldon, a hybrid town his late wife had been a detective in. Zelda's daughter was in law enforcement, too. It was now a matter of how many witches they could find who would first be willing to combat an untold number of Penhallows, and secondly, could get to Edgehill at such short notice.

Next, for the sake of privacy, she sent a text to Betty. *Hi, Betty. Can you tell my grandparents that the Penhallows are making their move in Edgehill tomorrow night? Do they have any advice on what we should do? We need all the help we can get.*

While she waited for a reply, she sent a group text to Kim and Jack.

AMBER: *We're headed to the airport. Raphael got his powers back and has gone rogue. He's heading to Edgehill with a Penhallow, and there are others already there. I need you both to get out of town. Convince as many people as possible to go with you.*

JACK: No way.

KIM: Ditto.

AMBER: *PLEASE. I don't know how many witches are about to descend on Edgehill.*

KIM: Coolest and scariest sentence you've ever said. Answer is still no.

JACK: Your aunt is working on Penhallow-specific tinctures, ya? Can non-witches drink those?

Amber had no idea. She didn't want to find out what effect that might have.

KIM: Oooh! What do they taste like?

AMBER: *Horrible. And you can't take them! I need you guys to pack your bags.*

JACK: Maybe I can add something from the bakery to make them taste better. Do you think cherry extract or vanilla would taste better?

KIM: Cherry, obviously.

AMBER: *You guys …*

JACK: Maybe I can bake the tincture into a scone. Would heat affect its potency?

KIM: Amber, ask your aunt if that would work!

AMBER: *Ugh. I'm turning my phone off. Please don't be in Edgehill when I get back. I mean that in the most loving way possible.*

JACK: See you soon!

KIM: You better be back in time for the parade!

Amber was about to drop her phone back into her purse when Betty wrote back.

BETTY: Message relayed.

AMBER: *Thank you. Things are about to get hectic there. You and Bobby should pack up Savannah and get the heck out of Dodge.*

BETTY: Nothing doing, sugar. I've been doing my best to look out for you since you were a foot tall. I'm not about to stop now. See you when you get back.

Amber was simultaneously touched and annoyed with her friends.

The last person she had to get a hold of was Chief Brown.

He picked up almost immediately. "I just got off the phone with your friend Agent Howe," he said in greeting. "She more or less suggested that I needed to batten down the hatches because a herd of cursed witches is going to be in my town. That accurate?"

"Yes," she said. "You, Jessica, Sammy, and Izzy should all—"

"You know dang well I'm not going anywhere, Amber," he said. "I've got an obligation to this town as its chief, and I have an obligation to you, my best bud."

She managed a laugh but sobered quickly. "I don't want anyone to get hurt, chief."

"I know," he said softly. "We'll get through this together though, okay? We might not have magic on our side, but our love of this town is pretty strong. Plus, no one wants to deal with the fallout if Kim's festival is ruined."

He was right about that. Bianca the Festizilla was likely even worse, which was a sobering thought.

"Anything of note happen while I was gone?" she asked.

"Garcia mentioned that he's seen a woman loitering near your shop," the chief said. "The town is completely overrun with tourists and Betty's bakery is swamped with people either waiting in line or fussing over that cat of hers, so I don't know what it is about this woman that stands out to him. Call it intuition, I guess. All he can say is that she's very intense, has jet-black hair, and 'dead' green eyes."

Amber got a flash of the dark-haired woman she'd seen at Balinese Park on Kids Day just seconds before all her toys attacked. Could it be the same woman? "Has she done anything other than creeping Garcia out?"

"He said the woman seems more interested in what's happening in Purrfectly Scrumptious than your shop," the chief said. "His best theory is that the woman is a disgruntled past employee. I'm leaning Penhallow, but that's not based on anything but a hunch."

"Is there any way you can station an officer outside the bakery until I get back?" Amber asked.

"You got it," he said, not asking any questions. Chief Brown was on a self-imposed need-to-know basis when magic was involved. "Give me a shout when you're back in town."

After hanging up, Amber slumped back against her seat, her throat a little scratchy from all the talking she'd done over the last hour. It was then that she realized the three men in the car with her were all silently brooding. It would be a long car ride.

Even if Edgehill was currently infested with cursed witches, Amber couldn't wait to get home.

They landed in Portland a little after noon. Banners hung above the escalators not only welcoming visitors to the city, but encouraging them to attend the Here and Meow Festival that weekend. Amber wondered if she could use a few wind spells to knock the signs loose. A pair of young ladies in front of her wore cat-ear headbands, and one had on a backpack shaped like a cat's head.

As she followed Agent Barker to the parking garage, she spotted no fewer than five people wearing cat onesies. A woman stood at the baggage claim carousel while holding a leash attached to a little boy who wore a felt lion mane and tail. He ran around on his hands and knees roaring at amused passersby.

So many innocent people who were traveling to her beloved town for a weekend full of feline fun, who had no idea what was brewing just under the surface. Her stomach churned.

Edgar hadn't said a word since they'd left Peaceful Meadows; he hadn't even asked her what had happened while she attempted to get his father's memories back. She supposed he didn't want to know. The details didn't really matter if his father had run out on him again.

Raphael had told Edgar that he'd never planned to come back to him. Amber was sure that was a fear that lingered in the back of his mind as constantly as Neil's disembodied voice. The decades-old "what if" had just been answered.

The answer sucked.

As they headed back to Edgehill, Amber rode shotgun in Agent Barker's SUV, leaving Edgar to brood alone in the back. Agent Barker didn't have much to say either, but his silence made Amber even more uneasy: she couldn't read him the same way she could read her cousin.

The closer they got to home, the more the Here and Meow Festival started to spill out beyond the town limits—a few roadside billboards featuring Ben's winning design, a speed limit sign with a stuffed cat flopped over the top, and a car zipping past the SUV with the windows decorated with drawings of cats. On the back window, someone had written, "A cat festival? You've gotta be kitten me!"

Within the town limits, banners hung from nearly every lamppost. An inflatable cat lounged on someone's lawn, its head oscillating slowly, as if watching cars go by. Colorfully decorated wooden cats peeked over fences, and statues and metal cat silhouettes decorated steps, porches, lawns, and roofs. Elegant black cat-shaped balloons bobbed from the low gate around the Manx Hotel.

Residents of Edgehill went all out with decorations for the Here and Meow like some people did for Christmas and Halloween—which Edgehill also fully embraced. The number of decorations had doubled since she'd been gone. Being away for two days made Amber even more aware of all the feline touches that graced the town on a daily basis. The cat-shaped mailboxes, the lounging stone cat statues outside the library that had spectacles perched on their noses and open books in their laps, and the cat fountain outside the Meowmm Yoga Studio, the centerpiece of which was a cat in an easy pose, a gentle spray of water shooting from between its upright pointed ears.

Balinese Park was a sea of white pop tents now, the area already swarming with tourists taking a gander at the early sales items. The ending line for the 5K had been erected not far from the pond, the peak of the balloon arch swaying just below the large "FINISH" banner. A few food trucks were parked in the grass here, but Amber knew most of them would be set up on Himalayan Way, near the fairgrounds not far from Angora Threads. That was where the parade would end in a few hours.

When Agent Barker pulled up outside The Quirky Whisker, he turned to her. "The best thing to do for now is to act as normal as possible. We don't know if Raphael—" Edgar grunted at this, "is in town yet. We don't know how many Penhallows are here, either. If you don't tip them off that anything has changed, then it might buy us some time to formulate a solid game plan."

Which meant the WBI didn't *have* a solid game plan.

Amber nodded, then glanced into the back seat. "Did you want to come up? We could have a family meeting since I'm sure Aunt G and Willow have a million questions."

"If it's all the same to you," he said, gaze focused across the street at the busy sidewalk outside Purrfectly Scrumptious, "I'd rather go home. I've had enough family today."

Amber frowned. "Call me if you change your mind."

He didn't reply.

Sighing, Amber thanked Agent Barker for the ride, grabbed her duffel that had been wedged into the seat next to her, and climbed out. She watched the SUV drive away, then scanned the sidewalk outside Betty's place, searching for the black-haired woman, but didn't see her. It didn't mean she wasn't there, though, as she could have been wearing anyone's face. Even the young boy walking down the sidewalk on her side of the street, headphones on and attention focused on his phone could be someone else.

Feeling exposed out on the sidewalk, she let herself into her shop, locked up behind herself, and then darted for the stairs, calling, "I'm back!" as she went.

She came up short when she reached the top of the steps. Her tiny studio apartment was quite crowded. Willow, Bianca, and Simon sat on the side of Amber's bed, and Aunt G, Kim, and Jack were seated at the dining table.

Kim let out an enthusiastic "Yes!" when she saw Amber and rushed over to envelop her in a tight hug. She pulled away a second later and peered behind her down the stairs. "Is…uhh…is Edgar with you?"

"He had a hard time with…everything," Amber said. "Agent Barker took him home."

Kim frowned.

Jack replaced Kim then and hugged Amber. She rested her chin on his shoulder and breathed in the familiar, comforting scent of him. He smelled like Purrcolate—coffee and sugar. "I'm glad you're back," he said.

"Me too."

He pulled away and kissed her quickly. A catcall went up behind them from Willow. They both flushed.

"I have good news," Aunt G said, redirecting their attention. "The tincture is done."

Amber glanced at the window, hoping the apartment still had an active noise-canceling spell on it.

"No one can hear us, little mouse," Aunt G assured her.

"Mine is done, too," Simon said. "After comparing notes, we're both fairly certain they work. We figure downing them before the parade might be a good idea. Some can drink mine, and some can drink Gretchen's to test them out."

"Glad you didn't blow up either kitchen," Amber said, wondering if the WBI had lied about the volatility of Penhallow blood.

Jack took a seat at the table again, while Amber stood in the middle of the room between her two sets of guests and wrung her hands.

"No, Kim," Aunt G said, pointing a finger at Kim, who had reclaimed her seat across from her at the dining table. Kim snapped her mouth shut before the question could leave her mouth. "Non-witches can't take tinctures. There's cursed blood in these things. You'll likely explode."

Kim gasped and grabbed at her imaginary pearls. Bianca and Jack both paled.

Amber highly doubted any of them would explode but was also glad Aunt G had scared them all out of taking it.

"So what's the plan here?" Bianca asked, crossing her arms. "Can't say I'm loving the idea of Edgehill filling up with witches—it's like my horrific childhood all over again." She winced slightly and offered her father a tight-lipped smile. "Sorry. But, well, horrific is the best word I have for it. I'm happy to help any way I can, though. I didn't put this much work into the Floral Frenzy only to have it ruined by Penhallows."

"Finally we agree on something," Kim said.

Amber cleared her throat and six sets of eyes swiveled toward her. She felt like a teacher in front of a classroom. She gave them a condensed account of everything she'd learned while in Washington.

"Isn't it a time travel paradox to meet your future self?" Jack asked.

"I thought that was only if you went back in time and killed your own grandfather because then you'd no longer exist," Kim said.

Amber's head hurt again. "Hopefully we'll have magical backup by the time the ritual happens tomorrow night. In the meantime, don't talk about any of this stuff with anyone outside the group unless it's in code or in a noise-canceling bubble. Penhallows can be anyone. Keep an eye out for strange behavior. Preferably every non-witch has a witch with them at all times. Bianca with Simon; Willow with Kim; and Jack with me. Aunt G, can you stick to Betty?"

Aunt G nodded. "Of course."

Simon stood then and fished two vials out of his pocket. "I think I should try Gretchen's and vice versa. It might help us troubleshoot better if we can see where the other possibly failed."

Aunt G got up and fetched two vials from the kitchen.

Amber and Aunt G downed Simon's tincture, while Simon and Willow took Aunt G's.

Simon's somehow tasted even worse than Aunt G's protection tincture.

Amber gagged and all the moisture in her mouth immediately evaporated. Aunt G hinged forward and placed her hands on her knees, nearly hacking up a lung as she did so. Willow and Simon's tongues both unfurled from their mouths, as if they'd swollen to twice their size. Willow shuddered uncontrollably for nearly ten seconds, while Simon had a fist pressed to his mouth, tears streaming from his eyes.

"Are they going to explode?" Kim asked from behind them.

"I hope not," Bianca said. "I really like this blouse."

Jack let loose a semi-hysterical cackle.

When they finally all settled, Amber fetched bottles of water for them all. For a moment, she'd been truly terrified Simon had poisoned them. She drained the bottle in seconds.

"I guess it's time for a parade …" Amber said, despite how ludicrous it felt to go to a parade at a time like this.

Kim looped her arm through Amber's. "We'll have fun, I promise! The line-up for this parade is great, even if we're sharing it with *Marbleglen*."

"I can hear you, you know," Bianca said, following behind Amber and Kim, who led the way down the stairs.

"Oh, so you *do* listen to other people when they're speaking," Kim replied, voice full of false cheer.

"There's nothing wrong with my hearing," Bianca said. "I just have a hard time understanding you most of the time because I don't speak Whiny Nonsense."

Kim dug her fingernails into Amber's forearm. As they reached the bottom of the steps, and Amber pushed open the Employee Only door, Kim whispered, "If I give you a thousand dollars, will you turn her into a hamster?"

CHAPTER 23

The kickoff parade was a joint venture between Marbleglen and Edgehill, mostly at the behest of the towns' two mayors. The fate of the parade hung in the balance for a short time after Marbleglen's former mayor got caught up in the murder plot of the town's previous police chief. The former Mayor Sable was now in a jail cell awaiting her sentence.

Neither festival committee had been happy about this partnership, but even Kim had felt awful about even considering bailing on their arrangement when the new interim mayor of Marbleglen not only had to take over so quickly, but had to do so at the height of festival season.

The parade started at Marbleglen's town hall. Bianca and Simon were there now. Bianca, as the Floral Frenzy Festival Director, was needed at the parade's start to make sure everything went off without a hitch. The parade would then make its way down Buttercup Road. Edge of Glen Pizza Parlor straddled the border, where Kim was stationed to oversee the midpoint checkpoint. Ann Marie and Nathan were positioned at the end, near the fairgrounds. They were all part of a group text message chain and were armed with walkie-talkies so they could keep in contact, in case something disastrous happened along the way.

Amber knew that "disastrous" normally meant something like a wardrobe malfunction, or a member of the school band misplacing his trumpet. She just hoped "disastrous" today didn't involve maiming by magic.

Amber parked on a side street a few blocks down from the pizza parlor, and then she, Jack, Willow, and Kim made their way to Sphynx Way on foot. Kim periodically said things like "We're almost at our destination, over," into her walkie-talkie, to which Nathan would reply, "All quiet on the western front, over." To which Bianca would reply with an exaggerated sigh.

They found a decent spot between two large families who had come prepared with folding chairs and a cooler. Orange traffic cones had been placed at the end of streets that led to Sphynx Way, and every so often there would be a volunteer in a reflective vest to further discourage people from trying to cross the parade street, and to offer directions to lost tourists.

Amber hadn't told Chief Brown where she and her friends would be viewing the parade today, so she was surprised to see him just down the street from where they stood. Excusing herself, she walked half a block to where the chief stood between the front of his cruiser and the line of orange cones blocking off through-traffic. He had a cell phone pressed to his ear.

Just as Amber approached, he hung up. "Hi, chief."

"Amber," he said, nodding. He eyed the people lined up on the sidewalk on either side of the cruiser. They weren't alone by any stretch of the word, but there was at least a few feet of distance between them and the waiting parade-goers. She stood beside him in front of the police car. "That was Agent Howe—again. She first gave me a call this morning to gently suggest I keep you in my sights as much as possible this weekend. She requested that I get in contact with her the second I see something fishy."

Amber scanned the crowd, not looking at the chief. They both only had eyes for the strangers lining the street. "And where is our friend Agent Howe now?"

"She said something about running a command post out of the Manx Hotel and that she had her hands full trying to keep track of all her agents," the chief said. "They're hunting Neil, Kieran, and now Raphael. She said, and I quote, I don't have the manpower to keep tabs on Miss Blackwood, too."

"Good to know I'm so low priority," Amber said.

The chief chuckled. "I saw Gretchen was holed up inside Purrfectly Scrumptious with Betty and Bobby, but I've got Garcia stationed outside the place, too. Agent Howe also gently suggested that it would be safer for the Harrises to keep baking today instead of attending the parade. The Harrises didn't put up much of a fuss. They're sending their new employees to represent them in the parade today. There will be fewer people over in your neck of the woods for the next few hours, so if someone is acting suspicious, it'll be easier to spot since the crowd has thinned."

Amber nodded, but she could hardly process how much her life had changed in the past few months. Her magical and normal worlds had collided and intermingled in a way she'd never expected. "Thanks for being here," she said.

"Of course," he said. "Give a shout if you need me."

Amber smiled at him, then headed back for her friends. Just as she arrived, she heard the crackle of Kim's walkie-talkie, and then Bianca's voice. "The parade has begun. The marching bands and the mayoral cars will reach your location in roughly twenty minutes, Kim."

"Roger, over," Kim said.

"Ugh," Bianca grunted. "Over."

Amber and her group chatted while they waited for the head of the parade to reach them. Jack slipped his hand into hers, grinning at her as he did so.

They listened while Kim grilled Willow about the afternoon she'd spent with John Huntley.

"His fans are coo-coo!" Kim said. "Did he, like, pour his soul out to you? I need you to know that I've basically written a screenplay in my head about your meet-cute. The Pop star and the Wi—wonderful lady."

Amber laughed. "Nice save."

Kim grinned at her.

"You're ridiculous," Willow said, smiling. "And, no, not really. He talked a lot about how much he loves his job—both the music and the acting—but that it can all be really exhausting sometimes. He was so tense when we first left the shop, but after a couple of minutes he realized no one knew who he was and he relaxed. He could just be a normal guy, you know? Thankfully, he doesn't seem to have a major ego problem. I was worried that once the adoration stopped, he would immediately miss it. But he genuinely seemed relieved."

Kim clasped her hands together and propped her chin on her fists. "So he's humble on top of being gorgeous and talented? Good grief. What else happened?"

Amber had heard all this already but was amused all over again at the deep shade of red that crept up her sister's neck and face. Willow was confident and self-assured ninety percent of the time, but every once in a while, her vulnerability shone through. "We just hung out. I showed him all the classic Edgehill landmarks. We got lunch at the Catty Melt and a gingerbread latte from Coffee Cat. We went on a stroll through Balinese Park. And we just…talked. He's really funny, too."

Jack asked, "How did the whole…uh…face thing resolve itself?"

Willow laughed. "Well, the…uh…makeup started to wear off, so I suggested that we go somewhere to get it touched up. He took me back to his tour bus."

Kim gasped and smacked Willow's arm. "Shut the front door!"

Flushing again, Willow said, "Several teens were loitering nearby, so I may have, you know, changed a hedge at the end of the street to look like John. When the teens went running, we bolted for the bus. The driver almost tackled us to the ground when we got on. John explained the situation, managed to convince the guy it was really him, and then the driver relaxed. I told John soap and water would work best, so we crammed into the small bathroom and I practically had to sit on his lap while I removed his…makeup."

Kim fanned herself with her hand. "All of this is going into the script. This is literally the best story I've ever heard."

"You said that about one of my stories last week," Amber said.

"You've said it to me at least once, too," said Jack.

Kim waved this away. "Literal isn't literal, guys. Geez."

Amber, Willow, and Jack shared an amused look.

"Anyway," Willow said, "once he was back to normal, he said he had a great time with me, yadda yadda. He, uh, got my number. Haven't heard from him since, though." She shrugged. "My love life is so sad that not being called by a celebrity is literally the most exciting thing that's happened in months."

"Sad? Weren't you and Connor dating?" asked Kim. Amber shot her a death glare.

Willow grumbled under her breath and abruptly turned to stare down Buttercup Road.

"*What'd I say?*" Kim mouthed.

Thankfully the parade reached them a minute later, breaking up the awkward silence. After the marching bands from both high schools, the mayoral cars, and a gaggle of adorable little flower girls tossing various petals to the ground, came a troupe of acrobats from the Cathletic Club. Attired in skintight black catsuits, they danced, twirled, and flipped. They would occasionally drop to all fours and gallop toward children in the crowd, swiping at them playfully with their "paws," then dart back into formation, their attached cat tails bobbing behind them.

Ben Lydon and Chloe Deidrick walked by next holding a giant banner featuring Ben's design. Behind them followed representatives from each of the twelve winning Best of Edgehill businesses.

A little girl beside her said, "Oh, Mommy! I think I see the floats!"

Amber craned her neck to look farther down Buttercup Road, and sure enough, the giant willow tree was trundling toward them.

When it was only a few feet away, Jack squeezed her hand. When she looked over at him, she realized the gesture had been involuntary. His mouth slightly hung open. He let out a low whistle and said, "Marbleglen really *does* know how to make a float."

After the garden float came a gaggle of Nine Lives Rescue workers in their signature green shirts. They all had their faces painted to mimic tigers, leopards, and house cats. The crowd, the children especially, gasped when they noticed how many of the workers walked cats on leashes. The man nearest them walked a slate gray cat who looked quite dapper in his forest green necktie and matching harness. Amber laughed, if only because she knew wrangling either of her cats into a harness would result in loss of limb. These cats, however, were pros, and only appeared mildly frightened by all the commotion. Amber liked to believe that these cats especially were descendants from Edgehill's population of familiars.

Kim glanced over then and squealed when the Edgehill float was visible in the distance. The giant cats somehow looked even better now than they had in the float barn. A few more Nine Lives Rescue workers walked around on the float itself, waving at parade-goers. A few live cats were on the float as well, either peering out from carriers, or held in the arms of the workers.

Amber was just about to congratulate Kim on how great it had all turned out when something on the other side of the street caught Amber's eye. The cat float trundled by a little more, the first cat's body blocking her view. In the next few seconds, the cat passed out of her line of vision and Amber saw it again. Saw *her* again. The woman with black hair and piercing green eyes. The woman who likely had been the cause of Amber's toys going rogue during Kids Day.

"Who is that?" Willow suddenly hissed in her ear.

So she'd seen her, too.

"I don't know, but I've seen her a couple of times now," Amber said, losing sight of her again as the next cat on the float moved past. Amber angled her head this way and that, and Willow got up on her tiptoes. "She's been acting shifty enough that even Garcia noticed her."

When the float passed out of view completely and a few more Nine Lives Rescue workers walked by behind it with their cats, Amber got a clear view of the woman.

And she gasped.

The woman's features were transparent, floating just over the surface of the ones beneath, as if two people were trapped in the same body.

It was Kieran Penhallow.

CHAPTER 24

Amber didn't think. She let Jack's hand go and started to push her way past people on the sidewalk. Willow was on her heels asking her what had her so spooked. Kim was asking, "What's happening?" every few seconds, while Jack shushed her, likely worried Kim would blurt something that would be overheard by the wrong person.

As Amber hurried forward, apologizing as she shoved her way through the crowd, she flicked glances to her left, checking to see if Kieran was still there. He merely stood there on the opposite sidewalk watching her. Amber needed a break in the parade so she could cut her way across.

The cat float had moved past them by now, but another handful of Nine Lives Rescue workers meandered behind it with their cats. The marbled rhododendron float was making its way up the street now. Men and women in elegant suits and dresses in various shades of blue walked in front of the rhododendron float, each holding a bouquet of Marbleglen's namesake. They walked slowly, waving at the crowd. Occasionally they'd walk to the viewers on the sidewalk to hand them one of the coveted flowers. Just as the last of the Nine Lives Rescue workers went by with their cats, Amber ducked under the caution tape and ran across the street.

"Amber!" Willow hissed, but Amber kept moving.

An alley ran next to Edge of Glen Pizza Parlor, the other side lined with a cinder block wall. A house sat on the other side. When Kieran, still wearing the face of the black-haired woman, saw Amber had spotted him, he ran a few feet to his left and then ducked into the alley. Amber took off after him.

He ran alongside the cinder block wall, then disappeared around the corner to the right. Amber braced herself as she picked up speed and rounded the corner too, and quickly slammed to a halt. The black-haired woman stood a few feet away in the narrow space where they were shielded on one side by the back of the restaurant, and on two others by cinder block walls. The lot beyond the restaurant was currently deserted, thanks to the parade. As long as no one came out the back door of the pizza parlor, no one would see them.

Willow, Kim, and Jack rounded the corner too, and nearly collided with her.

"Who is this?" Willow asked.

Which meant that Willow's tincture—the one Aunt G had made—didn't work. "Kieran."

A second later, the glamour sloughed off, revealing the familiar man beneath. He kept his hands out, placating.

There was a collective gasp.

A noise-canceling spell slammed down around them.

"I can explain!" Kieran said, glancing over his shoulder quickly. "I was sent here in large part to keep you distracted. The disguise I was wearing? That's the face of Patrice Penhallow."

Amber pursed her lips. "The woman who ran off with Raphael Henbane."

Kieran nodded. "She's one of the founders of the network. She instructed us to use her face as often as we could to make you think one woman has been following you around town. There are two of us here now. The witch who got me out, Henry Betel, is the one who made your toys attack a couple of days ago, not me. He was wearing Patrice's face."

"So the Betel clan is sympathetic to the Penhallows?" Willow asked.

"Most, but not all," Kieran said. "He's keeping tabs on the WBI agent—Barker, right?—who's stationed near the end of the parade route."

"Why should they believe a word you say?" Jack asked from behind her. It was the angriest she'd ever heard him. He moved to stand beside her. "Amber nearly died because of you the last time you were here. Why should she trust you now? I don't care that your magic is healed. Loyalty seems like something the Penhallows take very seriously."

Kieran gave Jack an elevator scan. "Because," he said, full attention shifting back to Amber, "I've been watching over Betty Harris since I got here. I overheard her conversation with you when you were in Washington. She was in her car and had no way of shielding her conversation from eavesdropping witches. Luckily it was me who heard her and not Betel. I know Ivy and Miles are alive. Don't you think the Penhallows would love that information?"

Amber's fists clenched. If the Penhallows did anything to Betty and Bobby or Ivy and Miles, so help her …

Willow must have sensed the rage pouring off Amber, because she asked, "Has Neil made any progress finding the spell?"

"The word in the network is that it's actually the WBI who's close to finding it," Kieran said. "I had my doubts Neil could do it. Sure, he'd been desperately in love with Annabelle and has a ring he took from the burned-down house—he took the ring the same day he took your father's watch."

The watch that had been strategically left for her to find under the porch of 523 Ocicat Lane. The watch that had been so infused with energy from the night of the fire that had killed her parents that the mere act of touching it had woken up Amber's memory magic. Exactly as Kieran had intended.

Exactly as the *network* had intended. Which meant Patrice had been the one pulling the strings dating back months ago, if not years.

"Even with that much energy trapped in the ring, I don't think it's enough to lead Neil to the book," Kieran said. "The WBI figured out when you three left town to hide the grimoires, and they've pulled up satellite images and have cell phone tower data from your phones. Old school, non-magical detective work that'll put them in the area close to the books' location. They'll use locator spells and scrying after that. Government-level Magic Cache. Several network witches are trailing the WBI. They're letting the WBI do all the work. It's their backup plan just in case Neil's plan to let *love show him the way* doesn't work."

It said a lot that even Neil's own brother thought the guy was out of his mind.

"Why are you telling us any of this?" Amber asked.

"You ended my curse," Kieran said matter-of-factly. He eyed Jack with an air of distaste. "Believe it or not, what you did for me trumps family loyalty. I'm forever indebted to you, Amber. My hope is you can find it in your heart to heal the rest of them."

Amber's gut wanted to believe him, but her gut was already doubting Raphael's loyalty. Did she now have a Penhallow as an ally and a Henbane an enemy? She supposed she could use a truth spell on him, but as she now knew, he could keep the truth from her if he was determined not to share it. She had the memory of a wicked sinus headache to prove it.

Could they use Kieran as a diplomatic force to sway the other Penhallows and their sympathizers?

Amber's phone buzzed in her pocket; she had a text from Chief Brown. Several, actually. And he'd called her, too.

Ten minutes ago: Answer your phone!

Nine minutes ago: Are you all right?

Seven minutes ago: Answer me in the next two minutes or I'm calling Agent Howe

Five minutes ago: Agent Howe is on her way

"Crap!" Amber said. "WBI is en route."

But Kieran already had a phone to his ear. He stared at her while he spoke. "Yeah, I had eyes on them, but Amber saw something in the crowd and ducked behind a building. Not sure how the WBI already knows that, though. I'm following her now and I've got the Patrice disguise on, so she doesn't suspect me of anything. I'll stay on her for now, but if anything changes in the WBI chatter, let me know and I'll head your way." He hung up and shoved his phone in his pocket. "We maybe have two minutes before we're found back here. Best bet is to break up the parade."

Kim gasped as if *this* was the most shocking thing said so far.

In the next second, Kieran changed from a black-haired man about Amber's height, to a six-foot-three television heartthrob. "I've got an idea."

Willow and Kim both turned a furious shade of red.

Jack laughed, rubbing a thumb across Amber's cheek. "Wow, you're even redder than that time Olaf Betzen made you forget your own name."

Amber flushed further and gently swatted his hand away. John Huntley's face was semi-less intimidating when she could see Kieran's just below the surface.

The sound-canceling spell dropped. Kieran flashed them an award-winning smile, pushed his way past them, and then started screaming "Help! Help!" as he took off at a run.

"It'll be nice to run after *him* for a change," Kim said, waggling her brows. "JOHN! John, my sweet baby angel, come back!"

"Ahhh!" screamed fake John, and he took off.

Willow, Amber, and Jack shrugged, then followed as well, calling John's name.

Fake John reached the mouth of the alley and then stopped abruptly. He looked left and right, gasping dramatically. "Goodness me! It is I, John Huntley, and I am in need of assistance!"

Kieran was even worse at this than Kim was.

A scream went up from their left and Amber glanced over to see a teenage girl hurtling down the sidewalk toward them.

"Oh my God," Kieran muttered.

From a few people over, Amber heard, *"Look! Is that …"*

"That looks just like John Huntley!"

"I think that is *John Huntley!"*

"He said on his socials that he might be at the parade today …"

Meanwhile, the sprinting teenage girl had gained four followers who were all running straight for them.

"Sweet mother …" Kieran said.

"Uhh…run," Amber said. "Now."

Kieran didn't need to be told twice. Amber, Willow, Kim, and Jack jumped apart to avoid being in a head-on collision with the sprinting girls. Amber recognized one of them from the grocery store—the girl who had a lawyer for an uncle. Tammy, maybe. She had her phone's screen in front of her face as she ran.

"Scuttle Hunters, I'm coming to you live from the Edgehill parade," she said into her screen as she went barreling past. "I have eyes on John. Today might be the day I finally catch him."

Amber almost felt bad for Kieran. She sent a quick text to Chief Brown letting him know where they were.

Then she addressed Willow. "What do we tell Agent Howe? We have to make a call on whether or not we trust Kieran, and then we have to stick with it."

In less than a minute, they were surrounded by Agent Howe and two other agents. They scanned the area around them, eyes wide and searching.

"What happened?" Agent Howe asked Amber. "What made you leave your post without informing your chief first?"

"Uhh …" Amber eloquently said, looking to her sister for help, but noticed the subtle movement of her lips.

"I saw John Huntley!" Kim yelped suddenly, drawing all the agents' attention away from Willow. She squeezed in between Amber and Jack, Willow slightly behind them. "I don't know if you know but I'm the head of the Here and Meow Festival and—"

"I don't see how this is relevant—" Agent Howe started.

"And!" Kim said, talking over her, "I was the mastermind behind getting John Huntley to the festival. He *loves* cats. Who doesn't love cats? I didn't expect to see him at the parade, so when I saw him, I said hi, but I did it with a little more intensity than a normal hello because I can sometimes be *a lot*, you know? He must not remember me though because he ran away when he saw me coming. I was like, Oh no, John, it's me! I'm in the here and now at the Here and Meow! Isn't that cute? I—oh my God, is that float on fire?"

Amber smelled something acrid a moment later and craned her neck to see past the agents. Someone ahead screamed. The agents ran toward the commotion. Amber's group followed, Willow continuing to mutter her spell under her breath.

A small patch of flames licked up the side of the rhododendron float. All those blue petals Amber had helped to attach to the replica of Lake Myrtle were starting to blacken and curl. As the last words of the spell left Willow's lips, flames overtook the sea of marbled flowers at the front of the float, too. Several people on the sidewalk stumbled back.

Amber and Willow shared a quick look and without discussing it, both cast wind spells, sending the air toward the flames, stoking them even more. That did it. The fire leaped even higher, jumping to the middle of the lake.

A commotion started farther up the parade route, in the direction Kieran had gone, and Amber glanced over just as the top of the willow tree on the garden float went up in a ball of flames. People started running this way and that, shouting about bombs and terrorists. Amber was sure Kieran had set the second fire as he ran past the float, presumably still being chased by John's fans. She was grateful he'd chosen that one, and not the one populated by cats.

Amber scanned the crowd, searching for Chief Brown. She could make out his cruiser still parked in front of the orange cones, but the man himself wasn't visible.

A horrible creak rent the air. Something was happening to the cat float now. She was just about to run toward it to free any trapped cats, when the frontmost, seed-covered cat *moved*.

"Oh my God," Kim muttered and sidled up next to Amber, the agents to their backs now. "Are *you* doing that?"

Which meant Amber hadn't imagined it. She had her reply on the tip of her tongue when the cat behind it moved too, and Amber nearly choked on the word "no." Then the third cat shifted, shaking its head like shucking off cobwebs. The wooden base on which the cats sat groaned as the animals, now fluid, got to all fours. The frantic crowd had slowed to watch the giant cats made of flowers and plant parts.

The black cat who had been at the front of the float—the one with the splash of white across its face, like Amber's own Alley—leaped onto the sidewalk. The two remaining cats tottered on their wooden perch. The people who had been nearby darted out of the way to avoid getting crushed by the six-foot-tall creature. It possessed the fluidity of movement that Amber's animated toys had, but it had an unnerving quality of otherness to it, due in large part to its massive size. Its wire-frame body creaked as it moved. Only a few feet of sidewalk separated Amber and the cat. It blinked its eyelids covered in black onion seeds, briefly hiding the sunflower petals that made up the yellow of its eyes.

"Consider this your final warning, Blackwood," the cat said, revealing its pink rose petal tongue and tapioca pearl-lined incisors. Its voice rumbled out of the cat's body. Amber could swear she felt the vibration in the soles of her feet. "You have until tonight to give us what we seek.

If you do not cooperate, it won't just be Henrietta's blood on your hands."

Amber's knees wanted to give out. Had they killed Henrietta because she hadn't handed over the Henbane book? Did that mean Kieran was wrong and the WBI wasn't close to finding it? Or was this another attempt to keep Amber distracted?

The cat then lowered its body toward the ground, its giant tail arched into the air. The two cats still on the float base had taken up a similar stance, each angled in a different direction. It was the same pose the rogue toys had dropped into before they attacked the children and parents at Balinese Park.

Kieran had said it was a witch from the Betel clan who had orchestrated that, not him. Heart hammering in her chest, she quickly scanned the crowd. Searching, searching—there, just past one of the cats on the float, was Patrice Penhallow. Amber was too far away to know if it was actually her, or Betel wearing her face.

"Willow," she hissed, and pulled her sister next to her. "Do you see that black-haired woman?"

It took Willow a second, but then she gasped. "It's the face Kieran had been wearing but …" She squinted. "It's a guy wearing a glamour. It's not Kieran."

"Simon's tincture really *is* Penhallow-specific then because I can't see the glamour," Amber whispered.

"And I can because Aunt G's is strong enough to detect high-level glamours, just not Penhallows?" Willow whispered back.

"I think so," Amber said. Then she took a step away from her sister. "We know you're there, Betel!"

The cat on the sidewalk cocked its head. "Perhaps you're more informed than they give you credit for," the cat said, still crouched. "The network needs to watch you more closely."

The cat sprang for her. Twin bursts of magic whizzed past her head. A moment later, the giant cat slammed into an invisible barrier mere inches from Amber and Willow. *Clang!* They both screamed. Seeds, petals, and other plant parts were knocked loose. The cat's wire neck didn't break so much as bend at an awkward angle.

"Get out of here now!" Agent Howe yelled from behind Amber.

Amber snapped to attention and turned around long enough to grab the hand of a wide-eyed Jack, while Willow grabbed the hand of an even wider-eyed Kim, and they ran.

CHAPTER 25

Guilt weighed Amber down and slowed her pace as she fled the scene. Edgehill residents and visiting tourists alike screamed behind her. She knew she'd left them in the hands of the capable WBI, who would not only do their best to protect the innocent in the crowd, but shut the attack down as fast as possible.

If you do not cooperate, it won't just be Henrietta's blood on your hands, the cat had said.

Heart in her throat, Amber let Jack's hand go so she could fish her phone out of her pocket as she ran. She called Thea Bishop.

"Hi, Amber," the woman said. "How are you? I heard you were back in town. I haven't gotten any word about a prosecuting attorney being assigned the case yet, but I'm building up an opposing one for you should it come to that. Is…do I hear screaming?"

"Yes…" Amber heaved, semi-relieved that Thea sounded so calm. "How is Henrietta?"

"Oh, you know, in a magic-induced coma," Thea said. "I'm here with her now. No changes, but she's steady."

Amber blew out a sigh of relief. It didn't mean that Henrietta was out of danger, though. "I'm sending an officer to stay with you."

Thea's tone changed instantly, as if she'd been causally slouching, and now sat upright. "Why?"

"The Penhallows are escalating," Amber said. "I still believe they targeted Henrietta only to rattle me, but I don't want to take any chances. Call me the second anything suspicious happens."

"Done."

The moment Amber disconnected the call, another one came through. Her pace had slowed slightly and she was now at the back of the pack.

It was Chief Brown. "Hi…chief …"

Screams rose in the background. "Amber! Where the heck did you go? What in the world is going on?"

She did her best to explain while she followed the group, Kim leading the way at a steady pace. Assuming the 5K still happened in the morning, Kim was sure to crush it. Willow and Jack kept shooting glances over their shoulders to make sure they weren't being followed.

"Are *you* okay?" she asked him.

"Carl and I are doing what we can to get people out of here," he said. "I've got all my officers on the way over here except for Garcia, who's still stationed outside Betty's shop. Your uhh…friends in suits seem to have the cat situation mostly under control at least. I say mostly because one of the cats took off; a few agents broke off to chase it."

Amber was sure this whole experience was going to scar the poor guy for life. "We're heading back over there right now. We can relieve Garcia when we get there. Is it okay if I send him to sit with Thea and Henrietta instead?"

"Fine by me," he said, knowing better by now not to ask questions. He cursed as a horrible crash sounded on his side. In a hushed, whispered tone, he said, "An eight-foot-tall cat just flipped a car. A *car*, Amber. My God."

The call ended. Yep, scarred for life.

Willow drove them back; Amber was too shaky. Hardly anyone said a word, which suited Amber just fine. Jack was in the back seat with her, his leg bouncing in time with her heartbeat.

Upon arriving at The Quirky Whisker, Amber was relieved that not many people were on the sidewalks here. Even the line for Purrfectly Scrumptious was relatively short, with only a dozen people waiting to go in, rather than the usual twenty-plus. Garcia had his cruiser parked directly outside, and he and Aunt G stood silently on the sidewalk, alternating their attention between foot traffic and Betty and Bobby inside the bakery.

Willow, Jack, and Kim went inside The Quirky Whisker while Amber ran across the street to let Garcia know he was needed elsewhere. He accepted this without a word and drove off.

Pulling her aunt aside, Amber gave her a quick run-down of events. "I think we can use both your tincture and Simon's. Maybe you two can combine recipes, though, and make a super tincture? Either way, we're going to need more of both."

Aunt G nodded. "I'll go get started on the next batch now."

"Amber, you're back," Amber heard and smiled as Betty came out the front door of her shop, Savannah at her heels. The Maine coon rubbed herself against Aunt G's leg, then sat and peered up at the three humans, as if she too were part of the conversation. Betty had walked out wiping her hands on a hand towel, which she now tossed over her shoulder. Her apron was dusted with flour, as usual. "Last I heard from you know who, they were making preparations."

Goodness knew what that meant. Were they planning to come *here*? They had to be in their mid-seventies at the youngest. "How much does Bobby know?"

"Oh, all of it," Betty said, wincing slightly. "Couldn't keep something like that from him."

"Are your employees able to take over for a while?" Amber asked. "Kieran knows that you know. He claims to be on our side, but if he lied or if he decides to divulge any of this, they might come after you to get information. If my mom and uncle both had the same, uhh…ability, and I have it as well, it's likely my grandpa has it, too—and only you know where he is. I don't think the Penhallows care at this point what path gets them to what they want—they just care about getting there."

Betty seemed to mull this over but nodded. "Give us ten minutes and we'll meet you up there."

Aunt G went into The Quirky Whisker to get started on her next tincture batch, while Amber waited out front for Betty. In those ten minutes, Zelda arrived with her daughter and two of their contacts. Amber felt like a bouncer at a nightclub checking IDs, but in this case, Simon's tincture was checking for Penhallows wearing glamours. Amber directed them upstairs.

Betty, Bobby, and Savannah arrived next. Savannah led the way, while Betty walked by with three boxes of cupcakes.

Bobby stopped in front of Amber while his wife went upstairs. "How you doing?" he asked, as he always did.

"Relieved to know you know my secret, honestly," Amber said.

His already dark skin turned a shade darker as he blushed. He ducked his head. "I can't tell you how many times I wanted to tell you I knew! But Betty kept telling me how important it was to keep it to ourselves. I hope you aren't cross with us."

"Of course not," Amber said. "But I am going to apologize now for how weird things are going to get up there."

He grinned. "Can't wait." He gave her arm a squeeze and then made his way across the shop.

Fifteen minutes later, Simon, Bianca, and three of their contacts arrived as well. Amber checked their glamours, listened to a tirade from Bianca about the destruction of her parade, and then locked up the shop behind the group, setting the alarm spell shortly after.

Her studio apartment was bustling with people. All told, there were eleven witches, five non-witches, and three cats. Amber was mildly concerned that the floor would collapse underneath them and send them crashing into the shop below.

Savannah sauntered around the place, greeting everyone in turn. Tom trotted along behind her, smitten. Alley, however, sat on the kitchen counter and surveyed the scene, managing to be hyper-aware and aloof at the same time, as only a cat could.

Simon, Willow, Aunt G, and one of Zelda's contacts were already fast at work in the kitchen, presumably comparing notes on the two glamour-revealing tinctures. Willow was currently doing most of the talking, periodically pointing at Amber as she did. Simon took note while the two women listened intently.

"Thank you, everyone, for helping with this," Amber said, a teacher in front of a class again. They all turned to look at her. She went through the details of the Penhallow situation, stating that it was unclear who Raphael Henbane and Kieran Penhallow were currently loyal to. "There's a ritual that will be performed tomorrow night at the ley line spillover. It's the fifty-year anniversary of the spell's creation."

"Is it true you cured Kieran's curse?" Zelda's daughter suddenly asked.

The witches in the room were especially interested in this answer. "Yes. He claims that's why he's loyal to me now. He hopes I can find a way to cure the others. Presumably, all the Penhallows will be at the ley line spillover tomorrow night. We need to come up with a game plan for how we can get that many witches shoved into the memory in 1971. I'm not strong enough to do it on my own. I was able to ask magic to help me to get two Penhallows transferred there, but just moving two of them almost knocked me out. I can't move a dozen or more at once. We need incapacitation spells and tinctures of every kind. Every defensive spell you've got. Maybe if they're all incapacitated at the same time, I can move them into the memory in waves. But they're all going to be on the defensive. We have to be as prepared as possible."

"A whole heck of a lotta things could go wrong," one of Simon's contacts said. He was an older, gruff-looking guy. He reminded Amber a little of Alan Peterson. Perhaps he was a detective who had worked with Simon's wife. "Penhallows are strong and unpredictable."

"You're not wrong," Amber said. "Which is why I want to hear every idea you all can come up with. You all have more experience than I do. I'm open to anything. The only thing I know is that we have to stop the ritual from happening. Who knows what could happen if they succeed in either turning back time *or* sending someone there."

The man seemed satisfied with that. In short order, nearly a dozen grimoires filled Amber's dining room table. After discussing the possibilities for several minutes, Willow joined the group. "I think you need a layout of the neighborhood to work from."

"Good idea." Amber grabbed her Edgehill map from the drawer in her coffee table and flipped it over, revealing the plain white back. She fetched a pencil for Willow. After clearing part of the table of grimoires, Willow sat at the table, closed her eyes for a moment, and then started to draw. Where her memory was fuzzy, Zelda helped fill in the gaps. Together they mapped out how many houses were on the street, how many were still intact, and a rough scale of the area. Then Willow added an X, marking the area just outside Zelda's house where most of the ley line activity occurred.

For the next hour, they worked in smaller groups. Some worked on sleep tinctures and spells that could possibly knock out a large group at once. Others worked on weather spells—everything from hurricane-level winds to flooding—to assess how feasible it was to create an event that would be quick and efficient enough to take out all the Penhallows before they could stop the spell or retaliate. One witch in particular was doing all she could to argue for the use of a blizzard spell she hadn't had an opportunity to put into action yet.

The non-witches, save for Betty and Bobby, had assignments, too. Kim and Jack went around the room asking for people's orders, while Bianca called them in to Catty Melt. Willow then glamoured Kim and Jack to look like a pair of cat-obsessed tourists. Jack was now a fifty-year-old man in a "Purranormal Activity" shirt, and Kim was now a middle-aged woman in a tiger onesie. Amber walked them to the shop's front door.

"Some people might be bummed out to get the job of gofer while everyone does all the hard work," Jack said, just before stepping out onto the sidewalk, "but I feel like I'm in the war room of a post-apocalyptic movie just before the alien spaceship lands."

"Oh my God," Kim said, holding onto her long, striped tail. "I was thinking the same thing!"

Amber laughed to herself as she watched them go.

Back upstairs, Amber floated between the groups while periodically checking on Betty and Bobby, who looked on in wild-eyed wonder. Amber supposed Kim, Jack, and especially Bianca were used to being around witches at this point, but it was all new for the Harrises.

Amber's phone buzzed on her nightstand, and she excused herself from the group, who were in a heated argument about the feasibility of reverse-engineering a headache tincture into a debilitating, airborne vapor. She expected it to be Jack or Kim calling about an issue with the large food order, but instead saw Edgar's grumpy face staring back at her.

"Hi, Edgar, is everything all right?" she asked in greeting. She could tell from the background noise that he was driving, likely with the window down.

"No," he said, voice tight. "Something is wrong with Neil. Well, more wrong than usual. He says he's close to finding the Henbane grimoire and when he does, he'll have to break the bond he and I have. And apparently the only way to do that is for one of us to die. He said something about a ritual and that in order for it to be successful, he has to be whole again."

"That's not happening," Amber said. "Where are you?"

"On my way to you," he said. "Maybe it's stupid of me to be moving, since I'm sure there's a way for him to track my location with this so-called bond now that he's loose in the world. I just couldn't stay by myself anymore."

"Well, you're heading to the right place because my apartment is currently full of witches. You'll be safe here. That guy would have to go through all of us to get to you," she said. "Kim and Jack just went to get food. I may or may not have told them to order you some pancakes just in case you decided you wanted to join us. It should get here the same time you do."

It took him a moment to speak. "I appreciate it, cousin," he choked out.

"See you soon."

Within fifteen minutes, Edgar and the food arrived, briefly disrupting the brainstorming session. Amber, Jack, and Kim passed out food while Edgar explained his connection to Neil and the message Edgar had just received from him. Because it was still unclear how and what Neil was able to view or learn from Edgar through this connection, they decided it was best to keep Edgar as far away from the discussion as possible. So, once everyone got back to work, he, Betty, and Bobby had a picnic on Amber's bed with the three cats, away from the group at large.

It was while Amber was walking around the studio with a trash bag, collecting sandwich wrappers, empty chip bags, and biodegradable containers, like an attendant at the end of a flight, that a horrible buzzing made her come up short. Something crashed in the kitchen and Willow stumbled out, her hands over her ears. The buzzing wasn't so much painful as deafening, like a swarm of thousands of insects had just poured into the room. Amber dropped the half-full trash bag to clap her own hands over her ears, but it didn't help. It was impossible to block out a sound that came from *inside* your head.

She was vaguely aware that the others had noticed. They were on their feet. Mouths were moving and brows were furrowed and the tension in the room was mounting, but Amber couldn't hear anything over the horrible buzzing.

No one seemed to hear it except for herself and Willow.

And then just as suddenly as it had started, it stopped. The silence left in its wake was almost as loud as the buzzing had been. Amber and Willow stood directly in front of each other; Amber didn't remember making her way over to her sister, but they'd been pulled together like magnets.

Before Amber could voice a question, Aunt G bustled out of the kitchen, put a hand on either of their stomachs, and violently shoved them apart. Amber stumbled back a step.

Willow yelped, "What the—"

CRASH!

Amber flinched.

There, on the floor, directly between Amber and her sister was the trunk of grimoires they'd hidden in Quill. A few seconds of stunned silence passed as Amber stared at the dusty box. Her wild gaze flicked from her aunt to her sister and back again.

She couldn't process what she was seeing.

Either the Penhallows or the WBI had found the chest, gotten through all the cloaking and defensive spells, and then triggered the boomerang spell that sent the books back to their owners: Amber and Willow.

Who had found it first?

Edgar let out a growl on the other side of the room. He was on his feet now, hands on his knees. "Neil is…*furious.*" He slowly stood and stared at Amber. "He knows it's in Edgehill now. He's coming for it."

"Hurry!" Aunt G said. "Every cloaking spell everyone has. Cast it onto the books—*now!*"

The room filled with spells, witches casting cloaking spells one after the other. The words flooded Amber's head like the buzzing had earlier.

A few minutes later, Edgar growled again. "The book dropped off their radar again. But they still know it's here. Geez. He's never been this angry." He started to pace in front of the window bench seat. "I have to get out of here. I'll do what I can to block him from reading my thoughts, but he knows how to get past my defenses. As soon as I get tired or slip even a little, he weasels his way in. It's only a matter of time. I need to get out so I don't put any of you or the books in danger. Maybe if I keep moving it'll help distract him."

Amber hated this idea. "Where would you go? You're safer here."

"Am I though?" he asked, stopping to stare at her across the small expanse of her apartment. "This is the first place they'd check, right? Sure, we can layer this place with as many soundproofing and alarm spells as we've got, but they could easily trap us in here. And we already know Neil isn't above burning a place to the ground with people still in it if he thinks it'll get him what he wants."

Amber's stomach churned.

"There's no need to be cruel, Edgar," Aunt G snapped.

"No, he's right," Amber said, holding up a hand. "Neil wants the spell and Edgar for the ritual. It's probably not smart to keep both in the same place."

Edgar visibly swallowed and lightly wrung his hands. "Where do I go?"

Before Amber could reply, Willow said, "Don't even think about it, Amber. You can't leave. And neither can you, Aunt G. You need to finish making those tinctures. Edgar and I can each take a Penhallow-specific one, glamour ourselves, and go hide out in the crowd. This is still the first night of the festival. I'm guessing the WBI took care of the giant cats. Where better to hide than in a sea of people? The Penhallows do it all the time."

Amber still hated the idea. But at least they'd have each other as magical backup. "Do it. Keep each other safe."

Aunt G went into the kitchen to grab the tinctures. Amber heard the crunch of glass as her aunt trod through whatever mess Willow had made when the sudden buzzing had incapacitated her and Amber. Amber noted how badly her aunt's hands shook as she handed a vial each to Edgar and Willow.

Within ten minutes, Willow and Edgar, wearing the faces of average-looking middle-aged men, and still shuddering from the aftertaste of the tinctures, headed for the stairs. Amber followed them out. She stood on the sidewalk and scanned semi-deserted Russian Blue Avenue. She didn't see any of the iterations of Patrice Penhallow lurking about or peering in windows.

As Amber watched Willow and Edgar drive away, she hoped that keeping Edgar as a moving target would increase his chances of not being found.

When she turned to head back into her shop, she found her aunt standing there, her face pale. "Am I too late?"

"What do you mean?" A moment later, Amber noticed that her aunt tightly held two tincture vials in her fist.

"I gave them my tincture, not Simon's," Aunt G said. "They won't be able to detect Penhallows. My premonitions keep changing because the variables keep shifting. If something happens to Willow because I'm not thinking clearly, I ..."

Amber quickly pulled out her phone and sent a group text to Willow and Edgar. *You have the wrong tincture. Trust no one.*

That ship already sailed, Edgar replied.

Despite the hollow feeling in her gut, Amber smiled faintly. Then she wrapped an arm around her aunt and guided her back inside. "It'll be okay," Amber assured her.

She just hoped that wasn't a lie.

CHAPTER 26

Amber had always known intuitively that contact with a subject made a spell that much stronger. What she didn't know was that powerful spells worked best when cast as a group. Some spells *only* worked that way.

"Forming covens was a more common practice in the days before the witch council broke magic," Zelda said. "Not only did the ley lines splinter that day, but so did families, covens, and communities. Witches felt safer spaced apart, since it made Penhallows have to work twice as hard to find them. Witches became scared to live in witch communities as well. After all, they wouldn't have suffered from magic sickness or been driven out of their homes had they been in magic-free towns and cities."

"Not to mention," Simon's gruff-looking friend, Gary, said, "the council had been a government-level coven, in a way. They'd argued that a group of witches working together would be in the best interest of the community as a whole. Yet, as a group, they'd made the worst collective decision magic had ever seen. It put a bad taste in everyone's mouth. Though there are still witch towns, there are far fewer than there used to be. Then, with the ever-present Penhallow threat—because they *had* shown up unexpectedly and picked off whole communities—people went their own ways. It's essentially what's happening right now. When Penhallows are around, it feels safer splitting up. They can't pick everyone off like fish in a barrel if there are multiple barrels."

It wasn't a comforting thought.

"Well, I'm grateful this many of you showed up to help," Amber said, "especially when the threat is so closely tied to my family."

"As far as I'm concerned," said a contact of Zelda's, "there are only two choices at this point: be proactive or stick my head in the sand. Too many witches for too long have chosen the latter. It doesn't really matter how we got into this mess—it only matters how we get out."

Amber smiled appreciatively at the woman, Irene. She was a kitchen witch like Simon and Aunt G, and was still convinced that a weaponized headache-causing tincture was their best course of action.

"I have to admit that's part of why I'm here," said Zelda's daughter Scarlett, "is because I've never met a time witch before. The possibilities of how your power could be used blows my mind. Have you ever *frozen* time?"

Amber had only done this once and it was largely by accident while at the junior fashion show. Kieran, wearing Olaf Betzen's face, had taunted Amber to the point that her frustration had bubbled over. She'd inadvertently poured all her magic into the word "Stop!" Everyone in the room had frozen in place—even Kieran had frozen, but not for long. "I don't know if I actually stopped time and Kieran was more resistant to it than others, or if *he* had frozen time and made me believe it had been me."

But then his words came floating back to her. "*You froze nearly a hundred people! And with only a single word. Annabelle had been a prodigy with time magic, and it seems she passed it on to you. It took three decades to unleash it, but here it is. I figured you'd need a highly emotional situation to wake it up.*"

It *had* been her. And it had been yet another way the Penhallows had been working behind the scenes to push her in the direction they wanted. All of it leading up to this ritual to manipulate time and history to get an outcome they liked better than the reality they were living in now.

"I can guarantee it wasn't Kieran who froze time," Zelda said. "I can't stress enough how rare time magic is, Amber."

Several others sitting around the table nodded.

"It's the type of magic most witches wish they could do solely because so many of us can't," Simon said.

Amber supposed a witch other than herself would have puffed up in pride at this. She was unique. She was rare. A unicorn like her mother. But the truth was, it felt like too much responsibility. Time magic would have been in better hands with someone like Simon or Zelda. Really, anyone sitting at this table with her would have been a better fit.

"I think what we should try to do instead of blizzards or a coordinated throwing of sleep tinctures or a widespread confusion spell," Scarlett said, "is a coven-driven power-funneling spell. If we can funnel all our magic into Amber, maybe it'll give her the equivalent of that strong emotion Kieran bullied her into. And then she can channel all that extra juice into a time-freeze spell."

"Turning me into a human super-charged battery. Got it," Amber said, mildly queasy.

"Magic from ten other witches flooding into someone simultaneously is just as likely to cause magic sickness as an eruption from the ley lines," Zelda said.

"But," Gary said, "Amber said the magic at the ley lines communicated with her, right? I'm sure you remember spells of permission, Zelda. Perhaps that could work here."

Zelda smiled ruefully. "Oh, how I hated spells of permission!" Addressing Amber, she said, "Back when I was a child, there was a school of thought that we needed to *ask* magic to use it. Scarlett has a really great analogy that people younger than me might better understand." She affectionately patted her daughter's hand.

"So, think of the ley lines a bit like the internet," Scarlett said. "It's out there for anyone to use as long as you have a way to access it. Magic is part of everything on earth, and witches especially have an easier time accessing it. But just like with the internet, things can get clogged up if too many people are using it at the same time in the same place. So, a way to keep things from getting clogged up—especially when witch communities were more common—witches used to ask magic if it was okay to use it. Spells were said to be more powerful when magic gave the witch permission first."

Emerging from the kitchen, Aunt G said, "Perhaps you have a bond with the magic there now, little mouse, because you asked for permission rather than making demands."

Amber pursed her lips. "Maybe …"

"I like this idea a lot," Simon said. "Once Amber freezes the Penhallows, they can be transferred to the memory where you can heal them."

They made it sound so easy. That much magic was sure to knock her flat on her butt—and she might not be able to get back up. But if it meant it could finally put an end to the Penhallows' reign of terror on the witch community at large, she was willing to give it a try.

She wondered how much the WBI knew about the ritual. Clearly they'd known why the Penhallows were ramping up this weekend, but did they know *when* it was happening? Were they chasing down leads? Had they abandoned Edgehill altogether when they lost track of the book? Were they on their way here now to tear the place to its foundations?

Shaking that thought loose, Amber got to work on a time-freezing spell, while Simon and Aunt G went back to their tincture-making operation, and the remaining witches settled into brainstorming the best way to funnel their magic into Amber without short-circuiting her system like the witch council had short-circuited the ley lines.

She stress-ate the three remaining cupcakes, even though one of them was an experimental sweet potato cupcake. Not even Betty could make that one work.

Jack and Bobby were crowded on the bed with the three cats draped over various laps. They'd set up Amber's laptop to watch a movie, but within twenty minutes, both men were passed out in a nearly identical fashion: heads tipped back against the wall, hands folded in their laps, and their mouths hung slightly open. Kim, Bianca, and Betty were sitting side by side on the window bench seat, deep in conversation about something. Bianca and Kim weren't currently trying to strangle each other, so there was that, at least.

As Amber wrote and rewrote the time-freezing spell, she cast furtive glances at the trunk of her parents' grimoires, still sitting where the boomerang spell had dropped it. No one had wanted to move it, worried that any shift in its location would also shift the cloaking spells layered on top of it. Amber wished she could study her mother's spells—she almost surely had something in there Amber could use as a starting point. But Amber knew it was too much of a risk. For all she knew, the building was currently surrounded by Penhallows waiting for a single pulse of magic from the grimoire to confirm that what they wanted was here.

Contacting the WBI meant admitting she had the grimoire. They'd likely conk her over the head, make off with the book, and never look back.

So she was on her own for this.

When her cell phone buzzed by her arm, she jumped; she'd been so lost in her task that everything else had fallen away for a while. Edgar's grumpy mug stared up at her. "Hey," she answered, wedging the phone between her ear and shoulder while she flipped the page on one of Willow's legal pads. Maybe she needed a thesaurus for the word "freeze." Too many of the words she chose had a temperature connotation attached to them.

"Willow is gone," Edgar said, voice edged with panic.

Amber dropped her pen and sat up straight. "What do you mean she's *gone*?"

"I mean…I woke up and she was gone," he said. "I'm…in her car, in the back seat. And she's not here.

Her purse and phone are gone. The keys are in the ignition."

Shooting to her feet, she called out, "Aunt G? Can you call Willow?" Then to Edgar she said, "Where is the car?"

"Uhh …" The sound of fabric on leather echoed through the phone and she could picture him adjusting himself on the back seat as he peered out the back windows of Willow's car. "It looks like I'm in a parking lot near the Manx Hotel. I'm near the alley by that weird brunch place that was only open until three."

"In Gravy?" she asked.

"Yeah, that one."

The place had recently folded. It had been the brainchild of some celebrity chef known for his decadent sauces. Every breakfast and brunch dish featured his sauce in one way or other, but the prices were so outlandish and the hours so weird that not even the high-end clientele that usually stayed at the Manx could keep the place afloat.

"It goes straight to voicemail, little mouse," Aunt G said.

Amber pursed her lips. None of this sounded like Willow. "What's the last thing you remember?" she asked Edgar.

"Uhh…we went to go meet…oh!" he said, his memory clearly returning in pieces. "John Huntley. You know, that famous guy? He and Willow hit it off or something and we came over here so I could meet him. I binged all of *Vamp World* recently, and meeting the star of the show sounded like a cool thing to cross off my bucket list before the lunatic Penhallow in my brain mur—"

"Don't be so morbid," Amber interrupted him. "So you went over there to meet John. Did Willow tell you to wait in the car while she went to go see him? Did you fall asleep while you were waiting?"

"No," he said. "Shut *up*, Neil, I'm trying to think! I don't care that my family has ruined your night. Mine's not going so great either." He grumbled. "Sorry, Amber, I'm trying to remember but it's really hard to focus when someone is basically scream-singing 'It's A Small World' in your head. Willow and I…uhh…Neil! *Shut. Up.*"

A sick feeling was washing over Amber. "Edgar," she said slowly, "do you think Neil is being extra annoying to keep you from thinking straight? Is he trying to make it harder for you to remember what happened?"

Edgar huffed out a breath. "Dang it. Maybe. I…okay, give me a second. I started using the noise-canceling spell in my head. It's like shutting a door in my brain. I can still hear him behind it, but it's not as loud. He's just good about knocking it back down."

Amber paced in a tight line while she waited for him to get his mind in order, at least temporarily.

"Oh. Oh, crap. Yeah, now I remember. I went with her," Edgar said. "John told her to meet him behind the Manx Hotel since that's where his tour bus is. He said he was going to take us into Portland for a nice dinner or something. He'd been at the parade and when all hell broke loose, he got into a fight with his manager, who wanted to pull him off the concert roster."

Amber let him ramble.

"Anyway," he said, taking a deep breath, "Willow knocked her glamour loose so we wouldn't freak the guy out, but we left mine on. We met him back there, but it wasn't really him.

His glamour came off pretty quick. It was that black-haired lady…Patrice, right? She hit me with the strongest dang sleep spell I'd ever felt. It was like being hit in the chest with a boulder. It knocked me clear on my butt. I swear I passed out before I hit the ground. Then I woke up in the back of this car, with Willow gone." He groaned. "Does the tincture not work? Why couldn't we see her glamour?"

"Aunt G handed you the wrong ones by accident," Amber said.

"What's happened, little mouse?" Aunt G asked, her voice rising an octave. "Where's Willow?" Amber held up a hand to quiet her.

"I'm really sorry, Amber," Edgar said. "I should have just stayed locked up in my house. I made everything worse."

"Stop it," she said. "I'm coming to get you. Don't move. We'll figure this out, okay? The ritual isn't until tomorrow night. We have some time."

"I don't think they ever wanted me," he said after a moment. "Neil is…laughing now. He's saying that part of their success is because of how predictable we all are."

Oh, she was so sick of these Penhallows! "Stay put." Then she disconnected the call.

She turned to find Aunt G just behind her, her eyes wide and her hands clenched in front of her. "Patrice took Willow."

Aunt G's bottom lip shook. "Let's go find her, then."

"No," Amber said. "I need you all here with the books. And I need you to start scrying and using locator spells to pinpoint where Willow is. They couldn't have taken her far. Call me when you find her. I'm going to pick up Edgar. He's not doing great, and I don't trust him to drive right now."

Aunt G grabbed Amber's hands. "I will be so angry with you if you don't come back."

Amber planted a kiss on her forehead. "We'll both be back, okay?"

With a nod, Aunt G went into practical mode, and started instructing the others on what to do now that the plan had shifted to locating Willow.

Why the heck was this happening to Willow *now*? Did this ritual require twenty-four hours of prep?

Amber rounded on her friends and Jack. He and Bobby were awake again and on their feet. Jack closed the distance between them.

"Please stay here," she begged him. "I'm going to get Edgar and come right back. You're safer surrounded by witches here than you would be with me."

"Yeah, but who is going to protect *you*?" Jack asked.

She leaned in quickly to kiss him.

Kim and Betty stood side by side in front of the window, their hands clasped. Kim looked like she might cry.

"Keep it together, Kim," Amber said gently. "I'll be right back."

"Famous last words," Kim and Bianca said in unison.

Amber grumbled. "Worst time for you two to be on the same page."

Then, before anyone could stop her, she grabbed her purse, keys, and phone, and hurried down the steps, across her shop, and into the darkening evening.

CHAPTER 27

Amber was just about to pull out onto Russian Blue Avenue when someone stepped in front of her car, a hand out like a crossing guard. Amber slammed on the brakes. "*Penhallow!*" her mind screamed, but Simon's tincture didn't reveal a second face.

It took a moment for it to register who the person was. When she rounded the side of Amber's car to stand at the driver's side door, Amber was more confused than terrified when she rolled down her window.

"Hi. My name is Tammy," the teen girl said. "You know John Huntley, right?"

Know was a stretch, but Amber nodded. "I do."

"Well, okay, so I've been tracking him around town the last couple days and I saw him with a lady the other day…a lady who I've seen come out of your shop a few times," Tammy said. "You two look pretty similar, so I'm guessing she's your sister?"

"Yeah," Amber said slowly, her heart thumping. "Willow."

Tammy nodded. "Thought so. My parents got a room in the Manx Hotel to increase my chances of running into him accidentally on purpose, but it hasn't been working. I knew he hadn't gone to the parade because he was doing phone interviews scheduled during the same time. Then a bunch of people went nuts on Scuttle saying he was at the parade, which I knew wasn't true since all his bodyguards were still at the hotel waiting on him. I got kicked out of his hallway for loitering, so I was in the bushes outside waiting for him to come out. He likes to check out his concert space the night before he performs, so I knew he was gonna have to leave eventually. While I was out there, I saw Willow walk behind the hotel with some old guy. I was trying to get up the nerve to follow them and then I heard all this noise like people were in a fight, you know? I almost ran over there to make sure John was okay, but like if a six-foot-tall guy was getting his butt handed to him, what good was a teenage girl gonna do? So I just waited and then this redheaded lady walked out from behind the hotel with Willow thrown over her shoulder like she was a sack of potatoes or something, put her in the back of a black SUV, and drove off with her."

Amber blinked rapidly at her, shocked more than anything. Someone had *taken* Willow? It was almost too much for Amber's mind to handle, so she focused on something smaller. "Red hair and not black?"

"Yeah," Tammy said. "It looked a lot like that lady who helped John escape the bathroom at the grocery store. I don't think you were there. She was Irish or Scottish or something? Her hair was in two braids."

Had Patrice donned a second glamour after she'd knocked out Willow and Edgar?

"I'm sorry I didn't stop her," Tammy said quickly, wringing her hands. "But I got the license plate. The plate was from Washington, though, not Oregon. Maybe you could tell the cops? I figured they wouldn't listen to a kid if I told them any of this."

"Holy crap," Amber finally said. "I could hug you. You absolutely did the right thing."

Tammy beamed.

"Where are your parents, by the way?"

Tammy shrugged. "Probably getting drunk somewhere."

"I'm heading back to the hotel right now," Amber said. "I need to pick up my cousin. Can I give you a ride?"

"Sure!" Tammy said. "It was kind of a long walk."

It was a *very* long walk. While Tammy ran around the car to get in the passenger seat, Amber called Chief Brown, putting him on speaker.

"Hi, Amber, I can't really—"

"Hi, Owen," Amber said quickly. "Willow was kidnapped and I have a teenage girl with me who saw it happen. Apparently it was *Sienna Tate* who took her."

"Uhh ..." he said.

"Yeah, I don't know either," Amber said. "Tammy got the license plate on the car. I've got several…um…people working to find her right now, but some old-fashioned police work could help, too."

"Good grief," he said, but immediately went into his by-the-book cop mode. "Okay, young lady, start at the beginning and tell me what you saw."

As Amber drove, Tammy told the story again, this time including the license plate number and a detailed description of the vehicle.

"I don't say this lightly, Tammy," the chief said. "But I'm very impressed right now."

Tammy beamed at the praise again.

"It's true," Amber said. "He's never impressed."

"It must be really cool to date a cop," Tammy said. "Do you guys have kids?"

Amber and Chief Brown let out twin shudders of disgust.

"We're just friends," Amber said.

"I'll get started on this on my end," the chief said. "Things are a bit chaotic here and our resources are stretched thin without Garcia, but I'll do what I can."

"Thanks," Amber said, then disconnected the call.

The drive to the hotel was like being in the car with Kim, but Tammy could somehow talk even faster and switched topics with a frequency that nearly gave Amber whiplash. But it helped distract Amber from how worried she was about Willow.

Amber pulled up outside the hotel and thanked Tammy again for all her help.

Tammy got out but poked her head back inside. "This might be nothing, but I think someone else might have seen Willow get taken, too."

Amber cocked her head. "What do you mean? Who?"

Tammy shrugged. "It's this lady I saw outside your shop a few times and around the hotel. I figured she was another Hunter like me, but I tried talking to her once and she was really mean and called me a child." Tammy wrinkled her nose. "Anyway, I'm like eighty percent sure I saw that same lady creeping around out front tonight. When Willow was taken, another car drove off like a minute after the SUV left. There was a guy driving. The windows were pretty dark, but I think it was her in the passenger seat 'cause she had really blonde hair—like almost white?—so it kinda glowed."

Amber pursed her lips. "Was she about five feet tall and her hair was really long? Blue eyes?"

"Yeah!" Tammy said. "Do you know her?"

"I think I do …" It sounded suspiciously like Molly Hargrove. "You're a real gem, Tammy. Truly."

Amber would never underestimate how resourceful and observant teenagers could be ever again.

The girl grinned. "Happy I could help. I really hope your sister is okay."

"Me too," Amber said, her chest aching. She watched as Tammy ran up the steps of the Manx Hotel before Amber made a U-turn and headed for In Gravy.

Sure enough, Willow's car was still parked behind the diner near the back of the oval-shaped lot. The cabin and rear taillights of Willow's car were dark. Evening was encroaching quickly. The second Amber stepped out of her own car beside Willow's, the back door flew open and Edgar poked his head out. His eyes were wild and red-rimmed, his hair was unruly, and his skin had paled. He looked terrible.

"Is Neil getting worse?" she asked softly.

He nodded. Voice cracking on the last word, he asked, "Any word about Willow?"

"Not yet," she said. "Hey, did you see Molly Hargrove tonight?"

"That Marbleglen reporter lady?" Edgar asked. "No, why?"

"I'm guessing you won't go back to my place?" she asked.

He vigorously shook his head. "No. I'm doing what I can to block Neil out, but I'm losing the battle. If I break while I'm near the others, I'm going to give up valuable information to Neil by accident. I already got Willow kidnapped. I don't need any more screwups on my record tonight."

Amber mulled over their options. How had Patrice managed to lure Willow and Edgar to the hotel? "We need to go check on John," she said.

They hopped in Amber's car and drove the few blocks back to the hotel. They sat at the curb, staring at the currently open gate that secured the back parking lot. From this vantage point, Amber could see a sliver of the tour bus's front. If something had happened to John, wouldn't there be more commotion? Wouldn't someone have called the National Guard?

"Let's go," she said.

They ran down the driveway, through the open gate, and around the hedge-lined cement toward the tour bus tucked in the back. Amber heard no voices and saw no one. When she and Edgar reached the massive beige and maroon bus, they stood before the door and shared a wide-eyed look. Swallowing, Amber knocked.

Nothing.

She tried the door, and found it unlocked. Opening it a crack, she called out, "Hello?"

Oh, if Patrice had murdered America's heartthrob …

Slowly opening the door the rest of the way, she crept up the four steps and peered inside. There were men collapsed on the floor, flopped over chairs, and one had face-planted in his salad at a small table. Thankfully, at least two of them were snoring, confirming they were asleep and not dead.

John was slumped on the floor in the narrow hallway in the back, flanked by bunk beds. Amber crept over sleeping bodies, careful not to step on hands or feet as she went. Edgar was playing lookout at the door.

Crouching beside John, she checked his pulse to make sure he was in fact still alive. Magic was the only way to wake someone from a sleep spell prematurely, so she called on her power and braced herself. When Amber had woken a drunken Bianca Pace from a sleep spell, Bianca had jolted back into consciousness…while screaming.

Casting the spell, she touched John's hand, then hurled her magic at him.

He sat straight up. "AHH!"

Amber fell backward.

On his feet in a second, he put up his fists. "Who the hell are you and what are—*Amber*?"

"Hi, John," she said, getting to her feet and brushing herself off. "Look, I can explain. Actually, no I can't. Did you call Willow earlier?"

"Willow!" he said, scanning the area behind him. "Yeah, she was going to meet me here and I was going to take her and her friend to dinner in Portland, but then some really terrifying woman broke into the bus and then—*bam!* Lights out."

Amber swallowed. "That scary lady kidnapped Willow."

"Wait, what?" he said. "Okay, I can send the three Ts out to find her. They're ex-military. They can track anyone. Give me ten minutes and I can mobilize a huge unit of—"

"Dang it," Amber said, realizing that this was all getting too messy. "You're so sweet and I love that you care this much about her. But you can't do any of that."

He cocked his head. "What do you mean? Don't you—"

"John Huntley," she said, "*sleep.*"

His eyes rolled back in his head and he tipped back onto the floor.

"Oh my God, I'm so sorry!" she said as she spun on her heel and gingerly made her way back across the bus. "I'll buy all your albums after this is over!"

Amber and Edgar bolted for her car again. She sent a text to Chief Brown letting him know that John Huntley and his staff had been put under a sleep spell and were currently unconscious in his tour bus.

My God, he replied. I'll see what I can do. We're swamped. One of the float cats is still on the loose. It tried to eat someone's dog.

You'll be more swamped if the Hunters catch wind of John's current unconscious condition. They'll run off with him.

I don't know how much more I can take tonight.

It'll be a national scandal if he goes missing, chief!

Sorry. I can't hear you. The reception is terrible. Insert crackle noises, he texted back.

Of all the nights for him to develop a sense of humor!

When she dropped her phone in a cup holder, Edgar asked, "Why did you ask if I saw Molly tonight?"

Amber's magic flared along with her anger. That Molly Hargrove! Without replying, Amber snatched up her phone again and called Connor Declan. He didn't answer. Amber hung up when the call went to voicemail, then dialed again. Voicemail. She called Molly, which went to voicemail after one ring. Then she called Connor again.

"What can I do for you, Amber?" he asked, then shushed someone. It sounded like he was on the move.

"Look, Connor, I know Molly is with you."

A brief pause. "Hello, Amber," Molly said, voice tight. "What do you want?"

Blowing out a breath, Amber steeled herself. "I know you know I'm a witch."

Connor cursed. Edgar cocked his head at her.

Molly said, "Are you both Cassie Westbottom and Sienna Tate? You can…change your face?"

Amber sighed. "Yes."

Now Molly cursed. "So it *was* you in the car that day I drove Sienna to Ma and Paw's. Ugh. I'm such an idiot. I spilled *everything* to you. Did you use a truth spell on me again like you did outside the float barn?"

Molly was more intuitive than Amber gave her credit for.

"No, there was no truth spell. You *really* hate me so all you needed was a willing audience and you talked freely," Amber said.

"They were right about you," Molly muttered.

"Who?"

"The Penhallows," Connor said, his tone matter of fact. "We know all about the feud between the Penhallows and Blackwoods, okay?" He awkwardly cleared his throat. "Just let Willow go. There has to be some other way than sacrificing her to perform this ritual of yours. She's your *sister*, Amber."

It took Amber a few seconds for all of that to settle in her mind. Molly had been there when Willow was kidnapped. Molly had seen Sienna Tate—a known alias and glamour of Amber's—walk away from the Manx Hotel with Willow over her shoulder. Molly just hadn't seen the full spectrum of the glamours Patrice used tonight.

"Patrice became your new contact after Kieran went to prison," Amber said, but it wasn't a question. "She's your witch source who gives you information no one else would know. Like my products malfunctioning."

"Don't blame Patrice for any of this," Molly said. "She predicted Henrietta's coma, your toys attacking those children on Kids Day, and that you'd sabotage the parade. All of it came true."

"Yeah, because she's the one who *made* all of that happen!" Amber snapped. "It would be like getting tips about fires set by the arsonist herself."

Molly laughed. "You *are* obsessed with fire, aren't you? She said you were. And she also said if I was outside the Manx Hotel at 6:15, I would have proof of how out of control you've gotten. You're so hell-bent on ruining this town and hurting everyone in it that you'd even turn on your own family. So where's Willow?"

Amber was so frustrated, her eyes watered. "I don't *know*. Patrice took her, not me."

Hitting the mute button on her phone for a second, she instructed Edgar to take her Edgehill map out of her glove box and to start scrying not for Willow, but for Connor. He found a pencil in the glove box, too. With the map laid out across his knees, he loosely held the pencil by its eraser to act as a pointing device. He closed his eyes, his lips moving quickly as he cast the spell. Amber hoped they'd get a hit quickly, since Connor and Molly couldn't have gotten far.

Amber's mind whirled. It wasn't running in any particular direction. It just ran and ran without going anywhere—like Thea had been in her wheel.

A soft tap drew her attention to the map. Edgar's pencil had landed.

"Looks like Feral's Diner," Edgar said.

Amber pulled out onto the street. Feral's was a good fifteen minutes away. She hit the gas. She knew she should be focused on the task at hand—namely coming up with the best way to stop the Penhallows' ritual—but she was so unbelievably angry in that moment that her vision tunneled out. How could either of them believe she would hurt Willow? It was so insulting, Amber saw red.

If Aunt G called with the hit on Willow's location, she would immediately change course. But with everything currently spinning out of control, with no clue where her sister was, or when exactly this ritual would take place or what it entailed, and with her fear of inadequacy scream- ing in her head, all she could focus on was how much she wanted to get to Connor and Molly if only so she could punch them in their faces for making a stressful day ten times worse.

"We saw you that day, you know," Connor said finally, cutting into her wildly scattered thoughts. Amber tapped the mute button on her phone that was now attached to her dashboard. "That day in the abandoned neighborhood when you made those two Penhallows disappear. Patrice told us you'd do something awful to them. We just had to be in the right place at the right time."

"Patrice said she needed us nearby so Damien and Devra could more easily create replicas of us," Molly said. "They were supposed to taunt you to see if you really had forbidden magic. And then you…made them vanish into thin air. Patrice said if we reported back to her about what we saw, she'd give us enough information to take all of this public. The story to set our careers in motion. The world needs to know that there's a bunch of evil witches in Edgehill who plan to burn their enemies to the ground. No one believed you that your parents were supposedly killed in a fire, so now you're going to use fire as revenge. Well, we're not going to let you do it, Amber."

What in the *heck* was she talking about?

"Patrice is hunting you right this second. You know better than anyone how extensive her scrying skills are," Connor said. "We can negotiate with Patrice on your behalf. She doesn't *want* to hurt you, but you're leaving her little choice. We have a secret meeting place with Patrice. We're there now. You can bring Willow to us, no questions asked. If you agree to abandon the ritual and exile yourself, like

Patrice has been begging you to do, no one will get hurt. But that can only happen if you give Willow up, Amber."

Amber shot an incredulous look at Edgar, who looked even more baffled than she did.

"Why on earth do you think I would do anything to Willow?" Amber blurted.

Molly laughed. "Don't play naïve with us. We know everything. Without Willow as your sacrifice, you won't be able to steal Willow's fire magic. Meaning you won't become the most powerful fire witch the world has ever seen."

Good grief. It sounded like the plot of a fantasy novel. Which was probably what Patrice had been going for, knowing it would appeal to someone like Connor.

"There has to be another way," Connor said. "Willow deserves better."

She had to keep them talking. In their eyes, this was the climax of their fantasy adventure. They'd rooted out the villain—her—and they were doing all they could to save the day. Save the world. "What do you even know about this feud between our families?"

The story Molly and Connor proceeded to tell Amber and Edgar was nearly identical to the truth. Amber's mother creating a forbidden spell, the Blackwoods being on the run for years, the Penhallows' curse, and the Penhallows' obsession with finding the hidden book with the coveted spell inside. Except there was one key difference: Patrice had convinced Molly and Connor that the bad guys in this story were Amber and her family. They believed Amber was the one who was cursed and that the Blackwoods were hiding the spells from the Penhallows because of the fire spell Amber's mother had written. A fire spell that was so strong, it caused flames that burned so hot, it melted metal like wax. According to Molly and Connor, the incident that happened on Edgar's property when Kieran had nearly killed Amber hadn't been a Penhallow attack, but an experiment with deadly fire magic that had nearly liquefied Amber's and Edgar's cars.

Patrice had convinced the pair that if Amber was to harness this fire magic, she would then be able to use it with such precision that she could burn people from the inside out without hardly lifting a finger.

No wonder they sounded terrified of her. Kieran had started the ball rolling with these two, but over the course of months, Patrice and other network witches had been slowly revealing "clues" to these reporters, preying on their desire for meaty, unique stories they could sink their teeth into.

And for what?

Kieran said he'd been sent to Edgehill a second time to distract her.

Earlier, Edgar had said, *Neil is…laughing now. He's saying that part of their success is because of how predictable we all are.*

Amber pursed her lips. Predictable.

Molly was still rambling about Amber's apparent nefarious plans. Nefarious plans that were supposed to come to fruition during a ritual scheduled for *that* night, not tomorrow. Amber's brain slammed to a halt.

She abruptly pulled over.

"Connor Declan," she said, then called on her magic—magic that was thrashing around inside of her, desperate to be released. "Why do you think I kidnapped Willow tonight?" Imagining her magic as that twisting coil of blue smoke, she sent it out. Down the familiar streets and sidewalks of her beloved town, around corners and down alleys and over fences until it arrived at Feral's Diner.

"The ritual has to happen at thirty-seven after midnight, the exact time your mother created the spell," Connor said.

"*Dang it*, Connor!" Molly said. "Where are you, Amber? Are you out here?" A slam of a door echoed through the phone. "Stop being a coward and show yourself!"

Molly probably thought Amber was lurking in the tall hedges that lined Feral's Diner's lot on three sides, casting her devious spells from the shadows. She pictured Molly with her arms out, yelling at the shrubbery. Rolling her eyes, Amber ended the call.

It was just after seven. They had *five* hours to find Willow, not a full day. *Dang it!*

Predictable, huh? Well, screw that.

She glanced at Edgar. "Sorry about this."

"About wha—"

"*Sleep*," she said, hurling her magic at him with all the force of her emotions behind it.

He let out a small gasp, doubling over as if he'd just been punched in the gut, and then his eyes rolled back in his head. He slumped in the seat. A soft snore sounded a second later. At least this would let Edgar get a little rest.

"Did you see *that* coming, Neil?"

Jaw set, Amber pulled back onto the road. She'd show these Penhallows predictable.

CHAPTER 28

Amber left her car—with Edgar passed out inside—in the parking lot beside her building. He would be out cold for at least twenty minutes, assuming Neil couldn't find a way to wake him up through their connection. She layered the car in an alarm spell similar to the one that was constantly on her building. If Edgar tried to get out, or someone tried to get in, she'd at least get a warning.

As Amber crested the top of her staircase, she found the place was in the same state of mild chaos as it had been when she'd left.

Kim took one look at her and popped up from the window bench seat. "Where's Edgar? Is he okay?"

"I'll explain in a minute," Amber said. "First, have you had any luck locating Willow?"

Aunt G stepped out of the kitchen, Simon close behind. "Not yet," she said. "Likely that's because she's unconscious, cloaked, or both."

Amber's jaw clenched. She imagined Willow lying in the middle of that dirt road in the abandoned neighborhood, unconscious and alone. She was so ticked off, maybe her emotions would be enough to freeze the Penhallows where they stood without her needing a spell.

"Well, we have a slight problem beyond that," Amber said. "The ritual is happening *tonight*, not tomorrow. I'm guessing Willow will be with them at the ley line spillover. The ritual is to take place at 12:37 AM. What I don't know is how many Penhallows there are or when they're going to begin prepping the ritual. For all we know, it's already started." Then she filled them in on the rest, including Edgar's current location.

It was silent in the room for a few tense beats of silence, then people were on their feet, asking a flurry of questions. Amber did her best to answer them.

When there was a slight lull, Amber said, "I don't know if Willow is part of the ritual, or if taking her is just another distraction. Neil said they've been successful so far because I'm predictable. He either said that as a passing comment, or he said it knowing Edgar would repeat it."

"Predictable for you," Jack said, "would be to abandon everything at the drop of a hat to go after Willow right this second."

He wasn't wrong. It was hard to think that anything else mattered when her sister was missing. But was that what the Penhallows wanted? For Amber to go searching for Willow, letting her emotions guide her more than logic? Would it be predictable to take the grimoires with her or leave them behind with the others? Was it predictable to storm the castle alone, or with backup?

A pair of hands gripped her elbows and she startled, finding her aunt in front of her. "It's also predictable for you to be overwhelmed by the possibilities and then shut down."

"We're being manipulated," Amber said, forcing her brain to settle on one thread of thought at a time. "Kieran was sent here as a distraction for me. They got Molly and Connor in my path, they probably got Thea in my path, and they first manipulated Willow and then me into tracking down Uncle Raph. Patrice *told* Molly when to be at the Manx tonight. She wanted Molly to see Sienna and make the connection to me. It's all been smoke and mirrors and misdirection to keep me out of their way."

"Then let's go to the ley line spillover right now," Gary said. "We'll have the element of surprise on our side, right? Stop them before they have a chance to get the ritual off the ground."

Something her uncle had said back at Peaceful Meadows replayed in her head then. "*If the Penhallows don't get me and that spell, they've got a Plan B,*" he'd said. "*It involves funneling large quantities of magic into the modern-day already broken ley lines. It'll be like a bomb; Edgehill will be a crater.*"

What if storming the castle and ruining their plans meant they'd trigger plan B and blow Edgehill off the map? Assuming, of course, that she could trust anything her uncle had told her.

Aunt G's calm, comforting voice cut through Amber's thoughts. "What does your gut tell you to do?"

Amber glanced around the room at all these people—many of them whom she'd never met before today—while she considered that. Her heart told her that they needed to go after Willow. Her gut told her they needed to be smart about it.

Unfortunately, her most persistent idea didn't feel smart at all.

Turning to Zelda, who sat at the dining room table, Amber asked, "How were you able to send me the message on the rock when you had never met me before?"

"A bit of your essence was still left on the guest book that got returned to me," Zelda said. "If I have an object belonging to the witch in question or have a picture of the witch, the message usually reaches its destination. What did you have in mind?"

"Our biggest problem at the moment is that we don't know the details of what we might be walking into." For all Amber knew, while the Penhallows readied themselves for the ritual, that Betel guy could be out in front of The Quirky Whisker with a clipboard, taking down notes on who was up here and what they'd been doing, and then reporting that back to the network. The Penhallows had sent out spies and scouts months before this—it was naïve to think they weren't all still being watched even if the soundproofing on the building kept them from overhearing what was being discussed. But, if he was to be trusted, Amber had a spy of her own. "I want to send a message to Kieran."

A wave of murmurs swept through the room.

"Just being devil's advocate here," Scarlett said from across the room, "but how do you know this isn't part of the whole predictable thing? You strike me as the kind of person who wants to trust people. What if that willingness means we're walking into a trap?"

"This might sound cheesy, but I think we *need* to trust him," Amber said. "If Kieran's magic truly is healed and being healed is the only thing that made him see the error of his ways, he's the answer to the Penhallow problem. It's in *all* our best interests to trust him. If the Penhallows are still monsters even after the curse is lifted, we're all doomed anyway. Not trusting him means we're giving up on the best solution anyone has come up with in decades. Not trusting him means we might as well just hand the book over and hope we're all still here when the Penhallows are done."

It was silent for a moment and Amber worried these people were going to pack up their grimoires and go.

"I really want to hate Kieran," Jack said from his spot on the side of Amber's bed. Everyone turned to look at him. "I was there the night he tried to kill Amber. I saw him use his magic to nearly choke her to death. The image still haunts me. But I was also there after the curse was lifted. He was like a different person. It's been hard to wrap my brain around the idea that someone like that could actually get past what he was, you know? It's like deciding whether or not someone who committed a crime could ever truly be rehabilitated. Some can't, but others can." He locked eyes with Amber then. "If we never give those people a second chance, then they never get an opportunity to make up for their mistakes."

She knew he was talking about more than Kieran in that moment and she smiled softly at him.

"All right," Scarlett said. "I'm in."

"Me too," said Gary.

Everyone else chimed in after that. Jack was right: they were all still with her even if her choice was risky. She heaved out a breath of relief.

"Okay, Amber," Zelda said. "What I need from you is something of Kieran's or a photograph."

Remembering how she'd shared memories of Edgar with Raphael, she held out a hand to Zelda. "Time for me to show you something," Amber said.

Zelda took her hand without question.

Closing her eyes, Amber called up the memory of the last time she'd seen Kieran—behind the Edge of Glen Pizza Parlor—and slid the virtual photographs into Zelda's mind.

When they broke contact and Zelda opened her eyes, she was smiling. "Oh, that's very cool." She went to the table to tear off a slip of paper from Amber's legal pad. "What would you like it to say?"

"Ask him the time of the ritual," Amber said. "And the exact number of rival witches in town."

Zelda scribbled the note on the scrap of paper, folded it up, and then placed the paper in the palm of one hand. She cast her spell, and then swiped a hand over the note. By the time her free hand had fully passed over her open palm, the note was gone. "Magical email," she said, chuckling.

"While we wait for an answer, let's keep working on that channeling spell. I would really prefer not to have my system short-circuit ..." Amber said. "And I'll keep trying to figure out the freeze spell."

Amber's heart still wanted her to spend all her time scrying for Willow, but her gut told her that was what the

Penhallows wanted. They wanted her as ill-prepared as possible.

Please be okay, Willow, she thought to herself, then went back to work.

Amber lightly thunked her head on her dining room table two hours later, hoping that would re-scramble her brain and make the words for her spell fall into place. Jack sat on one side of her, rubbing her back. Kim sat on the other side, offering Amber words of encouragement.

When Amber's phone started to buzz next to her, her head jerked up, giving her the temporary spins. She wasn't sure what method of communication Kieran would use to get back in touch with her, depending on how surrounded by Penhallows he currently was, but a phone call hadn't been what she was expecting.

But when she snatched up her phone, it was a number she recognized. Puzzled, she answered. "Hi, Alan."

"Hey, Amber," he said. "The chief is currently swamped so he asked me to look up a license plate number for you?"

"Oh, yeah," she said. "What'd you find?"

"The SUV is registered to a Stanley Johnson," Alan said. "Washington plates. The guy is an orderly at a private mental hospital in Washington. There was an APB out for Johnson today, since both he and a patient recently went missing—a Raphael Henbane. The staff speculated that Johnson and Henbane made a break for it together. But when police went to Johnson's house this afternoon, they found him dead inside."

"Oh my God," Amber said.

"Yeah," Alan said. "They thought it had been Henbane who did it—that maybe he'd gained Johnson's trust and then killed him when his guard was down—but Johnson clearly has been dead a while, though they can't currently pinpoint the cause of death. There's a giant black starburst on his chest. Oddly, they think it's possible he's been dead for years, and whatever was done to him basically mummified him. Apparently the seasoned medical examiner took one look at the body and then ran back out to throw up in the bushes."

It sounded nearly identical to what had happened to Wilma Bennett, the maid whom Kieran killed at the Manx Hotel.

"Law enforcement is very baffled," Alan said, "since Johnson, according to the Pleasant Meadows staff, has been coming into work as usual up until today. He doesn't have any living family, as far as anyone knows."

Just as Neil had assumed the identity of a family-less man in order to play a long con on Amber's mother, Patrice Penhallow had assumed the identity of Stanley Johnson, most likely in large part because if he went missing, no one would notice. How long had Patrice kept him alive so she could learn all she could about the man she was going to pretend to be?

"Isn't Henbane the last name of your cousin?" Alan asked, interrupting the very gruesome images she conjured up of Patrice sitting in Stanley Johnson's living room, eating a TV dinner while the body of the man in question wasted away in a recliner.

Amber had a feeling he already knew the answer to that. It wasn't the kind of interesting tidbit someone like Alan Peterson would hear and not look into further.

"Chief Brown mentioned something else," Alan said. "Garcia was out patrolling near the Marbleglen/Edgehill border near the scene of the parade attack, since someone called in a disturbance. While he was out there, he spotted Johnson's car. Willow's phone and purse were in the back seat. Any idea why your sister's belongings would be found in that car? A car that belongs to a dead orderly at a mental hospital that your uncle escaped from today? Doesn't Willow live in Washington?"

Amber mentally groaned as she followed the trail Alan was laying out. To non-witch law enforcement, it would look like Willow was connected to a murder *and* a missing patient. Was Uncle Raphael wanted by the police? Would the FBI get involved, since Raphael crossed state lines?

"Your sister is missing, yet you hardly seem concerned," Alan said. "You stalked me and got yourself into all kinds of trouble when Chloe, a girl you merely babysat for, went missing, yet your uncle is on the lam and your sister is gone and you didn't even pick up the phone to call me? What aren't you telling me, Amber?"

She didn't like being on this side of an Alan Peterson interrogation.

Zelda yelped on Kim's other side, and Amber leaned forward to see what had happened. A piece of folded paper lay in front of the woman.

"Thanks for your help, Alan, but I have to go," Amber said quickly and disconnected the call. When he immediately called back, she sent the call to voicemail.

Zelda gingerly picked up the paper with finger and thumb and handed it to Amber.

Several people crowded around Amber as she unfolded the small scrap of a note.

Ley line spillover. 12:37 AM. Twelve for ritual. Six others around town. Patrice will lie about time.

Or you're *lying about the time*, her mind replied. But, no, she had to believe that Kieran was on their side, even if her own uncle had quite possibly turned on her and his own son.

It was just after ten in the evening now. They had two hours to get their plan worked out.

While the others worked, Amber called Chief Brown.

"Hey, Amber," he said hurriedly after the fourth ring. "I put Peterson on the case of the missing car. And Garcia and Carl are looking for Willow. That's all I could spare at the moment. That dang cat is still on the loose. We've been swamped by calls all night about it. It apparently chased a man up a tree. Of course, by the time we get there, the thing is gone. And then there was some kind of noxious gas that was released in the community center? Ten teenage volunteers were in there with Ann Marie and Chloe doing last-minute prep for the 5K and a janitor found them all passed out asleep on the floor. Parents are livid. There's not a word for how angry Mayor Deidrick is. I'm sorry we haven't made any headway on locating Willow yet."

Wincing, she asked, "Did you call Garcia off Henrietta duty when I told you about Willow?"

The pause on the other end was prolonged and she braced herself, anticipating that he'd tear her a new one for micromanaging him when his night was clearly a chaotic mess. Instead he said, "Didn't *you* call him off Henrietta duty? He said you called, frantic that Willow had been kidnapped, and said that you were going to send Edgar to stand guard instead."

Amber's brow furrowed. That didn't even make sense.

"That wasn't you." It was a statement, not a question. "Dang it, Amber, I'm sorry. I've been run so ragged here that I didn't even think about it. Edgar would be a better guard than Garcia anyway, given everything." He sighed. "I'll get someone back over there as soon as I can. The good news is, if something *had* happened to Henrietta, I would have heard about it."

That didn't comfort Amber in the slightest.

A scream echoed through the phone, followed by what sounded like shattering glass. The chief cursed. "Sorry, Amber, the cat just crashed through someone's back door!"

Amber sagged as the call disconnected.

Her magic felt as anxious and buzzy as she did. She also knew that the more frazzled she was, the more likely her magic was to glitch. Which made crafting a spell even harder. A spell that she couldn't seem to get right, no matter what angle she used to come at it.

With only an hour until midnight, Amber felt no closer to having a viable spell than she had when she'd started. She desperately wanted to open the trunk of grimoires so she could leaf through the Henbane book for time spells. Maybe her mother's spell structure would get Amber on the right track. A little voice in the back of her head wondered why none of the Penhallows had even attempted to find the book here, but she had to hope Kieran was doing work behind the scenes to keep the cursed witches at bay.

She needed a break *and* she needed to recast the sleep spell on Edgar. Aunt G escorted her downstairs.

After successfully recasting the spell on her dozing cousin and reinforcing the alarm spell on the car, Amber and Aunt G went back into The Quirky Whisker. They were halfway across the shop when Aunt G's phone trilled.

"Who on earth would be calling me this late?" she muttered as she pulled the phone out of her pocket. Then her wide gaze snapped up to Amber. "It's Willow." She turned her screen toward Amber and a smiling image of her sister lit up the screen.

"Answer it!" Amber said.

Aunt G fumbled with the phone and managed to both answer it and put it on speaker. She and Amber huddled close to it, casting a bright blue glow in the dark shop. "Little bird?" Aunt G asked.

"No, I'm afraid not," a woman said. "But I have your little bird with me."

Aunt G's jaw tightened, as did her hold on the phone.

"What can we do for you, Patrice?" Amber asked, willing her tone to stay neutral.

"This is my final request that you hand over the book willingly," Patrice said. "We can make a clean swap—the book for your sister."

"No," Amber said.

"Predictable." Patrice sighed. "Since you refuse to do this the easy way, I will up the stakes. Bring the book to the location of your childhood home at midnight. If you do not, Willow dies by Neil's hand—seems fitting, no? It's a messier option, but it will suit our purposes just fine. Penhallows got into hot water with the council for siphoning magic, as you know, but the practice hasn't stopped. The death of your sister in a location already so charged with traumatic energy will allow Neil to absorb even more power, which will aid him well in his trip through time."

Amber worked her jaw. She was lying. She had to be lying.

"Don't believe me?" Patrice asked. "Willow, be a dear and say hi to your family."

There was a scuffle on the other side of the line and then Willow's high and light tone floated into the quiet shop. "Aunt G? Amber?" Willow asked shakily. "You can't listen to them, okay? It's a trap."

Amber pursed her lips. "What's the code word?"

"Logomark," Willow said quickly. "It's me. I swear it. You can't let them have the book, Amber. Just let them have me. I'll be with Mom and Dad again."

Tears sprang into Amber's eyes. "I can't let them kill you, Willow."

"What other choice do we have? Without the book, they can't complete their ritual," she said. "Mom and Dad worked too hard to keep this from happening. We can't give up now. Just let me go, sis."

Another scuffle and then Patrice was back on the line. "I will get the book one way or another. Believe that," she said. "At the stroke of midnight, be at 523 Ocicat Lane with the grimoire. If not, your sister's blood will be on your hands. Her death is preventable. The decision is yours."

Just before the blue light of the screen faded and the call ended, Amber caught sight of the devastated look on her aunt's face.

The Penhallows had won.

CHAPTER 29

When Amber and Aunt G went upstairs to tell the others about the ultimatum from Patrice, defeat settled on them all like a blanket. Amber couldn't allow her sister to die. End of story. Kieran had said Patrice would lie about the time—but what about the rest of it? Willow knew the code word. Willow had asked Amber to sacrifice her for the sake of keeping the grimoire out of Penhallow hands.

Kieran had told her 12:37, while Patrice had said midnight. What was the significance of the different times? Another thing piled on her plate to distract her and pull her mind in too many directions?

Predictable, Patrice had said.

The predictable choice was to save Willow.

"Who here is good at glamour spells?" Amber asked, not realizing she was going to say that until it was out of her mouth.

"I'm decent," Simon said.

"Me too," Irene said.

"Okay," said Amber. "I want us all glamoured to look like me. Patrice is sending versions of herself out all over town, so we will, too." She blew out a breath, hoping she was making the correct, least predictable choice. "We're going to the ley line spillover."

She was going all-in with her trust in Kieran.

But she knew if she was wrong, she'd never see her sister again.

The group left in three waves. Wave one, with three Amber clones, headed east. Wave two, with four Amber clones, headed north. And the biggest wave of nine clones, split between two cars, headed for the abandoned neighborhood.

The clock on the dash said it was just after 11:30 PM.

Amber killed the headlights a few hundred yards from the turn-off into the abandoned neighborhood. Pulling off to the side of the road, Amber angled the car into the overgrowth as best she could. The car behind her did the same.

11:45 PM.

Amber adjusted the settings on her phone to low brightness.

Once they'd all climbed out, the witches cloaked the cars so they wouldn't be immediately visible to anyone driving by. Then they made the rest of the way on foot. Amber's nerves were shot. Willow, Edgehill, and the fate of history were all relying on her to make the right choice.

No one spoke as they crept through the tall weeds toward the sagging house on the corner. Amber had never paid much attention to this house, seeing it only as a landmark for the start of the abandoned neighborhood. The white wood was rotting in places, the paint peeling and splattered with dried dirt. Now it felt imposing, like it was sentient and watching her. If Amber hadn't made the right call, and the Penhallows got spooked and went to plan B, the whole neighborhood, this house included, would be gone.

She ran a hand along the side of the house to help keep her oriented in the dark. When she stopped at the corner of the house, pressing her back against the worn, dirty wall, her companions did, too. Her heart hammered.

Peering around the side of the house, she spotted about a dozen people milling about in the middle of the neighborhood's main dirt road. A few crates were scattered among them. Witches lit tall, chunky candles, a few others were bent over something on the ground, and a group of four stood in a small huddle, presumably deep in conversation. Lanterns sat on the ground in a wide circle, providing an abundance of warm orange light. Anything more than a few hundred feet away from the group, though, was in deep shadow. It looked like a spotlight shone down from the thick canopy of leaves above.

Amber dropped to her knees, touching a hand to the ground, letting the magic know she was here. She could feel it humming faintly beneath her hand, but it didn't make her woozy. "All right," she said. "One at a time."

Thanks to everyone's identical glamours, she honestly had no idea who was behind her. A clone of herself crouched low, rounded the side of the house, and then headed forward. A second Amber went past her, then ran across the dirt road before moving in the direction of the Penhallows. Once the Amber clone had crossed the road, the darkness swallowed her up. The Amber clones alternated then—one rounding the side of the house they stood beside now, while the next darted across the dark street.

By the time it was Amber's turn, with two Ambers left to follow after her, six witches wearing her face had already disappeared into the darkness. Blowing out a steadying breath, she rounded the side of the house and crept forward. Her eyes had adjusted enough to the dark at this point that she had a rough idea of what was in front of her, but she stumbled often. Her attention shifted from the dark ground in front of her, the slow, methodical movement of the Amber clone several feet ahead, and the group of Penhallows preparing for their ritual.

The Penhallows had mostly been quiet, working on their assigned tasks like busy little monster ants, but there was a sudden halt in their movements. Amber stilled, seeing that the clone in front of her had, too. Amber was still far enough away from the Penhallows that she couldn't make out the details of anyone's face yet.

Suddenly, the headlights of a car that had been parked in the shadows at the other end of the street flicked on. A dark SUV emerged from the shadows, drove around the amassed group, and then headed for the exit. Amber hit the ground as quickly as she could, hoping the shadows and the tall grass would shield her from the searching beams of the car's headlights. She hoped the others had ducked out of the way in time. Something sharp poked her side, and something even sharper dug into her elbow, but she didn't dare move until the red taillights of the SUV were around the corner and out of sight.

Darkness settled on her. She waited for her eyes to readjust.

Pulling her phone from her pocket, she hid it behind a large chunk of broken concrete and cupped a hand over the screen before she tapped it. Its dull light still felt too bright.

It was 12:01, and she had a text from Irene who had gone to 523 Ocicat Lane.

It was a bluff. Willow isn't here. I got to use my blizzard spell after all. We nearly knocked the two witches into the next state.

Amber heaved out a breath. Kieran hadn't steered her wrong. She thanked Irene, then checked in with Jack's group. He was with Edgar, Aunt G, and Bianca, as well as the trunk of cloaked grimoires. They were hightailing it north as fast as they could. Neil would know where the books were now, since Edgar had been instructed to give him clues about their location.

Patrice had a decision to make, too: go after the grimoire speeding toward the Washington border, or attempt a complicated ritual without the key ingredient. Perhaps Amber's unpredictable decision had just bought them another fifty years to solve the Penhallow problem.

When Jack didn't reply to her text, Amber stuffed her phone back into her pocket and got to her feet. She slowly crept forward again. The Penhallows seemed to have finished setting up. None of this core group had left, nor did it look like they had any plans to. Neil had surely relayed the information about the book's whereabouts, hadn't he? Would Patrice move forward with the ritual without the grimoire?

The witches stood motionless now, hands clasped in front of their laps. They weren't adorned in black, hooded robes while chanting around a bonfire or anything as dramatic as that. They had, however, placed a ring of tall flickering candles around a form on the ground, creating their own circle just behind the candles. From this vantage point, it most assuredly was a person—a female with long brown hair.

It had to be Willow. *Please, please let her still be alive.*

As she crept forward, Amber spotted Kieran among the group of twelve, and the back of someone who was possibly Patrice. When Amber reached her designated spot, she was directly across the street from Zelda's house, as were the ring of witches. Amber wondered if Patrice knew this was the prime spot of the ley line spillover because she could sense the magic the same way Amber could, or if the location had been supplied to Patrice by Connor and Molly.

Within another minute, all her witches were in place. It had to be about ten after midnight now, which gave Amber and her witches roughly twenty-five minutes to stop the ritual in its tracks. Something shone in her peripheral vision and she glanced back the way they'd come. A car sat at the end of the street now. Its headlights winked out a moment later, but the car remained in place.

"You may begin," a woman said, pulling Amber's attention back.

She bit her lip as she watched a man step out of the formation and stand near the body on the ground. Amber was positive now that it was Willow.

Her jaw clenched at the sight of Neil Penhallow—the man who had murdered her parents. Her magic ignited, like someone had just poured molten lava into her veins. It wanted to retaliate, to make this man pay for not only turning Amber and Willow into orphans, but for putting Edgar through hell and back for years.

Don't storm the castle, she had to remind herself. *Be patient.*

"The day the council decided to strip our family of our powers was the day the council turned its back on magic," Neil said. "The council felt threatened by our growing power. They saw us for what we were—not dangerous, not reckless, but superior. And that superiority threatened the system they'd forced witches into for too long. We hide in the shadows among the magic-less like cockroaches scurrying from the light. But you know what cockroaches are? Resilient. We are a resilient clan and have waited years for the stars to align so we can take back what is ours. In this new future, *we'll* be the head of the council. Fifty years ago, Annabelle Henbane crafted a spell that was the answer to all our problems as a clan—as a people. Today, we'll acquire that same spell to give magic—and the witches who wield it—the freedom it deserves."

The witches around him nodded and muttered their agreement.

Neil stepped back into the circle, and Patrice stepped out of it. "Do you feel the magic here? This is one of the six spots where magic ruptured. It's raw, untapped power. It's enough to literally make your head spin. The council knew how much magic was in the ley lines, yet regulated its use as if it were a limited resource. The WBI is worse still. We need to return to a time when magic was free to use, and make sure we build a future that lets witches thrive."

If the Penhallows had put this much work into keeping Amber and the chief distracted, what had they been doing to the WBI? Were they not here because they were off chasing a wild goose?

Patrice gestured to someone in front of her, nodded once, and then stepped back into her spot in the circle.

It was somehow both a shock and not to see her uncle step into view. He clasped his hands behind his back and slowly walked the track made between the circle of witches and the ring of candles. "Many of you likely think I blame Annabelle Henbane, my sister, for ruining my life. And I do, in a way, but I blame the society we're in more. The council, and then the WBI, spent so much time telling us what we can and can't do with our magic that now we fear the very thing that makes us who we are. Traveling back to the moment of the spell's creation is going to cause changes here in the present but look where we are now. The collective decisions of others have given us a world where none of us truly belong. I was blessed by magic itself with the rare ability to manipulate time and memory. Why would magic allow such an ability to exist, only for others to tell me how to use it? Had we valued magic more, the council never would have done something as egregious as stripping away a whole clan's magic. A time-travel spell like my sister's should have been applauded, not hidden. So, today, on the eve of the spell's creation, we're taking history back."

The collected witches cheered.

Raphael moved back to his spot in the circle.

Patrice then turned to Kieran beside her. "I'm glad you're with us again. We all worried you'd betray us, you know. That the time witch had poisoned your loyalty."

Kieran kept his features neutral as he said, "I am loyal."

"Yes, I believe that's true," she said. "But to who, that's the question."

Patrice tipped her head back and the crisp, clear words of a spell left her lips. Amber's stomach sank to her feet like a boulder when she recognized the spell as the same one Kieran himself had used on Edgar's property the night he attempted to kill her. Déjà vu washed over her, and she futilely scanned the darkness she and her companions stood in, searching for a place to hide.

"*Give me the book, Blackwood*," Kieran had growled at her as she'd run for her life. He'd pursued her as if she were a defenseless rabbit.

A moment later, the whole neighborhood lit up in a burst of blue light as if lightning had just struck. Her arm shot up to shield her eyes. When Amber lowered it, Patrice was smiling at her from the middle of the road. The light had chased away not only the shadows, but Amber's hiding spot as well.

Then Patrice's gaze skipped a bit to the left, and then swung to the right. "How quaint! You all came wearing the same face. But you can't really expect to out-glamour *us*, can you?"

"I *am* loyal," Kieran said. His eyes jumped to Amber for a moment and she held her breath. He sidled up next to Patrice and whispered something in her ear, pointing to the Amber to the right of her.

Patrice thanked him, and he stepped back into his position. "Raph, dear, can you do the honors?"

Several of the Penhallows cast more lightning spells, filling the neighborhood with so much light, it gave off the illusion of daylight.

Raphael turned around, facing the side of the road where Amber and her companions stood several feet apart. He looked first to the witch to Amber's right, the one Kieran had pointed out. With little warning, the witch beside him spun around and hurled a mass of magic at the Amber-lookalike. It looked like a thick black tendril of smoke, the end forming into a clawed hand. It was cursed magic manifested into something physical. And it was a killing blow. Amber had seen magic used as a weapon like this before: in her memories of her mother's and grandfather's altercation with Neil and his own father in Delin Springs.

Neil's father had sent this same kind of attack at Miles Henbane. Amber's mother had stopped it—had frozen the magic in place—just seconds before the cursed magic slammed into Miles' chest.

The memory flashed through Amber's mind in a split second, but that second was enough to cause her own magic to rise up in her. Her instinct to stop this from happening overrode all else.

"No!" she screamed, thrusting her hands out toward the cursed smoke careening for the Amber clone. Instead of freezing the cursed magic as her mother had done, Amber knocked the witch out of the way with a force of wind so strong, it knocked her clear off her feet.

The burst of cursed magic hit the wall of an abandoned house, cracking one of the porch's support beams. The wood held, but the roof sagged dangerously in one corner.

The fallen witch Amber had knocked into the brambles struggled to her feet. And revealed that she wasn't Amber at all, but Gary. The gruff man managed a smile at Amber, silently thanking her for saving his life even though she'd just given herself away. As had Kieran.

Amber heard the whoosh of air before it hit her—hit all her companions—and simultaneously sent nine witches airborne. She managed to curl herself into a ball before she hit the ground, rolling a few times before her shoulder connected with the edge of a rotted porch. Amber was glad Aunt G and Zelda weren't here, being the oldest in the bunch. Amber knew everyone's glamours had been knocked loose.

She had just gotten herself into a standing position, her shoulder aching, when someone grabbed her forcefully by the arm. "Hi, Amber," he said in her ear. "I'm glad you could make it, my gullible little fool."

She recognized the voice instantly. Uncle Raphael.

Just like back at Pleasant Meadows, his magic allowed him to travel from one spot to the next in the blink of an eye. Was this a facet of his time magic?

A shocking jolt of cold hit her. She blinked and a moment later, she was in the circle, standing beside the body on the ground that was very much Willow's. Amber, briefly forgetting that she was literally surrounded by Penhallows, dropped to her knees. She checked Willow's pulse, and was relieved to feel a steady, if slow, beat below her fingers. "Willow," she said softly, patting her cheek. "Willow, can you hear me?"

"She can't."

Amber shot a glare over her shoulder; Patrice stared down at her. "What do you want with her?"

"Don't worry," Patrice said. "Willow is a bargaining chip. We needed you here, but we also needed to know who the rat was in the organization. My bets were on Raphael, honestly." She smiled at Amber's uncle. "I'm glad it wasn't you, pet." Then she rounded on Kieran, who shrank back a fraction.

Amber quickly scanned the dark neighborhood, squinting to see beyond the shadows now that the bursts of light had faded. She heard a faint rustling from both in front of her and behind. Were her witches regrouping?

Neil clucked his tongue, pulling Amber's attention back to the world of trouble she was in. "You'd really turn on family, brother? After everything the Blackwoods and Henbanes have put us through? They want us rounded up and caged, Kieran."

"She freed me," Kieran said. "My magic is healed. The curse has been lifted. It's not all or nothing for us like we thought. Our curse will be gone, but our magic won't be."

Neil's lip curled. "You've gone soft over the years. You've lost sight of what's important."

"I agree," Patrice said. "Shall I?"

Neil nodded.

Amber, with a hand still protectively on Willow's arm, glanced over her aching shoulder again just as Patrice lunged forward and grabbed Kieran by the neck with both hands. Amber was convinced Patrice was going to snap it like they do in the movies, but instead she cast a spell. As the words poured out of her mouth, something seemed to be oozing out of her hands and into Kieran's skin. He clawed at her hands as he gasped for breath, black tendrils running up the sides of his neck. His back arched as he screamed.

"Stop!" Amber called out, scrambling to her feet.

But Raphael blinked into existence behind her again and yanked her back. He wrapped an arm around her middle, pinning her arms to her sides. "Do you want Willow cursed as well?" he hissed in her ear and Amber shied away from his hot breath. "No? Then hold still."

Amber's jaw clenched as she watched the cursed magic continue to snake up Kieran's neck and into his face. Abruptly, Patrice let him go and he slumped to the ground in a heap. He didn't move. Amber choked out a cry. Had Patrice reinfected him with the curse, or had she outright killed him?

"Now," Patrice said cheerfully, turning back to the group.

Raphael still held Amber in place near Willow's motionless feet. She ignored the death glares Neil sent her from across the circle.

"Now that Amber is here, we can get started. But first, we'll need some privacy," Patrice said.

The Penhallows all held hands again. They tipped their heads back, speaking in unison.

"*No!*" someone called out.

Amber craned her neck to see Scarlett and Gary running toward her.

"*Get out of there, Amber!*"

"*We won't be able—*"

A noise-canceling spell snapped down around the Penhallows like a bowl, immediately cutting off the shouts of alarm from her companions. When they reached the invisible barrier and started beating their fists against it, Amber knew with a sinking feeling that this was more than a dome of silence. She was trapped in here with a dozen Penhallows, and her only two allies on the inside were both unconscious.

Amber's time-freeze spell wasn't complete. Patrice had successfully distracted Amber out of finishing it. And now, ironically, she'd run out of time. How was she supposed to combat twelve Penhallows all on her own?

"Amber," Patrice said, not at all fazed by the muted shouting and fist-pounding happening around their invisible dome by the eight other witches trying to get in. "I'm sure you're wondering how we plan to complete this ritual when we're missing the key piece of the puzzle, yes? What on earth are we going to do when the spell we need is in a car speeding toward—where are they now, Neil? Portland?"

"Close to it," Neil said.

Patrice laughed lightly. "Well…you see …" She snapped her fingers and just in front of her, the cloaking spell that had been shielding a leather-bound book from view dropped away.

Amber struggled in her uncle's grasp as she realized that her mother's grimoire sat at the feet of Patrice Penhallow. "How…what …"

"Ah, we've surprised her!" Patrice said, grinning. "You really need to thank Thea for this."

Amber cocked her head.

"Agent Garcia! Willow has been kidnapped!" Patrice said in a perfect imitation of Amber. "Hurry, you have to find her! Edgar is coming to take your place." Switching back to her own voice, she said, "I dropped by the hospital where Henrietta is being treated, and I told Thea that if she didn't tell me every detail she remembered you and your family discussing while she was imprisoned in your care, I would kill her sister. She called my bluff. I activated the poison tincture in Henrietta's system that was keeping her stable, yet comatose. There was some writhing and alarming beeping from the machines."

Amber struggled in her uncle's grasp again, but it did little good.

"Anyway," Patrice said, "non-witches aren't made of the strongest stuff, so when she was convinced her sister would die if she didn't give me the information I needed, she started babbling. Took us a while to get there, but with enough pressure, she remembered the name Quill."

Which was how the Penhallows had been able to swoop in and snatch the grimoires out from under the WBI's nose. She shot a disgusted look at Neil. His supposed connection to her mother hadn't been the reason the book had been located. It had been Patrice's nasty interrogation techniques.

But it still didn't explain how the book was now in Patrice's possession if the books were triggered to return to Amber or Willow the moment they'd been found.

"The boomerang spell was a nice touch," Raphael said from behind her. "But I was with the team when we got word that the books were in Quill. Locator spells got us to the dead zone—also a nice touch. After we cracked through your layers of spells, I sensed the boomerang just before it was triggered and I froze time. After breaking the spell, I took the Henbane book out of the trunk, unfroze time, and then let the trunk with just the Blackwood grimoire go off on its merry way. We figured you'd be so worried that the uncloaked books would alert us to the grimoires' location that you'd immediately cloak the trunk again without opening it. After all, your magic was sound, and your aunt would have assured you the plan you'd crafted had been foolproof. You Blackwoods were always so arrogant."

"The only little problem now is that the book *does* have a rather powerful spell on it that won't allow us to open it," Patrice said. "It's a binding spell that protects it from being opened by anyone who is doing so with ill intent, yadda yadda. So I'm going to need you to open it so we can get this show on the road."

"No," Amber said.

"Who thought she'd say that?" Patrice asked, and the Penhallows around her rose their hands in the air, smirking. "Of course you'd say no. Which is why Willow is here."

It was Willow's arm that twitched first, followed by a foot. Amber thought she might be waking up, but then realized her back was arching off the ground. Her neck twitched awkwardly. Then she began to seize.

Amber lurched for her, but her uncle held her so tightly now, Amber was sure she'd bruise. "What are you doing to her?"

"She was injected with the same poisoning tincture I gave Henrietta," Patrice said. "But since it was injected rather than consumed in tea, like it was with your friend, the coma came on faster, and the poison will work more quickly when activated."

Oh God, Willow. I'm so sorry.

Willow jerked more violently now, a faint cloud of dust rising from the road as she thrashed.

"Fine!" Amber screamed, nauseated. "Just stop whatever you're doing to her."

Patrice waved a hand in the air and Willow immediately stilled. Raphael let Amber go. After Patrice gestured at it, Amber reluctantly grabbed her mother's book off the ground. Even though she'd only held it a few times, the weight was familiar in her hands. The feel of the smooth leather cover, the deeply ingrained letters spelling out HENBANE. Her mother had spent most of her adult life trying to keep this very book out of Penhallows' possession, and now Amber had to hand it over voluntarily.

"I told you I'd get the book one way or another," Patrice said.

Forgive me, Mom.

Willow twitched slightly in Amber's peripheral vision, and a soft, agonized groan whispered past pale lips.

Amber's hands shook as she opened the book, flipping to the back where the time-travel spell was located. Willow settled again as she did so. Amber attempted to flip the pages slowly, searching discreetly for any sign of a time-freeze spell—any spell—that could get her out of this.

"Stop stalling, Blackwood," Patrice said. "You have ten seconds to find the page, or I'll instruct Neil to torture Edgar until he runs his car off the road."

Defeated, Amber opened the book to the spell the Penhallows wanted, then held it out to Patrice. Amber watched in disgust as the woman's dark eyes alighted as they scanned the words on the page.

"This is really it," Patrice said in awe. Then she looked past Amber to where Raphael stood. "Are you ready?"

"I've been ready," he said.

Patrice took Amber by the shoulders and spun her to face her uncle. "Give him permission to take the book from you. That should break the pesky spell."

Teeth gritted, Amber stared at this man she'd once called family. "I grant you permission to use the Henbane grimoire."

With a look of joy on his face that rivaled Patrice's, he took the book from Amber. The moment the familiar weight was gone, her knees nearly gave out. It was as if a vital organ had been violently torn from her body.

Patrice, Neil, and Raphael huddled together to go over the plan one more time, Amber guessed, but she didn't care. She dropped to her knees beside Willow and gave her a gentle shake. Willow's forehead bunched in discomfort, but she didn't open her eyes. How had Amber managed to screw this up so badly?

She'd failed everyone who'd believed in her. She'd failed her parents.

And somehow in that moment, the worst part of it all was that she'd failed magic itself. She agreed with the Penhallows that what had happened to them and the ley lines had been wrong. She agreed that the council had made terrible choices. But what the Penhallows planned to do now was no better. The Penhallows could claim that all they wanted was balance, and for magic to be free, but it was a self-serving desire. Magic shouldn't have been forced into the situation it had been in before, and it certainly shouldn't be forced into the one it confronted now.

With tears running down her face, Amber placed a hand flat on the earth. She swayed from the intensity of the energy below her skin. *I'm sorry*, she told the magic. *I don't know what to do. I don't want to ask anything more of you either, though. I'm just sorry.*

And just like the first time Amber had been in this abandoned neighborhood and had communicated with the magic in the ley lines, a force of energy slammed into her. The world around her went black and she happily allowed it to swallow her whole.

CHAPTER 30

When Amber came to and found herself standing on the intact front porch of 523 Ocicat Lane, she was convinced she'd died. That, or the time-travel spell had worked and somehow the fire had never claimed her house. Which would mean—

She quickly let herself into the house, scanning the familiar front room that was just as she remembered it from the last day she'd been here. "Mom? Dad?" Running up the steps, she poked her head in every room. "Willow? Is anyone here?"

No answer.

She ran back down the steps, grabbed hold of the knob at the end of the banister, and swung herself around the side and toward the kitchen, just like she'd done hundreds of times as a teenager. She peered into the garage, the downstairs bathroom, the backyard. The house was deserted.

She turned around and yelped. Her parents stood there in the doorway of the kitchen, wearing twin expressions of confusion. Amber's breath caught in her throat. "Am I dead?"

Her mother shook her head. "Something has happened with the book, hasn't it? Did the Penhallows succeed?"

"I'm sorry," Amber said. "I tried—"

"Hush, pumpkin," her dad said. "Now, listen to us. We're here, but we're also not. Magic is trying to speak to you, and it's choosing forms that will help you best understand."

"Whether intentional or not," her mom said, "our families have become protectors of magic. We've made choices that, while traumatic for our family, have been necessary for magic's survival. Your grandparents chose to protect magic over allowing Raphael to give into his bitterness. We chose to protect magic over accepting a deal from the WBI, as well as choosing it over staying with you girls."

"But I chose Willow over magic," Amber said.

"Yes, but it was you against twelve," her father said. "If you had fought back, do you know what their backup plan was? Using Willow as a conduit for another magic-severing spell. But they planned to sever magic from the Blackwood clan, thereby cursing you, your aunt, and Willow—were she to survive. But magic knows that if they did that, it would destroy it completely. You not only chose to save Willow, you chose the option safest for magic."

A moment later, Willow appeared in the kitchen beside her.

"Oh my God, Will!" Amber yelped and the two collided in a fierce hug. Amber could feel her there—her warmth, her tight embrace—and heard her tinkling, watery laugh. "Are you okay? How are you here?" she asked, holding her sister's face in her hands.

But Willow had just seen her parents and had burst into tears. She broke free from Amber to hug her parents, too, but her hands moved through them. They smiled sadly at her. "Are you…ghosts?"

"No," her mother said. "We're no longer of this earth so we don't have a form anymore. Our essence was absorbed back into the ley lines when we died. We're part of magic now."

Willow moved back beside Amber and looped her arm through hers.

"What do we do?" Amber asked. "It's me against them; Willow isn't conscious."

"Your plan is a good one," her father said. "Accept that even if you feel clueless, you know what you're doing. You're a protector of magic, and magic will protect you, too."

Amber swallowed. "Okay." She still felt vaguely nauseated, but seeing her parents—even if they weren't flesh and blood anymore—bolstered her. "Oh, and Mom? Neil is the worst."

Her mother laughed. "He really is. I'm glad you have Jack."

Amber flushed.

"Give Edgar a hug for us, even if he'll hate it," her mother added.

"By the way, John Huntley isn't the worst choice you could make, peanut," Theo said to Willow, then winked.

Amber and Willow were still sharing a wide-eyed look of shock when the cheery, familiar atmosphere of their childhood kitchen melted away. The ground was cold beneath her knees and palms. She was still a little woozy from the magic below her hands, but it wasn't as debilitating as before. Willow, however, was still unconscious.

Neil, Patrice, and Raphael still talked behind her. Her friends and family still ringed the invisible dome. Had anyone noticed that she'd traveled…somewhere else? She cast a quick look at Kieran's collapsed form and sucked in a breath to see his eyes were open. The black lines of the cursed magic were still writhing around under his skin, but that dead-eyed look she associated with the Kieran she'd once met wasn't there. The real Kieran—the healed one—was still the dominant force, but Amber didn't know how long that force could fight until he had to succumb.

Accept that even if you feel clueless, you know what you're doing.

Amber quickly cycled through all the spells she'd used over the last few months, and the training she'd done with Edgar. The key things for her—even when she didn't have a spell in front of her—had always been contact, intent, and channeling emotion. And, when in doubt, she asked magic her questions, letting it guide her when she felt lost about what to do next. It was a cobbled-together technique, but it was the best she'd come up with without formal training.

Shooting another quick look at Kieran, she whispered, "Is your magic okay? Healed still, I mean."

"I think so," he croaked out.

That wasn't reassuring, but she was running out of options. "Do you trust me?"

He managed a nod.

"Think of your magic like a physical thing you can put in a shoebox," she said. "When I grab onto you, hand it to me."

He cocked a brow at her, clearly worried that she'd finally cracked under the stress, but nodded again.

She quickly worked through the words of a noise-canceling spell in her head, swapping out "noise" for "privacy," and then worked backward. She didn't want to create a dome around them; she wanted to knock one down. When she had it worked out, she nodded once at Kieran, reached out a hand to wrap around his forearm, and then firmly placed her other hand on the earth. At the same time that the ley line magic ignited under her skin, Kieran shoved his own magic at her. It was like a caffeine rush or a sugar high. Her head buzzed.

Then she pooled both sets of magic with her own, mentally cast the spell, and then funneled it all down and out. Through her limbs, into her hands, and into the earth. Into the ley lines.

Shouts rushed in, like a crack in a dam that had first let in a trickle, and then a flood.

"What in the—" Patrice called out.

Her exclamation wasn't cut off intentionally. The sound around Amber had snapped off too. Was the dome of silence back? Had the spell not worked? There was something off about the quiet now, and she scrambled to her feet and whirled around.

Everything was frozen in place. Simon was in mid-run next to Scarlett several hundred feet away. The Penhallows all had varying expressions of confusion on their faces. Patrice and Neil glared Amber's way, fingers pointed in her direction.

And Raphael, with the grimoire still propped up in his hands, stalked toward her. She stumbled back, hands out.

"Amber, stop," he said. "I froze time. Hurry, we don't have long."

She stared at him.

He groaned in a way that was so Edgar, it almost made her relax instantly. But she didn't move. "I told you before. I needed this to be believable. Now, come here. From what Kieran told me, your time-freeze is instinctively stronger than mine. But I think between the two of us, we can execute your plan."

She figured she had no other choice than to believe him, then ran over to look at the spell he had the book opened to. It was a spell like the noise-canceling and privacy spells—it created a dome, rather than freezing everything in the vicinity. Keeping *everything* frozen was a strain on the witch who cast the spell. Amber guessed that his teleportation-like skill only allowed him to travel through time in short distances, as it was too much energy output to maintain a spell as complex as this for very long. Raphael already looked like this one was zapping him dry and it had been less than a minute.

She studied the spell as quickly as she could, memorizing it.

"When I get back to my spot, time will start up again," he said. "Funnel everything you've got into that spell and I'll do the same."

Amber nodded, still not fully believing Raphael hadn't betrayed their family.

"I know changing the past isn't the answer," he said, a bit reluctantly. "No matter how unhappy I am with the present, I have to make the best of it." Then he ran back to his location and she did her best to lie back down where she'd been when the neighborhood had frozen around her.

The sound flooded back in.

Amber called on her concern for Willow and Kieran, her hope that Edgar would be able to live a life free of Neil, and her fear for the safety of her town and all her companions here. Then she slapped both hands onto the earth, the magic in the ley lines making her head spin. She squeezed her eyes shut and uttered the words of the spell. She heard Raphael do the same.

Patrice and Neil called out something, but it was drowned out by a loud rumbling that shook the ground as if a mini bomb had just gone off. Amber glanced over her shoulder just as a thick spray of dirt, grass, and cement chunks erupted into the air.

Amber heard Simon cheer, "Aha! It worked!"

Good grief! She'd known that he'd been working on a strength tincture, but she hadn't realized how effective it would be.

She tried not to let the sound of battle around her distract her as she called out the words of the spell in almost perfect rhythm with Raphael. Dust rained down on her, and rocks and large chunks of debris slammed into the ground. Shutting her eyes, she focused only on the words of the spell.

And then the sounds abruptly stopped.

Amber cracked open an eye to see Willow and Kieran in the same positions they'd been in before, but now covered in a fine layer of dirt. She quickly got to her feet, listing sideways a bit. Her head spun so badly, she had to place her hands on her knees for a moment and take a deep breath. It would do no one any good if she passed out.

When the feeling passed, she turned and gasped.

It was like someone had hit the pause button on the action scene of a movie. Simon's arm was still in the air, his face screwed up mid-battle cry. Amber followed the arc of his throw to a small crater in the ground at the feet of a Penhallow who was in the midst of being blown backward from yet another exploding tincture. Scarlett was airborne, sailing backward from a burst of air thrown at her by Neil.

Raphael was a few feet away from her, the grimoire on the ground. He'd dropped the book and fallen to one knee. Amber hurried over to help him to his feet.

"You okay?" she asked.

He nodded and leaned on her heavily as he stood. His skin had paled and sweat beaded at his temple as if he'd suddenly come down with a horrible case of stomach flu. She wanted to tell him to sit, but she knew they didn't have time for resting.

"A few of them have thrown killing blows. We need to move people out of the way," Amber said, then used a wind spell to knock a witch out of the way of Patrice, who had the witch pinned to the ground and had sent a blast of cursed magic straight for her heart. Raphael did the same with a couple of others.

Once they'd done that, Amber grabbed the grimoire, studied the freeze spell one more time, reversed it, and cast it at each of her companions, unfreezing them. By the time she'd released all eight, she was nauseated and lightheaded. She slumped to the ground.

"Nope," Scarlett said. She and Gary forced Amber back to her feet. "We're not done yet."

Simon and a woman were crouched near Willow and Kieran. Amber watched as Simon handed a vial to the woman, who then tipped the contents into Kieran's mouth, while Simon did the same for Willow.

"Revitalizing tincture," Simon called over his shoulder at Amber. "I usually put it in my coffee when I need an extra pick-me-up. It might not be enough to wake them, but it's all I've got. She needs a hospital. I'll text your aunt."

The rest of her companions gathered around her, Scarlett and Gary still propping Amber up by looping their arms through hers on either side. Why wouldn't they just let her sleep? She watched through bleary eyes as the others started to link arms, too. Simon stuffed his phone in his pocket, then joined the circle. They made a ring with the original nine, plus Raphael.

Scarlett said, "Remember what she said…after the channeling spell, visualize your magic. Picture it like a gift you're handing to her. A box, a bag, a plastic leftover container—doesn't matter what. But we're all giving our magic to her to make her stronger. And she needs it now."

Muttered words of agreement floated into Amber's ears, but it was a soft, faraway sound. Something jolted her and her eyes popped open.

"Stay with us," Raphael said.

"You're the only one who can do this," Simon said, "but we'll help you get there."

Amber managed a faint nod.

A cough sounded behind her and she managed to turn around enough to see Kieran struggling to his feet. "I can help, too."

Two links in the circle broke to let Kieran in, then the circle was reformed.

"All right," Gary said, "here we go."

Amber, as the recipient of the magic, only had one task: stay conscious. A task that grew increasingly difficult. It felt like she'd just run a marathon—through molasses while wearing a weighted sweatsuit. She had her doubts about moving this many people into the memory even when she'd felt healthy. If she were successful at this, it would almost assuredly knock her flat. And she might not be able to get back up.

But as her companions started passing their magic to her, she felt her strength returning. Her aches diminished, her legs were strong enough to hold her up, and her exhausted magic reinflated. Her senses heightened and her mind cleared.

She could do this.

She felt invincible.

As her companions all let go, each one drained and now holding each other up, Amber eyed the frozen Penhallows a few feet away. Her eyes skittered over the ones she didn't know by name, and then flicked back and forth between Patrice and Neil. The woman who had orchestrated all this and had been slowly driving a wedge between Amber and her beloved town. The man who had murdered her parents and had been torturing her cousin.

Her magic crackled under her skin. She could end both of them right here and now. She didn't know any killing spells, but with this much energy in her system, with her own magic this eager for a purpose, Amber could be resourceful. And, since the ley lines were ticked off, Amber was sure the magic below her feet would help her, too. The world needed to be rid of people like Patrice and Neil. The kind who preyed on the innocent to get what they wanted.

A face swam into view, breaking her concentration. It was Kieran.

"I speak from experience when I say you're on a dangerous path right now, Amber," he said. "I can see it on your face. This much power might temporarily solve your problems—but it'll create even more. And they might be my family, my clan, but they're monsters right now. They need to be stopped—but in a way that doesn't destroy *you* in the process."

Devra's words from a few days ago flooded back in then. "*You call us monsters, but what does this make you?*"

Somehow the Penhallows were right this time.

"Okay," she said softly, and Kieran nodded and stepped out of her line of vision. "Okay," she said, louder. "If you see me start to struggle, push more of your magic at me."

She turned to check on her still unconscious sister. She hoped Willow would wake up once Patrice was in the memory of 1971. Maybe the poison tincture would lose some of its potency when Patrice was removed from the timeline.

With that, Amber dropped to her knees beside her mother's book. The sight of it gave her another jolt of confidence. Placing both hands on the ground, she said, *I need your help again. What happened to the Penhallows was a punishment that didn't fit the crime. I'll never forgive Neil for taking my parents from me, for what he's done to Edgar, but it's also not his fault that the people who came before him cursed his magic. It's not fair to him or to you. Help me move them the way you helped me move Damien and Devra. I'll give them all a choice. If they want to be healed as Kieran was, I'll do it.*

Amber took one hand off the earth to pick up her mother's grimoire and hold it to her chest. "Anyone willing to travel with me, hold on," she said out loud.

Hands landed on her back, shoulders, arms. It gave her weakening magic a little espresso kick.

She pooled all the magic her body held—hers and the gifts from the others—and imagined it as a gift she was giving back to magic. It was equal parts apology, offering, and request.

White light tore through her vision.

When it cleared, she was in the neighborhood from 1971. Her mother's book was in her arms, and her companions—including Kieran and her uncle—stood beside her. They were in a horizontal line, eleven of them standing shoulder to shoulder. The transported Penhallows were all conscious. Some had landed on their feet while others had collided with the dirt road. Confusion overtook them in waves.

It was Patrice who came to her senses first and whirled toward Amber. Her piercing gaze went from grimoire to Raphael to Kieran and back again. She thrust her hands in Amber's direction, but nothing happened. She thrust them out again and again, like a mime trying to push open an invisible door. She looked at her hands as if they had purposefully betrayed her.

"You're in the memory of a day in 1971, when the ley lines unexpectedly erupted," Amber said. "Magic calls the shots here. You can't use it unless magic gives you permission."

Patrice scoffed, crossing her arms. "Magic isn't a physical thing. You just have to be strong enough to use it."

A great rumbling shook the earth then, and a moment later, Patrice was airborne. She hit the ground a few feet away, rolling into a patch of unmowed grass. The Penhallows flinched, startled out of their side conversations and schemes.

Thanks, she silently told magic. A vibration tickled the soles of her feet in response.

A door slammed in the distance. Damien and Devra came running. They had changed clothes since Amber had last been here, so now they both looked like they'd just stepped off the set of a 1970s sitcom.

The group parted to let Damien and Devra through. Patrice still lay unconscious in the grass. It said a lot that no one made a move to check on her.

"Welcome, all, to the time witch's prison," Devra said, standing just inches from Amber.

Damien, however, had noticed something else. "Kieran? You're…with her?"

Amber glanced down the line at him just as his features shifted from his own to a mirror of Damien's.

"How …" Devra asked, taking a step back. "How can you do magic here when we can't?"

"She healed me," Kieran said. "She didn't take my magic away. She returned my magic to its pure form. She can do it for you, too."

Devra shook her head as she stepped back several steps, until she was lined up with the Penhallows standing across from Amber's group. "You can't trust her. They want us locked up and stripped of our powers. Being a witch in a world with people like her and the WBI is just as bad as being trapped in this time loop."

Damien had been watching his sister's retreat, but then slowly turned back to Kieran, who wore his own face again. His gaze shifted to Amber. "And once you heal me, you let me back out? Just like that?"

"Just like that," Amber said.

"Do it," he said.

"*Damien*," Devra hissed, but he didn't even look back.

Amber looked past Damien to address the rest of the Penhallows. "The agreement is this: choose to have your magic healed, and you get to leave; if you choose not to, you stay here in this memory indefinitely. Your magic won't work here, and you're confined to this neighborhood. It *is* a prison, but you can choose to leave it voluntarily.

Make your choice and then come see me if you want to be released—both from this place and your curse."

Amber turned to her group then. "That house over there is Zelda's. I say we set up shop in there. I need you all to be my backup in case they try something. At least we've got magic on our side and they don't."

For the next few hours—Amber assumed—she healed Penhallow after Penhallow. They were brought in one at a time and Amber, with her mother's grimoire as her guide, traveled into the minds of these troubled witches and severed their insatiable desire for more power. She assured them that their magic would come back, like a green sprout poking its way out of the soil come spring, but that it might take a while. Each one emerged from the experience in a daze, as if they'd never seen color before. Kieran became their temporary therapist, explaining what it would feel like as the magic returned.

But of the fourteen Penhallows transported to this place, three had yet to enter Zelda's house. None of them were a surprise to Amber: Devra, Neil, and Patrice. Even with the extra boost in energy from magic itself, and her companions offering their own magic when she felt weak, as well as supplying her with whatever food and drink they could find, Amber's energy was fading, and fading fast. If the last three didn't want to be healed, she had no problem leaving them here to sort out their demons on their own.

Just as Amber had decided she was ready to pack up and head back to the present, Kieran poked his head into the room Amber had been conducting her work in.

"Uhh…my brother is here," Kieran said.

Amber pursed her lips. She'd been hoping that Neil's stubbornness would allow her, with a guilt-free conscience, to leave the man here to rot for all of time. "Okay."

Kieran ducked back out.

Scarlett, Simon, and Gary were in the room as well, and clearly recognized Amber's expression for what it was.

"If you refuse to help him," Scarlett said, "no one would blame you."

"If he so much as looks at you funny," Simon said, "I'll blast him into next Tuesday. Well, not literally, since you're the time witch. Oh, you know what I mean."

"You're a better person than me for even considering healing that guy," Gary said.

Neil stepped into the doorway and Amber's stomach clenched. Her mind flashed back to the memories she'd watched of her parents' last day on earth. The way Neil had trapped them in their own house and then had set it on fire. All for the book that now sat on Zelda's coffee table. He eyed the book, that hungry glint in his eye still there.

"I suppose I'm the last person you'd want to offer aid to," Neil said, looking at her now.

"You're not wrong," she said. "I can't say that if you hadn't been cursed, that you would have acted differently, but being healed will give you the opportunity to make decisions that are wholly your own now."

He smiled a little. "You're so much like Anna, you know. She would be proud of you."

"Don't speak my mother's name as if you have the right to use it," she snapped.

He winced slightly, and just behind him, Scarlett, Simon, and Gary wore matching grins.

Neil coughed awkwardly. "Fair enough."

Amber gestured to the blue-and-white checkered fabric couch she'd been using for what felt like days on end now. "Lie down and we can get started."

Once he was lying down, he folded his hands over his lap. "See you on the other side, I suppose." He closed his eyes. Amber thought about how easy it would be to end this man here and now. The body would be left in this loop in time and no one would ever find him again. It would be like he'd just disappeared off the planet.

But she believed what Jack had said about Kieran. *It's like deciding whether or not someone who committed a crime could ever truly be rehabilitated. Some can't, but others can. If we never give those people a second chance, then they never get an opportunity to make up for their mistakes.*

Consulting her mother's spell one more time, even though she'd now cast this spell eleven other times, she placed a hand on Neil's arm, closed her eyes, and entered Neil's mind.

As with all the others, there was no light, no sound. There was just a *pull*.

She followed the pull as if walking through an invisible maze whose walls you could only find by bumping into them. In every Penhallow, the desire for power was more obsession than anything else. Illogical, all-consuming obsession that was so bone-achingly deep, it made Amber want to scream.

In Neil's mind, it wasn't just magic he was obsessed with. It was Annabelle, too. Images of Amber's mother started to flash in Neil's mind, like a film projected onto the side of a building. Annabelle laughing, crying, lying beside Neil as she slept. A reel of fights, and kisses, and quiet moments. Hints of a life he could have had with Annabelle Henbane if his obsession with reversing the curse hadn't consumed him so completely that it had driven him to kill the woman he desperately loved.

Amber understood on some level, watching these images swirl around her, that Neil had killed Annabelle partly because his obsession with her had gained the same fever-pitch level as his obsession with reversing the curse.

I killed her because I loved her so much. I couldn't live without her, the obsession seemed to say. *I had to kill her because my love for her interrupted my mission.*

Everything in his mind slammed to a stop.

The world went black. Amber stilled. This had never happened before. Though she didn't have a form here, somehow she still felt rooted to the floor. Trapped. Bound. Unable to move.

"Now you're *my* prisoner," a voice said. A voice that seemed to come from all around her. "You let me out of here fully as I am, and I'll do the same for you. If you don't, well, I can just replace Edgar with you. You'll have me in your head day and night, day and night, until you give me what I want."

Amber thrashed out with her magic, but it was as if her arms were bound to her sides.

Something yanked her back with such force, it zapped the air from her lungs. Light and sound and feeling flooded back into her body and she toppled backward out of her chair, hitting the ground. There were shouts of confusion, and rapid footfalls on the wood floor. Amber's ears rang.

As hands grabbed her under the arms and helped her to her feet, she found the couch was empty. All that lay there was a small golden ring—her mother's wedding ring. Amber recognized it instantly because it was a combination of diamonds and rubies. It hadn't been a promise ring at all. It had been the ring her father had given her. Neil had even lied about that.

Once on stable footing, she made her way to the couch and picked up the ring, turning it over in her fingers. Palming the ring, she turned to face the now-full room of startled witches. "What happened?"

"I don't know," Simon said. "He sat up on the couch and said that you were our only way out of here, and now that he'd taken you hostage, no one was getting out unless you agreed to his demands."

"And then he just …" Scarlett said, eyes wide, "vanished. And when he did, you fell out of the chair."

"Patrice vanished, too," Kieran said from the doorway.

"And Devra," Damien said, his arms crossed tightly over his chest.

Amber opened her palm to stare down at the ring. "I think magic took them…broke them back down to their magical essence. They're gone." Slipping the ring into her pocket, she scanned the room full of witches, some friends, and some healed foes. "What do you say we get out of here?"

But Amber hardly had to lift a magical finger and suddenly they were back in the present. The second Amber's very large group touched ground, two bursts of warm yellow light flooded into the dark, abandoned neighborhood. Energy leached out of Amber then and she swayed on her feet as the adrenaline and magic stabilized in her body.

The lights were cabin lights. Aunt G, Edgar, Jack, Kim, and the others were here.

"Is Willow okay?" Amber managed to croak out.

"She's resting peacefully in the car, little mouse," said Aunt G's voice from somewhere far away.

"Good." Amber collapsed.

CHAPTER 31

When Amber awoke, it was in a bed that wasn't her own. Absently, she patted her chest, where something metal rested against her skin. Her searching fingers wrapped around a ring at the end of a chain. Angling her head the best she could, she smiled faintly at her mother's ring that now hung from her neck. A throb of pain went through her head and she dropped the ring, where it landed back against her skin. Her head was fuzzy and her mouth was dry.

Wincing, she tried to sit up, only to find something poking painfully in her arm. She squirmed, trying to pull the thing free, but a warm hand landed on top of hers to still her.

"Easy, little mouse," a familiar voice said.

Amber rolled her head toward the sound and found her aunt smiling down at her. "Hey, Aunt G." She sounded like she'd swallowed a frog.

Aunt G's eyes welled up. "You gave me quite the scare, you know. You both did." Then she jutted her chin toward Amber's other side.

Willow lay in the adjoining bed, sleeping peacefully. Amber's bottom lip shook. "She's okay?"

"Yes," Aunt G said. "Simon and I came up with a detoxifying tincture for her that I snuck in an hour or so ago. Without Patrice around to reactivate the tincture Willow consumed, it will eventually break down and pass out of her body. The detoxifying tincture will just make sure that happens quicker."

"Have I been asleep a long time?" Amber asked, unable to take her eyes off her sleeping sister.

"About twelve hours," Aunt G said. "Time passes differently in that memory, so though I'm sure you were in there for hours, in the present, it had only been an hour tops before you were back. Between the amount of magic that had been pumped into you, and the number of spells you cast in the memory, you exhausted yourself rather completely."

The door to Amber's hospital room opened. Kim's gaze jumped from Willow to Amber to Aunt G, and then quickly back to Amber. Her eyes lit up. "Oh my God! You're finally awake! I can't believe I missed it."

Kim wore a tank top, athletic pants, running shoes, and a bright pink headband. Her long brown hair was up in a messy ponytail, and her face was flush. The running bib was still attached to her tank top with safety pins.

"How'd you do?" Amber asked, trying again to sit up.

"Twenty-six minutes flat!" she chirped. "I beat Bianca's time by thirty-nine seconds."

Amber smiled at that.

Slowly, people started to trickle into her room. Jack, Simon, Bianca, Betty, Bobby, Scarlett, Zelda, Irene, Gary, and several other witches who had helped her that night.

None of the Penhallows she'd healed were there, but she wasn't surprised by that. They all had to process that they were in the world curse-free. Her friends and loved ones crowded around her bed, all expressing how glad they were to see her awake.

The door swung open yet again but Amber couldn't see who had walked in. "Is she awake?" came a gruff voice.

The group parted as Edgar strode toward her. He stood there staring at her for a long moment, his grumpy expression hard to read. Then a small smile inched up his face, and even more shockingly, tears sprang up in his eyes. "He's gone."

Amber choked out a laugh. "Yeah?"

Edgar quickly closed the distance and gave Amber a tight awkward hug, Amber unable to move without all her muscles screaming in protest. "Thank you, cousin," he whispered in her ear. "I didn't think you could do it."

She laughed. "Always so optimistic."

But he still didn't let her go. "Thank you," he said again, but softer this time.

"Of course," she said.

Edgar and Jack were in the middle of telling the group their story—how they'd nearly gotten into a high-speed chase with the police because Jack was driving 90 miles per hour on the highway in an effort to get the grimoires as far away from Edgehill as possible—when the door opened yet again.

A hush almost immediately swept over the group. Several people backed away, moving closer to the windows and further from the door. Aunt G got to her feet.

The sinking feeling in Amber's gut was so acute, even the monitor keeping track of her vital signs reacted.

"Dad?" Edgar asked softly, his back to Amber now.

Raphael stopped at the foot of Amber's bed and smiled weakly at her. "Welcome back."

Amber's gaze flicked between Edgar and Raphael. "Thank you for your help," she said, keeping her attention focused on the tight jaw of Edgar's profile even though she addressed Raphael. "I couldn't have done any of that by myself."

Edgar's fists clenched by his side.

"Is Neil gone?" Raphael asked his son.

Edgar nodded.

"I needed it to be believable," Raphael said quickly. "I knew Neil would take anything you said or did or thought and use it against us. I asked Amber not to tell you."

"To be honest," Aunt G said, "she had more faith in a Penhallow than she did in her own uncle."

Raphael grimaced. "Can't say I blame any of you for thinking that way. I wouldn't trust me either." He took a slight step toward Edgar, who was still wound so tight, Amber was half convinced he was gearing up to deck his father in the face. "The FBI also doesn't trust me. I'm apparently under suspicion for the murder of Stanley Johnson and possibly kidnapping my niece and taking her across state lines. I've been informed by the WBI that a Thea Bishop will be my attorney."

Yikes. Amber had managed to forget about *that* whole mess.

"I know I have a lot to make up for, son. But I'd like to try. I was angry and bitter when I was your age. I see the same rage in you that I had—for different reasons, I know, but I don't want that for you. All I'm asking for is the right to earn a second chance."

Edgar didn't say anything for what felt like ages. The tension in the room was nearly claustrophobic. Everyone's focus was on the two Henbane men staring each other down.

"All right," Edgar said tightly.

Raphael sucked in a shaky breath. "Yeah?"

"Yeah," he said, then crossed the distance and pulled his father into a tight hug. "You can start by buying me all the pancakes I can eat at the Catty Melt."

"Deal," Raphael said.

"Your wallet is going to regret that," Amber said.

Letting his dad go, Edgar craned his neck until he made contact with Kim. "You wanna get pancakes with us?"

Kim, eyes wide, nodded so vigorously, her head nearly snapped off at the neck and rolled away.

"Is this a party or something?"

Amber grinned. A very sleepy, very confused Willow was sitting up in bed.

"You feel okay?" Amber asked.

"Yeah," she said. "But I'm *starving*. Can I get some of those pancakes, too?"

An agonized cry sounded next to Amber and she looked over in alarm to see her no-nonsense, practical-in-all-ways aunt full-on sobbing. Amber had never seen such a sight in all her life.

"Aunt G!" Amber yelped, turning so abruptly toward her that her back muscles temporarily seized up. "What's wrong?"

"I'm just so relieved!" Aunt G wailed. "My girls are okay!"

Thanks to another round of detoxifying tinctures slipped to them by Simon, and a muscle repair concoction from Aunt G—which was basically a magically enhanced protein shake—Amber and Willow were able to leave the hospital by that afternoon.

From the bits of information Amber got from her friends and family, the WBI had descended on Edgehill while Amber slept and had indeed used devices to wipe memories of magic from the non-witches' minds. The timing was suspicious, according to most, as if the WBI had been hiding in the wings while Amber and her witches did all the heavy lifting, and the WBI materialized only to be the cleanup crew.

Chief Brown had been reported to say, "I thought the mind-wiping tools were a myth!" Thankfully this revelation hadn't made him faint the same way he had when Thea had been turned into a hamster.

Memories of the giant cats who terrorized the parade, the noxious gas that had knocked out the group of volunteers at the community center, and Amber's rogue, vicious toys were all stuff of weird dreams now.

When she got back to The Quirky Whisker, under the tutelage of Aunt G, Amber's apartment turned into a toy-making workshop. The non-witches were assigned the tasks of assembling plastic flower wreaths and sanding the plastic discs needed for Amber's various spells.

An assembly line of witches was then set up to layer spells on plastic discs, fusing the discs to the body cavities of the toys, and then fusing the plastic parts together. It took a few tries to get the kinks worked out—the giraffe that had accidentally been enchanted to bark like a dog being the happiest of mistakes.

Amber, who was functional but barely so, divided her time between managing the line and working on a single animated toy: a blue Pegasus for John Huntley. She hoped he too had his mind wiped of the strange evening where a black-haired woman had stormed his bus and put him and his entire staff to sleep.

Somehow, by five in the evening, all the pending toy orders had been filled and Amber had finished her line of exclusive Here and Meow designs, and John's custom toy. Which meant she could actually enjoy an evening at the festival without worrying about getting her inventory done on time. Tomorrow, she would be able to set up her booth for the last day of the festival.

All the visiting witches agreed to stay for the evening as well. Zelda was thrilled about sharing the festival with her daughter. Up until a few months ago, Zelda had been convinced she'd never set foot in Edgehill again, let alone attend the town's beloved annual festival. Even Bianca agreed to attend the Here and Meow that evening, as long as Amber and Kim agreed to go to The Great Seeding the following morning.

Though Melanie Cole's rose garden memorial would be unveiled in the morning at Balinese Park, they'd be able to attend both events. Neither Kim nor Amber had any idea what The Great Seeding was, and they were both scared to find out—especially when Bianca instructed them to wear rain slickers.

Amber had easily succeeded in convincing Jack to join them, but Kim didn't have any luck with Edgar. Edgar had a good excuse, though—he and his father were going to begin repairs on the house. Amber had sent the trunk of grimoires off with the men, too, knowing the books could be better stashed in Edgar's house than in Amber's tiny apartment. The Henbane men weren't sure when the FBI was going to come for Raphael, so they wanted to spend as much time together as possible.

Amber had all the faith in the world that if anyone could find a way out of this mess for Raphael, it was Thea Bishop.

As the group all piled out of The Quirky Whisker, splitting off into groups that would caravan to the fairgrounds near Angora Threads, Amber noted that a black SUV was parked at the curb a few doors down. Amber stood in the middle of the still-deserted sidewalk outside her shop as she stared at the vehicle.

Jack realized a moment later that she wasn't beside him and turned back. "You okay?"

The driver and passenger side doors opened and out stepped Agent Howe and Agent Barker. They moved toward her.

"Yeah," she said. "I'll meet you guys at the car, okay?" She was riding to the fairgrounds with him and the Harrises. Willow and Kim were riding over with Simon and Bianca.

Jack kissed her cheek, then headed after Betty and Bobby who had already crossed the street.

The agents, still in their black suits, stopped before Amber.

"Good to see you up and about," Agent Howe said, hands in the pockets of her slacks. "That was a lot of magic use for someone as untrained as you."

Agent Howe clearly had never issued a compliment in her life.

"What she means," Agent Barker said, "is that the WBI is grateful to you for the work you did."

"With no help from you, I might add," Amber said. "You were too busy trying to get your hands on my mother's grimoire, and the Penhallows stole it out from underneath your nose anyway. Then when we needed you, you were nowhere to be found."

Agent Howe pursed her lips. "We were cleaning up the mess in your wake. This whole thing was a PR disaster waiting to happen. Do you know how many memories we had to wipe? Our backup needed backup."

All this talk of memory wipes got Amber thinking. "Is the WBI the reason why so many witches forgot the truth of what the council did?"

The agents exchanged a look, but neither answered. Which was answer enough.

"We're heading back to headquarters now," Agent Howe said. "Know that the WBI isn't *currently* planning to get the Henbane grimoire into our custody. The higher-ups are willing to admit that your actions kept Edgehill and magic safe at the same time. The book is safest with you. The WBI is hard at work trying to track down the network and who was in it. Kieran is getting his sentence reduced in exchange for coughing up the names of those in the network. If the Penhallows—or their sympathizers—become a threat again, we'll be back. And we probably won't ask nicely next time."

With that, Agent Howe turned and walked away.

"Nicely?" Amber muttered.

Agent Barker shrugged. "Enjoy the festival, Amber."

She remained in the same spot on the sidewalk until the agents got back in their car and drove away. Amber truly hoped she never saw either one again.

The entrance to the fairgrounds was marked by an arch made of cat-shaped balloons. Amber, hand-in-hand with Jack, followed Willow, Aunt G, Kim, Bianca, Simon, and the Harrises. On one side of the entrance were the restrooms, and booths to buy tickets for games and rides. To the left was a fenced-off area lined with human-sized cat beds where tired festival goers could rest. A giant screen had been erected near the front of the enclosure that played a perpetual loop of funny cat videos.

The first of the food sections came up next. The staples of popcorn, giant pretzels, and lemonade were there, but so were elaborately decorated cat-shaped sugar cookies, a Coffee Cat food truck, and a Mews and Brews stand. Rumor had it that there were elaborately crafted hamburger buns that had been dyed with food coloring to look like cat faces.

Cheers and shouts drew them to the game section, which featured carnival games where only cat-related items were available as prizes. Basket toss, lawn bowling, and sack races were the most popular options. Kim, Bobby, and Amber entered a very competitive sack race. Bobby smoked them all, winning Betty a giant stuffed cat. When Jack gallantly volunteered to try his hand at winning Amber one from a ring toss game, she declined. She wasn't emotionally ready for more giant cats just yet.

At 7 PM, they grabbed seats at the Cat Stage for the last show of the evening. Amber sat between Jack and Kim, and Kim kept up a steady commentary on how much work she'd put in booking the cat troupe.

"Shows like this often feature dogs who can walk on their hind legs and bark on command and whatever," Kim said. "Well, these cats can do all that and more. And the coolest thing? They're all previously feral cats or cats that were days from being euthanized. The organization donates at least a third of its proceeds to cat shelters and spends a lot of time in the community offering education on spay and neuter programs, and encouraging people to adopt adult cats, who need homes and love just as much as kittens."

After the show, Amber wondered if she started today, how long it would take to train Alley or Tom to do a back-flip. She was working through the logistics of such a task when someone called her name. Jack and Simon were deep in conversation ahead of her, and Bianca was passionately explaining the ins and outs of The Great Seeding to Kim, so none of them noticed when Amber lagged behind and turned around.

It was Connor Declan. "Uhh…hey," he said, wringing his hands as he closed the distance.

Amber stared at him, wondering if the WBI had paid him a visit. "Hi."

"So…uhh …" he said, giving the back of his neck a scratch. "I talked to an Agent Howe earlier."

Amber felt Willow sidle up next to her.

Connor swallowed. His gaze skittered to Willow for a moment, then back to Amber. "She straightened things out for me. I know now that the information Molly and I got was flipped. You guys—both of you—were the good guys and Molly and I were manipulated."

"We've been friends for *years*, Connor," Willow said. "Why didn't you just talk to me when you doubted me? I can't tell you who to spend time with, but there's a dif-ference between being dedicated to your job and having tunnel vision. Molly is so relentless in furthering her career that she doesn't care about consequences. I know your career is important to you, too, but you let it go too far this time."

"I know," he said quickly, his hands held up, placating. "I broke things off with her."

"Really?" Amber asked.

"Yeah," he said. "Well, the WBI also sort of hired her. They apparently work with…uhh…*people* like her because she can get insider information in ways they sometimes can't. She's leaving for a hybrid town next week."

Amber and Willow shared a bewildered expression.

"Willow, I know I haven't always handled things the best way with us," he said. "But I was hoping maybe we could give this—you and me, I mean—a try." He looked so hopeful, so vulnerable, Amber almost ran screaming in the other direction. The emotion on his face was so raw, Amber felt like she was seeing something too intimate. Not to mention he was doing so while they were surrounded by bustling tourists.

"You mean you want to give me a try now that Molly is leaving," Willow said. "I'm your backup plan *again*."

"No," he said urgently. "With everything that's happened…it's made me reevaluate everything, you know? Made me really think about what's important to me. *You're* important to me."

It took Willow a moment to speak. "I've waited since high school to hear you say that," she said. Connor grinned so wide, it looked like it hurt. "But you should have known I was important to you before all this."

"I did know," he said. "Honestly. All I want is a second chance to prove it to you."

Willow looped her arm through Amber's. "Sorry, Connor. I need to be with someone who thinks I'm important from the start." Then she turned Amber around with her, and they walked away.

"I know that wasn't easy, Will," Amber said after a minute. When her sister didn't reply, Amber glanced over to see tears running down her face. Amber let her sister have her quiet moment with her thoughts, but she didn't let her go.

At 9:00 PM, Amber and her companions were at the back of the fairgrounds before a stage. Aunt G and Zelda were together in the nearby food court with alcoholic beverages, exchanging stories about the good old days. Amber already knew those two women left together were going to be trouble.

Kim—since she "knew his people"—had snagged a bunch of tickets for the John Huntley concert. There were a good two rows of bouncing, prematurely screaming teenage girls lined up before them, but Kim had gotten them premium seats.

Just before the concert started, Amber spotted a girl in a front-row seat turn around and scan the crowd. Amber guessed she'd been looking for a parent or friend, but she spotted Amber instead.

"Amber!" Tammy cheered.

"Tammy!" Amber cheered back.

Then the lights on the stage came to life, and the members of John Huntley's band started to make their way out. The crowd went nuts, and Amber and Tammy shared another delighted squeal.

Willow and Kim sang along to all of John's songs, note for note. Amber and Jack realized they only knew a few of them, so they just danced extra hard when they were clueless.

"You're amazing, Edgehill!" John called out after a few songs. "This next song is for a girl I met recently." The crowd of girls before him booed, but John didn't seem to notice. "I'm only just getting to know her, but I can already tell she's pretty special. This one is for you, Willow."

Amber, Kim, and Willow screamed as if *they* were sixteen-year-olds.

It was a good night.

EPILOGUE

Early on Sunday morning, Daisy and Lily Bowen arrived at Amber's booth in the fairgrounds to help her set up. Amber hugged them both fiercely in turn. It had only been a few days since she'd last seen them, but it felt like it had been half a century. As they worked, the sisters mostly wanted to know if it was true that Willow and John Huntley were "a thing." Amber didn't know what they were. All she knew was that he was going to come by to pick up his custom animated toy later that night, and then was going to take Willow out for dinner next week—just how that would work with a celebrity as big as Huntley, Amber didn't know. Maybe Willow could hire out a WBI agent whose sole job was to keep the public from finding out any information about Willow.

Amber buzzed with nervous energy. She knew the WBI had wiped the memories of the rogue toys from residents' and tourists' minds, and she also knew that her magic hadn't been the reason why Toast the Bear exploded. Yet she was concerned that the events of the last few days had ruined her business.

Amber was partially underneath the tablecloth on the long table in her booth, checking her supply boxes underneath, when someone cleared their throat. She had a sign on her table that said she wasn't open for business for another ten minutes, but she tamped down her mild wave of annoyance and stood up, mostly pleased that someone wanted one of her wares so much that they wanted to try to get one early.

She gasped.

"Hello, Amber."

"Grandma?" she ventured.

Then her gaze jumped to the man next to her. Her grandfather. And beside them were Betty and Bobby. Her grandparents grinned at her.

"Oh my God," she said and ran around the table to hug them both in turn. Something about them, even though she'd never met them before, felt so much like home—like her parents—that she burst into tears. The next thing she knew, she and four elderly people were all sobbing. Daisy and Lily, who had dark teal blue hair today, went about their setup tasks as if nothing about this situation was strange.

When they'd all managed to calm themselves down, Ivy Henbane took Amber by the face, her hands a little cold but soft. "Please don't be cross with Betty for keeping us a secret."

Amber shook her head. "It's impossible to be upset with Betty about anything other than withholding cupcakes."

"Oof," her grandma said, letting Amber's face go. "I tried one of her German chocolate cupcakes. That was your mother's favorite, you know. Perfection!" She made a chef's kiss with her fingers.

Amber laughed.

"Now, young lady," her grandpa said, his voice shaky with age, "the Harrises are going to take us around this festival for a bit. Don't worry about entertaining us. We've got a lot to catch up on, but we can do that tonight, hmm?" Then he and Ivy both kissed her on the cheek.

Betty and Bobby hugged Amber again.

Over the next couple of hours, Amber's business was so steady that her concerns melted away entirely. Sally Long came by with little Noah and bought a walrus he named Cement. Sally showed no sign that she remembered anything about the altercation from a week ago.

Amber knew she had the WBI to thank for that, but she refused to do so to their faces.

Claire Petrie came by the table too, and Amber handed her daughter Wendy a sea green, exclusive Here and Meow cat. Amber was certain the color was still a little too close to "seasick green," but Wendy gasped when she saw the toy and said, "Thanks, Miss Amber! I love Minty!" And off she went, stopping after a few feet to show off her toy to a friend.

Amber was still smiling to herself when her phone buzzed in her pocket. She and the Bowen sisters had been so busy, she'd hardly had a chance to slow down, but she was a content kind of exhausted.

A text from Jack had popped up on the screen. You need to get back to The Quirky Whisker as soon as possible!

Her heart lodged in her throat.

After confirming with the Bowen sisters that they could man the booth alone while she dealt with an emergency, she grabbed her purse and hustled for the exit to the fairgrounds. She called Willow on the way to her car.

"Hey, Amber," Willow answered, her tone calm and light. "We—"

"Are you at the shop? Is everything okay there?"

"Everything was fine when we left. Aunt G and I are going to grab lunch with…*our grandparents*! That's so weird to say. They told us you already met them. Thanks for the news."

Her heart rate slowed a little. "I figured you were too busy canoodling with a pop star."

"There has been no canoodling," Willow said. "Yet."

Amber laughed.

"Also, gird your loins because we're having a family reunion dinner tonight," Willow said. "We haven't chosen the restaurant yet, but both Edgar and Raphael said they're coming."

"Oh wow," Amber said, realizing how charged a reunion between Raphael and his parents could be. It would be the first time they had seen each other since they'd dropped him off at Pleasant Meadows. Yikes. She hoped the restaurant had insurance. "Are you sure everything was okay at the shop?"

"*Yep!*" she chirped, then immediately hung up.

Amber's anxiety only got worse the closer she got to The Quirky Whisker. What was going on?

When she turned onto Russian Blue Avenue, she found a ton of people milling about on the sidewalk. She parked on the street a door away, then slowly approached. Jack, Simon, Bianca, and Kim were all there, but so were Ben Lydon and Chloe Deidrick—and they were holding hands, Amber noticed.

She also spotted Henrietta, Thea, Nathan, and Jolene. Ann Marie and Alan Peterson were here, too. Even from this distance, she could sense how Alan's intense quiet energy didn't match the vibe of the rest of the group. Amber had just reached the mouth of the parking lot when Jack noticed her approach. He and the others scrambled to arrange themselves in some semblance of a formation. The long line of people snaking out of Purrfectly Scrumptious across the street were eyeing this spectacle with curiosity.

Four of her friends were holding something long and white, like a small rolled-up rug.

"Now," Jack said, and then unfurled what turned out to be a banner that said, "Grand Reopening!"

Chloe, Ben, and the Bishops shot off party favors. Kim, Ann Marie, Nathan, and Jolene blew noisemakers. They all cheered as if Amber had performed a great trick. Alan Peterson clapped politely.

She smiled awkwardly as she reached them. "What's all this?"

"You're too scared to open your shop again," Jack said.

Amber flushed a little. "I'm not *scared* …"

"You're totally scared," Kim said.

"Yep," Bianca agreed.

"Time to fix that!" Jack said. "A few of us can hang up the sign and set up out here. Put the rest of us to work. Ben said he can help you keep the place running until you can get one of the Bowens back over here."

Amber bit her bottom lip but nodded.

"Woo!" Kim cheered again, giving her noisemaker one more excited blast before everyone got to work. Balloons materialized from behind Nathan.

Jack, Nathan, Jolene, and Kim stayed outside to spruce up the entrance, while the rest filed inside. Amber asked the others to straighten up the shelves, though she'd kept the place in decent shape over the course of the week. In short order, Ann Marie had pulled a folding table out of storage, and she, the Bishops, Ben, and Chloe worked to create a display of Amber's cat toys, the extra Here and Meow exclusives prominently arranged in front.

Amber was behind the counter while they worked, restocking and straightening up the apothecary wall. The baskets along the bottom were still in disarray from the day she and Aunt G had rifled through them all in search for the escaped Thea in her hamster form.

"Amber?"

She stilled on her hands and knees, wide eyes focused on the apothecary wall, at the sound of Alan's voice. Amber had no idea if the WBI had gotten to him with their memory wipes. Knowing Alan, he'd stayed off their radar, since avoiding notice was one of his best skills as a private investigator.

Standing, she brushed off her knees and turned to face him. "What can I do for you, Alan?"

He stared at her a beat, then cast a quick look over his shoulder to make sure the others were still occupied. "You know I like you, Amber. I don't like many people. And I'm forever indebted to you for convincing Ann Marie to give me a chance."

Amber, slightly relieved, opened her mouth, only to have Alan cut her off.

"But," he said, "you and your family are now tied not only to a murder, but potential kidnapping. Not to mention a number of other incidents in town that warrant an investigation. I hope there's nothing for me to find when I start digging and that there's a reasonable explanation for all of it—but I just wanted you to have a heads up that I *will* be looking."

Amber swallowed. The WBI definitely hadn't gotten to him. He'd evaded their attention, and now he was focused on her weird past. "I'm a witch," she blurted, then quickly scanned the people milling around the shop. No one seemed to have overheard.

Alan opened his mouth, closed it, then cocked his head at her like a curious cat. "Like…*magic*?" he whispered.

Nodding, Amber stared at him intently, hoping her gut was right about him.

"Huh," he said after a moment. "You know, that checks out."

Amber heaved out a sigh of relief.

"Does Ann Marie know?"

"Not yet," Amber said.

"Fair enough. Thanks for telling me," he said, taking this news in stride just like he did with everything else. "Congratulations on the grand reopening."

Within half an hour, everything was ready to go except Amber's welcome sign. She took the small chalkboard off its hook on the door and stared down at the forlorn cat logo. "*Sorry. We're closed for the rest of the week.*" Taking the board to the counter, Amber squatted behind it.

She cast the familiar spell and then slowly waved a hand over the board. The cat's downcast eyes were now focused out at his audience. A little smirk lit up his whiskered face. "*Welcome!*" the sign said now.

As she emerged from her hiding place, Henrietta headed her way, her face as red as her hair. "Amber, can I talk to you about something?" She wrung her hands.

"Sure …"

Lowering her voice, she said, "So Thea filled me in on everything. I mean…*everything*. Including how you found out about my failed tea business. But, I mean, of course it failed if the missing ingredient is *literally* magic!"

Amber fought a laugh.

"I just wanted to say I'm so sorry about all of it," she said. "Me trying to steal from you started this whole mess."

"Henrietta, no—"

"Just…let me finish," Henrietta said, face still flush. "When I met with Molly for our 'business meeting,' I realized I'd been duped. She offered to pay me to spy on you. I said no. She started harassing me. She'd show up all over town, threatening me and saying if I didn't get dirt on you, she was going to expose me for the thief I was. She said she had evidence that I was complicit in my ex-husband's schemes and that she could get me thrown in jail." Henrietta sighed. "Molly and I had this bad, blow-out fight in your parking lot and I screamed at her that my sister is a lawyer and if she didn't leave me alone, I was going to file a harassment suit. As I was leaving, I looked in my rear-view mirror and Molly was standing there glaring at me, and then I swear to you, for like ten seconds, she was someone else. She was taller, had black hair, and crazy eyes. She was grinning at me and waved, then turned back into Molly. I swear I thought I imagined it. Then a few nights later, I saw the black-haired woman loitering in my neighborhood. Now I know she was Patrice Penhallow. I just don't know how often it had been her, and when it had really been Molly."

Amber frowned, feeling terrible that Henrietta had been pulled into all this because of her. "I'm so sorry, Hen."

"*You're* sorry?" Henrietta asked, incredulous. "If I had just tried getting a job like a normal person, Molly wouldn't have found out about my dumb idea and—"

"Stop," Amber said, holding a hand up. "The Penhallows had been manipulating people for months, if not years. If Patrice hadn't used you, she would have used someone else."

Amber still hadn't wrapped her brain around the fact that Molly was going to be working for the WBI, which was possibly just as bad as Molly working with the Penhallows.

"Anyway," Henrietta said. "I hope you can forgive me and I swear when I purchase your *magical* tea, it'll be for personal use only." She started to back away from the counter.

"Where do you think you're going?" Amber asked. "There's an opening on the staff if you're still interested."

Henrietta's eyes lit up. "Really?"

"Yep. I can make it work," Amber said.

"Thank you," Henrietta said. "Truly."

"Ben and I can get you started today, if you're up for it."

"Yes!" Henrietta said, and hurried across the shop to tell Thea the news.

Amber walked to her front door and hung the welcome sign there. Just as she pulled the door open, a man rounded the corner of the recessed entry. His blonde hair was a bit unruly for him, and he breathed heavily.

"Did I miss the grand reopening?" Chief Brown heaved.

"Perfect timing," Amber said.

Little footsteps sounded and then Sammy appeared around the side of his dad's leg. Jessica, with baby Isabelle, joined them a second later.

"Sorry we're late," Jessica said. "Sammy wanted to make sure he had on the perfect outfit for the occasion."

"Thank you both for coming," Amber said, feeling foolish that all these people were making such a fuss over her when her shop had only been closed for a few days. Then she looked down at Sammy and noticed that not only did he wear a button-up shirt, but he also wore a rather snappy clip-on paisley bow tie. "Do you know what kind of toy you want today, Sammy?"

"I want a bear, Miss Amber," he said, then took off into the shop.

Chief Brown smiled, squeezed Amber's arm, and then followed his son inside. Jessica trailed after them, Isabelle's bright blue eyes widening as she took in the sights and colors of Amber's unique shop.

"Excuse me?" someone asked behind Amber, and she turned to see a woman standing on the sidewalk with her young daughter. "Are you open again?"

Several people milled about outside, peering in the windows or watching Amber hopefully.

Amber smiled and held the door open wider. "We sure are. Come on in."

ThE End

Thank you for reading *Pawsitively Betrayed*! If you enjoyed this story, please consider leaving a review. Reviews mean the world to authors. Reviews often mean more sales, and more sales means more freedom to write more books.

Other books by Melissa Erin Jackson:

If you're looking for a slightly darker tale, consider *The Forgotten Child*, a haunting paranormal mystery starring a reluctant medium.

The dead can speak. They need her to listen.

Ever since Riley Thomas, reluctant medium extraordinaire, accidentally released a malevolent spirit from a Ouija board when she was thirteen, she's taken a hard pass on scary movies, haunted houses, and cemeteries. Twelve years later, when her best friend pressures her into spending a paranormal investigation weekend at the infamous Jordanville Ranch—former home of deceased serial killer

Orin Jacobs—Riley's *still* not ready to accept the fact that she can communicate with ghosts.

Shortly after their arrival at the ranch, the spirit of a little boy contacts Riley; a child who went missing—and was never found—in 1973.

In order to put the young boy's spirit to rest, she has to come to grips with her ability. But how can she solve a mystery that happened a decade before she was born? Especially when someone who knows Orin's secrets wants to keep the truth buried—no matter the cost.

Acknowledgements

Ahh! The series is complete (for now)! It has been such a fun experience. Thank you to all my readers who have been with me from the beginning. When I started to feel daunted by the task of wrapping this series up, hearing from people eager for this latest installment kept me going. I hope you all have enjoyed your time in Edgehill as much as I have.

As always, thank you to my beta readers…Mom, Krista Hall, Margarita Martinez, Brittany Gray, Christiane Loeffler, Jennifer Laam, Lauren Sprang, Garrett Lemons, Jasmine Warren, Kara Klemcke, Mary Studebaker, Samantha Lierer, Quinn Nicols, Cynthia Sandusky, and John Parker—y'all are the best!

Thanks to my design team. Maggie Hall for my covers, and Michelle Raymond and Clark Kenyon for all the feline flair.

Thank you to Justin Cohen for being my favorite proofreader. Can't wait to work with you on the next one!

I'm delighted to have found Victoria Villarreal, my audiobook narrator. Edgehill and Amber Blackwood will forever be more real to me thanks to you.

To my new Sunday accountability group, thank you for being the support I didn't know I needed during quarantine. Whether we laugh or cry (and sometimes both!), our meetings help give me a boost to get through the week ahead. Rebecca, Michelle, Cecilie, and Lauren, you ladies are great.

A huge thank you to Sam for the emotional support, the hours of video games, the energy drink runs, and keeping me from falling apart. Times have been rough, but you make them better. And we haven't murdered each other yet, so that's a plus!

I had to say goodbye to my best friend of the last twelve years shortly after I finished this book. Diamond lived to the ripe old of fifteen, which doesn't feel like nearly long enough. When is someone going to figure out how to make dogs live longer? She helped me through a breakup, took countless weekend trips with me, and went on a cross country road trip with me, Sam, and Boorito. Both our girls are gone now, and the house feels so quiet without them. I miss you like crazy, sweet girl.

Finally, I want to thank my readers. Whether you've been with me from the start, or if you just binged the series, I'm so happy that I get to share these books with others. I'm still floored whenever readers tell me how much they enjoy them. I have many more stories in the works, and I can't wait to share what's coming up next!

About the Author

Melissa has had a love of stories for as long as she can remember, but only started penning her own during her freshman year of college. She majored in Wildlife, Fish, and Conservation Biology at UC Davis. Yet, while she was neck-deep in organic chemistry and physics, she kept finding herself writing stories in the back of the classroom

about fairies and trolls and magic. She finished her degree, but it never captured her heart the way writing did.

Now she owns her own dog walking business (that's sort of wildlife related, right?) by day…and afternoon and night…and writes whenever she gets a spare moment. The Microsoft Word app is a gift from the gods!

She alternates mostly between fantasy and mystery (often with a paranormal twist). All her books have some element of "other" to them…witches, ghosts, UFOs. There's no better way to escape the real world than getting lost in a fictional one.

She lives in Northern California with her very patient boyfriend and way too many pets.

She's currently fast at work on her newest cozy mystery series.

You can find out more about her upcoming books and join her newsletter at: https://melissajacksonbooks.com